Sharon Ellery was born and raised in London and still resides there. This is her second novel.

Her first novel, *Siblings*, was published by Austin Macauley Publishers in May, 2022.

Fatima,
I hope you enjoy this book.

Sharon Ellery.
x
x

I would like to dedicate this book to the head and staff, past & present, of Queensmill school. For all of their care and support over the years. Also, to Full of Life family support and parents forum for all of their help, care and support over the years and may they continue to do so.

Building Bridges – Between Special and Mainstream

No two children are the same. Autism is a huge spectrum so not all children and adults have the same symptoms but have their own quirks and traits, which should be celebrated as individuals.

Sharon Ellery

SHADOWS IN THE RAINBOW

AUSTIN MACAULEY PUBLISHERS™

LONDON • CAMBRIDGE • NEW YORK • SHARJAH

A CIP catalogue record for this title is available from the British Library.

ISBN 9781035804030 (Paperback)
ISBN 9781035804047 (ePub e-book)

www.austinmacauley.com

First Published 2023
Austin Macauley Publishers Ltd®
1 Canada Square
Canary Wharf
London
E14 5AA

I would like to thank Elaine and Sharon for their specialised input for this book, which has been very helpful.

I would like to thank Nakita for reading *Shadows in the Rainbows* first, which she enjoyed immensely.

Table of Contents

Chapter 1

"It's a negative, Mel," said the nurse. "I am sorry," she added.

"Not too worry, Susie, it can't be helped. Better luck next time," Mel added. She got up out of the seat and left the room. She said goodbye to the receptionist Jill and then headed onto work. She was so sure this time.

She had been late and feeling rather unwell, she should be used to it now, but as she said to the nurse, better luck next time. It was only a few minutes' walk from the surgery to her shop, a florist. Mel had been working at the florist since she left school and loved it.

Later on, when things were on the up, and up for her and Terry, an opportunity came up for her to buy the florist, the shop and the flat upstairs. Her and Terry had stayed there when they first got married, but now she was renting it out to two students who studied locally.

She walked in through the front door and said hello to her staff, Julie and Fiona. They were both part time and she also had Lesley who was full time, but on her holidays to Spain at the moment. "Much going on, girls?" Mel enquired.

"We have a wedding order come through about an hour ago, but it's not until June. Want a cuppa, Mel? I was just going to put the kettle on?" Julie asked.

"Mmm, that sounds good, coffee for me please," replied Mel. She was still thinking about the result this morning. But that wasn't going to get the work done; she had a funeral to get ready for the morning and it was only because both of the girls were in this morning that she was able to go to the doctors.

She ploughed through the orders for the rest of the week and before she knew it, it was time to pack up for the evening. "Night, you two, see you in the morning. Oh sorry, Julie, you're in the afternoon. I don't know where my brain is at the moment, night," she added.

Both the girls said night and made their way out of the door. Mel only had a couple of things to do before she could also leave for the night. She got in just after 6.30pm and Terry was already in from work.

He worked for the local bank, in the mortgage dept and loved his job; saying yes to the people who wanted to make a new life for themselves with owning their own home. "Hi, love, how was work?" Mel asked.

"Yes, it was great, I think I have nearly hit my targets for this month," Terry remarked.

"Oh, that's good, love. Erm it was another negative test again," said Mel.

"What?" Terry shouted.

"It's a negative result again, Terry," Mel added.

"Another test, Mel. What's going on? I thought we were going to leave this baby business and concentrate on our careers now," demanded Terry.

"I thought we were still trying, Terry; I mean it's what we both want, isn't it?" Mel asked rather tearful now.

Terry came over to comfort her. "Sorry, love. I just thought that we were going to have a break from it all now, after all of the tests we have had and what you have been through. That we had done with it now!" Terry suggested putting his arms around his wife to console her as her tears were turning into sobs now.

Terry patted her head and held her close. He hadn't wanted to continue trying for a baby. He wanted them to have a bit of a life, after all of the test tubes, blood tests and everything else that went with it. He couldn't understand what it was with women wanting babies so much.

"I'll put the kettle on, tea?" He asked Mel she nodded. She had hoped he would have been as upset as she was. She couldn't understand why he wasn't more sympathetic that she wasn't pregnant. Maybe it was just a man thing. Terry returned with two mugs of hot steaming tea.

"I was going to get Fish and Chips for tea, that alright with you? Save you cooking tonight?" Terry prompted. Again, Mel nodded, she didn't want to cook; not now with her outburst and Terry's reaction to her test. Maybe he had just had a hard day.

Terry popped round to the chippy and got their dinner. They sat in front of the TV eating it out of the paper, saving on the washing up, Terry suggested. He seemed to want to make their life a little easier. He just wanted to try and distract Mel from talking about babies all night…again. He knew that Mel had wanted a baby just as much as he did in the beginning.

They had been married for just over eight years and didn't start straight away. They had brought their own place, because Terry got a good discount from the bank for their mortgage. They both talked and said they wanted to try for a family. It was great at first, early nights, bubble baths together, relaxing evenings and sometimes mornings, if Mel didn't have to be in work first thing.

But after two years and nothing happening, Mel suggested they go to the doctors to see where to go next. He suggested they take her temperature every morning, when it goes up for a few days, on the first day, then to have intercourse. That way they had a chance of conceiving within those couple of days. They had done as the doctor had suggested, but nothing had worked in 3 months.

The doctor had told them it would take longer than just 3 months, but to continue for a few more before trying the next step. When that didn't work a further 3 months later, he wanted to send Mel off for blood tests at various times of the month, just to see how her hormone levels were. Once they had done that, they found it wasn't that great and she would need some tablets to help stimulate her ovaries to make sure she was ovulating.

As from the results of the blood tests, she was only ovulating once every 3 months. So even though they had been trying with the two sets of 3 months of temperature taking, they only really had two chances and nothing had happened. The doctor suggested Clomiphene or Clomid for short. He had suggested they try if for 6 months and see how they got on…again nothing.

So by then, they had been trying for three years and two of them were with the help from the doctor with different solutions, that didn't seem to work. Their doctor had then referred them to see a consultant at the hospital, who had suggested that they continue with the Clomid for a further year, BUT they would start to do other tests as well, to see what was going on with them. First of all, he asked for Terry to be tested to make sure there wasn't any problem with him, which Terry was a little embarrassed about and then he got annoyed.

But as the doctor had said, it could just be a minor thing that needed sorting out. In the meantime, they would give Mel a laparoscopy, which both Mel and Terry were a little concerned about. The doctor had explained to them, that Mel would be put under general anaesthetic; they make a small incision under her tummy button and they would put a long needle with a camera on the end of it and have a good look around.

Which is exactly what they did, thankfully she was asleep while this procedure was being done, but when she came round, she felt like she had been kicked by a horse. Terry was waiting there for her with a big smile on his face. "You, ok?" He asked her.

"Fine, a little sore," she added, but he knew that.

The doctor's registrar came round and pulled the curtains round Mel. "Mel, we have done a bit of digging. I am sorry, you will be very sore, but we think we know the problem. Apart from only ovulating every 3 months or so, your fallopian tubes are both blocked. Now we can sort that out and hopefully you will be able to have the family you want," said the registrar.

"We can arrange for that to happen if you want. We will make an appointment for you to go back to clinic and then arrange for a little while as you need to recover from this procedure first," he added. Mel and Terry both broke into big beams on their faces and both nodded yes.

"Well, when you feel ok in a little while, have something to eat, then you can go home and wait for the appointment for outpatients to come through the post. But go home today and relax, no heavy work for you. Can you take a couple of days off from your job?" He asked her.

"Yes, that won't be a problem," added Mel. Terry had brought her a sandwich and she ate it. The nurse came to check she had a cup of tea also before she left. She got herself off the bed, and Terry helped her into her clothes as she was struggling a bit.

***

A couple of weeks later, her appointment had come through. She and Terry went along and came back out with a date for her small operation. Mel was excited, where Terry was nervous, his test came back fine, and he was well, relieved. He knew that put the pressure on Mel. If she was starting to feel it, she never let on.

Her date came for the OP and Terry was there when she went down to theatre and still waiting when she came back up a little while later. The surgeon said that the OP was a success, so all Mel wanted to do was go back home and start trying. The doctor warned her against that for a little while, as the tubes would be very tender. So, they both waited for a couple of weeks.

Terry was glad with that news, but they both had hoped it would solve their problems. In the meantime, Mel's business was really starting to flourish. Orders were coming in all the time. She wondered how she would be able to cope with a baby and a business; but she had good staff, who didn't really know what was going on, but Mel was pleased with that.

They had been trying for a year or so once they knew it was safe too, and that's why Mel had gone to the doctors, but again a negative result. Terry, on the other hand, was getting fed up with the baby palaver. He wanted them to start living, not in and out of the doctors. So the next morning after they had their quiet evening in with their fish and chips, he was glad to get out of the house.

They only lived a few streets away from their work; the florist and the bank were on the same street but at other ends. He kissed Mel on the forehead; she was still asleep. He wanted to get into work early, there was some stuff he wanted to finish up from the day before. He slammed the door shut and Mel woke up, she felt wet.

"Oh no!" she thought, now the test definitely made sense. She ran to the bathroom, grabbed her supplies and sorted herself out. She jumped into the shower, she had looked at the clock. She didn't have to be in until ten this morning, so she got herself a coffee when she got out of the shower.

They had that funeral for that lovely old gentleman, Mr Cole. His daughter came in to order the flowers for him. Mel hadn't seen her before, but that was OK. She knew Mr Cole, but also didn't know he had any children. He had two daughters; one had emigrated to Australia, the other the next town on. His funeral was at eleven thirty, so she thought she had better get out the door.

***

Terry was hard at it. His head was down and he was checking some figures. Yes, all correct, he thought. A lady moved closer towards him, she looked familiar but he couldn't think where from. He got up and introduced himself, "Terry Humphreys," he said to the lady holding out his hand to shake it.

"Hello, Terry Humphreys, don't you remember me?" The lady asked.

Terry thought, he couldn't remember where he had seen her…but yes she was. "Clare, Clare Baxter?" Terry said.

"Yes, that's right. Well, it's now Clare Proctor," she told him.

"Ok then, Clare Proctor, what can I do for you?" Terry asked.

"Well, I moved out of the area, when I got married, but I am now divorced and would like to buy my own house after my husband left me for his floozy who worked for him. I have my half of the house and I wanted to see how much I would need for a deposit for a new flat I have seen," she stated.

"Erm, well, where is the flat and how long do you want the mortgage for, Clare?" Terry asked.

"Well, I have 75K, but I don't want to put it all down, as I want to re-decorate it and maybe put in a shower…I don't know I haven't decided just yet," Clare added. Terry offered her a cup of something and they sat down to talk business. Terry found out that yes that even though Clare's husband was no longer around, she had a good head for business. She had her own company in her own right, but she didn't want to tie up all of her cash into something that she could borrow so much for.

Terry had asked Clare if she wanted to go to lunch with him and they could talk more. So they did. Whilst having lunch in a very nice restaurant, Terry realised that they had lots in common. Like they both didn't have children. Terry was already going off the idea of babies.

They liked to travel and both liked trying new things. Mel only stuck to what she knew, never got out of her comfort zone, but Clare, Clare was different. She had it all, money, an ex-husband, her own business, and lots and lots of positive ideas about her future.

By the time Terry got back to the bank, he knew lots more about Clare, but he wanted to know more. He gave her his office desk phone number and told her to call him anytime, he was always there. When Clare left, Terry seemed to have a spring in his step. He had liked Clare at secondary school but forgot about her when he met Mel.

Soon his day's work had finished, he wanted to go and meet Clare, but knew he had to go home to Mel. She had this big funeral on today. He also knew that he left Clare's phone number back at the bank, and that was now shut. He would have to wait until tomorrow to get her number and give her a call. He wanted to see her again.

Mel had just got in from work, the funeral flowers were lovely. Mr Cole's daughter dropped by on her way home from the wake at the local pub to thank Mel and her staff. Mel always liked to do a good job. It's the last nice thing you can do for a person, give them a great send off and lovely flowers can make a big difference. Also the other mourners like to look at them and then moan at how tight some people can be.

Terry wasn't home yet, so she ran herself a lovely bubble bath, put the kettle on, so she could have a cup of tea in it. She felt nice and cosy and not all uncomfortable these times made her feel, like a failure really. Terry popped his head around the door; he was in a good mood.

"You alright, love?" Mel asked.

"Yes, good. I had a new client today. Clare, Clare Baxter. Do you remember her from school?" Terry asked.

Clare Baxter. It didn't ring any bells with Mel. "What year was she in at Fox bury Manor, Terry?" she asked.

"Oh, I can't remember if she was in the same year as me or the year above!" he replied.

"Oh, I don't know her then, Terry. I didn't really know many of the kids in your year, apart from you that is," she laughed.

"What can I smell coming from the kitchen, Mel?" He asked her.

"I put a pizza in the oven, a little while ago. It must be nearly ready, let me get out of the bath and I will check on it," she added.

"It's fine, I will have a look. Yes, it's nearly ready." He told her. Mel got out of the bath, wrapped a towel around her and went into the kitchen downstairs. Terry was just taking the huge pizza out of the oven. He put it on the side and pulled out two plates.

"Yes, she looks really well, does Clare," Terry said.

"Oh, OK, so has she moved back then?" Mel quizzed.

"What? Yes, she's just getting over a divorce, so she has seen a flat she wants to buy, but not sure how much mortgage she will need," Terry added, delighted at a new client. Mel took her plate and went to sit at the table. Terry brought his in and then two glasses of wine.

"We don't normally drink in the week, Terry, not when we are you know…trying," said Mel.

Terry sighed. "Mel, I have a new client, which means if she goes with the mortgage, I set up for her, will give me a great commission and even maybe a bonus. Just be pleased for me, huh?" Terry said.

Mel thought whatever. She took a sip of her wine, then a bite out of her pizza. Meat feast, her favourite. She liked to have pizza when she was feeling a bit not right. Once they finished eating, and the wine drunk, Mel wanted to get an early night. She was tired and her tummy was feeling rather tender.

The next few weeks whizzed by. Mel was really busy with work and Terry seemed to be busy at work and now in the evenings. He was wining and dining Clare, when he should have been home with Mel. He told her it was just business, but Terry knew it was something more.

He had changed when Clare had come back into his life, not that she was in his life much before. Even when they were kids, he always liked Clare, but it was Mel that he wanted and he got her. Now he doesn't even give her a second thought.

It's not because Mel isn't pretty, she is very attractive. Terry was very lucky, but he felt they had nothing in common anymore. But Clare, now she was different. She liked life. She liked having a great social life, which is what Terry was now getting, she liked to go to faraway places and Terry was starting to think he wanted to go to faraway places, as long as it was with Clare.

The thing was, Terry didn't tell Mel he was with Clare, but work colleagues or his friends from the rugby club, where he went sometimes to play rugby, but also the social side of it. Not that he took Clare there. It wasn't good enough for her as far as he was concerned. Terry was changing and not for the best as far as Mel was concerned.

He had become rather moody and annoying; would have a go at her for nothing. She couldn't work it out. She couldn't put her finger on it, but she knew it was over something recent. She was at work arranging some flowers for a lady's birthday, then it dawned on her.

Terry has changed, ever since he met up with that Clare. She was a client, but what if she had become more than just a client. Mel didn't want to challenge Terry just yet, she needed evidence first. Proof or he would say that she wasn't right in the head or she was imagining it.

She thought about it, she would keep an eye on him and see when he would be moody and when he would be in a good mood.

She didn't have to wait too long. Tomorrow was Sunday. The banks weren't open and the florist was only open on a Sunday if it was a holiday, Mother's Day or something like that. He woke up in a bad mood. Nothing she did for him was good enough; her cooking, his clothes weren't ironed properly, which she thought were fine.

She was starting to hate being at home on a Sunday, but Monday, that was different. On a Sunday night, he would perk up. Go to bed in a good mood, be up early the following day and out the door as soon as he could. Also, the fact that they weren't really sleeping together, spoke volumes.

On Monday afternoon, Terry started calling Mel at the florist with one excuse or another, saying he was going out with the lads from work or the rugby club. Thing is, him and Mel used to have a good social life, but that went out the window. So Mel was really suspicious, when Terry said that a couple of the guys from work were going on a conference on a Friday, but not back until the Saturday.

He had been working at the bank for over five years and this had never happened before. She didn't say anything to him about it but let him go. He would trip himself up, she thought to herself. Men are too stupid to think that what they are doing isn't right and they do get caught out in the end eventually.

So Mel went out with her friends, Paula, Jodie and Samantha, on the Friday night to the local pub. She hadn't been out with the girls in ages with all of the hospital appointments. They knew what was going on. Mel had watched every one of her friends have their babies while she watched on the side lines, happy for them, but gutted for herself for not being able to have one.

As they say the most natural thing for a woman to have, but it's not possible for all women sadly. Mel was up at the bar getting her round of drinks, where she saw Tony, one of Terry's works colleagues and also a fellow rugby player. "Hey, Tony, didn't you go to the conference for work?" Mel asked him.

Tony who looked a bit puzzled replied, "Oh no, that's next week, and I can't make it. Maxine and I are away at her parents for the weekend. It's been arranged weeks ago, for their wedding anniversary or something. Say hello to Terry for me!" Came his reply.

A little sheepish, Mel thought. So she knew for sure now. "You OK, Mel?" Jodie asked.

"Yes, why?" she replied.

"It's just that you look like you have seen a ghost!" Sam remarked.

"No, I am fine," she told them unconvincingly. She tried to have a nice time with her friends. You need your friends, they keep you sane, keep you level headed unless you all have the same amount to drink, then it's everyman for themselves in this case every woman for themselves...Mel laughed to herself.

When the night out ended, she turned her key in the door. She called out, just in case Terry had come back, but no, silence. "Oh well, I can go straight to bed, work tomorrow." She thought to herself. Mel knew now though; Terry was definitely up to no good and she was going to have it out with him when he got back.

For now though, her pillow was calling her. She walked slowly up the stairs. She forgot how much wine she had drunk and the stairs seemed never ending. She flopped into bed and fell asleep. She got up the next morning, got herself ready for work and out the door.

She knew when she came back that evening, Terry should be home. She would tackle it, depending on his mood. But for now, she had orders to finish and they wouldn't do them on their own. Lesley was back in on Monday, so if she had a rough Sunday, she knew she would be able to take over for the day and cope with everything.

When 5pm came round, she told Julie and to go home, she would lock up. Julie said goodnight and left. Mel checked everything was off and closed. The till empty, she put the closed sign on the door and then locked it.

She had been dreading it all day. She knew she would have to tackle Terry about what was going on and who with, but she now knew, but she wanted him to tell her. She walked home; it was really only around the corner, but she walked slowly. She didn't want to rush, because even though she was right, she didn't want to be.

She had hoped it had all been in her head. She turned the key in the front door, he called out. He was home. She gulped and then closed the door. "Hey, love, how was your day?" Terry asked her.

"Fine, I went out last night with the girls, but even so, yeah good," she answered him. "How was your conference?" she asked.

"Oh, that was good, yes, very informative." Terry said, happy with his reply.

"Oh, that's funny, Terry, because I bumped into Tony in the pub last night and he told me the conference was next weekend and he can't go because it's

Maxine's parents wedding anniversary. So where were you, Terry, and who with, because I noticed you have put your washing straight into the machine rather than leave it out for me to do. Lipstick on it, is there?" Mel demanded.

Terry was rumbled and he knew it. How would he get out of this one, he has actually been caught. Well, not actually caught, but yes, he knew the game was up. What did he do, he was stalling now? Does he tell her everything or does he just make out that she doesn't know what she's talking about?

No, he would have to come clean, there was no way out now? "Well, I'm waiting," demanded Mel, she was sick of this.

Finally, Terry spoke. "Mel, there's no easy way to say this, so I am just going to say it. I'm leaving you. I am seeing Clare and I am moving in with her. I just wanted to put a couple of things in the wash before I left."

Mel interrupted him, "Excuse me, you wanted to put a couple of things in my washing machine, before you go round to your fancy woman. Are you for bloody real, Terry? Are you for real? I tell you what, just go and get your bloody bags packed. I tell you what, I will pack them for you and throw them out of the window," she said, but he bolted up the stairs to their bedroom and grabbed the suitcase.

Mel followed him up there, screaming and shouting at him. "Bloody cheek, you want to wash your crappy gear in my washing machine so you can go to Clare. Clare, that stupid bitch, who left her husband, for what? You? Oh my god she must be desperate." Mel said.

"She didn't leave her husband for me, you stupid dingbat, he left her for some floozy," Terry replied.

"Oh he left her. He must have got something right then and now you're going to her, well go then," said Mel as she was pushing Terry. She couldn't believe she wasn't putting up more of a fight, but she was so angry. "So why are you leaving me then again, Terry, to be with your floozy?" Mel asked.

That is when Terry turned on her. "Leaving you to be with Clare, too right I am. All you think about is babies, babies, babies. You don't think anything of me anymore, just babies and getting bloody pregnant. I'm sick of it. You only want me to get you pregnant, not because you want me. Clare doesn't; she wants me for me, not have babies. SHE doesn't want them," Terry declared.

That was it. Mel's whole world was falling apart. Terry wasn't leaving her because he had met someone else, but because of her obsession of becoming a mum. With that, she burst into tears. Did he really not want children with her, obviously not.

Terry grabbed the rest of his stuff and left Mel crying on the edge of the bed. He ran to the kitchen and grabbed his shirt and underwear he had just put in the washing machine but hadn't had the chance to turn it on yet. He stuffed it into a carrier bag, opened the door, took his stuff and shut it tight behind him.

Chapter 2

Mel put the receiver down; she had spoken to Lesley asking her to take over for the day. She couldn't cope, not with what had happened the day before. She sat in a crumpled heap on the sitting room floor, still in her pyjamas from Saturday night once Terry had walked out the door with his belongings.

She still couldn't believe it; she burst into tears again. Her eyes were already red from all of the crying. Why hadn't she challenged him more, or fought harder, maybe he wouldn't have gone…no he was going. This was his excuse. She had made it easy for him without even realising it. What was she going to do now?

The phone rang. She ran to it, maybe it was him. Terry calling to say he was sorry and he was coming back to her…"Hello, Mel, its Mum. You, ok?" she asked.

"Oh hi, Mum," responded Mel.

"Mel, what's wrong? You sound either ill or you have been crying," Mel's mum asked. "I'm coming round," she told her and put down the phone. Mel's mum, Jean, had a key just for emergencies. Ten minutes later, she was opening the door to the house.

"Mel, Mel, where are you?" she asked.

Mel came out of the sitting room, looking like she had been dragged through a hedge backwards and sideways. "Mum, I'm here and I'm fine!" Mel exclaimed.

"Look at the state of you. What if Terry could see you like this?" Jean trailed off.

"Mum, Terry's left me, he went on Saturday evening," Mel said.

Jean's mouth was wide open. "Left you? Why? What's been going on, Mel?" Jean asked her.

Mel wasn't in the mood to tell her, but her mum wasn't budging, "Terry has met someone else and he's moved in with her. He said that all I wanted him for was a baby. That's not true, Mum, I love him," Mel said, starting to cry again. Jean put her arms around her daughter and held her close.

Once Mel had stopped crying, Jean smiled at her and went into the kitchen. She opened up the cupboards and put the kettle on. She made some tea and was looking for something for Mel to eat. She looked like she hadn't eaten in a month of Sundays. She came back in, Mel had just finished blowing her nose.

Her mum handed her a mug of tea. Tea was always good in a crisis; it seemed to put the world to rights. "So what do you want to do now then?" Jean asked.

"I don't know, he took everything with him, and left his keys on the side, Mum. He's not coming back," Mel said.

"I wasn't talking about Terry, but you, my girl. You still have a house and a mortgage and a business, who's running the shop today?" Jean quizzed.

"Lesley is running the shop for today and I will see how I feel in the morning. The house, I can still afford, if I have to I will get lodgers in to help it the cost. Other than that, Mum, I haven't thought about it."

"I will go upstairs and run you a lovely bath and sort you out something to wear and then we can go into town!" She said.

"No, no, Mum I can't, I may bump into Terry and I don't want to see him yet," Mel retorted.

"Well, listen to me, young lady. The best thing for you to do is pick yourself up, dust yourself down and show Mr Big Ideas, what he is missing not being with you. You sort yourself out, and don't tell me it's too early. You're not auctioning off yourself. You're getting back out there and you say he has left you for someone else."

"Well, I think you need to get a solicitor. He's committed adultery, that's grounds enough for divorce and as you say this mortgage needs paying, or you sell the property and halve the money. But you cannot sort this out on your own, you need help," Jean told her.

"Mum, STOP. I can't think of any of that just yet. I am still trying to come to terms with it. I want to lick my wounds and take it slowly," Mel told her mum.

"Look, Mel, I'm on your side and these things need to happen quickly. You have to get in before he does and if he has a bitch. She's going to push for the money, those type always do. I don't want to sound like I am nagging you, love; I just don't want to see you getting the bad end of all of this," she spoke.

"I know, Mum, but I need to take this a step at a time," said Mel.

"Have a bath, I will put some lovely bubbles in it and some soft music to relax and you have a think about what I have just said. I don't want you to come out of this in a worse state especially financially…" Mum said to her. Mel did as she was told.

Mum went up to the bathroom to run her a bath, while Mel was choosing something to wear. Her mum wasn't going to let Terry take liberties like her husband did. He left her with two young girls to bring up. He took the money and ran.

Jean had to turn to her own mum to house the three of them, which her mum, Marge, did willingly. She didn't have a good word to say about the girl's dad, but never in front of them, only when they were out of earshot. Jean didn't want the same for her daughter, even though there weren't any children involved.

Mel had worked hard for a long time, to build up her business and home. There was no way some floozie was getting her hands on it. She would see to that.

Mel climbed into a lovely hot bubble full bath. It looked so luxurious, it made her skin feel like silk. Thankfully, her monthly had already finished. She wasn't very heavy at the best of times, so she felt lovely in this hot relaxing bath. Her mum had been right. The last couple of days, her head had been all over the place.

She wanted to go in and see Terry at work and scream and shout at him for leaving her and for another woman, probably a blonde bimbo, who had no sense. Her own marriage had broken up and now she had broken hers and Terry's marriage. Mel felt nothing but hatred for the two of them for making her feel like this.

She was hoping that her and Terry would start trying again properly for a baby, but that wasn't going to happen. Her mum was right though, she decided. She couldn't stay cooped up in this house and things had to be sorted out properly and correctly. Her business and the house, the belongings, his belongings he had taken everything.

He must have taken some stuff out when she wasn't there, but at work, because his records had already gone and she hadn't noticed them until today, he didn't take them on Saturday. Anyway, she was trying not to think about Terry; this was about her now.

There was a knock on the door. Mel opened her eyes, she was relaxing with her eyes shut. "Mel, you ok?" Her mum asked.

For a split-second, Mel had forgotten that Terry wasn't there. "Yes, fine, Mum, just soaking. I will be out in a minute!" Mel shouted through the door. She got out of the bath, wrapped a lovely big soft towel round her, put her slippers on and opened the door.

Her mum was waiting for her on her bed. "You ok, feel better?" Jean asked.

"Yes, I do," handing her the empty mug. "You're right though, I can't leave this until later on. I don't want his new bird getting her hands on my home or my business. So, Mum, if I get ready now, will you come down to town? I can pop into the solicitor's office and make an appointment. Then I don't know," said Mel a bit stuck.

"Well, we can have a bit of lunch if you want and do you need any new things by any chance?" Mum said looking at Mel's wardrobe.

"Errm, I don't know. I don't think so. I mean everything fits me still, I haven't put on or lost any weight," Mel commented. Jean took the mug downstairs to the kitchen, so Mel could get changed, actually when she put on her suit, it was a bit loose on her. *Never mind, that will be the stress from the last couple of weeks or so*, she thought.

Mel dressed and went downstairs. "Mum, I forgot to ask how's nan and Tina?" Mel enquired.

"They are both fine, worried about you," Jean said.

"Why?" Mel replied.

"Because the way I shot out of home that's why," Jean replied. Mel picked up her handbag, checked she had her keys and then shut the door and walked down the path and made their way to town. It wasn't far, the solicitors were only a few doors away from the bank. As long as she didn't see Terry, she was fine. She didn't know how she would cope if she saw him.

***

They walked into the reception of Johnson and Carey Solicitors; Mel asked the receptionist if she could make an appointment to see a solicitor about divorce. The receptionist told her that would be Mr Johnson, but he was unavailable for a few days. She could see him on Friday at 11am. Mel nodded and that was set now.

She had to come back on her own unless her mum came with her, but sometimes there are only certain times you want your parents with you. When they left, Mel wanted to pop into the florist to see how Lesley was coping, as they were nearly there. When Mel opened the door, Lesley looked surprised to see Mel in a suit.

Fiona was working this morning; both ladies had their mouths open. Not that Mel was ever scruffy, but she looked very official. There wasn't anyone in the shop, so she asked her mum to go and put the kettle on. She had already closed the door and put the sign up to say they were closed.

Lesley and Fiona looked at each other. "That's it," they thought, that was their jobs gone down the pan.

"Lesley, Fiona, don't look so worried. I haven't died you know," said Mel. They both knew that because she was standing there. "Right, something's happened, which I feel I can tell you now. Don't worry, your jobs are not in jeopardy."

"Terry left me on Saturday after I came home from here. I have been holed up indoors until mum came round today and talked some sense into me. If I had my way, I would still be sitting in the middle of the sitting room in a heap. So as he told me he left me for another woman, I am going to divorce the bugger. I have just made an appointment, hence the suit," Mel told them.

Both of the other women breathed a sigh of relief. "It's just I wanted to tell you myself, before you hear it from elsewhere, but I don't want it common knowledge just yet. As I said, I have to sort out the legal stuff first and take it from there."

"Do you know who Terry is with then?" Fiona asked.

"Yes, some woman called 'Clare'. She was at school with us, but I don't really remember her."

"Clare Baxter?" Fiona asked.

"No idea, Fi. He just said that she's recently divorced and she doesn't want any babies," choked Mel. She grabbed for a tissue as she thought she would blubber at any minute.

"Don't, Mel," said her mum, wiping her own eyes. Mel composed herself and then Fiona piped up.

"Clare lives down the same road as me, Mel, and she's not very nice. Too business like, but she has just come into a lot of money, Mum told me. She jets off all over the place, so I am surprised she's settled down here again. I am sorry, too much information," said Fiona.

"No, don't worry, love, it's fine," said Jean. "Now let's make that tea," Jean said. She left the shop and went out the back to make the tea. She returned with two cups for the girls and then one for Mel and herself.

"Are you coming into today then?" Lesley asked.

"Oh no, I just wanted to pop in and let you know what's what, then Mum wants to take me for lunch. Mind you, I might pop into the shops. My clothes are getting a bit big as Mum said earlier," Mel remarked. They finished their tea. Mel told Lesley that she would be back in tomorrow and would just enjoy the day off.

Lesley nodded in agreement and said her goodbyes to Mel and Jean and went out to wash the cups up. They went along to some of the boutiques to see if there was anything suitable; they ended up in C and A and British Home Stores Mel saw a couple of pairs of slacks that she liked in black and navy blue, also a couple of shirt/blouses that would go with both, so she grabbed both of them.

She found a couple of pairs of comfy trousers, more combat ones, a pair in Khaki and beige, a couple of tops to go with them. She was done, she didn't need any shoes. They went to the till and paid for the items and left the shop. They had only walked down past a few shops, then she stood still.

He was there with her laughing at something she had just said; he was laughing his head off. He hadn't noticed Mel or her mum. Her mum then spotted him, she went to say something out loud, but Mel put her fingers to her lips. They had walked on. They hadn't spotted them.

Mel didn't want him to see her until he really had to…she felt like her heart had been ripped out again. It only happened a few days ago and now again. Her and her mum carried on walking. "Mel, you should have let me say something," Jean said a little upset. He had hurt her little girl, she didn't want him to get away with it.

"No, Mum, let me hit him where it hurts, his wallet. Then let's see how long little miss Clare will want him," replied Mel. They finished their shopping, had a quick bite of lunch in the local café and then Mel decided she had done a lot today, she wanted to go home. Her mum was a little wary as she didn't really know how Mel was feeling, but she had to let her go. She was a woman and not a little tot needing protecting, well she needed protecting, but to be treated like a woman and not a kid.

Mel headed home, popped upstairs to put her new purchases away. She liked what she bought. She didn't realise she was losing a bit of weight. Next she changed out of her suit, put her blouse in the dirty laundry. The suit was still clean, she hung that back up and put it away in its cover and then in the wardrobe. She changed into something more comfortable to wear around the house.

She tidied up the bedroom, now it was only used on one side the bed seemed too big. Last night, she had put all four pillows in the middle of the bed and slept like that. She hadn't slept well. Well in the recent circumstances in a while, but she felt a bit better about being alone in a big bed.

Anyway, after a quick tidy, she went downstairs. She did the same, then had a look in the fridge and then freezer. She had some food in but didn't really want to go out again. She took out a chicken pie, some veg and yes, she found them, some frozen chips, that would do for this evening.

She started to prepare dinner. While she was stirring the broccoli, her mind wandered to earlier today out with Mum. It had only been two days since she saw Terry, but he looked so different already. He seemed happy. She hadn't seen him look like that for quite some time. Maybe he was right; maybe this baby business was getting too much for both of them, but Mel never noticed it.

I suppose, she was in a bubble. She went to the drawer, grabbed her cutlery, plate and a glass. She didn't want anything alcoholic this evening, so she grabbed the jug of squash in the fridge. There was always a jug of squash in the fridge, they went through so much of it.

She laid the table, put the TV on and sat down to eat her meal. There wasn't much on TV, a couple of films, but she didn't fancy watching anything romantic. She did have a book she got recently. She grabbed that and thought she would have an early night and a bit of a read.

She put the dinner things in the dishwasher, there was enough there for a load, so she put one on and then went upstairs with book in hand and got into bed. She jumped back out of it. She hadn't checked she had turned everything off…lights were off anyway, but the back door, front door, windows. It only took a couple of minutes and then she was back cosy in the bed.

She had already learnt, when you get out of bed, put the covers back over, so when you got back in, the bed was still warm. She turned the night lamp on and started. This looked alright; she didn't want to read a thriller in case she couldn't sleep, but she found a book that looked quite a bit of everything. She made a start on it, got to about twenty pages in, then decided she would go to sleep. She turned the corner over at the top of the page that she was reading and turned off the light. Then snuggled down to sleep.

Next morning, Mel jumped out of bed. She felt so refreshed. She felt better than she had in a long time. She turned the radio on, as she went to the bathroom, then went downstairs to make a cuppa. It was still only 8am, she had a little while before she had to leave.

She put the toaster on, and the kettle had boiled so she made the tea. Toast popped out, so she buttered it, took it in the living room, so she could have that before getting ready. She put one of her new outfits on that she got the day before. She grabbed her keys, checked everything was off, locked the door and made her way to work.

She walked in the door, there wasn't anyone there yet, but that was fine as she was still early. She went to the notepad up on the wall, to see if anyone had put any more orders in. Yes, there was a few bouquets wanted for birthdays and anniversaries, but nothing really more than that.

Lesley was walking through the door when Mel came back out to the shop. "Morning, Lesley, I have just put the kettle on," said Mel.

"Cheers, Mel. I would have done that, let me put up my jacket and I will make the tea. How are you feeling today?" Lesley enquired. She knew that Mel was not right at the moment, but she had seen her looking good and confident the day before.

"Yes, not too bad, had a good sleep last night. Saw Terry and her yesterday, after we left here," Mel told her.

Lesley had her mouth open, "Oh what happened?" she asked.

"Nothing, I just stood there. Mum wanted to say something, I told her not too. I am glad though I made an appointment though with the solicitor, as I need to get stuff sorted, Les, otherwise she may make a play for the house or even the business," Mel commented.

Lesley looked horrified. "Don't worry, Les, they won't get anything. Even if they get the house, they can't take away my livelihood, and there is a flat upstairs, but I'm not worrying just yet," Mel said with a reinforcing look.

Julie was working this morning and Fiona this afternoon. "Morning, Mel, morning, Lesley," said Julie.

"Kettle's boiled, want cuppa, Julie?" Lesley asked.

"Yes please, I could do with one!" Julie smiled.

"Much on today?" Lesley asked.

"Not really. A couple of birthday bouquets and anniversary one for Mrs Finch down the road, you know in that charity shop," suggested Mel. "You should know, Les, you took the booking," laughed Mel and then Lesley. Julie came out with her tea and her tabard on, so she wouldn't get her clothes wet. Mel was getting on with it and it felt good for her to be with people than on her own at the weekend.

Her and Lesley were having a laugh about some flowers that Mel had seen, that she thought looked awful and wouldn't know what to put with them. A young lady came in with her mum, they both looked excited and were looking around. Mel asked them if she could help at all. "Well, it's for my wedding in four weeks. I was wondering what flowers would be best for June. My colours are pink and white," the young lady said.

Mel's head was reeling, white, that's the colour her face went, then she burst into tears. The young lady and her mum looked at each other, wondering if they came into the right shop. "Julie, please could you see to these two ladies for a few moments, until I come back," Lesley said smiling at both of the women.

Julie pulled out a book for them to look at. Lesley took Mel out the back. "Mel, maybe you shouldn't be here. Maybe you should go home. You can't keep bursting into tears when a customer wants to arrange their wedding flowers; you will scare them off. Now you stay in here for a little while, I will send Julie in while I deal with the customers," demanded Lesley.

Mel nodded. Lesley left and Julie came in. "Mel, are you OK?" she asked her. Mel sniffed into a hankie and then said that she was fine. She thought she had better tell Julie what's happened. She wasn't there the day before, so was unaware of the situation.

Mel explained and at first she thought the same as the other two, that she was for the chop, but Mel said that wouldn't be the case. They still had enough work for all of them, especially when there was a funeral or a wedding. She rolled her eyes. It wasn't that ladies fault in the shop, it was just the timing.

Lesley came back into the back room. "It's fine, the young lady has chosen her flowers, pink roses and carnations for her bouquet. Smaller versions for her two bridesmaids and then white carnations for the wedding party, except for the men in the bridal party, that's red carnations. She preferred the carnations to the roses as buttonholes. It's fine, Mel. There's plenty of time to get it all from the wholesalers, I can do that if you want?" Lesley asked.

"What would I do without you girls, eh?" Mel asked.

"You couldn't," reported Lesley, with a cheeky laugh to follow. "I just filled Julie in with what's going on with me at the moment, now you know why I had that little outburst, shall we say?" Mel suggested.

***

Mel continued with work for the rest of the week and she seemed to be getting into some sort of routine without Terry. She had her up and down days, but she was getting there. A couple of weeks later, Terry had been gone for over three weeks now, a letter came in the post, from Terry's solicitor, saying that he was going for half the house. Mel was fuming, she had already gone to her solicitor, which went very well.

He could go for the house, but not really the business, because even though they both put their name to it, Mel had it as a business. The flat would be handy. She could move in, but she would have to check as she had rented it to two student girls. She thought that this year was nearly up, as they finished a little earlier than school, so she may be alright.

If the house got sold, she would have some money, but she could pay off more of the mortgage to the shop and flat upstairs. She had paid a lot, but this would put her in a position to nearly own it outright and hopefully have a bit left over for maybe a holiday. My goodness she would need it after all of this. Her solicitor said that this was standard practise though for the husband.

Even though he left her, he wants his share, so the house would have to be sold. Oh and he put in divorce papers. "On what grounds, he left me for a tart?" Mel screamed down the phone. "Sorry, Mum, I didn't mean to shout," she said.

"Mel, don't worry, either call your solicitor or go down there and see what can be done. If he asks for the divorce, he pays for it," said Jean.

"Yes, but if I get representation, which I think I will have to, it will cost me too, but not as much as him," replied Mel.

"Mel, what grounds is he divorcing you on?" Mum asked.

"Unreasonable behaviour? How does that work, he left me for another woman, Mum. I will call the solicitor and see what he says, OK. I will let you know what he says!" Mel said hanging up the phone. She looked at the time, she had to get going for work, she would call from there.

When she got in, she was already late, but the solicitors would be open when she got to work. Lesley was already there, sorting out the orders and Julie was making up some flowers for the display in the window. "Morning, girls, I will be out the back if you need me," said Mel, looking a little flustered and frustrated.

Lesley popped her head around the door. "You OK, Mel?" Lesley asked.

"Yes, yes. I have a letter from Terry's solicitor with divorce papers and he wants the house sold and half the money," reported Mel.

"Cor he didn't waste any time. I'll leave you to it, see you in a little while," said Lesley, closing the door. There was a phone in the shop, but also on in the little room in the back, like the office bit.

"Yes, oh OK, yes, that's fine. Yes, I can pop in on Friday again. Yes, 10.30am, that's fine. I have put that in my diary, OK. Thank you, Mr Johnson, see you then, bye," Mel replied putting down the receiver.

"Well, what did he say?" Lesley asked with her head just inside the door.

"Well, if I let Terry go ahead with his divorce petition, it won't cost me as much. It looks like the house has to go but I should be able to keep the shop and flat above and as he suggested and I said to you earlier, if I can pay more of the mortgage off this place and above, that will go in my favour. Terry can't leave me without the means to earn my living," Mel told her.

Mel felt better after that. She went into the shop, saw a bright sunny day out of the shop window and thought, that she may just come out the other side of this. Friday was soon here. She saw Mr Johnson and Mel felt brighter when she left his office. She did suggest that she could divorce Terry on grounds of adultery, but then he told her she needed proof.

Apart from things that had happened and her gut feeling, that wasn't really enough, so he suggested she let him divorce her. The judge might not understand it. I mean continuing to try for a baby, may not be grounds, but to see what happens when the paperwork comes in. It was only the petition, it didn't have much on it, which Mel and her solicitor felt was very sloppy.

Mel went back to work, after the solicitors meeting. She got stuck into the invoices and what needed to be paid into the bank. Her mum kept popping into the shop daily, just to check Mel was doing OK, which she was. Jodie popped in and asked Mel how she was doing.

Apparently, it was now common knowledge that her and Terry had split up. "What are you doing this evening, Mel?" Jodie asked.

"Oh I don't know, staying indoors with a good book I started," replied Mel.

"But it's Friday night, you can't stay in on your own. Why don't you come out with me and the girls. You look like you need cheering up," suggested Jodie.

"Do I? Do I look that bad?" Mel said looking in the mirror. She hadn't really taken any notice of her appearance recently. She thought she looked OK.

"Oh come on, Mel, it will do you good. Us as well, we haven't seen you in ages. Since we went into the pub that Friday," said Jodie wishing she hadn't. That was the weekend, Mel had split with Terry.

"Oh come on, we will have a right laugh. Pleeaaassssseeeeee," begged Jodie.

"Ok, you're not going to leave me alone otherwise. What time and where?" Mel asked.

"Same as usual and between 7.30–8pm!" Jodie told her, with a beaming smile on her face.

"Now go, I still have work to do," Mel told her. Mel rolled her eyes at Lesley, as if to say, can you believe her.

"You need a good night out, Mel, and you need a good shag too!" Lesley retorted.

"Excuse me, missus," argued Mel.

"You're so uptight at the moment, you need it, Mel; believe me…" replied Lesley as she left Mel thinking. At least Mel had something to look forward for the evening now. The rest of the day flew by. Julie wasn't working this morning, she was at the dentist, so Fiona worked all day.

If she knew anything about Clare, she was keeping it to herself. Her and her mum had seen her and Terry out and about and coming and going, but she didn't want to upset Mel about it, so kept her mouth shut. "It's 6pm now, girls, time to go home," Mel told them.

"Yes and you too. You have to get ready for tonight. Don't forget to eat something before you go, especially if you're having a drink or three," said Lesley.

"Yes, Mum," replied Mel. Mel shut up shop. The girls had gone ten minutes before. Everything was locked up, so she made her way home. They were right, all of them. She needed a night out more than anything. A chance to have a laugh and a good drink with the girls.

She darted home, threw a microwave meal in, while she ran a bath and grabbed something to wear out. Some of her stuff was a little big, but her mum kept popping into the shop with sandwiches and some fruit, and sometimes a coffee from the local café. She definitely wanted to make sure Mel was eating properly.

She pulled out a pair of jeans and a lovely new top. She had some lovely flats that would go well with both. She returned to the bathroom to turn the bath off. By the time she had her bath, the food would be ready. Then she would do her hair and make-up, then she would be done.

Once she had eaten, she put some music on to getting ready to. The radio was good for that, save her looking for CDs. She hadn't been near them since Terry had gone, but maybe another time. She would see what he had left her behind.

She put the finishing touches to her hair, it was wavy tonight. A bit of perfume behind the ears, down the top and on her wrists. She grabbed her purse, her keys checked everything was off. She was getting good at that now, it's amazing at the habits you pick up or start when your now on your own.

She opened the door, closed and locked it and off down the garden path. It was quite a warm night and she was excited for the first time in a long time.

***

She walked in the door and Samantha was up at the bar getting the drinks. "Hi, Mel, glad you got here alright?" Sam shouted. Jodie and Paula looked round and beckoned her to the spare seat at their table, they had only just got there. Sam came back over with the drinks.

"Half a lager and lime for Paula; Vodka and Orange for Jodie; Vodka and Lime for Mel, and Gin and Tonic for me," said Sam putting down the drinks and then taking the tray back to the bar. "So thankfully, you listened to Jodie and came out, yessss," said Sam.

"Well, I couldn't stay in now could I? Not when Jodie had made the effort to come and see me at work. Anyway, let's forget work and everything else and have a great time," said Mel.

"I will drink to that," said Sam. They all chinked their glasses together and had a sip. They had a great night. Mel was glad she came. When the evening was over, they asked Mel if she was up for it again next Friday.

"Oh I don't know, girls," she replied.

"Yeah like you have other more important things to do, like read a book at home. Come on, Mel," coaxed Jodie.

"Oh OK, why not, as long as it's not too late, I do have work the next morning as you lot don't working in an office..." replied Mel. They all said their goodbyes and went in the directions of home. Mel got in safely. She stripped off, put her clothes in the dirty laundry, put on her nightshirt and then crawled into bed.

She wasn't drunk but very merry. Thankfully, when she got up the next morning, she didn't have a hangover, like she did last time she went out. But maybe that was because last time she wasn't on the vodka.

Mel went to the shop a little earlier. She was in a good mood. Good company last night, a real laugh with the girls, which was what she had needed, but didn't admit to. Lesley walked in right behind her. "Hi, Mel, how did last night go, did you enjoy yourself?" she asked.

"Yes, it was great. I haven't had a night like it in a long while. I'm glad Jodie twisted my arm yesterday," Mel replied. They had that wedding in a week, so Mel was writing down her list of what stock she needed from the wholesalers in the week, so they can get prepared early enough. Julie came in, with a bit of a headache. "Heavy night last night then?" Mel asked.

"No not really. Just once you start on the wine, you never seem to have an empty glass for too long where my sister is around, so yes feeling a bit rubbish this morning, but once I have another coffee, I should be alright. Mel, do you want one?" Julie asked.

"No, I'm fine thanks. Lesley has just made some tea. Are you out tonight then as well?" Mel asked.

"No chance, early night for me tonight, hot bath, maybe a takeaway and then bed, depending on what's on TV first," Julie replied. Mel put her head down to continue with this list. The day went rather quick, lots of bunches of flowers bought by young men or rather husbands who looked like they had been out too long the night before. Otherwise, the day went OK, no more orders, but there wasn't normally many on a Saturday.

Jodie called Mel in the week to see if she wanted to go out again on Friday. She said yes as she had had such a good time the week before. Jodie said she and the others would meet same place and roughly the same time. Mel had picked up the flowers on Wednesday for the wedding, so she and Lesley could make a start on them on Thursday.

They were being delivered on Saturday morning, that way they would be still fresh. If they got them on Thursday, they may have a rush on and not time to make them. Even with two full timers and two-part timers, it could be daunting sometimes.

Mel was rather pleased with what her and Lesley had done. The bridal bouquet was rather beautiful, with pink and white roses with a few carnations with some baby's breath. The bridesmaids were smaller versions of the brides. Mel was going to deliver them on Saturday, but Lesley thought they had better see if she had a hangover first.

So they waited, by Friday afternoon, all the wedding parties flowers were finished. Mel took a few photos of the bouquets, the bridal one then all of them together, with the buttonholes. She left them in the refrigerated area, well the massive fridge in the kitchen. To keep them fresh, Mel would spray them in the morning.

But now she was off, it was 6pm. She locked up and turned on her heels and made her way home. She was getting used to this new life she was getting for herself and she was enjoying it. She put her bath on, checked the freezer. She had done some shopping the day before and there was a nice-looking lasagne that she was going to have this evening. So she pulled that out, left it on the side and went back up to turn her bath off.

Mel pulled out a dress to wear this evening. It was a lovely evening and jeans and a cotton top was not going to do it tonight. She pulled out her sandals and a white cardigan she could put over her shoulders if it turned cold later on. The girls again were there already before her.

This time Jodie was up getting the drinks. "Vodka and Lime, Mel?" Jodie asked.

"Yes please, no hangover last time," Mel reported. She took her seat, and Jodie came back with their drinks. And again, they had a great time. This time there was a band on, not that they liked the music they were playing, but they still enjoyed themselves. Mel left when it was closing time and she felt a bit merry, but still had a good night.

She climbed into bed and before she knew it the alarm had gone off. Time to get up, but this time, her head started to hurt. She didn't know why, she hadn't drunk as much as last week. She got herself ready for work, and left the house. She thought she may have heard something from Terry's solicitor, but nothing all quiet, which she was grateful for.

She opened the door. She knew they had a lot to do today, she went to the fridge and collected the flowers, put them in their boxes. Then Lesley came in, she said good morning, then told her she had a visitor. Mel wasn't expecting anyone this morning. She was expecting to go out and deliver the flowers for the wedding in half an hour.

She went into the shop and there stood Terry. Mel saw him and gasped. She stood for a couple of minutes in shock. "What do you want, Terry? I have a busy morning and I don't really have time for this!" She told him.

"Oh OK, I just wanted to see you," he said but then Mel interrupted him.

"Why?" She snapped at him.

"I just wondered if you had signed the divorce papers yet, that's all?" He asked rather coyly.

"Are you in that a rush to get the divorce done then? All of them years, flushed down the toilet?" Mel demanded.

"It's just that me and Clare, well we really want to get married," he explained.

"What?" She said, as if she hadn't heard his answer.

"We want to get married, as soon as really," he told her.

"Again WHY?" Mel asked. This time she was getting annoyed. They had only been broke up a few weeks and he wants to get married again.

"No, I haven't had a chance to sign them. I'm afraid, you will have to wait, unless it's that urgent that you get married. You could marry her anyway, but then that would make you a bigamist. So if you don't want to do that, I'm afraid you have to wait. Now, I have things to do, good day," said Mel, rather abruptly, but she felt good for it.

He had treated her awful, and now he wants something from her. Terry left the shop and Lesley came into it from the back. "Did I hear right? Sorry, Mel, I couldn't help but overhear," she said a little embarrassed.

"Yes, Les, you heard right. He wants to get married. He's only been gone for a few weeks, divorce can take a long time, so why would he want to rush it?" She told her. "Come on, we have to get these flowers delivered. Julie, can you cope on your own for a few minutes, while we deliver these. Actually, Les, can I take Julie and leave you in the shop, just in case wonder boy comes back?" Mel asked.

"I know it was you who had sorted this out for me. I just wanted to wish the bride the best and apologise for my behaviour when they came into the shop," she quizzed.

"Go on then, I can manage and as you say wonder boy might come back to see if you have signed your life away," Lesley retorted.

Mel and Julie picked up the boxes and put them in the back of the little van. They hopped into the front and made their way to the address on the order. Ding dong, went the doorbell, "Hello, Mrs Jackson, Mel from 'Blooming Marvellous'. I have the wedding flowers for your daughter."

Mrs Jackson was over the moon with them. "Lizzie, the flowers are here," shouted up Mrs Jackson.

"Mrs Jackson, I wanted to apologise for the way I behaved when you came into the shop with your daughter to order your flowers. So in a way of an apology, I know your daughter's theme was pink and white, but I have upgraded your buttonholes for the mothers of the bridal party to roses, instead of carnations and made your daughter Lizzie's bouquet larger than you asked for. I hope that was OK. I was just having a very bad day, but that was no excuse, so I apologise for that day," said Mel.

"Oh not to worry, lovie, everyone has a bad day now and then and thank you for that, for my Lizzie's bigger bouquet. She will love it, I know she will. Thank you again," said Mrs Jackson.

"Have a great day all of you and congratulations to the bride and groom," Mel added.

"Thank you," said Lizzie, who had just appeared at the door. "Uncle George wants another brandy, Mum," Lizzie told her. "Thank you for the bouquet. It's beautiful, I just had a look," said Lizzie.

"Bye," Mel said as her and Julie got into the van again. They got back to the shop in record time. "Any surprises?" Mel asked looking round before entering the shop.

"No, none. How did it go with Mrs Jackson?" Lesley asked.

"Fine, they were delighted with the larger bouquet, so that's a good thing. Now what else have we got on today?" Mel asked.

"Not much, I'm afraid," replied Lesley.

"Well, do you think we should let a young lady go home, who isn't feeling too great," suggested Mel.

"No, you can stay with me, we can send Julie home," tittered Lesley. So Mel let Julie go home. Mel and Lesley didn't do much for the day, but you can't just shut up shop, so they had to stay there. There still was no more from Terry, but Mel thought it was funny, this morning she realised that she hadn't heard from him or his lawyer, then he turns up at the shop.

She knew her solicitors were shut today, but was going to call Mr Johnson on Monday, to ask if she should sign the papers. At least it would start the ball rolling, but that was for Monday. When she finished work this evening, she was going to take a leaf out of Julie's book and chill and get a takeaway.

When Mel got up the next morning, she knew why she had headache the day before. She ran to the bathroom, got out her supplies. At least this time, she knew she wasn't pregnant, she hadn't done anything. So that day, she stayed in bed, most of the day with a hot water bottle on her tummy and hot milk topped up with pepper, that sometimes helped.

Her mum called her to see if she wanted some dinner, but Mel explained that she wasn't feeling up to it, as she had them again. She turned up later on with two dinner plates, one on top of the other with a roast dinner on it, and a small jug with gravy in it. She had literally took it round after dishing it up. Mel was grateful for the dinner; took it, ate it and then washed up the plates to take them round later on in the week.

Work went rather quickly because all of a sudden there were lots of christenings and parents wanted flower arrangements at their do's, which Mel was grateful for, but also that she didn't have to be around on the day to see the little darlings. Mel was feeling fine to go out with the girls on the Friday. She didn't stay as long as normal. She was rather tired as she had had a busy week.

The following week though, she felt as fit as a fiddle, even though this week was just as busy as the last one. She was looking forward to going out. It was now the end of July. She had spoken with her solicitor and decided to sign the divorce paperwork. It would still take a while, so she got on with her life.

When Mel got to the pub, for a change, it was only Paula in at this time. Mel was a little early. She ordered drinks for her and Paula and then Jodie and Sam came through the door and Mel got their drinks, brought them over to the table and sat herself down. Mel looked round, then she looked again. "Oooohh," she thought, whose he?

Standing at the bar was a tall, blonde haired muscly guy. He looked round at Mel and smiled at her. She noticed it and smiled back, but so did the girls. "Go on, Mel, he's gorgeous. Get his number at least," said Jodie.

"Jodie, you're terrible. I have only just seen him, he may not be interested," Mel said, really telling herself.

"Don't be daft. He smiled at you and you smiled right back at him. Go on, up to the bar. We will just sit here and watch," urged Jodie.

"I'm not accustomed to asking men out, Jode," Mel said.

"No need, he's coming over here," said Sam.

"Hi, I'm Andy. Can I get you a drink? Well, all of you?" He said looking round at the other three.

"We OK, thanks, Andy," Mel replied.

"No, that's a vodka and orange, a vodka and lime, Gin and Tonic and half a lager and lime, Andy. Mel can help you at the bar, can't you, Mel?" Jodie coaxed. Giving Mel a nudge on the elbow.

"Ok then, Mel," escorted Andy. Andy got up to go to the bar and Mel went with him. He got the drinks and put them on the table. Mel and Andy stayed at the bar. Jodie brought Mel's other drink over, so she could stay talking to Andy. He was lovely, as well in looks, Mel thought. He was just a dream.

He worked on the building sites as a bricklayer, which made sense to his physique, he was well toned up. He made Mel laugh a few times. "Hey do you think we should have kept Andy for ourselves, Mel seems to be having too much fun with him at the bar. Oh no their not at the bar anymore, have they left?" Jodie asked.

"No, silly, they are over the other side, look?" Sam suggested, they all raised their heads to have a look. Mel and Andy seemed engrossed in conversation. Mel thought he was fascinating. He didn't live around here, but was meeting up with friends, who hadn't turned up and saw Mel, and thought he would chat to her.

Mel didn't return to her seat with the girls for the rest of the evening. She stayed with Andy. He was telling her about his job and how he didn't always stay in one place for long because in the building trade, you took the work wherever it was. He was nearly finished in the area he was working, just had another week, then was off to somewhere over the other side of town.

He liked all sorts of music, like Mel, no particular band or group. She was trying to find some mutual ground, apart from the jobs they do which you couldn't get any further apart. They got on well, but goodness knows what they would talk about the next time she saw him. He looked like he went to the gym, they could talk about that, but he didn't he got his workout at work, lifting the bricks.

'Hod carrying', she thought he said. Makes sense with the muscles. He was single and she was estranged from her husband, but she didn't tell him that. He liked fine wine though, even though he was drinking lager. When the pub was closing, Andy asked Mel if he could walk her home.

She was delighted. She said goodnights to the girls, they all sat there with their mouths open. They replied their goodnights. Jodie was going to be straight on the phone to Mel in the morning. Andy asked if it was far enough to need a cab or did she want to walk home.

It was still a nice evening, warm, the summer was nearly in full swing, so she had her cardigan round her shoulders. He put his arm around her as they walked. Mel had all sorts of feelings going round in her head. She hadn't thought she would meet anyone again, especially so soon to Terry going, but what the hell.

They got to hers, and she asked Andy if he wanted to come in for a coffee. He said yes. He didn't have to work in the morning, so it would give them time to talk. Mel opened the door, she turned the lights on in the sitting room, shut the curtains, and went into the kitchen to make the coffee.

Andy made himself at home in the sitting room. Mel made the coffee and came back into the room. Andy took the cups off her and for the first time, Mel was able to see Andy's bright blue eyes. They had a sparkle to them and she looked like she was drowning in them.

Andy moved forward and bent down to kiss Mel. Mel responded and let Andy take control. That kiss seemed to go on forever and ever. Mel sunk into Andy's arms. He picked her up and made his way to the stairs, which he spotted when they walked through the door. He carried her up to her bedroom, which was open, he walked through and put Mel neatly on the bed, closed the door and started to undress himself and then her.

Mel pulled the covers off the bed and turned off the light by the bed. Andy laid down next to her and pulled her close. He kissed her again and caressed her body. She felt herself tingle all over. She couldn't believe what was happening. She thought she had died and gone to heaven, in this moment.

Andy stroked her body softly. Terry was never this tender with her. Mind you she had nothing to compare Terry too. He was the only man she had ever been with. Where had Andy been all of her life?

Andy kissed her again and this time, he got on top of her, while still stroking and kissing her body now. He entered her and she felt his thrust, it was wonderful. She hadn't felt like this in a very long time and Terry was definitely nothing to be compared to. This was the best sex she had ever had. It seemed to last all night, but it didn't.

Mel didn't want it to end, but it did, and then Andy, laid next to her cuddling her until she slept.

Mel woke around 10am. 'Oh no', she thought, she looked over, next to her was empty. Did she dream this or did it really happen? She grabbed her dressing gown and ran downstairs. The two cups of coffee from the night before had gone. Andy was in the kitchen making tea.

"Oh I was going to bring this up to you. How are you this morning?" He asked her caressing her forehead, smoothing her hair out of the way.

"I'm fine, but I am really late for work. Do you have to go anywhere today? You could stay here until I come back about 5ish?" Mel asked, well pleaded really.

"No, I have to go soon. Sorry, Mel, but if I can take your number and we can go out again, if you want to?" Andy asked her.

"Yes, of course I want to and I just wanted to add, that I don't normally really do that sort of thing like last night?" She said rather embarrassed.

"Oh don't be silly. I won't hold it against you. Yes we can go out again, leave your number for me and I will take it with me," Andy said. Mel ran back upstairs after taking a mouthful of tea, put on some clothes, brushed her teeth and then ran out the door, leaving the number for Andy. Andy left just after Mel, she had told him just to pull the front door closed. It didn't matter if she didn't lock it, nobody could get in, it was like fort knocks.

She practically bumped into Fiona when she ran through the door. "Hey, where's the fire, Mel?" Lesley asked. "So did you have a nice time last night then?" Lesley asked.

"Er yes I did, it was great fun," replied Mel.

"Liar, Jodie has already been on the phone asking about Andy," said Lesley. Mel went red. "So what happened then, Mel?" Lesley asked.

"What do you think happened, Les?" Mel said.

"Jodie has been on twice asking about the gory details. I said I didn't know what she was talking about, so she may pop in, sorry," Lesley said to Mel.

"Not too worry, all three of them had their mouths open last night when I left with Andy," said Mel.

"Well, what's he like then?" Lesley quizzed.

"Well," Mel started to tell Lesley all about him, but she left out that she slept with him, that was her little secret for now; plus she didn't think Andy was the type to kiss and tell. So she held that bit back from the others too. Jodie kept her promise and popped in wanting all the details. Mel did the same, she kept out the crucial details, they were hers for now.

Even though she was late in, Mel couldn't really concentrate and the day was dragging. There weren't doing much so let Fiona go home. Her and Lesley could cope. Mel left the shop to go home. She had to tidy up, it wasn't a mess, but she had had someone there the night before.

Andy didn't leave the place untidy, but she wanted to strip her bed. No she didn't, she wanted to leave it like that forever. He was in her bed and he had made love to her. She loved every minute of it…she didn't want to wash those bed things ever again, but she knew she had to. She jumped onto the bed and smelt the pillow that Andy laid on.

She could still smell him on it. She laid there for a little while, then realised she had to get up and sort herself out. She jumped every time the phone rang thinking it would be Andy. He had taken her number which she had left on the side for him. Sunday came and went, no call.

Monday she went to work, he still hadn't called. Maybe he was busy and hadn't had chance. She didn't have an answer phone, so she may have missed his call.

Tuesday, Wednesday, Thursday, still no call, but she thought never mind, tomorrow was Friday and she would be out with the girls and he would be there again. She had told Jodie she was going out Friday night as always. When she got there, the girls were already there.

Sam ordered Mel a drink, she had sat down on her regular seat. She looked out for Andy but couldn't see him. When she went to the loo, she went round to the other side of the bar, no sign of Andy. "Come on, Mel, he probably hasn't had time to come over this way and you did say he was moving onto the next job sometime next week. Maybe he had to pack up early and go already," said Jodie.

'Yes, that would be it', thought Mel. She was a little disappointed. She wanted to see him or at least hear from him. She stayed for a couple of hours with the girls then had an early night. It was a far cry from the week before, but hey ho.

She went to work as normal, as in time. Lesley looked a little disappointed too, when Mel walked through the door. They had a busy day today. Getting a hall ready for the evening do, so that took her mind off Andy. Sunday, Mel just chilled at home. Her mum called her and asked if she wanted to come round for Sunday lunch.

Mel thought about it and then said yes. She hadn't seen her mum in a little while and it would break up the day. The Friday nights were coming round rather quickly now, and Mel still hadn't seen Andy since that night about 6 weeks ago. Jodie went up to the bar and ordered their usual round, but Mel didn't fancy a vodka, but just an orange juice.

"Huh?" Jodie asked.

"Sorry, Jode, I don't fancy a vodka and I have an early start in the morning," said Mel. So Mel got an orange juice, then another, then another, then made her excuses to leave. She was shattered. She got home, checked everything was locked at went straight up to bed. She didn't even take her clothes off, she fell asleep with them on.

When Mel woke up in the morning, she felt like she hadn't even been to bed. She pulled herself off the bed, grabbed some clean clothes and went to the bathroom to get washed, really to splash some water on her face also. She felt so tired. She didn't fancy breakfast and she wasn't hungry. She shut the door and made her way to work.

When she got there, Lesley thought Mel looked awful, but didn't say anything. Mel went into the back and put the kettle on. "Anyone want one?" Mel asked. Everyone had a hot drink. She went back into the office and put her head on the table.

"Mel, Mel, wake up," said Lesley, nudging Mel.

"What sorry?" Mel said, not sure where she was.

"Mel, you were asleep!" Lesley said.

"Asleep, I couldn't have been. I have not long got up and come straight to work," she replied.

"Mel, what time did you go to bed last night?" Lesley asked. "Er, 9 I think?" She said scratching her head.

"And you got up at what time?" Lesley enquired.

"I'm not sure, what time did I get in here?" she asked Lesley.

"After 10," Lesley said.

'After 10, that means I have been asleep for 12 hours and now I am falling asleep at work, that's not right', thought Mel. She went into the kitchen to make that coffee. She thought she had better have coffee to stay awake. She drank that and was nodding off again.

"Mel, go home, we can manage and you need the sleep," demanded Lesley looking stern.

"Are you sure, I am knackered," Mel told her. Mel didn't need telling twice with the look Lesley was giving her. "Thanks, Les." Mel took her keys and went straight back out the door again. She went home and straight up to bed, she was so tired.

She didn't wake again until gone 12 the next day. 'What on earth is wrong with me?' She thought. Her mum had called but Mel didn't hear the phone. Her mum thought she had gone out, so didn't call again until later on, but Mel was again in bed and didn't hear the phone ring.

The next morning, Mel woke early, all of a sudden she fancied something to eat. She looked in the fridge. 'The bacon, sausages, eggs, no eggs', she thought, 'bacon sandwich would do'. So that's what she made herself before going to work. She ate it with such gusto, she thoroughly enjoyed it.

She got herself ready then left for work. Lesley was already in, that poor woman seemed to live at that place at the moment. "Kettle's on, Mel, tea or coffee?" she asked.

"Oh tea please. Oh I just need to pop along to the café for the minute, anyone want anything?" she asked looking at Lesley and Julie.

"No thanks, we are fine," said Les. Mel went to the café and picked up two bacon sandwiches. She went back to the shop, where with her tea made by Lesley, she could enjoy her sandwiches. Lesley looked odd at her, in all the time she had known Mel, she had never gone to the café for breakfast or lunch or anything else.

'Oh well', she thought, 'she must be hungry'. Mel enjoyed her sandwiches and started on the orders. Fiona popped in to say that she would be a little late for her shift as she had to go to the doctors for an appointment. "Nothing wrong is there, Fiona?" Mel asked.

"Oh no, it's just a check-up that's all. See you at 1.30pm." Mel went back to the office and sorted out the invoices that had to be paid and then went back to the shop. Fiona came in just as Julie was finished her shift. She picked up the broom to start sweeping the leaves and twigs from the fallen plants and flowers on the floor.

"How did your appointment go then, Fiona?" Lesley asked.

"Oh it was OK, nothing wrong. I just kept getting terrible period pains, where I would be laid up in bed for a few days. When I was at work, I would spend the morning in bed and then bundle up with strong pain killers, but now the doctor has given me something for it. So hopefully that will work better for me. Eh, Les, guess who was in the surgery? Terry and Clare!" Fiona said.

Mel's ears seemed to prick up at the mention of Terry and Clare. "I wonder what they were there for?" Lesley asked, trying not to make a big deal out of it.

"Oh that's easy, Clare's pregnant, probably there for her first check-up," said Fiona matter of flatly.

"PREGNANT!" Mel screamed. "Pregnant. I don't believe it, that bastard couldn't get me pregnant and he dips his wick with her and then along comes a little Terry or Clare…Oh now it makes sense to rush this bloody divorce. So he can marry her and give THEIR baby his name, so it's all proper," Mel shouted.

Lesley was surprised next door hadn't come in to see what was wrong. Mind you the noise Mel was making, it wasn't difficult to hear her. Mel got up from the floor, with a little difficulty and marched straight out the back. Lesley gave Fiona such a look.

"Sorry, Les, I forgot," apologised Fiona.

"You OK, Mel?" Lesley asked, a little worried she had asked.

"I'm fine, Lesley, honest. It's just hearing those words that SHE is pregnant. He knew there was nothing wrong with him, but this now confirms it. Do you think you could manage here for the rest of the day?"

"I know I am asking a lot of you. You have been great these last few months, but now hearing that, it's just difficult, that's all," Mel told her.

Not that Mel needed to say anything, Lesley knew the score. Mel picked up her keys and her bag, said goodbye to the women and then left. She didn't want to go home, so she popped round to see her mum. Tina was at work but her nan, Marge, was there as well.

"Tea, Mel?" asked Marge.

"Yes please, Nan," replied Mel.

"You OK, Mel?" Her mum, Jean, asked.

"No, not really, I found out today that Terry and Clare," she made a face, "are having a baby. I'm just a bit sad that's all. I will be fine, please don't worry," she added.

Marge and Jean looked at each other and then Marge said, "Mel, these things happen I'm afraid. You can't change it. It does make sense now why he wanted you to sign the papers. Well that's a thing, he divorces you on grounds of unreasonable behaviour, but he's the one committed adultery and the reason he's divorcing is because of your wanting of a baby and now she's pregnant."

"I would get in touch with your lawyer. This may make it easier for you, because he's now done the thing he blamed you for. It's worth looking into. Try not to worry about it, things will all come right in the end, you'll see," Marge said.

Mel hugged her nan. She knew she was right. All of a sudden Mel was really tired. "Mum, do you mind if I go and have a lie down on your bed. I'm tired all of a sudden, maybe the shock," Mel commented.

"Go on, do you want me to bring you up another cup of tea?" she asked.

"No thanks, I don't think I can drink any tea at the moment. It's starting to make me feel sick," she added.

Marge looked puzzled. "Since when has tea made our Mel feel sick? Sleeping all the time. Jean, how many times did you call her yesterday?" Marge asked.

"About 4 or 5," Jean replied. "But she was home, just asleep. Oh, I see what you mean," Jean added.

Mel slept for over two hours, when she came down, she had found her appetite. "Mum, is there anything to eat?" Mel asked.

"Well, I was doing dinner. I was going to do egg, chips, beans sausages," said Mum.

"No eggs please, Mum, they make me feel a bit queasy now," Mel told her.

"Mel, have you had anything to eat today?" Marge asked.

"Yes, I had a bacon sandwich, I made for breakfast then when I got to work. Lesley put the kettle on and I popped along to the café for a bacon sandwich, but got 2, I felt so hungry," she said.

"And what else?" Jean asked.

"Oh that was it, until now," she added.

"But you have been sleeping an awful lot, love, you're not eating properly, tea and now eggs make you feel sick. I think you should go to the doctors," Jean told her.

Mel went into the kitchen. She hadn't thought about it. She was tired a lot of the time and had kept falling asleep. She dismissed it, she would see how she felt tomorrow and if she didn't feel any better; she didn't feel ill or sick, but not her usual self, then she would make an appointment.

Chapter 3

"Sorry, Susie, could you say that again. I don't think I heard you correctly," said Mel.

"Mel, you're pregnant!" Susie told her.

"Are you sure, Susie, you're not pulling my leg?" Mel asked quite nervously.

"Mel, look, it's a positive test. You're pregnant. You're going to have a baby!" Susie said, jumping up and down. She was as thrilled as Mel would be if she wasn't in shock.

She had made an appointment with the doctors, but they had all gone, so she saw the nurse. Mel couldn't believe what Susie was saying. "Susie, are you positive?" Mel asked.

"No, Mel, you're positive and yes, you're pregnant and if I'm right on your dates of your last period, you're about eight weeks. So now what I will do is work out roughly your due date. Now, your due date is 15 April. So you have plenty of time to plan things, so if you go into reception, and Jill will give you a date for the ante-natal appointment. Then you can be referred to what hospital you want," said Susie.

Mel was still in a daze. She got up, grabbed her stuff and then went to leave the room. "Congratulations, Mel," added Susie.

"Thank you, Susie," Mel replied. She went to reception and made an appointment for the next day, that way it could be sorted and she could be seen before her dating scan. This was too much for Mel to take in. She said goodbye and left the surgery. She felt like a zombie.

She should have gone straight back to work but felt she should go and see her mum and tell her the good news. It didn't take long for her to get to mum's. She pressed the doorbell, she could hear her mum coming to open the front door. "Mel, what are you doing here and why didn't you use your key? Come in, you look dreadful," Jean said to her.

Jean went to the kitchen, Mel followed her. Her nan was already in there, she was sat at the table and was making a cuppa for Mel, then remembered she had gone off tea, so pulled the coffee jar over to her. "Mel, are you ok?" Marge asked.

"Er yes, but I think you had better sit down, Mum. I've got something to tell you both," she said. Mel had tears in her eyes as she was about to start. "I have just left the doctors, and I have news. Good news, well great news really," she said as she was starting to smile.

"I'm going to have a baby! I'm pregnant," she added. Jean jumped up and grabbed her daughter and gave her the biggest hug.

"Are you sure, Mel?" Marge asked.

"Yes, I even looked at the stick they use POSITIVE. Mum, is it really great news?" Mel asked, looking for approval or support.

"Of course its good news, its great news," she added.

"But, Mum, I'm going through a divorce. I could lose my house. How on earth am I going to provide for a baby, another human being on my own?" Mel begged.

"Now who says you're on your own, eh? You have us, your mum, me, Tina, your friends. So you don't have a no-good husband, who frankly wasn't worth anything if you ask me, but now your nearly rid of and what's this about having a baby on your own. What are we? Your family and if you lose the house, that will give you some money."

"You still have the business and the flat above you. We will all help out and don't forget, it will be your mum's first grandchild and my first great-grandchild. It will be fine, Mel, you'll see," said Marge getting up to hug her granddaughter. Mel hugged them both back.

Her nan was right, they would manage somehow. "The house will have to go and maybe the shop and flat above if he wants half of everything. Good job we didn't have a dog!" Mel added, with that they all burst out laughing.

"Mel, it will sort itself out. Don't worry, have faith," nan added. 'Why were older women so wise', Mel thought. Mel stayed for a little while then headed back to work. Even though she had only been told a few hours ago about having a baby, she wanted to tell her staff.

Mainly so they made sure she didn't do too much lifting at work, if she forgot all of a sudden, not that she was likely to. It's just a shame what she wanted more than anything in the world with Terry was a baby and now she was having one, all on her own. But she was a strong woman, she knew she could do it.

Besides, she had dealt with a lot these last few months or so, not always great, but she got there in the end. She walked in through the door. Lesley was writing up an order and Fiona was sweeping up the floor. "Hiya, ladies," Mel said.

"Hi, Mel, you OK, you look a bit er… peaky," said Fiona, that girl just said it as it was, no filter.

"Thanks for that, Fiona. I need to talk to you both, if I shut up for a few minutes. Les, could you put the kettle on, coffee for me please. I need to talk to both of you," Mel told them. They all went out the back. Mel had put a 'Back in 15 mins' note on the door.

Lesley handed her a piping hot coffee, then handed a tea to Fiona. Mel sat down and thought for a moment. "Now, you both know that I have been to the doctors," she said.

"Yes," they replied.

"Well, I found out that I'm going to have a baby," with that both of the women jumped up and screamed.

"Oh, Mel, that's wonderful news!" Lesley said.

"Yes, it is. I am now thrilled. I have been in shock most of the morning. The baby is due 15 April. The thing is for now, please can we keep it quiet?" Mel said, who wanted to continue but Fiona interrupted.

"Why, Mel?"

"Because, I am in the middle of a divorce. My estranged husband is about to become a father and has a new partner, so it is rather delicate, at this moment. I don't want him to know about my baby," Mel said looking at Fiona. "Now, Fiona, I know they live on your road, but please don't say anything about it not yet, at least until I am showing?" Mel said pleadingly.

"I won't, Mel," Fiona promised.

"I don't need him having a go at me. Anyway he doesn't know that I had slept with someone else, so he will be wondering…" Mel said with a coy look on her face.

"Oh I forgot about that, Andy?" Lesley quizzed.

Mel nodded her head. "Well, I haven't been with anyone else," Mel snapped. "Sorry, I didn't mean to do that, Les," she apologised. "Have you seen him?" Lesley asked.

"No, not since that night," Mel replied.

"Oh, so you had a one night stand, Mel?" Fiona asked.

"Fiona, is there anything you can be doing now, tea break is over," said Lesley.

"Oh OK. Congratulations, Mel," she said and grabbed her hand and gave her a warm smile. Mel smiled back. Fiona let go of her hand and then picked up the two empty cups and went to wash them.

"So it's Andy's then? Don't worry, no judgement here, but, Mel, was it worth it?" Lesley quizzed.

"Oh, Les, yes it was. It was the best ever. Terry was rubbish compared. It's a shame I haven't seen him since, but what can you do?" Mel replied.

"As you said tea break over, let's get back to work." Mel agreed. The week went rather quick. When Julie came in the next morning, Mel told her, but also to keep it quiet. She didn't want any hassle from Terry, even though she had signed the paperwork, she hadn't heard anything since.

***

Mel went to her appointment the next day and saw the doctor. She congratulated Mel on her pregnancy and then asked her what hospital she wanted to go for, as it was now shared care, which took a bit of the strain off the hospitals. Mel opted for St Augustines on Lemon Tree Road. Paula's sister had her daughter there and had said that they were wonderful.

She had to go there for an initial appointment the following week, and to also arrange her date scan. Which would be two weeks later on. Mel was delighted with her choice of hospital and the doctor referred her when she left. It was all done on the computer nowadays, so within a couple of days, she received a letter from St. Augustines that she was accepted to have her baby there.

That was what she wanted. A confirmation that she was having a baby in writing.

***

Friday night soon came round and Mel wasn't sure about going out, but thought she owed her great friends the same consideration she told her staff. So thankfully when they went out. The pub was empty enough for Mel to tell them without too many people over hearing. Jodie, Sam and Paula were all sat there with their mouths opened, stunned.

Then they all ran over to Mel, cheering. They couldn't believe it. She had also asked them to keep it quiet for the time being. "But why?" Jodie asked.

"Because, dummy, I'm in the middle of a divorce, that my estranged husband has asked for and as we now know, she's pregnant, now me. We know who the father is, but Terry has no idea. Even though it's not his business, like nothing I have done since he left the marital home has been."

"I don't want his unnecessary attention, because he will think he can divorce me for adultery, even though he was the one to go off with that woman," Mel told them. "So thank you for whoever is buying the next round, mine is an orange juice," she commanded. Mel stayed for an hour or so more, then headed home.

She hadn't had to do too much this week, but it had been a whirlwind of stuff going on. She had gotten used to living on her own, checking everything was locked up before she went to bed. Her work days were rolling into the next ones, everything was going great.

***

It was the morning of her appointment at the hospital. Her mum came with her, for moral support. Both of them sat down in the waiting room. "Mum, would you mind if I go back to my maiden name of Shaw?" Mel asked.

"No, love, that would be great, but why?" Mum asked.

"Well, this baby isn't Terry's, so I can't really call it Humphreys, so I thought if I went back to using Shaw, the baby can take that name too. What do you think?" Mel asked a little nervous.

"It's a great idea and it will be lovely to have you as a Shaw again!" Jean added.

"Mrs Humphreys," called the nurse. Mel got up from her seat, and followed the nurse. "Did you bring a urine sample with you?" The nurse asked. Mel gave the nurse her sample. She did her checks with it and put it down the sink and the container in the medical bin.

She then asked Mel to get on the scales, they wanted to keep an eye on her weight throughout the pregnancy. Then she did Mel's blood pressure. "I need to take from blood from you, is that ok?" The nurse smiled. Mel held out her arm. Thank goodness she didn't faint at the sight of blood.

"Er, nurse, can I ask you something?" Mel asked.

"Yes, of course," she replied.

"Well, I want to be known as my maiden name, how can I do that here? I can inform my GP, which sadly I forgot to," Mel said.

"Well, if you go over to reception and tell them the correct information, it will go on your paperwork before it gets too confusing eh," replied the nurse. "All finished, do you know when you're here next?" she asked.

"Yes, in two weeks for my dating scan," Mel said all happy.

The nurse smiled again. "First baby?"

"Yes, very much wanted baby, been trying for years, no luck," Mel said.

"What did you do?" The nurse asked a little nosey.

"Slept with someone else," Mel said happily. The nurse was dumbstruck. Then she said goodbye to Mel and went to call the next patient. Mel went up to reception and gave her details, as she was told to by the nurse. "Just so there's no mix up," Mel suggested.

Mel left the hospital with her mum and headed back to the doctors to do the same there, as she said, just to make sure there's no mix up. "Ok, Mel, thank you for letting us know," said the reception. They didn't care that Mel's baby was by someone else, they were just delighted she had got pregnant. Everyone knew about Terry and Clare it had got round like wildfire about Clare being pregnant.

But everyone who liked Mel, had changed their attitude about Terry, so they were going to keep her secret until Mel said otherwise. Mel was always respected in the community, but with what has happened, her respect was higher, because how she had dealt with it. She hadn't screamed at Terry at his workplace and shown him up out and about. Even though she wanted to in the beginning, she didn't dare go down to his level.

Now she was going to have her very own baby, without Terry or without its dad, Andy, but that didn't matter. If Andy ever did turn up again, he was going to be in for a big shock. But Mel wasn't worried about that, out of that one night, she was going to be a mummy. There she said it, Mummy. It was a word, she never thought would be associated with her, but now it was.

The next two weeks flew by, and she was now 12 weeks pregnant and starting to show a little belly. She was thrilled a few of her things that didn't fit her anymore, had started to, but she knew not for long. It was the morning of the scan. Her mum had called round to her a little early.

Mel had decided once she knew she was having a baby, that she wanted her mum to come with her for everything, mainly for support, but she knew her mum was as just as excited as her. They got there a little early. Mel had only just sat down when she was called into the scan graphics room. "Ms Shaw," she called. Mel felt better about that.

"If you could take your bottom half off, but leave your underwear on, and hop onto the bed, unless you need help," she said.

"Not yet, I don't, but thank you," Mel said smiling, she was so excited. The scanographer put some gel on the bottom of Mel's tummy and then put the tool attached to the machine over her tummy.

Mel's mum was standing to the left of her, so one she didn't get in the way and two, so she could see properly. "Oh, Mel, look, that's your baby," said Mum squealing like a little girl. Mel was mesmerised, she couldn't stop looking at her baby.

"Would you like a photo of the baby?" she asked.

"Yes please," said Mel.

"Can I have one as well please?" Jean asked.

"Yes, of course, but I'm afraid it's a two-pound charge for yours though, sorry?" The lady told her.

"That's OK, thank you, I can show nan when I get in," said Jean.

Mel couldn't stop looking at the screen, she was so happy. "I don't suppose you can tell what it is yet, can you?" Mel asked.

"No, not this time, but you will be able to at the 20-week scan, in eight weeks' time, then we measure everything. I'm afraid you will have to wait until then." The lady said. "Right then, that's done. Until next time in eight weeks. Believe me, Mel, they go so quickly," she added.

Mel thanked her, she had already given her tissue to wipe her tummy with, then she got off the bed. The lady gave them both their photos. Mel still couldn't believe it. She thanked her and then they left. "Oh, Mel, I still can't believe it," said Mum.

"What? Me finally having a baby or that this little one is in me?" Mel asked.

"Well both really, but I am so happy, because I know you're so happy," Mum added.

Mel went home with her mum to show her nan the scan picture. Her nan was as delighted as they both were. She stayed a little while and then went home. She hadn't been there all morning and wanted to drop off stuff like her new hospital notes, she didn't need them with her just yet.

She put the key in the door and picked up the post. There right on top was a letter from her solicitor, Mr Johnson. She opened it up, he said that things were going well so far. She had already given them all the information that they had needed, but now both parties had signed, they had been given a date for court, 10 October at 11.30am.

Mel thought she had better put the date in her diary as she was getting a bit forgetful. She picked up the phone to call Mr Johnson, she had better tell him her circumstances. They had changed and what was her best strategy now as she was going to be a single mum?

When she got through, Mr Johnson was at court on a different case, so Mel made an appointment to see him on the 8 October. She knew it was a bit short notice, but she couldn't really do anything else. She then called her mum. "Mum," said Mel.

"Mel, what's wrong, love. There's nothing wrong is there?" Mum said panicking.

"No, Mum, I'm fine. I thought you would want to know," she then relayed the situation to her mum, but also told her about the appointment to get things straight before court.

"Clever girl that Mel, Mum," said Jean. "She thinks of everything, but then mind you, she's getting awful forgetful though," Mum added.

Mel, still in a good mood, even though about court, she wanted to pop into the florist. She opened the door and they were still serving customers. Mel took her things out the back and came back when she knew the shop was empty. She still hadn't said anything about it.

She had the photo in her hands. "Who wants to see my new bubba then?" she asked. Both of the ladies, Lesley and Fiona, came over and oohed and ahhed over the new baby in the picture.

"Oh, Mel, how are you feeling?" Fiona asked.

"I'm great, thanks. It's so amazing to see that little one in my tummy on a screen. I was mesmerised." She told them.

"How was Jean holding up?" Lesley asked.

"Oh she was loving it the doting grandma," Mel replied. They were sitting there talking. Fiona had gone to make drinks. Mel was no longer on coffee as she didn't think it fair on the baby.

She had switched to herbal teas, they were better for both of them and if she was tired, just have a chamomile tea and she would fall asleep. She told Lesley that she needed to be out of the shop, with one thing and another, the pregnancy, hospital and doctor appointments, but also now court, and the extra appointment. "If you want, I could get Julie in full time to help you if you want?" Mel asked.

"If we need her later on when it gets busy, it's the beginning of October now, so maybe nearer Christmas, but I will let you know. At the moment, Mel, you have enough on your plate," Lesley told her. Lesley was right, but at this time, Mel wasn't too worried, even with the legal side, she was having what she always wanted and nothing was going to upset her. She wanted this pregnancy to go as smooth as possible.

***

Mel was sitting in Mr Johnson's office and was telling him her situation. "Now I know that this could be a bit of a blow to the divorce, but I thought you should know because I don't know if it changes anything? Terry is divorcing me, under unreasonable behaviour, but as you know as well as me, he's got her pregnant and now I am pregnant by another man. Does this give him more ground to change the divorce grounds?" Mel asked.

"Now, Ms Shaw, Mel, as both parties had signed to carry on with the divorce, before you got or knew you're pregnant, the information cannot be changed, so you have nothing to worry about. But it may give you a bit of leeway," he said.

"Pardon me?" Mel quizzed.

"Well, as a married couple, who have their own house, a business with a property above, that normally would be half and half straight down the line, but as the petitioner and now the responder are both going to becoming parents but with other people, it shouldn't change, but circumstances can change. Let see what happens tomorrow. Please, Mel, don't worry, that's the last thing you need at the moment," he said to her encouragingly.

Mel said thank you and left his office. Her mum was waiting outside for her. "What did he say, Mel?" she asked.

"Well, even though I am having a baby with someone else, and so is Terry, he cannot change the original reason for the divorce. He can't now change it to adultery, because I have met and lost someone else, not that he knows that," Mel told her mum.

"Let's go and have a drink? Oh I forgot, you can't," Mum said.

"Oh yes, I can, a very small one, Mum, with lots of ice," Mel retorted. They went to the pub. Mel ordered a vodka with lots of lime and tons of ice, so she only got a little of the alcohol. She didn't really want it, but felt she needed it. It was only one of course.

Mel had her mum with her. She wanted to wear her suit, but that didn't fit her anymore, so she had to buy some elasticated smart trousers, that would grow with her belly. They walked into the court room and then was told that the petitioner couldn't be there and could they postpone for a later date.

Mel was really annoyed. She had to gear herself up for this and he couldn't be bothered to turn up, bloody typical. The judge agreed with the postponement as Terry's solicitor had a quiet word with him. They re-scheduled it for a month later, 10 November. Something must be wrong for this to happen.

Well, Terry hadn't died, she would have been told, then none of this would matter. So her and Mum left with Mr Johnson. He knew why Terry couldn't be there today, but didn't want to tell Mel just yet, he would tell her later on. So Mel and her mum went to have some lunch in the café just along from the florist. She went back to work afterwards but didn't have to do much.

It was still that time, where not much was going on in the flower world. People wanted Halloween Wreaths for their front doors, but not much else. Mel went home as there wasn't much going on. The next day, Mel was walking along to work in the morning and spotted a new baby boutique opening up not far from the shop. She popped her head around the door, but there wasn't anyone there, except a workman who was painting behind a door.

Mel asked him when the shop was going to be open. He thought about 2 weeks, but the lady wasn't there and there would be a sign going up on the window with an opening date. Mel said thank you and walked happily away, singing to herself. Mel was starting to show now, not a lot, but you had to look and then thought was she? Wasn't she?

Mel told Lesley about the new baby shop opening up. She was really excited about it. They were on a high street, but it wasn't in town. The main shopping centre was literally that in the centre of town, not too far away. She had seen Mothercare, but not had the chance to go just yet, but she thought she would do so with her mum, in the next week or so.

She had to start thinking about buying baby stuff and things for herself, she was running out of clothes. She couldn't go on Saturday but asked her mum if she would go with her on Monday, then they could have a good look around. Mum was delighted with that, she couldn't wait to get her hands on baby clothes and prams and things. So they made that their special day to do that.

Monday came around very quickly. Mel had put on her loose slacks and top to match. She was uncomfortable in heels nowadays, so she put on her flats. It was only a little walk into town. Lesley was taking hold of the reins at work.

Mel was having what she had always wanted, so she indulged while she still could. Her mum knocked for her and they made their way to town. Now she was happy buying some baby clothes, but nothing big just yet, she didn't want to tempt fate. So for now she was happy with that and some new bigger things for herself.

They walked along the road happily, they both made a head for Mothercare. They were both excited, giggling like a couple of kids going into a huge toyshop for the first time. There were prams up on shelves near the ceiling. Mel's eyes were like saucers. She looked at the cots, the cribs, the highchairs.

"Oh, Mum, look at this stuff, it's wonderful in here. Look at those cots and those tiny cribs, they look like dolls cribs," said Mel.

"Mel, they are dolls cribs, look," said Jean. Mel burst out laughing. "You silly cow, trust you to be looking at the toys rather than the ones for real babies," Jean said laughing to herself. Then she spotted it. "Mel, look at this pram, it's beautiful," she told Mel.

It was navy blue, with big wheels and a big chassis. "Look, it has a big bounce on it when its pushed," said Jean.

"Mum, I live in a house. How on earth and I going to get that inside, yes it's beautiful, but it's far too big. Now this one, this is beautiful. It's like that big things baby. It's the same, but just smaller. I think I could get this one in and out of the house." Mel thought to herself. She was pushing it.

"Yes I can imagine this one at home," she added. Mel looked at the price, £450.00. "That's not bad, Mum, I think I will ask about this one!" Mel told her. Mel went to find an assistant.

"Yes, madam. Yes we have that item in stock, did you want it now?" she asked her.

"No, not yet, I just wondered how often you changed your stock and would I be able to get this one after Christmas?" Mel enquired.

"Well, that really depends, you see, what we have here and in the warehouse, is all the stock we have. So if you wanted it after Christmas, we may not have it still in stock at all. We have a huge turnaround of prams and this is the winter one, by February our stock changes over for the spring/summer collection," she told Mel.

"Oh OK, thank you," Mel added. She wandered back over to her mum. "Once they have sold in the shop and the warehouse, they may not get that one in again, Mum. What do I do? I don't want to have it in the house just yet. Come on, let's have a look at the clothes and I can have a think about it!" She said.

Mel picked up some baby vests, baby gro's. Her nan had already started knitting cardigans, a hat and mitten set. Then she looked over at the maternity clothes. She saw a pair of trousers that had elastic round the middle. She picked a pair in her size and looked at the tops, she looked quickly. She thought, 'No, it can't be, she must have been mistaken'.

She picked up her basket with her purchases in and went to the till. While she was paying, her mum was looking at the pram again, the one that Mel wanted. "Mum, are you ready?" Mel asked. She had paid for her items and was ready to leave. Jean looked lovingly at the pram.

"Coming, Mel," she said and left the pram and said goodbye to the assistant and they left the shop. "Mel, do you fancy a coffee and maybe a cake?" Jean asked.

"Yes, why not, but nothing with fresh cream, Mum, I'm not allowed," Mel told her.

"I know," Jean reacted. They found a little coffee shop. Mel found a table Jean went up to the counter to order them both tea and cakes, well Mel fancied apple pie with custard. She hadn't noticed who was in the café, then she spotted him, and her. Terry and Clare. Terry had spotted Mel when she walked in with her mother, but like Mel, her mum hadn't noticed them.

Mel hid her bags. She didn't want Terry to see them, it wasn't any of his business. They both got up to leave. Terry stopped to say hello, but Clare encouraged him out of the door. Mel sank in her chair. That's the first time she had seen him in a long time.

She had her coat over her lap, so he didn't see her ever growing bump. That she was thankful for. Her mum came back with apple pie and custard and a huge cream cake for herself. "Did you see who just left Mum?" Mel quizzed.

"No," replied her mum.

"Terry and Clare!" Mel said.

"Why didn't you ask him why he didn't bother to turn up to court last week?" Jean quizzed.

"No, he looked like he was going to say something but Clare took him away. He left without speaking, which was odd. He hasn't done that to me before, but who cares," she retorted. But Mel did care. Terry, her Terry would never have done that to her before, but he did do that to her before. He changed and he left her when he met Clare. So now she thought good riddance.

"Did you notice, Mum, that Clare has a flat tummy. I thought she was pregnant?" Mel enquired. *She was further on that me. Oh that must be why they didn't come to court, maybe she lost the baby, Mum. Oh they must be really hurting,* thought Mel.

"Tommyrot," said Jean.

"Pardon? Tommyrot?" Mel asked.

"Mel, he didn't give a second thought when he went off with that Clare. Why should you feel anything for them except contempt. He, they treated you badly, wants a divorce, then doesn't turn up to the court for the hearing. If they have lost that baby, then it's them getting their just desserts and don't you go worrying about them."

"You have your own baby to worry about. So here's your tea, sorry coffee, and your apple pie and custard. You enjoy it and don't give them to a second thought, hear?" Mum demanded.

Mel knew her mum was right, but it didn't make her feel good, it made her feel bad, not that she had anything to feel bad about. She was having the one thing she wanted and he or she was growing inside her this very minute. So she took notice of what her mum had said and started eating.

"That's it, my girl, you're eating for two," Mum smiled. They finished their food and drinks and left. Next thing Mel needed the loo. She ran back in and asked to use their toilet. It wasn't a problem. She said thank you on her way out, then she couldn't find her mum.

She went to the next shop, she wasn't there and she went to the one before the café and she wasn't there. She turned round and she was walking towards her. "Mum, where did you go? I came out of the café and you had disappeared?" Mel asked.

"Oh sorry, love, I thought I saw something I liked the look of when we came past but when I went into the shop, it wasn't as nice. So I didn't buy it. Anyway I'm here now. Where do you want to go next, British Home Stores? They do some lovely baby stuff?" Jean asked.

"Yes, we could do, but I don't want to be out too late, I'm feeling a bit tired," Mel replied.

"Ok, love, would you rather leave it for today?" Mum asked her.

"Do you mind, I mean I know we were going to make a day of it, but I feel tired now, so maybe in couple of weeks or so," Mel asked.

"Not a problem, as you said we can do it another time," Mum replied and they headed home to Mel's.

***

Mel continued to work and time was passing by slowly. It was nearly Christmas. Mel had given more responsibility to Lesley as the orders were coming in thick and fast, especially as the Christmas trees were being delivered in the next week or so. Mr Johnson, her lawyer had told her a couple of weeks ago that the next court date was at the end of November, and it was nearly that now.

Her bump was still growing nicely, and everything with the pregnancy was going well. Mel was starting to feel a little sick, not where she wanted to vomit, but her head was hurting her and she was starting to sneeze all over the place and her throat was sore. The doctor told her to take paracetamol and that was really it; fluids if she can't eat or soup if she wants to have food where she doesn't have to chew.

The morning of the court hearing, Mel had called Mr Johnson, who didn't recognise her on the phone at all, said she thought she had the flu and couldn't get out of bed. He said he would go to court and see if it can be adjourned and will let her know later on that day. Jean had popped into see Mel, who was fast asleep on the bed when she got there.

She had found the half-eaten soup on the side and tons of tissues and honey and lemon that had gone cold on her bedside cabinet. The phone rang. Jean ran downstairs to answer it; it was Mr Johnson. He had wanted to speak to Mel, but Jean told him she was fast asleep. She could pass a message on for him, but he told her to tell Mel that he would call again the following day.

Jean put down the receiver and Mel appeared in the doorway. "Who was on the phone, Mum?" she asked.

"That was Mr Johnson. I told him you were asleep, he said he would call you again tomorrow, that ok?" Jean asked.

"Yes, I can't be doing with that today. I'm going back to bed," Mel told her.

"Is there anything you need, sweetheart?" Mum asked.

"Er yes, could you make me another honey and lemon if you don't mind?" Mel asked.

Mel went back upstairs to bed and Jean went to the kitchen to make the hot drink. Jean took it upstairs to her and she was trying to get comfortable in bed. Jean had already taken down the dirty cups and soup bowl, so there was room for this cup.

Jean sat on Mel's bed. "Are you OK, love?" Jean asked.

"Yes, well as well as I can be like this. It's a shame I can't take anything stronger," Mel added, but that wasn't what Jean was talking about.

"No, I meant about today, did you want to go to court?" she asked.

"Yes, well no, not really, but I would have done if I hadn't been sick with the flu," Mel admitted.

"Are you worried about this court thing? Do you think that's why you got ill in the first place?" Jean asked her.

"No, not at all, Mum. I don't feel run down or anything. It's more than likely just busy with the shop and now bubba," she said looking down at her bump. It was getting bigger now. "Mum, you know what it is next week, don't you?" Mel said.

"No what?" Jean said, a bit oblivious to what Mel was talking about.

"My 20 week scan. God that's come round really quick. Will you be there?" Mel asked.

"Yes, but will you?" Jean asked.

"Huh?" asked Mel. "Of course I will be there, it's my tummy," Mel replied.

"You won't be going anywhere if you're not better. You not infecting all of those other mums and babies, so back to rest, my girl. Do you have enough tablets?" Jean asked then checked.

"Right, I'm off now so get some sleep and in a couple of days, you should be as right as rain, don't worry," putting her hand up. "I will pop into the shop and tell Lesley, that girl is like gold dust. She is taking on the shop for you, now get some sleep," said Jean, kissing Mel on the forehead and heading downstairs. She let herself out and then went along to the florist.

***

"He's what?" Mel couldn't take it all in. "He wants the business and the house. How dare he, who does he think he bloody is. It's my blood sweat and tears gone into the shop not him. He works in the bloody bank and he thinks he can take my living away from me."

"Just wait until I see him, that shyster. Well he has a fight on his hands, I can tell you that, Mr Johnson," Mel was fuming. She put the phone down, she was so angry. How dare that bastard take away the only way she can make money for her and her baby. If he takes half of it, what the hell was she going to do.

She was feeling better than she had in the last few days, but you could still hear she wasn't quite back to normal just yet. She got herself washed and grabbed some clothes. She got dressed, brushed her hair, grabbed her keys and her handbag. He was not getting away with this. She pulled the door shut, locked it and off she went to the high street.

She was so angry, she was talking to herself all along her way there. It was lunchtime and the bank was full. Terry had a client, so when he stood up to shake their hand he spotted Mel, then he spotted her growing tummy. "Mel, what are you doing here?" He was shocked at seeing her and that she was pregnant.

"Me, what am I doing here," Mel was shouting and she didn't care who the bloody hell heard her. "Me, I have just heard from my solicitor that you not only want my house, but also my business, so how the hell am I supposed to make a living? Eh you tell me that, Terry," Mel screamed at him. Everyone in the bank was looking at him and then her and then her belly.

"Mel, I'm sorry, I didn't know, you see," Terry started.

"Sorry, you didn't know, it's none of your fucking business. You left me for another woman and expect to wait around until you're fucking bored with her. I don't think so, chummy, so what about my business?" Mel demanded.

"Mel, you should sit down. You're rather red in the face, you don't want to do any harm to your baby," Terry suggested rather sheepishly.

"My baby, Terry, yes not yours. So what the bloody hell are you going to do about it?" Mel pushed him. She wanted answers, NOW.

"Look, I will have a word with my solicitor. The house has to go, Mel, I can't afford it, but the shop. Yes, well, even though I sorted out the mortgage, you have been the one making the payments. Let me talk to him and I will get back to you," Terry pleaded.

"No, I would you rather go through the solicitors than speak to you again. At this moment, Terry, I am too bloody angry with you," Mel spat, then she turned on her heels and left the building.

The people in the bank, all clapped and cheered Mel, but then looked at Terry as if he was a terrible human being. Terry's manager came over and told everyone that there was nothing to see now and could they all resume to their business. He then called Terry to have a word with him in his office.

"Terry, what on earth is going on? I knew things were bad for you, but this. This isn't good you know and now the whole bank knows your business. You're going to have to do something about this? Now you said that you sorted out the mortgage, so Mel has been paying them for the shop, yes, it's all here, she hasn't missed a payment. Now the house?" Tom said.

"The house is in both of our names, Tom, I have been paying my half and Mel has been paying her half," said Terry, who was still in shock at seeing Mel's tummy. "That's what we both wanted you know, a baby?" Terry changed the subject. He looked into space as he said it.

"Yes, but you just lost yours, Terry, and sadly that baby won't come back, and Mel is having her own baby. Look you have to just get past this bit, this phase of time. It will get better, I promise. Now what are you going to do about the business. Legally Mel has paid everything up to date, you haven't contributed, so I don't know if you have any claim on any of it."

"Talk to your lawyer, use my office, but I suggest you let Mel keep the shop and flat above and sell the house. That way you get your half and she has her half, for her and her baby. Unless you want her to pay off the flat and shop, that way, it's totally hers. Have a think about it."

"I need to get back out front and make sure it's quiet again. Go on call your lawyer from in here, that way no disturbances." Tom told him and then left him to it.

***

Mel left the bank, still fuming. She made her way to the florist. "Hey, how are you doing?" Julie asked.

"Cor you look rough," said Fiona.

"Thanks, Fi," replied Mel.

"Hey what are you doing here?" Lesley asked. "Your mum said that you were still sick," added Lesley.

"I still am, but a lot better than I was. Mum has been a dream, but I'm out for another reason," Mel said. Julie put the kettle on and left their drinks in the office for the two of them to have a drink. Her and Fiona were alright in the shop still, there was customers that needed serving.

Mel regaled her tale to Lesley, who looked horrified. "Mel, are we going to lose our jobs then?" she asked Mel.

"Not if I can help it. Terry hasn't put a penny to this business or the flat above. Anyway if the house has to go, I need somewhere to live and this is all mine, unless he decides different and with what I have just done in the bank, I don't think I will lose," Mel told her.

"Everyone will now know what a shyster he really is. I told him to talk to his lawyer then he can talk to mine. I don't want to talk to him for the time being. I don't want to stress the baby out with his crap," Mel snapped. Mel had her drink and then left.

Lesley was left wondering, but she knew Mel wouldn't take this from Terry. Since she found out she was pregnant, she had changed and for the better, she took no rubbish from anyone. So she was hopeful that everything would be alright.

Mel got in. She thought she had better call her mum. They would need to start getting rid of everything they didn't want and Mel couldn't do this on her own. Jean was round in a matter of minutes. Mel had got her notepad out, they would have to do this room by room.

So when Mr Johnson called at 5pm that evening, just before leaving the office, he told her that even though normally the shop and flat above would have to be sold and halved with the now circumstances, Mel would be able to keep both the flat and the shop, but her share of the house, would have to now go to paying off her mortgage of the said properties. Mel said that should be fine. They would need to get an estate agent in first to see what the house was worth, but that shouldn't be a problem.

She thanked Mr Johnson. "Oh before you go, Mr Johnson, I don't really want to talk to Terry, Mr Humphreys; so could you relay to his lawyer, what contents he wants from the house, before it goes up for sale, many thanks," Mel told him, then put the phone down.

"Mum, I can keep the shop and the flat above. I think I need to sort out what's at the flat and see what I can take. I think I need to sit down, this is too much excitement for me," Mel said, excited she still has somewhere for her and the baby to live, without it having anything to do with Terry.

The next day, Mel went to the flat early. Her mum and her sister, Tina, both came with her, to see what was there, what needed to be thrown and what could go to the charity shop. The furniture was OK, but if she could take some from the house, then it would be a bit cosier and a bit more like home now.

"Right, the sofa and chairs can go; the curtains need sorting, they are really awful; the kitchen stuff is fine; the bathroom the same; the bedrooms need sorting out, but I can donate a lot of this stuff to the charity. I think they have a van and can collect it. Mum, will you have a look, I think they are in the yellow pages."

"Then once I have heard from Terry's solicitor, I will know what he wants, then bring the rest here. Then again, charity gets what's left at the house. What do you think, Mum?" Mel asked.

"Mel, whose going to be there when Terry collects his stuff he wants. I can do that for you if you want, so you don't have to see him. If mum's there, she may lamp him one," smiled Tina.

"Teen, are you sure?" Mel asked.

"Yes, because there's nobody else and if nan is there, she will do the same as Mum," laughed Tina.

"Ok, Tina, that would be great, love; thank you," replied Mel. Once they had sorted out what was going and what was being kept.

"Now what about decorating. It could do with freshening up, Mel," suggested Jean.

"Oh, I don't know," said Mel. "It's a lot of work, Mum, that I really don't have the time to," Mel added.

"But you want to get the baby's room decorated for the nursery. Oh and once you have had the scan, you will know what colour to go with," Jean said excitedly.

"Yes, that's on Tuesday. Are you still coming, Mum?" Mel asked.

"I wouldn't miss it for the world," said Jean.

"Can I come too?" Tina asked.

"If you want. I don't think they would mind. If it comes to it, you may have to wait outside, then send Mum out and you in. Sound alright to you, Mum?" Mel asked.

"Hmmm. I was just thinking about these curtains, they may do for your room."

Chapter 4

It was the big day, when Mel was going to have her scan. She would be able to find out what sex the baby was. She was so excited, she had already been to the toilet at least three times. Tuesday had come round really quickly. Ding dong, went the doorbell. Mel knew it was her mum. She had her keys but Jean didn't really like using them unless she really had to.

"Ready, Mel?" Jean asked.

"Er yes, I have my sample wrapped with tissue round it. Yes, I have my handheld notes, so yes I am all set. What about you, Mum?" Mel enquired.

"Yes, I have been waiting for this my whole life," she chuckled. Tina was going to meet them there, but she was running late. Her new boyfriend, George, offered to pick her up and take her to the hospital but he had broken down and she was now getting the bus.

Mel walked up to reception and handed the receptionist her appointment card. She was glad that she had changed it over to her maiden name, Shaw, rather than have her married name. She wouldn't be giving the baby her married name, so it made more sense to do it now rather than later on.

The receptionist gave Mel back her card and asked her to take a seat, they would be with her shortly. She gave her mum's arm a squeeze. Tina came running through the door.

"Oh I am so glad I didn't miss you two," she smiled as she told them what happened and her reason for being late.

The nurse called Mel. Her mum and sister both got up. "This is only for her appointment checks, not for the scan. We will let you know when that's happening," replied the nurse. Mel sat down. She had already taken off her coat and it was hot in the hospital.

The nurse beckoned Mel to the scales. "Yes, that's fine. You're putting on the right amount of weight, you're not eating for two, are you? Lots of women think once they are pregnant, they can eat what they like, but they have a job getting it off later on," the nurse told Mel. She took Mel's blood pressure that was fine; checked the specimen that was all OK. She told Mel to go back and take a seat, she would be called as soon as her space was free.

Mel didn't have to wait long. "Ms Melanie Shaw," called the scanographer. Mel, her mum and sister all got up and followed the lady. "You all coming?" she asked.

"Yes please," said Jean.

"Well, it's not a big room, so if you can stand in the corner until your mum sees the baby, is that OK?" she asked. Tina nodded. She wasn't wrong, you couldn't swing a cat in that room, not that anyone would have tried. Mel laid down on the bed.

Her mum the opposite side to where the monitor was, so she could get a good look and the scenographer in front of the machine and keyboard. She asked Mel to pull down her bottoms, so she could put the gel on. She struggled a bit, but got there in the end. The gel was freezing cold, then the lady put the tool on Mel's tummy, she started to push it across Mel's tummy.

Mel and her mum were both mesmerised. "Why do you keep stopping?" Jean asked.

"Oh that's so I can get the measurements of the baby. Its head, the organs, heart and just to make sure baby is growing properly," she told them.

"Wow, it's amazing. They never had this sort of stuff when I had you, Mel, or you, Tina," Jean said with wide eyes.

"Can you see what it is, nurse?" Mel asked.

"What boy or girl you mean?" she replied.

"Yes," said Mel excitedly.

"Do you want to know what the baby is?" she asked but by the look on Mel's face.

"Yes please," Mel said and nodded at the same time.

"Well, you're going to have a baby boy, pleased?" she asked.

"Oh yes, I was fine with whatever, boy or girl, but now you have confirmed it and I can see him. I can start to get things ready," replied Mel.

"Mum, my turn now, you have been there for ages," Tina said, bursting to come over and have a look.

"Ok, love, your turn. Oh can Mel get a photo of this please. Well, me too, if that's possible," Jean asked. She desperately wanted a picture. She moved over so her daughter could come over and Jean walked over to the corner. Mel was beaming.

Jean had never seen her eldest daughter so happy. She got a clear picture of Mel's face. The lady finished what she was doing, gave Mel some tissue to clean herself up. Her sister was just in awe as her mother was. "How many photos do you want then, Mel?" The lady asked.

She looked at her mum and her sister. "Can I have three please," she replied the lady.

"Yes, but I have to charge you for the second two, is that OK?" she asked her.

"Yes, that's fine," said Jean pulling out her purse before Mel even got off the bed. "How much is that then?" Jean was looking in her purse whilst she asked.

"That will be £2. Please?" she asked.

"Is that all, I thought it was at least a five?" Jean asked.

"No, just a pound each. Maybe in a few years it may go up to a couple more, but I wouldn't have thought five pounds," the lady said. Jean handed her the money and thanked her so much. They helped Mel with her coat, said their goodbyes to the nurse and went over to reception for Mel to make her next appointment.

"12 January?" The receptionist asked.

"Yes, that's fine. What time?" Mel asked.

"11am, that OK, Mel?" she asked.

"Yes. Mum, you coming to the next appointment, the one next is at the doctors, but the hospital. Mum?" Mel asked.

Jean was staring at her photo, she didn't actually hear Mel. "Yes, honey, that's fine with me. Just let me know nearer the time and at least we can have Christmas soon," Jean answered. Still not looking up from her photo. They made their way out of the hospital.

Jean finally put her photo away in her bag for safe keeping. They then went along to the bus stop. George had pulled up. He got the car started and wanted to collect them from the hospital. "Sorry about this morning, Mel and Jean, you too, Tina," George said.

"Not to worry, George, you're here now and you can drop us home. Your nan will want to see you, Mel, now that you have had your scan," Jean told her. Mel wasn't going to argue, she wanted to just get back and take off her shoes.

***

"Hi, Mum, we're home," said Jean when she opened the front door. Mel and Jean walked through it. Tina went off with George somewhere. She didn't have to go to work today, which is how come she could make the hospital for the scan. "Put the kettle on will you, Mum?" Jean asked.

Marge was already in the kitchen, cups were done and she just had to put the milk in. Mel was still on the coffee, tea still made her feel sick. "All done, Jean. How did it go at the hospital then?" Marge asked.

"Oh, Nan, you should have seen him. He is so big," Mel told her.

"Oh so it's a him then? Well, that's great, Mel. It's about time there was a boy in the family. We always have girls…" said Marge as she went back to the kitchen to make the refreshments. Mel had already taken her coat and shoes off. "You back at work today, Mel?" Nan asked.

"No, I'm going in tomorrow. It's only a few more working days until Christmas, Nan, so I had better show willing, I suppose," Mel reported.

"Just you take it easy. Did they say anything at the hospital, Mel? Apart from him being a boy," Nan said as she pointed to Mel's stomach.

"Well, they measured him. Blood pressure is fine, urine is fine, weight is ok; so yes, it was a good visit," said Mel, who had handed her nan the photograph. "Nan, we only got three copies, but I am going to photocopy one for you. Is that ok?" Mel asked.

"Mel, that's great. They never had anything like this in my day you know," said Marge. As she said that, she wiped a tear from her eye. "He's beautiful, Mel. What are you going to call him?" Nan asked her.

"I have no idea yet, but now we know he's a boy, I can start having a think about it and get a baby naming book," Mel replied taking her coffee from her mum.

"Now, Mel, you're here for Christmas, aren't you? I mean you're not staying in that house on your own, are you?" Nan asked.

"No, Nan, I won't be staying at home, but with you guys. I have to work for a couple of hours on Christmas eve, but closing the shop for Christmas day and boxing day. Open in between and then off again New year's day. That way the girls who have been working extremely hard have some time off and they are going to get a bonus. We have done really well."

"I think the public who were in the bank when I had it out with Terry have started to come into the shop. Probably to see me, but maybe to help support us as a local business. I don't think Terry was going to be very popular after I left."

"Speaking of Terry, Nan, has he called here by any chance?" Mel enquired.

"What in person or on the phone?" Nan replied.

"Either?" Mel answered.

"No, not here. Maybe he left you a message at home on your answer phone. Why?" Nan asked.

"It's just that he has to make arrangements for him to take what he wants from the house. Tina has taken photos of what she thought I would want but also made up a list. She's going to give him coloured stickers, so he can put them on the things he wants and me the same, if we both want the same thing, we will see who bought it or if it was a gift. Then if it was from our side, I get first dibs and vice versa." Mel remarked.

Jean and Marge just looked at each other and drank their hot drinks. Mel left her mum and nan and made her way home. She did turn the answerphone on when she got in. There weren't any messages to speak of, but she wasn't too worried. It was still a little early for the house to be put on the market, but it would be in the new year, so hopefully Terry wasn't going to drag his feet with this.

Mel needn't have worried about Terry. He was on the phone the day before Christmas eve. He wanted to come over, but Mel didn't want to see him face to face and asked him if he would come over the day after boxing day; that way he could have a look through the house, without her being there. Tina would be instead. She didn't want to have to talk to him while he looked at her ever growing belly.

Mel went into work the next day. The girls were all pleased to see her. She showed them her scan photo and told them all that she was having a boy. They were delighted for her. Lesley gave her a huge hug, so did Fiona and Julie. Both girls were working full time while the holidays were on, they were so busy.

Mel really wanted to give them their bonuses, but in envelopes. They both got the same, Lesley got a bit more, because she had taken over the reins as such. Lesley was locking up. Mel would get the takings the next day. They had a great hiding place even the other two didn't know about. Not in the fridge or freezer like most people, but they had a cupboard in the office, well next along from it, they had space behind the skirting board.

It was getting more difficult for Mel to climb down there now with her big tummy. So Lesley would put it away at night and Mel would come in the morning, take out and bank the takings, but left enough for the float and for whatever bills needed paying. At the end of the week, the girls' wages came out of it. Then Mel took her salary.

She was hoping to live upstairs before the baby came, because she wouldn't have to keep paying the mortgage. She was having a coffee with Lesley. She was drinking decaf, would be better for the baby. Mind you no coffee would be better for the baby, but Mel couldn't bring herself to drink tea of any kind even herbal.

Lesley was going to leave the takings overnight well until the day after boxing day. Nobody knew where the money was kept. So she locked up, and then left the florist until she was due back to work after boxing day. She was knackered. Taking over from Mel wasn't hard work, but she wasn't as young as she would have liked to have been.

***

"It's Christmas morning. Come on, you two, get up. Don't you want to see what Father Christmas has bought you?" Nan asked. She had handed them both a cup of something; Mel coffee, Tina tea. They both drank them and then went downstairs to open their presents, well Mel waddled down.

Jean was already in the kitchen making bacon sandwiches. Her girls both had great appetites, so she thought they can be opening presents and eating at the same time. Mel had realised she had a taste for bacon sandwiches since she was pregnant.

Mel couldn't sit on the floor anymore, so Tina handed her presents to her. She got some lovely stuff for herself and for the baby. She was still trying out names, but not for now, she was busy with some big boxes. Her mum had already bought her pram which was upstairs waiting to come down, but not yet.

Mel hadn't seen it yet. Jean was going to take her upstairs when she had opened everything else. Tina had got her some bath stuff to have once the baby was born. "So you can really treat yourself. I know it's hard getting in and out,

Mel, but once he's here, it will be great to get in and out of the bath..." laughed Tina.

She also bought the baby some baby gros in blue. Now he was confirmed as a boy, there was no stopping any of them. Lesley had dropped off presents for Mel yesterday before Mel had got there. Lesley had also got Mel some stuff for herself, but some baby vests, socks and her mother-in-law made her some cardigans. Mel ooh and aahed at them and so did her mum and nan.

Jean took them off Mel and put them in the washing machine, just so everything was soft for him to wear, when the time came. Julie and Fiona went halves on a baby bath and set for Mel. They thought she could do with that, it would be easier at the flat for her. Mel was quite touched by their gift. By the time Mel had opened everything, she had new slippers, dressing gown for the hospital, skincare, a couple of new nighties, again for the hospital.

Her bag was nearly ready with what she had received. Nan had bought her the baby's moses basket. "They didn't have anything like that Mel and I thought he would look so cute in it. I know it won't last long, but it will be great," said Nan.

Mel hugged her and said 'thank you'. She didn't know where she was going to put it all, but once Christmas was over, she was going to get started with the flat. That way, it would all be ready for her to move into before he came, because the house had to go.

Once they had finished opening all of their presents, and they all had a good haul as Tina said, Jean took them upstairs to the spare bedroom, which makes sense to why Tina and Mel shared the room the night before. Mel thought it was funny. Jean waited until they were all standing there. She opened the door and ushered them inside. Mel's eyes were closed as it was still a surprise.

They had already gasped when they saw it but Mel hadn't. "Open your eyes, Mel," Jean told her. Mel understood their gasps, she gasped too. She saw the pram that she had her eye on in the pram shop.

"Oh, Mum, it's beautiful. It's the one," Mel said.

Jean interrupted. "Yes in the shop, do you like it, Mel?"

"Like it? I love it, Mum. Thank you. So that's where you went when I came out of the shop and couldn't find you," Mel said, wagging her finger at her mum. "Very naughty, but ever so nice, Mum. Thank you," Mel told her. She gave her mum a final hug and they all went downstairs. "You don't have any more surprises for me, do you?" Mel asked.

"No, that's the lot, for now anyway!" Jean said.

Off they went back downstairs. Marge had already peeled, scrubbed, cut and prepared the vegetables for dinner. Some of it was already on. Turkey was cooked, that was done the night before and was covered in kitchen foil to keep it fresh. Mel sat down, that was all that Mel was doing nowadays.

She was too tired to do much, even though she had just under 4 months to go until she was due, but this really took a lot out of her. She had got washed and dressed, same as everyone else. They liked to wear something a little sparkly on Christmas day. They had the TV on, but no-one was really watching it, but it was great for a bit of background noise.

They sat down just after 2.30pm for their Christmas dinner, so they would be finished just before the Queen's speech, which both Jean and Marge liked watching. "It only used to be on the wireless, Mel, Tina, we had no telly in them days," remarked Marge with a huge smile on her face. Marge had brought up Jean on her own. Her husband had died in the second world war. She had it hard, but as the women did then, she just got on with it.

After dinner, Mel felt a bit sleepy, so she went up for a snooze. She was doing that a lot lately. Mel had only gone up about an hour when the front door bell went. Tina looked out the window. "Mum, it's Terry. You had better get it before he wakes Mel up," Tina said looking a little worried.

Jean went to the front door and opened it just as Terry was about to press on the doorbell. "Hello, Jean, I was wondering if Mel was here. I have already been to the house, but there's no answer," Terry quizzed.

"Yes Mel is here, Terry, but she's fast asleep. What do you want?" Jean said defiantly.

"I just wanted to wish her a Merry Christmas and just to give her this!" Terry said, he held out an envelope.

"I will give it to her when she wakes up, Terry. Merry Christmas," Jean said then she shut the door. Terry turned round and walked away, looking up as he did so. Mel was fast asleep and didn't hear the doorbell ring, which Jean and Marge were grateful for.

Mel slept for a further hour or so, but when she woke up, she made her way downstairs and said that she had had the weirdest dream ever. "I was in the middle of cleaning the windows, when my waters broke, but Terry came running in and wanted to take me to the hospital. I told him, I was fine I was going with my mum."

"He didn't want you to take me, he wanted to take me, but he was so insistent, but so was Mum. In the end, she punched him on the nose and called for the ambulance. Then I burst out laughing and couldn't stop, then the baby came and I was still laughing. It was very strange!" Mel said.

All three of them looked at each other then at Mel. "What's wrong? What's going on?" Mel asked.

"Mel, Terry turned up while you were asleep. He left this with Mum to give to you," said Tina. Tina handed the envelope to Mel, who slowly opened it. It was a Christmas card, and inside a £50 note fell out.

The card read, 'Merry Christmas Mel, I hope you have a great one and new year. You deserve it. The money is to get something for the baby from me. All my love, Terry'.

Mel put the card and money back into the envelope, she then handed it to Tina. "Here, Tina, have a night out with George, on Terry. I don't want his money. He is nothing to do with my baby!" Mel told her and left the room. Tina put the envelope back up on the mantelpiece, she didn't want it either.

Mel went into the kitchen to get a cold drink. Jean and Marge looked at each other and shrugged. "It's probably for the best anyway, Mum" said Jean. Marge nodded. Her girl was strong, she didn't need a man to make her happy. Well one did or she wouldn't be in this condition, she thought to herself.

***

Boxing Day came and went like any other, sitting down watching TV, eating and drinking, not in Mel's case but that didn't matter. "Teen, you still ok for tomorrow?" Mel asked.

"Huh?" Tina replied.

"Letting Terry into the house to choose what he wants from it," reminded Mel.

"Oh that, yes, that's OK. I don't go back to work until the day after new year. So it won't be a problem," replied Tina.

Mel was relieved, she hadn't wanted to see Terry especially after his little stunt on Christmas Day. Tina was doing her a real favour. She was enjoying staying at her mum's and being waited on. It's not that she was lazy but it was difficult getting round at home, because she was getting so big.

She was hoping she was more water than baby, but as long as he was OK, she didn't care. She was getting her dream, becoming a mum.

Soon it was time to get up to bed. She took her time, up the stairs. Her mum was starting to come up and check on her, just to make sure she didn't fall over really. Mel got into bed and got herself comfortable. She was glad she could stay there for the next few days, especially after Terry was going to be at home, looking round.

Mel soon drifted off to sleep and before she knew it, it was morning. Jean had made her some breakfast, coffee, juice and toast. She thought Mel would have bacon and eggs but eggs were out of the question. Jean brought her up a cuppa and sat it down on the bedside cabinet, Mel turned over.

"Morning, Mum," she said.

"Morning, love, sleep alright?" Mum enquired.

"Yes, really well. What time is it, Mum?" she asked her.

"It's just after 9.30, love. Yes, Tina has already left, with her clipboard, pen and pad in hand!" Jean told her.

"Oh good, I was a little worried," Mel added.

"Why, Mel. Our Tina is a match for Terry. She won't let him take liberties, don't worry," Mum told her. Mel knew her mum was right. Tina took no rubbish from anyone and woe betide anyone who did. She was definitely a tough bird, but then again so were all the women in their family.

Mel got up out of the bed, she needed the loo. She put her slippers on, so she wouldn't slip. "Mum, could you take my coffee back downstairs, I'm coming downstairs," she said to Jean. Jean nodded, took the cup and made her way back down.

Mel made her way downstairs when she finished in the bathroom. She had wanted to have a bath and it was safer at her mum's as there were so many people in the house, if she got stuck in it. At home, she would be on her own struggling. Marge was just finishing her breakfast.

The phone rang, it was just one of Marge's friends wanting to know if she wanted to go to Bingo. She went every once in a while, and they were open. Marge declined, she wanted to wait until Tina came back; so she made her excuses, thanked her friend and then put the phone back down.

It was gone 2pm before Tina made an appearance at home. Mel had just come out of the kitchen. "Hi, Teen, have you just finished at my place?" Mel asked.

"Yes, oh my goodness, Mel. It was horrendous."

Mel interrupted. "Why? What happened? Was Terry out of order, did he do something he shouldn't have done, Teen?" Mel quizzed getting ready to call him and have a go at him.

"Oh no, nothing like that, Mel. How on earth you stayed with him all this time is beyond me."

"Tina, come on what happened?" Nan asked.

"He was…I'm not sure if I want this, do you think Mel would want it? Or I like the vase bottles we got when we went to Greece, but I don't know if Mel would want them, what do you think, Tina?" Tina said.

"Mel, I wanted to throttle him. He was driving me mad. Also he didn't know if what he was taking was going to suit where he was now, but he was saying that under his breath so I couldn't hear him. But you know me, ears like radar. Anyway, he has chosen quite a bit, but has left you some lovely things still," Tina told her.

"So come on what have I got left then? What has he left me?" Mel asked.

"He left you the cut glasses in the unit, he wants the unit; the dining table he wants you to have. He already took the stereo, he wants the videorecorder. Oh yes he also wants a couple of the wedding photos, that you have in your bedroom, but I couldn't find them. He said he would like them when you find them."

"Oh yes, he also wants the carriage clock his nan brought you for a wedding present. I think that's it, you can have a look at the list afterwards if you want?" Tina said.

Mel squeezed her hand. "Thank you for that, Teen. I know he can be a pain, but at least I didn't have to do it. I don't know if I could have handled him keep looking at me with those big sad eyes." Tina agreed. She took the list from Tina and started to scroll down it.

"There's nothing really here you know, he only wants sentimental stuff, hardly any furniture…how on earth am I going to get the rest of this stuff up to the flat above the shop?" Mel commented.

"Mel, we can sort that all out at a later date. You still have to decide what you're keeping and what your selling. Don't be giving any of this stuff away, you're having a baby, you need all the money you can get," said Jean.

"I know, Mum, it will be fine. It will work out, it always does," Mel replied. She knew her family had her best interests at heart, thankfully. Mind you she had good staff and a great group of friends and it was all women. What a huge amount of support from women you could ask for.

They were all there for her and the baby, especially the baby, but he would be the only male. Oh no George, Tina's boyfriend; Mel had forgot about him, but he was a good bloke and he really took care of Tina. That's all she wanted for her sister to be happy and the love of a good man.

***

New year was over and so were the holidays, everyone was back at work. Mel had managed to get herself over to the florist. She hadn't seen her staff except on Christmas eve. She wanted to get there a bit more. It just wasn't possible, even though Mel still had a little while to go, she was waddling everywhere. She looked like a big fat duck, waddling from side to side.

She walked into the shop and the staff were pleased to see her. Lesley had seen her coming along and asked Julie to pop to the café and pick up a bacon sandwich or two for Mel. She was quite partial to them since she fell pregnant. By the time she walked through the door, Julie had just returned. "Cuppa, Mel? Bacon sandwich?" Lesley asked.

"Oh yes, thanks, Les. How did you know?" Mel asked.

"Well, it's all I see you eat anymore, and the coffee."

Mel interrupted. "Julie, do we have any herbal tea. I think the baby is wide awake with all the coffee I have been drinking lately," Mel enquired.

"Yes we have lemon and ginger or peppermint," Julie replied.

"Lemon and ginger. I think that will calm him down a bit," Mel said. Julie made the drinks, she made one for everyone. "Have you been busy lately?" Mel asked directing the question to Lesley really.

"Yes, it's been OK up to Christmas, now though it's dead. Oh sorry, Mel, we have a couple of funerals this week. Old Mrs Jessop died you know from up the bingo hall," said Lesley.

"Oh yes. Nan was saying that the other day. Ah, when did she go?" Mel asked.

"The day after boxing day!" Julie replied.

"Yes that's when nan spoke to Lil down the fishmongers, she called and told her then. Is it a big order? She was a popular lady. She had worked down the hall for at least thirty years or so," Mel added.

"Yes, it is. We need six wreaths, two pillows, a cross. Goodness knows how many sheaths."

"Sheaths?" Fiona enquired.

"I thought that's what men wore…" Lesley continued, "well big bouquets then," finished Lesley.

"Well you girls have a lot on then. Are you still able to cope without me? I'm sorry, I know I haven't been here half as much as I had hoped to. It's just there are so many hospital and doctor's appointments. I didn't realise…" said Mel trailing off.

"Mel, its fine, we all knew if this ever happened, your mind would be on your baby and you. You know your health as well, not this place," replied Lesley.

"You're amazing, Les. I don't know what I would have done without you?" Mel said to her trusted and loyal colleague who had become her great friend.

"You couldn't. You would have shut up shop, but you need to stay open, Mel, for as long as you can. You still need to pay the mortgage and you need money coming in," Lesley told her. By now, Fiona and Julie had already got back to their work.

"Les, I really appreciate all that you do for me, especially these last few months. You have had a lot land on your head practically overnight. I'm just glad you have been able to cope with it all. Have those two given you any trouble at all?" Mel asked.

"No, they are great girls and now they are both full time. Sorry, Mel, I wouldn't have managed if they were still part time, especially to go and get the orders, pick up the stock," said Lesley.

Mel put up her hand. "Now listen, I appreciate everything you do and no you couldn't have done it any way, with me completely out of action. Who would have thought pregnancy would affect a woman so much. Yes, I know it's not an illness or sickness, but this has really taken over my body, Les.

Anyway, you're already manager, but I want to give you a pay rise, but also the girls."

"It won't be much for them, but maybe an extra tenner a week. I can still sort that out and it won't affect the bills to be paid. So if I can give you say forty a week extra, is that ok? Don't worry, I have already checked it out with the accountant, and it's all doable."

"Plus there is extra money coming in and when I pay most of the mortgage off, it should bring the bills down a bit. So what do you think; is £40 a week ok?" Mel stopped talking. Lesley was flabbergasted with what Mel had said.

Not about the mortgage being paid on the shop, just £40. She thought she would get a tenner like the girls. Lesley beamed. "Yes, Mel, that's great, fantastic even. When do I tell the girls?" Lesley enquired.

"Not until they get paid on Friday. Put it in their wage packet and they will think there's a mistake. Look at their faces when they realise they are getting a rise," Mel added. She was so grateful for such great work colleagues, even if Fiona did drop herself in it a lot of the time, she knew she was lucky.

Mel drained her cup of herbal tea. "Hmmm, that's not bad, think I will need to stock up on these until I have the baby. Don't know if I will be back on normal tea by then. Right, I'm off. Are you ok to carry on?" Mel asked.

"As if you need to ask," replied Lesley. Mel said goodbye to the girls and made her way home. She hadn't been there since Christmas eve morning, so she thought she had better have a look at what she wanted from the house, before it all got sorted to be sold.

She knew they would have to leave stuff in the house, but why? Some houses were shown empty. She needed to get this stuff sorted out before she had the baby. So the more she got done, the better, as far as she was concerned.

Mel opened the door. There was some post on the floor. The rest was on the coffee table, which had a lovely blue sticker on it, that's what else Terry wanted. She added the rest, as she was just about able to bend down and get it. 'Well that felt like a workout, picking up the post', Mel thought to herself.

She sat down on the sofa and looked round. Tina was right, there were more blue stickers in the unit than anywhere else. She went into the kitchen and saw a few more stickers on various items. She hadn't noticed most of this on the list.

Maybe Terry put them on without Tina's knowledge. She would ask her later on when she got in from work. She managed to make a hot drink, but put it down on the coffee table, because now she needed the toilet. She made her way upstairs and went to the bathroom. There was a big blue sticker staring right back at her, stuck on the bathroom cabinet.

She was fuming. She loved that cabinet, that and the mirror were a set, but no sticker on the mirror. She opened the doors and found stickers on a couple of things.

"Bloody hell, Terry," was all Mel could muster. 'Has he even left me anything?' Mel thought to herself. She left the bathroom and then went to the bedroom. Not many blue stickers in there. She looked in the spare room which would have been the baby's room, but not now.

Terry had put some stuff in there, with blue stickers on. Mel knew she would have to make up a list of what she wanted and what was to be sold. She had already seen what was at the flat. Some of her furniture was going to the flat but packing up a house and getting everything split into two was going to be a nightmare.

The best thing Mel thought would be to take what she wanted, sell the rest and leave Terry's stuff to be collected last, so it would be an empty house and he wouldn't know what she actually kept. Yes, that was a good idea. She would relay this to Tina, her mum and nan. George would help and then she could get a company in the take the rest.

It didn't take long for Mel to get this stuff all arranged. The house was already up for sale and it wasn't long before they had an offer on the house. Mel and Terry, through their solicitors arranged the price and what they would accept. The couple gave the asking price, so they were all pleased.

Mel had two weeks to get everything out. Contracts had already been exchanged and they needed to hand over the keys soon. George had a few friends from work come over and take Mel's stuff to the flat; including her bed, which came in two pieces then the mattress. What Mel didn't need or want got sold and she got a good price for it. At least when Terry came to collect his stuff, that's all that would be left.

Mel and Tina had gone over and put all of the ornament things she wanted into protective bubble wrap and wrapped up the items and put them in the old tea chests; so once he got the little bit of furniture out, it was only the tea chests left. Once Terry had taken his stuff, he had a final look round the house. It was completely bare, as if nobody had lived there. He closed the door behind him and put his keys through the letter box. Mel and Tina went over later on that day and did the same thing.

Tina picked up Terry's keys. Mel could no longer bend down; picking up that post a couple of weeks before gave her terrible tummy cramps. Like Terry before her, they both went upstairs to do a final sweep of the house. It had already been cleaned throughout. Mel looked in every room.

She stayed in the bedroom a little longer, but not thinking about her and Terry, but her and Andy, the baby's father. That was one night she would never forget; it was the best sex she had ever had. She took one last look and then shut the door. Checked the bathroom and the spare bedroom, all empty and clean.

They both went back downstairs. Mel took her time. Tina went to the kitchen, checked all the cupboards; empty and clean, yes every last one of them. The larder or pantry, whatever you prefer, nothing, completely empty. This had been a happy house until it all went wrong, but Mel was about to start a new chapter of her life. Terry was part of her old life, with this old house.

She was now glad that it had been sold. She just had to wait a little longer for the divorce to come through, then she had Terry out of her hair and her life and she couldn't wait. One last sweep of the sitting room, and then she closed the door. She checked she had all three sets of keys, they had to go to the estate agents in the morning. That was one job she was looking forward to do, because he knew that was the last of the fine tuning that had to be done.

The money had gone into the bank, the mortgage was paid up completely and now with her share of the money, she had practically paid up the mortgage on the shop. Business was booming. She was going to live above the shop, so she only had to pay the bills on the flat and that would come out of her salary from the takings, then everything for the shop to be paid out of that as well. Once Mel had handed the keys in, the estate agents were giving them to the new owners later on that afternoon.

"Mr Davidson, here's the keys. The place is spotless and empty, ready for the new owners. I hope they are happy there as I once was," Mel said. She gave the guy the envelope and he shook her hand, and she left the building. Her mum was waiting outside for her.

Mel had a doctor's appointment, just a check-up, to make sure everything was how it should be. They were going to head off for a cuppa. Mel had got quite accustomed to these herbal teas and had them every time she went out.

The peppermint was great if she was having heartburn, which she was more frequently now. They were a boon for her.

Once they left the doctors, they headed only to the café. She sat down and her mum ordered; also a slice of apple pie and custard, cream was off the menu for Mel. She was happy with that. "It's going to be weird, Mum, staying at the flat now," Mel stated. Jean and Tina.

Tina was so good, she was helping with everything she could. Mel didn't know what she would have done without her this last month or so. They had gone over to the flat once George and his friends took over the stuff Mel wanted and they tidied up, aired the place and put everything where she had said she wanted it.

Mel was going over there later on, but popping into the shop first, just so they don't think they have burglars and call the police. Once Mel and Jean had finished at the café, they made their way over to the flat. Jean wanted to make sure it was aired enough. She had already brought her some shopping to put in the cupboards and the fridge/freezer.

Thankfully, Mel had that there already. George and his mates would have done themselves an injury taking that up the stairs. Mel called into the shop quickly. They were pleased to see her and were glad she was moving in. They had been hearing lots of noises coming from the flat above.

Lesley handed her a bunch of carnations. "What are these for?" Mel asked.

"I thought they would brighten up the place," replied Lesley.

"Thank you, you're nuts, but thank you," said Mel. She closed the door and then went to the side door. She opened it up. "Mum, I have had two sets of keys in my hands today; the ones from the old place and the ones to my new place," Mel beamed.

Jean just smiled at her. She knew her daughter had been through so much these last few months, but she was about to start a new adventure. She had a lot to look forward to and she was grateful for that. They both made their way upstairs, opened the door and Mel just stood there and sighed.

She was home.

Chapter 5

Mel had settled in these last few weeks. She was waddling a bit more now and she didn't have long to go, but she wasn't worried. It seemed everything was in slow motion, then time sped up and now it's in slow motion again; she couldn't keep up. Once she handed her keys to her house back to the estate agent for the final time, this was it.

Anyway, she didn't want to dwell on it. She had made her new home so cosy, for the two of them, her and her new baby, when he put in an appearance. Mel was having weekly appointments at either the doctors or the hospital, and Jean, her mum, was there every step of the way. Mel had all of her scans now and she was getting too big to be scanned, and she had trouble getting on and off the hospital bed couch thing. It was so narrow, she had to be steadied onto her feet with her mum's help last time.

The spare room, well the baby's room, was next to Mel's. Not that she was putting him in there on his own for a long time, but she wanted to make it nice. She had the walls painted cream, and had pale blue accents around the room, lampshade, curtains. Her sister, Tina, had helped her a lot.

Actually, Mel didn't realise how much she would become reliant on her. "Coooeee, Mel, it's only me, love," shouted up Jean. She didn't want to worry Mel.

"Kettle's on, Mum, see you in a sec," Mel replied with a chuckle. Jean walked in through the opened door, full of bags. "Oh, Mum, what have you bought now?" Mel asked.

"Oh I just picked you up some food shopping and a couple of things for bubba. You know, I just couldn't resist it, Mel. Please don't be annoyed!" Jean added. Jean loved buying things for Mel's baby, well her grandchild. It was her first one and she was excited. Especially as she thought that Mel wouldn't ever have one.

Mel handed her a cup of hot steaming tea. "Cheers, love, aaahhh," Jean muttered. "There's nothing better than a hot cup of tea," Jean added. Mel would normally agree with her, but before Mel knew she was pregnant, she couldn't stand the sight or taste of tea; it made her throw up. "So what are you up to today then Mel?" Jean asked.

"Nothing really. The place is clean and tidy, thanks to you and Tina. I don't have any appointments today, so I was hoping to put my feet up and rest. I mean now the weather is getting better, Mum. It's a shame to waste the blue skies and beautiful sunshine," Mel said.

"But you're going to be inside, not out in it, Mel," Jean sounded a little surprised.

"Yeah I know, but it's nice to look out and see the sky, Mum, and the lovely colours outside, whilst looking out of the window," Mel said dreamily.

"Ok, Mel, whatever you say," Jean thought. "So how long do you have now, Mel? Is it 4 weeks or 5, I can't remember?" Jean asked her.

"It's 4 weeks, Mum, not long now," she said.

"Have you decided on any names yet? What did you think of David or are you still stuck on Jonathan?" Jean quizzed, looking a bit puzzled.

"Nicholas!" Mel said.

"Nicholas? Is that what you have decided on then?" Jean asked, not sure if she liked the name or not.

"I think so, I will wait and see what he looks like first and see if it suits him. Jonathan and David, no, Mum. They have become such popular names. Lesley said they keep getting orders for christenings for David and Jonathan. I want something a little different, something you don't hear of very often," Mel answered.

'Fair enough', thought Jean. She knew her girl was right, she mostly was with these things. "Have you been in the shop much lately?" Jean asked.

"No, not really. It takes me all my time to get up and down those stairs, by the time I get to the bottom, I'm too knackered." Both women laughed at that.

Just over a week later, Mel got up and she was having pains in her back, her lower back. It didn't feel like cramps, she normally got that in her calves, this was like a dull pain at first. Mel reached over her bed and got her phone. She pulled it onto the bed, thankfully the cord was quite long, so she didn't hurt herself.

She got another pain in the back, but this time it was sharp. 'Oo oh, I don't like this', she thought while dialling her mum's number. "Nan? Hi, Nan, yes is Mum there? What oh OK. Can you get her to call me when she gets back?"

"Oh no, I think I have wet the bed. Oh bloody hell, what OK, Nan. See you in a few minutes then!" Mel replied putting down the receiver. Within less than ten minutes, her mum, her sister and her nan were scrambling up the stairs.

"Mel, Mel, where are you darling?" Jean asked, well screamed.

"Mum, I think I wet myself. It's all over the bed and the floor," said Mel looking rather upset.

"No, Mel, I think that's your waters breaking!" Jean said.

"What, you mean the babies coming? Is that why I was getting sharp pain...sssssss," Mel said as she grabbed hold of the door handle.

"Mel, we think you're starting, love. Where's your bag and let's get you dressed. We need to call for an ambulance," said nan.

"Got Mel's bag and I have just called for an ambulance and called the hospital and told them that you're starting your labour." Mel looked like she was in a film, where everything was going on around her and she didn't have a clue.

"Mel, where are your handheld notes, the ones you take with you to the doctors and the hospital?" Jean asked.

"Oh, they are already in my handbag, Mum. I don't take them out, just in case they are needed, like now. I need to get cleaned up and washed and dressed," Mel replied. Tina went into Mel's bedroom, stripped the bed and put the wet bedding into the washing machine and cleaned up the floor. She didn't want Mel to trip and hurt herself.

She grabbed some clean bedding from the airing cupboard in the hall landing and re-made the bed, so it was nice and fresh. Tina had taken Mel's bag downstairs to the hallway, so it was there ready for when they were leaving. Thank goodness Tina was organised, normally it was Mel, but her head was all over the place.

By the time Mel got washed and dressed, you would never know there had been an accident in there at all. Mel had protectors on the mattress so it only went on the sheet and duvet cover. Mel couldn't believe how organised they all were. She had just put her shoes on and then the front doorbell went.

"That will be the ambulance, Mum," said Tina. Jean went to check in on Mel and the ambulance driver and assistant walked through the door. They asked Mel a few questions and Mel held onto the door again. The pains in her back were becoming more frequent. They told her to breathe, she was fine now.

Mel answered her questions and asked her where her bag was. Tina told them it was downstairs in the hallway, they should have passed it on their way up. They nodded that they had done. Mel grabbed her keys. Her nan had already made her way downstairs, she didn't want to be in the way.

Tina had already called George and he was waiting downstairs to take her and nan to the hospital; they wouldn't all be able to go in the ambulance. Mel made her way down slowly. Lesley was outside with Fiona and Julie. When they saw the ambulance, they knew it had to be Mel. They all waved and Lesley told her good luck.

Mel looked back and grimaced, she was having more pains again. She was helped into the ambulance and her mum followed behind her. The driver shut the back door and the assistant took the relevant information they needed for the hospital, like her hand-held notes and how often her back pain was lasting for and how often.

They got to the hospital rather quickly. It wasn't that faraway, and the assistant ran out of the ambulance to get a wheelchair to save Mel from walking. She said thank you to the ambulance men and the assistant took her inside and then returned to the ambulance as they just had another call come in. He told Mel good luck before he left her.

George, Tina and Marge got out of George's car and followed into reception. Mel was still waiting there with Jean. A porter came over and took Mel upstairs to the labour wards. They all followed her up to the wards, but they couldn't all stay. "Tina, what if I come back in a couple of hours, if nothing's happening. I can take you and nan back home and we can scoot right back if Mel has the baby. Is that ok?" George asked.

"Nan, what do you think?" Tina asked who was listening to the conversation. "I think that's a great idea, because I don't think we can stay here all day, love. I don't think the nurses and doctors want that. So yes, George, that would be great. I don't think we will be moving from here. So OK, love, thank you," said nan.

George gave Tina a kiss, said goodbye and then left. "You have got a Gooden there, Teen. Make sure you keep hold of him," said nan. She was proud of both of her granddaughters. They had so much going on in their lives.

Their mum bringing them up on her own, having two jobs at a time to get them what they needed and on the odd occasion a treat each.

Mel was taken into a delivery room. There were two nurses and a midwife. Jean went in with her bag and stood out of the way. Once they got Mel settled. They hooked her up to a baby monitor machine, with a big elastic around the Mel's huge tummy, then clipped it together and this read the babies heartbeat.

It was exciting but Mel looked a little nervous. "Mum, he's not due for another three weeks, surely he can stay up there a while longer?" Mel asked naively.

"Mel, your waters have broken which means there's no longer any fluid around him. He wants to come out and by judging of the size of you, I'm not surprised," said Jean. She could tell her girl was getting nervous. She wasn't expecting him just yet, so wasn't quite prepared, but she couldn't put him back.

This was it, her baby that she had waited for many many years was going to put in an appearance very soon. They gave Mel gas and air, that's what she wanted for now. She was dealing with the pain. She was also getting contractions, they were a little further apart. The next time the midwife came back in, she went over to the monitor machine and had a look at the readout.

Jean noticed her look of worry on her face. "Mel, I want to have a little look down there and see how far you have dilated, is that OK?" she asked Mel. Mel was nodding. She was having the gas and air, it did keep her calm. The midwife came back up and left the room. She returned with a doctor, who also looked at the readout and then spoke with the midwife, who was also called Tina.

"Mel, we have had a look at your readout, and Tina has just examined you. I'm afraid your baby has turned and is now breech, so it's impossible for you to have this baby naturally as your pelvis isn't very wide and baby is a big baby. So I'm afraid that we are going to have to prepare you for a caesarean section."

"So Tina, if you could help Mel onto her side and pull her legs up to her knees, so she can have the epidural injection into her spine. Now, Mel, please think about if you're on the escalator in Debenhams and you think you're going to poop yourself and you need to hold it in," the doctor said. Mel did as she was told, even though she was thirty, she felt like a little girl at the doctors.

With the needle administered in Mel's back, they wheeled her off to theatre. Tina and nan left a couple of hours ago, but Jean had to quickly call home and tell Tina and nan that Mel was going in for an emergency caesarean and could they both get back here as quick as they could. She had to go, she didn't want Mel to think she was leaving her on her own.

Jean had quickly changed into her scrubs and was taken into theatre. Mel was OK. They were just going through the procedure with her and she was taking it in. Jean was so proud of her elder daughter, going through all of this on her own, well her own body, but she had all of them around her.

Actually when Jean thought about it, the only man in their lives was George, the rest around Mel were women. A good structure of strong women, was all she needed, but once in a while a shelf had to be put up.

Jean had walked up to where Mel's head was, really so she wouldn't be in the way. "Mel, we are going to put up a screen, so you won't be able to see, and I want to spray you with water, and tell me if you can feel it," said the doctor, who sprayed her practically straightaway.

"Ooh yes, that was cold," replied Mel.

"You OK, Mel?" Jean asked, holding out her hand for Mel to grab it if need be.

"Yes, a little nervous!" she replied.

"Not to worry, Mel. We will be as gentle as we can. Now once we are able to get started, you will feel a bit of tugging, but that's all!" The doctor said who seemed to be in charge. He sprayed Mel again, but this time she didn't feel it.

"Right we can get started," he said to his team. The next half an hour or so went in a blur for Mel. She did feel them tugging a bit. Her waters had already broken, so they didn't have to worry about getting them out of the way. The next thing Mel knew the doctor was holding up her baby.

"Mel, it's a boy and a big one at that!" The doctor remarked. He handed him over to the midwife once the cord was cut and she took him over to the scale to be weighed. "9lbs 4oz," she called out to the nurse taking down the information, to go on the white board.

"9lbs 4oz, Mel. He's a whopper," said Jean.

"Would you like to see him, Mum?" The doctor in charge asked.

"Yes, but what about?"

"Just around to where the incubator is," the doctor interrupted Jean mid-sentence. Jean went over to her new grandson, where the nurses were just cleaning him up to bring over to Mel to look at. She couldn't hold him just yet until she was sewn up and able to move.

"Would you like him to have the Vitamin K?" The midwife asked.

"Oh yes, please," replied Mel. She had read up on that and thought it would be important to give him the best start.

"Mel, he did a little wee and then a huge fountain of one," Jean told her. Mel was laying there patiently waiting to see her young baby. The midwife brought him over in a towel and saw that he had a huge mop of black hair, just like Mel did. He scrunched up his nose, and looked straight at Mel. He had beautiful blue eyes.

The midwife handed him to Jean, so she could hold him. "Hello, Nicholas. It is Nicholas you want to call him, Mel?" Jean enquired.

"Yes, yes, I do," mumbled Mel. She was already full of tears. She couldn't believe this little well big bundle of joy was hers.

"Nearly done now, Mel, just finishing stitching you up. Then you can go on up to the ward."

"Mel just think if you would have had him tomorrow, it would have been April Fool's day," laughed Jean.

"Oh yes, but he is three weeks early," Mel piped up.

"Actually he's only two weeks early, should have been here on 15 April. You were further than you thought, Mel," said the midwife.

"Right ready, one two three," said the doctor. There were that many staff holding onto Mel's sheet to transfer her onto a hospital bed, thank goodness they had those metal poles in the edge of the bed to help.

"Thank you, everyone. You have been great," she said before she left theatre. By now, she was holding her new baby son. When they opened the double doors to theatre, nan, Tina and George were all waiting outside. Mel, Nicholas, Jean and the staff taking her to the ward all walked down together.

Mel was beaming from ear to ear. She didn't care she had just had abdominal surgery, she couldn't be happier than she was right at this moment. They were both taken up to the post-natal ward. Even though Mel hadn't really had any complications, the hospital still wanted her to stay in for the week, for rest mainly, but also to adjust and to make sure she was healing well with her scar.

The week went really quickly. Mel had adjusted to feeding Nicholas no problem and getting up for the feeds in the night. It was a little awkward at first, especially with her feel like she had been cut in half. But she managed with help from the nurses and midwives and of course her family.

Jean was there as soon as she could be when visiting hours had started and she stayed as late as possible. Before they all knew it, Mel and Nicholas were coming home. "Mel, we have had a bit of a change around," said Jean.

"Huh," commented Mel. "How come?" she asked.

"Well, we think that you going up and down all of those stairs considering you have just had major surgery, may be too much for you. So what we have done is, moved you back home and Tina and George are taking over your flat, for the time being unless you say otherwise. Now I know we should have run it passed you first, but we wanted to help and didn't want to worry you."

"So all of your stuff nick nacks and that, are in your old room. Nicholas has Tina's room when you want to put him in there, even though we know it won't be for months. We just wanted to take the pressure off you, is that ok or are you annoyed?" Mum suggested.

"No, of course not, Mum. It makes more sense and I will have you and nan there, and of course it gives Tina a chance for somewhere to live. I don't know why we didn't think of it before really. So no, Mum, I'm not annoyed. It's a great idea," Mel replied.

"And we will be paying you rent of course," Tina told her.

"We?" Mel quizzed.

"Me and George. We are going to live together, is that alright?" A nervous Tina asked.

"Of course it is. I feel better that you're going to have George there rather than be on your own and the money will help out lots. So congratulations, you two," Mel said excitedly. Tina grabbed Mel's bag. Jean had picked up a lovely baby car seat for Nicholas, but she didn't think he would fit in it for too long as he was already a big baby.

George asked Mel if he could carry the car seat with Nicholas in it, as he was a big boy, but also the weight of the car seat. She shouldn't really be carrying anything too heavy now, at least for the next six weeks or so. Nan wasn't there to collect Mel and Nicholas. She was at home waiting for them to arrive.

George drove very carefully, more to Jean's approval than Mel's really, but he got them home safe and sound. Nan had seen them drive up and rushed to open the front door, with her arms opened wide. "Welcome Home, Mel, and Nicholas, of course!" Nan said.

A few of the neighbours came out of their front doors to see Mel and the baby. They were oohing and aaahhing over him. Nicholas was none the wiser, he was fast asleep. When they all left, they went indoors and nan asked if anyone had wanted tea. "Yes please, Nan," said Mel.

Nan looked a little shocked. "Since when have you been back on the tea?" Nan looked confused.

"Since the nurse brought me a cup once Nicholas was born," she laughed.

"I wonder if Nicholas will ever drink tea then?" Nan asked.

"Well, he definitely likes his milk," replied Mel and they all burst out laughing.

Once they had all drank their tea, nan put the kettle on again. George had already taken up Mel's bag and then had to go back to work. They all went upstairs to have a look where Mel and Nicholas were sleeping. Mel had opened the door to her own bedroom and it was just the same as before.

George and his pals had got a van and brought Mel's bed and a few other things, like Nicholas's wardrobe and chest of drawers and other baby stuff. Also his lamp, curtains and other blue stuff from his bedroom at the flat and put them in his room. George at the weekend had decorated his room white and put the stuff up for Mel, but had opened the windows, so the smell of paint surely disappeared pretty quick.

They had then replaced the stuff needed at the flat with stuff from Tina's room and from George's place. He also had lived at home with his parent's and they were happy to help with anything him and Tina needed. "It's amazing what can be done in a week, when everyone pulls together," said nan, and she was sure right.

Mel took Nicholas out of his car seat. He was due a feed and would be waking up at any minute. Jean, nan and Tina had helped her get her stuff together in her new bedroom. Her clothes had been brought over too and Tina had put it all away, but Mel wanted to go through it.

She may need to wear some of her bigger things until her figure was back to normal. Not that Mel was worrying about that, she was just happy she had her baby. So she was going to do that, when Jean came in and told her not to just yet. She looked rather tired, so once she had fed Nicholas or her, Mum could feed and wind him and Mel could have a little rest and maybe sleep.

Mel had gotten used to sleeping in the day in hospital. She didn't want it to be that she continued, but as Jean had told her, she has only just home from the hospital. So Mel decided Mum was right and yes she could feed him and change him if he needed it.

Jean was in her element. She couldn't wait to get her hands on Nicholas for cuddles and feeding him would just be great. She was floating on a cloud. She had no idea where she was going, over mountains and oceans, but she felt so weightless. It was an amazing feeling.

Then she felt that she was under water, swimming with the fishes and the corals. "Mel, would you like a cuppa?" Jean asked. Mel stirred from her dream and opened her eyes. Why is it that when you're having a lovely dream, someone always wakes you up?

"Coming," Mel replied. Mel took her time to go downstairs. She didn't want to fall and she hasn't walked downstairs without being able to look at her feet in a long time. She opened the door to the sitting room and Jean popped out of the kitchen with a steaming hot mug of tea for her.

Nicholas was fast asleep in his new pram. Mel looked over at him and sighed a long sigh. "You OK, love?" Nan asked.

"Yes, Nan, I still can't believe he's mine," Mel chuckled.

"Mel, I have sterilised his bottles. Do you want me to make up some bottles and put them in the fridge to keep them fresh?" Jean asked.

"Oh OK, Mum, I was going to do that," Mel said.

"I just thought it would help and you wouldn't have to worry about it and sleep for longer. Next time and in the future, you get into your routine, and we will follow what you want. He's your baby, we don't want you thinking we are treading on your toes!" Jean exclaimed.

"Mum, it's fine. Honestly, I think I need all the help I can get," Mel replied.

"No, you don't, Mel. You see, it will become natural. You just need to find what works for you. So now Nicholas is asleep and you have had a rest, do you want something to eat and do you want to sort out your clothes?" Jean asked.

"Well?" Mel started to say then the doorbell went. Jean went to see who it was.

It was Lesley. "Hiya, Mel, how are you?" Lesley asked her.

"I'm fine," Mel replied while Lesley hugged her. Lesley had visited Mel in the hospital, but now she was home, she wanted to pop in when she had time, rather than when it was visiting time. She looked over at Nicholas who was fast asleep.

"Oh, Mel. He's such a beautiful boy and so big. How on earth did you manage getting about when he was still inside you?" Lesley asked.

"Well, I had no choice really. I had to take it slowly. Anyway how is it going at the shop?" Mel enquired.

"Mel, the business is doing well; lots of orders. There are lots of babies being born, so lots of floral tributes, which is why I brought you these instead of flowers," Lesley added handing her a big box of chocolates. "I thought you would be sick of flowers, Mel," Lesley said, looking round at the lovely flowers she already had in vases all over the place. Lesley gave Mel the books to have a look through. "Oh I hear we have new tenants upstairs?" Lesley commented.

"Er yes, Tina and George have moved in. They won't be any trouble, Les, but at least the flat isn't empty and there is money coming in, so a win and they can keep an eye on downstairs, when the shop is closed," Mel replied.

"Well, I have to make a move, I'll pop in again later on in the week," Lesley said.

"Actually, Les, I may pop in instead, if that's ok? I can bring these with me. I need to get some fresh air and Nicholas can start going out into the outside world," chuckled Mel.

"Ok, Mel, see you then," replied Lesley.

"Mum, can you keep an eye on Nicholas, while I go up and start sorting out them clothes. I have to keep moving or I will take root I think." Both Mum and daughter started laughing and Nicholas stirred.

"Ooops," chuckled Mel, she then left the room to sort out her wardrobe.

Chapter 6

Mel had seen the midwife for a couple of weeks and she had now been transferred to see the health visitor. Nicholas had regained his baby weight and was doing well. He was now 6 months old and he was laying on the floor, trying to roll over.

He hadn't tried sitting up at all, but Mel wasn't too worried about that. The health visitor made a note of it on her last visit at home. Mel would take him to see her at the clinic once every couple of weeks or so, just really to check on Nicholas's progress, weight and make sure he's doing what he is supposed to and when. Not that you're supposed to compare to other babies as each baby is different and they do catch up to the same level as the other babies and children by the time they go to school.

Mel was pleased that Nicholas was doing well. She was a little anxious, but she's a new mum. An anticipated mum, who thought she would never have a baby. So some of the things even though new are a little daunting.

Mel left the clinic on this occasion and met up with her mum. Nicholas was laying in his pram. He didn't have much on as it was still very warm for September, so just a long vest that did up under his nappy, and it had little cap sleeves. They walked along the high street and went into a small café.

Mel had been there lots of times before. Even when she had not long found out she was pregnant, that was the time she saw Terry with Clare.

Terry seemed a very distant memory to Mel. So much had happened in the last two years, but she knew things couldn't carry on as they were. Anyway Jean went up to order two teas and two slices of apple pie and cream. "Ice cream for me please, Mum!" Mel exclaimed.

She did like a bit of vanilla ice cream with her apple pie. There wasn't much time left of the summer, so she wanted to have ice cream while it was still warm enough to get away with it. Jean sat down and they were discussing Nicholas's last visit at the clinic.

"Well he's putting on his weight, Mum, he's meeting all of his targets," Mel said as she looked down at a fast asleep Nicholas in his pram. Tina and George had settled into Mel's flat lovely, it's like they had always been there.

"Mel, are you keeping up with the bookkeeping for the shop?" Jean asked.

"What? Oh yes, Lesley has been my right-hand mum. She drops them off on a Saturday and I return them back on Monday, which is great. Everything is going with the shop and the rent from the flat is helping out as well."

"Nicholas doesn't need a thing for about five years with what you, nan, Tina and George, and the girls have bought him. So this is the money to be put away once the bills and wages have been paid. So yes, I am happy how things are working out," Mel told her mum.

"Mel, don't you want a night out once in a while, you know with the girls. You haven't seen them in a long while?" Jean suggested.

"Oh I don't know, Mum. Nicholas needs me," said Mel.

Jean held up her hand. "Do you think me and your nan, wouldn't be able to cope for one evening, Mel. I raised two girls on my own after your father left us for that you know what, and so did your nan. She raised two of us after the war, on her own."

"So please for your own sake and a bit of sanity, call up Sam or Paula and go out for a night out. You don't have to have a lot to drink, but I think it would do you the world of good. Because I mean, if you didn't go out with the girls, we wouldn't have littleun in the pram there, would we eh?" Jean chuckled.

Mel laughed. "Ok, Mum, I will call the girls and see when they are next going out. I know you two just want cuddles with Nicholas, don't you?" Mel teased.

***

Mel went out to the pub with the girls on Friday as she used to. She hadn't been out in over year and the girls were great. They had been to see her once in a while when she was home before Nicholas came along and then when he was born. There's nothing like a new born to make you feel alive and happy and broody.

Jodie and Sam had decided that they were thinking of having babies now. Mel looked so happy, so complete, they were feeling a little out of it. Jodie had just broken up with Paul, so she wasn't too interested in men or babies at the moment, so she wandered off on her own for a little while. "Are you still talking about babies or can I come back now?" Jodie asked.

They all giggled. Samantha and Mike had been dating about two years, and had recently got engaged, but she wanted the wedding first. "Oh, Mel, we are talking about dates," said Sam.

"Dates? Oh I don't want a date," Mel said.

"No not those sort of dates, silly, but dates for the wedding. Would you do our flowers for us, for the wedding?" Sam asked.

"Oh, Sam, but of course, mates rates though?" Mel winked.

"Are you sure, Mel?" Sam quizzed.

"Of course, anyway, let me know what sort of flowers you want and how many buttonholes. If you're having a church or registry office, because sometimes they do their own arrangements and we don't want to step on anyone's toes," Mel suggested.

"I will when we have the necessary organised. You will be the first to know, well apart from my mum and dad and Mike's mum," Sam added. 'She want us to have the works but it's going to cost a fortune', thought Sam.

Mel enjoyed her night out with the girls. Even Jodie who was on a wind up all evening, well she hadn't expected to break up with Paul, but she was fed up with his humming and haring about whether or not to get a flat together. If they stayed with his mum, they could save. His mum didn't want him to move out just yet.

She was a lady who lived on her nerves and as her husband had died this last year. She was anxious all the time. He did everything for her. She was struggling with everything and became to rely on Paul a hell of a lot. So he asked Jodie if they could cool it for a while and see how his mum would be in the next few months.

Jodie wasn't sympathetic about June. She loved Paul so much, but there would be three in this relationship until his mum, June, got herself together.

***

"Mum!" Mel called when she opened the door. "It's only me," she said.

"Well, it wouldn't be Father Christmas would it, Mel. He doesn't have a key," Jean laughed.

100

"How was Nicholas?" she asked.

"He's been a little lamb, Mel, fast asleep he is!" Nan said. They both loved looking after him. "He's upstairs, thought it would be easier than up and down all night," said Nan.

"Up and down, has he been any trouble then?" Mel asked, a little nervous.

"No, Mel, he's been fine. You have to remember nan can't do up and down, the stairs are too much. So it was a figure of speech, so to speak," said Jean. "Did you have a good night?" Jean asked.

"What, oh yes. Samantha and Mike are getting married and asked if I could do the flowers for the wedding, which I said yes of course. Once they sort out the date and where they are getting married, we can take it from there. So that will be something to look forward to eh, Mum?" Mel asked.

Mel kissed her mum and nan on the forehead and said goodnight. She made her way up to bed and checked on Nicholas before getting into bed. He was sleeping through the night now. So Mel was able to get decent sleep now.

She settled herself into bed and drifted off into a lovely sleep; dreaming her and Nicholas were holding hands and running through a meadow, picking up some daisies as they were going along.

September was now over and October was already here, with a bit of a chill in the wind. Mel had been popping into the shop every week, really just to drop the books back for Lesley. She had told Lesley about Sam getting married and they would be doing the flowers, but they won't know what's what until they had spoken with their parents.

Lesley knew they would manage it, they always did. Mel had started to sort through Nicholas's clothes; what no longer fitted him, what she could take down to the clinic. There was a big container of children's clothes, that no longer fitted; they could be donated for families who didn't have great income. Mel wanted to donate the stuff that he no longer wore.

While she was there, she spotted a notice board, with various stuff on it. Baby Clinic Mon-Weds 1pm–3pm, she knew that, because that was when she took Nicholas to be weighed. Prams that were no longer needed being sold for a fraction of the price, coffee mornings for the mums-to-be, and then she saw something that she thought would be a great way to meet other mums.

Get out for a morning a week and for Nicholas to engage with other babies and children, a mother and baby group. Mel had a smile fixed on her face until she got home. "Hi, Mum, we're back," Mel shouted out. She was taking a rather wriggly Nicholas out of the pram.

He had a Babygro on, with a cardigan and a lovely navy lightweight jacket. He wouldn't need anything warmer at the moment, but Mel had acquired rather a lot so she had lots to choose from. "Mum, guess what?" Mel teased.

"What?" Jean replied.

"They are running a mother and baby group down at the clinic once a week on a Thursday morning. I was thinking it would be great to go. I can meet other mums and Nicholas can be around other babies and children. What do you think?" Mel asked her mum.

"Mel, I think it's a great idea."

"What a great idea?" Nan asked, before Jean could reply.

"I am going to be taking Nicholas to a Mother and Baby group on a Thursday Morning, Nan. It will be great for both of us," said Mel.

"Yes, it will save you both being cooped up in here all the time," added Nan.

"We are not always cooped up in here. I take Nicholas to the park. We go to the shop once a week and I do go shopping you know. I don't just sit down on my backside, Nan," Mel retorted.

"Mel, I didn't mean it like that. I know you're always out, but sometimes it's nice to be home, but you're only here with me and your mum. You need to get out there and meet other mums and make some new friends. Your pals, Sam, Paula and Jodie, don't really have much in common with you now."

"So you have to go with what your situation is and now it's to be around other mums. You can share stories and get tips and that, that's all I am saying," said Nan proudly. She knew her girl had done so well these last few months, but it didn't really give her much input from anyone else but them. She knew it would be great for both of them.

Thursday morning soon came round and Mel was excited. She hadn't been to one of these things before and had high hopes, to meet other mums with tots.

Mel made her way to the clinic. When she got there, she parked Nicholas' pram where the other ones were. There were only a couple of mums inside. Mel said hello to both of them and they reciprocated.

One of the mums, Emma, told Mel where the kitchen was and to make herself a hot drink if she wanted one. The mums all put in 50 pence in a jar when they got there, that would cover tea, coffee, etc. Mel took Nicholas's coat off him and sorted out his hair. It was all stuck together and matted from the heat of his hood. She settled him down on her lap.

There were toys ranging from ages 6 month to 4 years. Emma handed Mel a mug of tea. "I didn't know if you wanted sugar or not?" Emma asked.

"No, that's fine, thank you. Where can I put it out of his way?" Mel quizzed. There was a shelf higher than the seats they were in.

"Just put it at the back, so no little ones can get up there to grab it," suggested Julie, another mum. Mel did as she was told. She didn't want any of the little ones getting burnt by her drink. Emma sat next to Mel.

"So who is this little one then?" Emma asked.

"This is Nicholas and I am Mel," said Mel, very proud of her son.

"Well, I am Emma and that little tiger over there in the dungarees is David. He's 6 months old, and that other mum going to the changing room is Maria and her little one, Safia, is 2 years old. She's a real sweetie," said Emma. Emma touched Nicholas' feet which he pulled away. He didn't like them stroked. Emma apologised.

Mel said it was fine, he just didn't like certain stuff. But he was fine. Nicholas was looking all around at his new surroundings, with big wide eyes. A couple of other mums came with their children. Some were carried in their mother's arms but wanted to get down as soon as they saw the toys to play with.

There was Sophie, Ann, Jackie, Rachel, Tracy and Julie. Then Lynn popped her head around the door. "Hello, everyone. Ooohhh we have a new mummy and a little poppet. Hi, I am Lynn and this is my session for mums and babies to come and have a jolly good time, meeting new faces, and you are?" Lynn asked.

"Oh sorry, I am Mel and this here is Nicholas," Mel replied.

"Oohh, he's a little darling, how old is he?" Lynn asked.

"He's 6 months old and a content baby, thank goodness," replied Mel.

"Now help yourself to tea and coffee, but there is a small fee from everyone, just fifty pence, just to help cover the tea and coffee," suggested Lynn.

"Er yes, is it Emma, told me, I have done already!" Mel told Lynn.

"Did you sign in as well?" Lynn asked.

"Oh no, I didn't know I had to," said Mel a little flustered.

"It's nothing to worry about. Just so we know who has come, and just in case we do have a fire alarm test, which happens once in a while. We want to make sure everyone is out of the building!" Lynn said.

"Thank you. I'll do that now, thanks, Lynn," Mel replied. Mel sat down again and another couple of mums and tots came through the door.

"You know what his reply was, I would have to apply again in a year or two. There's nothing they can do at the moment. Our review had just gone through and even if we appealed against it, it doesn't mean they would do it again until next year!" Jackie said.

"Hi, everyone," said Jackie, everyone responded. "Oh hello, you must be new? I'm Jackie and this is Ben," Jackie said, putting Ben down to play with some bricks.

"Hi, I'm Mel and this is Nicholas," Mel said showing off Nicholas.

"Oh he's gorgeous. Look at those chocolate brown eyes. He is going to break hearts when he is older, and look at those lovely long lashes," added Jackie. Mel and Nicholas stayed for the full two and a half hours. Nicholas was just watching what was going on.

"Now you have broken the ice with the other mums, it won't feel so daunting the next time you come," said Lynn as Mel was getting ready to get up and leave. Mel got Nicholas in his pram, he was fast asleep, far too much excitement for the day. Mel took the long way home, just because it was a lovely autumn day and the leaves had already started falling from the trees and the beautiful colours of them, reds, golden brown, hardly any green left on them.

Mel pushed the pram up the path and Jean who had been watching them up the road, had opened the door. "So how did it go?" she asked.

"Oh, Mum, it was lovely. Lots of lovely children. A couple of babies and some lovely mums. I am so glad we went," Mel told her.

"So I suppose you will be going back then?" Jean asked her.

"Oh yes, even though Nicholas was watching what was going on, he seemed to enjoy it. So yes, we are definitely going back next week. Put the kettle on, I am so parched. We had a walk the long way round, through the park, looking at the leaves. Well, I was looking at them, Nicholas was asleep," Mel added.

She took Nicholas in, left him in his pram for the time being, because she has found lately, that if she moves him while he's sleeping, he will wake up.

She did move the top cover off the pram though, as it was quite warm at home. Jean brought her a cuppa over, which Mel was grateful for and she sat down in the big armchair next to the fire…

"Mmmm, just what I needed, Mum. You can tell winter is on its way, there's definitely chill in the air," Mel said.

***

"Mel, hi, Mel, it's Tina. Can you hear me. This line keeps going funny. Anyway, I was wondering if you would like to come out with me and George this Saturday night. They are having a band down at the club. It would be a great chance to have some fun for once?" Tina asked.

"Oh I don't know, Teen, this Saturday?" Mel replied.

"Well it's not like you have tons to do and it would be great for mum and nan to look after Nicholas. What do you say?" Tina encouraged.

"Well, I don't think Mum and nan would object, do you? So yes, if I can find something to wear then it would be great to come down with you and George," replied Mel.

"Right so that's a date. I will let you know Friday the final arrangements, because we go at different times at the weekend. Have to go now, see ya," said Tina putting down the receiver.

"Who was that, love?" Jean asked.

"That was our Tina, calling to ask me to go down the club with her and George on Saturday night. Would you mind watching Nicholas, Mum?" Mel asked her. "I'm not taking liberties, am I?" Mel added.

"No, of course not, and you know we love having our Nicholas anytime you want us to," Jean replied, adding a gentle kiss on her daughter's cheek. 'Well, that would be great for a change', thought Mel. She had just finishing Nicholas' washing and he was due a feed in about half an hour, and was trying to get ahead of herself.

He was trying to get up off his back. He had started rolling around the last month or so, but now he's trying to lift himself up. Mel was really pleased with his progress. They were going to the Mother and Baby group the next day. She had been going for a few weeks now and she was enjoying it.

Nicholas, on the other hand, was just lying there watching the other children and babies. A couple of them were already sitting up and even starting to hold their bottles, but Nicholas wasn't really interested. Mel wasn't too worried. She had started seeing a lot of Emma and Jackie out and about, which was lovely.

A couple of times they had met up and had a cuppa at the local café, so Mel was getting to make new friends at last, and Mum and nan were over the moon and now she was going out with Tina and George. She was starting to get a bit of life again.

Mel had got there first. She had put the kettle on, put her money in the tin and signed in. Nicholas was on the floor on one of the massive mats, that were soft and spongy; he wouldn't hurt himself on it. Mel had given him some soft bricks to play with, but he wasn't interested in them at all.

Emma, Maria and Julie walked through the door. "Kettle's already on, ladies, help yourself. Oh and I brought in some chocolate biscuits for everyone!" Mel told the women.

"Oh, Mel, don't be starting that. We will all start getting big backsides and hips, not that they were small already," chuckled Julie. Everyone brought snacks in once in a while, but no pressure. It was just nice to have a biccy with a cuppa. As long as it was away from the children.

"How are you all doing then?" Mel asked.

"Well, Steve has just his promotion at work this week, so we are due a holiday soon. So I am going to be booking something hot for next year, because once Christmas is over, it's just damp, dreary and depressing times ahead for the rest of winter. Anyone have ideas where I can look for?" Julie asked.

"What about Spain or Portugal?" Maria suggested.

"We went to Spain this summer, not that I look like I have been anywhere. I was thinking further afield, maybe the Caribbean, or even America, that maybe a nice change," said Julie.

"Well, it must be a good promotion, Julie," said Emma.

"Oh yes, it was, thankfully. He earns it, I spend it…a good mix really," Julie laughed. Mel left the group when it finished. Everyone was going in different directions, she was just going home. Tina was going to be popping by later on for some dinner. George was going to be working late and it was a chance to catch up with everyone.

"Mum, we're back," Mel called when she walked through the door with the pram. Thankfully there was space in the hall to store it there. She didn't like leaving it outside the front anymore. Prams had been stolen outside a couple of people's homes and she just loved Nicholas's pram; Mum had treated her to it.

Jean came rushing in from the kitchen with her pinny on. "Did you both enjoy it again today then, Mel?" As she was cooing to Nicholas.

"Yes, he seems to enjoy it, but he doesn't really engage, Mum. Maybe he's just a bit slower or behind some of the other kids. He wriggles around on that mat, but he's not interested in any of the toys or bricks. Think I may mention it to the health visitor when I see her next," Mel said.

"When are you next there, Mel?" Mum asked.

"In two weeks," Mel replied.

"Maybe he would have picked up by then. I wouldn't worry, Mel," Mum replied.

"Oh I'm not worried, Mum. It's just some of the babies are moving around a lot more than him and they seem to be able to sit already," Mel told her.

"Now, Mel, you can't compare babies and children. They all seem to do things at different times, but by the time they go to school they all catch up," Mum said. Mel knew she was right and she wasn't really worried, but she was noticing it a bit more. Nicholas had woken up.

The fresh air always sent him off to sleep, but now it was lunch time and he wanted some food. Mel was still giving him milk, but he was onto solids a bit more, nothing with lumps in as he hadn't started getting his teeth through just yet, soft food. "Mum, could you get one of those jars out of the cupboard, maybe the chicken dinner one and maybe the chocolate pudding for afterwards," Mel asked her mum.

Jean brought both of them over, but she then remembered that the chicken one would need heating up. She took it back to the kitchen and put on a small pan of water, put it inside and kept an eye on it. Mel was getting Nicholas out of his outerwear. He looked so snug in his quilted all in one.

She sat him on her lap. He could sit that way, but not on his own yet. "Mel, I was thinking Halloween has just gone and it will soon be Bonfire Night. Do you want to take Nicholas at the local display or do you think it will be too noisy for his little ears?" Jean asked.

"No not this year, Mum. It will be too loud for his ears, but what if we just watch out of the window. Some of the families round here normally get fireworks. We could watch from inside, that way it will block out some of the noise. What do you think?" Mel asked.

"That's a good idea. The Jones a few doors away normally do some in their garden, so yes we could watch from the kitchen window. Me and your nan could go outside and watch them and you two stay inside," Jean said. "I'll tell your nan. She loves a good bonfire," Jean replied.

***

Tina came round that evening and stayed for dinner. It was a great evening. She, like nan and Mum, enjoyed cuddles with Nicholas. He was smiling at Tina. He had a lovely smile, where his whole face lit up.

"Now, Tina, you're going out with George and Mel on Saturday. You're not setting our Mel up with a man, are you? You're not trying to be matchmaker here, are you?" Nan asked.

"No, Nan, of course not. Don't you think Mel has enough on her hands without a man. She has Nicholas," and as she said that she nuzzled her face into his and he squealed. Mel loved to see him happy. He had already had a haircut as his hair was quite thick; not at the barbers, one of the mums at the club was a hairdresser and she did it for him. He sat very still.

He did still have some wavy curls left on his head though, and Mel was chuffed because she loved his curls. "Mel, I had better be going," said Tina.

"Isn't George collecting you, Teen?" Jean asked.

"Oh yes, I just heard him pull up, sorry," Tina told her. Jean looked out of the window and Tina was right, George had just pulled up and was getting out of the car. He waved to Jean and she waved back. He then pressed the doorbell, Tina went to answer it. He came in and said hello to everyone including Nicholas.

"George, would you like to stay for a cuppa?" Nan asked.

"Oh yes please, Marge, it's been a long day," he replied. George then sat down next to Tina and held onto her hand. These two were so much in love and were so good together. "Oh I spoke to Jim this evening, he's going to the club Saturday night," said George.

Mum raised her eyebrows at Tina. "Oh no, Mum. Jim is married, they will both be there. Oh, Mel, you will love his wife. She's so nice and they have a little tot as well, Bonnie. She's a little darling. They don't get much chance to go out, so when Jim's mum will babysit they go out. As we know it's hard looking after a little one," Tina commented.

George drained his cup. They both got up and kissed everyone goodbye and then left. Mel took Nicholas up to give him his bath and then put him to bed. Mel was a bit tired it had been a very eventful day, so once she sorted him out and put him to bed. She jumped in the bath herself, then went to bed and slept well, dreaming of Nicholas running around the garden chasing rabbits.

Saturday night was here and Mel had chosen a black dress to wear. Nothing special cocktail or anything, but she felt comfortable. She left her hair down as it was always put up, really because of Nicholas he liked to hold onto Mel's hair. She had styled it with hair curlers and put on some make-up.

Tina and George were picking her up at 7.30. She was just putting the finishing touches to her make-up and the doorbell rang. Nan opened it and it was Tina and George. Mum was holding Nicholas who seemed wide awake at these late visitors. He cooed away at Tina and blew bubbles at George. Nicholas was definitely starting to teethe.

"Now, Mum, you know where his milk is for later on. He has already had his dinner. He's been bathed, so when he's tired put him up to bed and don't forget to put the baby monitor on," Mel instructed.

"Now, Mel, do you think we haven't done this sort of thing before? So I suggest you leave little Nicholas with me and your nan, and go and have a lovely time this evening. He will be here when you get back. So off you go, you too Tina, George, now take her away please," Mum retorted.

Tina grabbed hold of Mel, before Mel could say anymore. Jean put her hand up, "Now go," Mum commanded.

"Bye then," they all said as they were leaving the house. George opened up the back door of the car. Tina got in the front and then George got in the driver's seat. The club was a short distance away, so it didn't take long to get there. George parked the car and they got out and he locked the car door.

The three of them went to the entrance of the club. They had to sign in and then they went into the hall. Jim and Angela were already there and Angela was talking to another lady. Jim waved over to George and met them all at the bar. Jim said hello to Tina, and Tina introduced Mel to him.

"Come over when you're ready. We have saved you some seats," Jim said. George grabbed their drinks and handed Mel hers. She wasn't breast feeding so she could have a drink once in a while. She had started to drink white wine, it didn't go to her head as much as the spirits.

They made their way over to the table. Jim stood up, to move the chairs nearer. They had great seats, not too near the stage, so they could hear and also speak, so the music wouldn't drown out their conversation. Jim introduced Mel to the ladies. "Ange, this is Mel, Tina's sister and Mel, this is Angela, my wife, and her sister, Elaine," Jim told her.

They exchanged their hellos and took off their coats and sat down. Elaine's scooted over and started talking to Mel. "So, Mel, what do you do, if you don't mind me asking?" Elaine asked.

"Well, I am a full time mum to Nicholas."

"So what about his dad then?" Elaine interrupted.

"Well he's not on the scene and I own a florist in town, 'Mel's Flowers'." Mel had recently changed its name from 'Blooming Marvellous'. "So yes, I am kept pretty busy. What about you, Elaine?" Mel asked.

"Oh I am also a single mum. My ex decided once Todd was born that it was too much trouble taking care of a baby and he legged it. So I have been doing it really since I came home from hospital on my own. Oh I have a wonderful family and they have been great. I used to be a secretary before I had him though, but this is a completely different experience, motherhood," Elaine told her.

The band had just started up, so conversation was difficult at first until they found their momentum. Mel and Elaine chatted away the evening. Mel had a couple of glasses of wine, then changed to orange juice. "Are you sure, Mel?" George asked. "I know you're not driving," he chuckled.

"No honest, George, I'm fine, still have to get up to Nicholas in the night you know," replied Mel. Angela was chatting to Tina, talking about weddings. George and her hadn't set a date yet, they were still trying to sort out what they wanted.

"Mel, we should meet up, you know with the boys," suggested Elaine. They exchanged phone numbers, when they were putting on their coats. It had been a welcome change to go out for Mel and she had made a couple of new friends.

"We normally meet up once a week or so, Mel, the club do have some nice bands and that play. Once in a while they have a disco, so maybe see you again sometime?" Angela suggested.

"That would be lovely, yes thank you. Let Tina know what's on and I will see how things go. Thanks everyone for a lovely evening," Mel said. Her, Tina and George, all left the hall and went to the car. George had one drink of a very watered-down lager, well a shandy really. He didn't drink and drive and he stuck to orange juice like Mel.

Tina had a few vodkas and oranges and a slight worse for wear. They got into the car and George dropped Mel home. "Night, Mel," said Tina.

"Night," replied Mel. They waited until Mel opened the front door and then drove off. "How was Nicholas, Mum?" Mel asked.

"A little angel, Mel. He had his bottle, before you ask, drank the lot and now he's tucked upon his cot fast asleep, look," Jean said pointing to the baby monitor. It was on, only lightly lighting up. "See, that's showing us he's breathing," Mum told her.

Mel said goodnight to her mum and nan and kissed them both. "I'm off to bed, Mum, Nan. I can't hold my drink anymore," Mel chuckled again. She grabbed her coat and left the sitting room. She held onto the banister going up the stairs.

She felt fine in the club and again in the car, but the night air had hit her both times getting home and once out of the car. She looked in on Nicholas who was fast asleep. Mel didn't want to breathe her drink infused breath on him, so just gave him a pat on his arm. He stirred a little but not enough to wake him up. Mel undressed and fell into bed, with her head slightly buzzing.

Chapter 7

Mel and Elaine only had the chance to meet up once. Since it was only a week away to Christmas and they both had a lot on their plates. Mel had been buying stuff for a few months now and was wanting to really get stuck in with the rest. Nan and Mum had been watching Nicholas so she could dart in and out of the shops and he could be with them at home in the warm.

Not that it was freezing but going round the shops with a pram could be a bit of a pain, especially as everyone was rushing about. The tree had gone up about a week before and Nicholas loved the Christmas lights, so that kept him entertained for a while, especially when they were flickering on and off. Mel had already sorted out Mum and nan. She had got them both new jumpers and slippers, different colours of course so they didn't get mixed up.

For Tina she had got some of her perfume she liked, she wore it all the time but was going through it so quickly now. Mel was just finishing up. She wasn't sure what to get George, she thought of aftershave. Mum and Nan had brought him a jumper, slippers and some socks. Underwear was a personal thing, they left that up to Tina to get sort of stuff for him.

So Mel did pick up aftershave and she also got him a dressing gown. Not that the flat was cold at all, but it's nice to snuggle up in the winter. This time last year, Mel was heavily pregnant, looking forward to this Christmas more because she knew Nicholas would be here. She had quite a few bags and thought, right I need a coffee if I need to get any more stuff.

She ducked into her little café that her and Mum used to frequent so much. It wasn't very busy, they had just had the lunch rush. Mel found herself a table, put her bags down and then headed over to the counter. "Erm can I have a coffee please. Yes, and a ham salad sandwich. Yes, I will be sitting near the back over there," Mel pointed to where she was sitting.

"Ok, I'll pay when I'm done, thank you," she told the lady at the counter. She hadn't met this young lady before, maybe she was new. Mel settled herself down and waited patiently for her beverages. "Thank you, Jackie. Jackie, who is the new girl?" Mel asked.

"Oh that's Susie, she's new. I think she's Donna's sister, just filling in for the holidays!" Jackie replied, leaving Mel's food and drink. Mel was ready for this.

Christmas shopping can really make you hungry. She had a sip of her coffee. 'Ah that's better', she thought. She ate her sandwich. Jackie came over and took her plate. "Apple Pie, Mel?" she asked.

"Oh yes, please. I shouldn't really but what the heck?" Mel told her.

"Yes it's nearly Christmas and if you can't have a treat at Christmas. When can you eh?" Jackie replied. Mel chuckled. This was a real treat, apart from doing her shopping without Nicholas which felt weird enough, but to have something nice to eat and taking a time out for herself from the hustle and bustle of the shops.

Mel checked through her bags. She had picked up a couple of bits for Nicholas as well, but also something nice to wear for Christmas day. A navy checked shirt and navy dungarees, with white socks. He still didn't like to wear shoes, even pram ones, so she gave up with that idea.

Jackie brought over her apple pie. "I forgot to ask if you wanted custard, Mel, but you normally do anyway and it's a bit chilly today, was that?" Jackie asked. Mel had already put her spoonful into her mouth. She put her thumbs up while she was chewing and savouring the taste of the apple pie and custard running down her throat. Well not running but going down a treat.

Mel finished her coffee and went up to pay. "Mel, this is Susie. Susie, this is Mel, our local florist," Jackie introduced. Both ladies said hello to each other.

"Oh you're Mel. You're the lady that split up with her husband and shouted at him in the bank?" Susie told her. Mel was quite taken aback at this remark and wasn't sure how to answer it.

"Susie, you don't say things like that, apologise to Mel, now!" Donna said, who heard Susie out the back. Donna came out to the front.

"I'm sorry, Mel. I didn't realise," said Susie, blushing red.

"Oh don't worry about it, Susie. It felt good actually to shout at him in the bank, because he worked there and he was really embarrassed. So don't worry, to be honest I had forgotten all about it. You have cheered me up no end," Mel replied, trying to not make Susie feel awful. Mel smiled at her and Susie smiled back.

Jackie and Donna were trying their best not to burst out laughing. Mel left the counter, grabbed her coat, said goodbye to the girls and would hopefully see them before Christmas. Mel chuckled again to herself. So much has happened in over a year, no wonder she had forgot that little escapade in the bank.

Funnily enough, she hadn't thought about Terry or Clare in a long time either, but not to worry. Mel made her way home, she had done enough for the day.

Mel put her key in the door. She could hear Nicholas laughing. Tina and George were there and they were making shadows on the ceiling with the Christmas lights flickering on and off, and he thought it was hilarious. Mum and nan came out of the kitchen. "Mum, how has Nicholas been?" Mel asked, but she didn't really need a reply, he was having a great time.

"George tried to blow raspberries on his tummy when he had his nappy changed but he screamed the house down. Nicholas was looking at the ceiling, so George started to make shadows with his fingers, and he was mesmerised then he started laughing," Tina told her.

"Mel, I am sorry. I didn't think he would react that way, but I changed it as quick as I saw he was intrigued with the lights on the ceiling. Sorry again," George said.

"George, it doesn't matter, you changed it straight away, so he wasn't distressed. Mum, I'm going to put this lot upstairs, back in a minute," said Mel. Mel hid the presents in her spare wardrobe and went back downstairs.

"Cuppa, Mel?" Nan asked.

"Oh yes please, its freezing out there now!" Mel added.

"Mel, we wanted to see if you wanted to come over to the club on Christmas eve, they are having a disco this time," asked Tina.

"Thanks, Tina, but no, not Christmas Eve. Maybe another time," Mel said.

"Ok, it was just a thought. I know you enjoyed yourself last time," Tina added.

"Yes, but it's also Nicholas' first Christmas. I would rather be here, but thanks for asking. You never know, I may surprise you next time and say yes," Mel replied. Nan brought in the tea. Tina and George were heading off soon.

"Are you both here for Christmas day then?" Mum asked. Tina looked at George and then back at her mum.

"Mum, it will be me Christmas day and then we are going to George's mums on boxing day, is that?" Tina asked rather nervously.

"Yes that's fine, George, you know you can come anytime. If you want to pop in over the holidays, you know you're more than welcome," said Jean.

"I know, Jean, thank you," replied George. "Teen, we should make a move you know. Jim is calling later about the tickets for Christmas eve!" George told her.

"Tickets?" Mel asked.

"Yea tickets, Mel. They try and keep the riff raff out if they can, I know it's only a little club, but all the un-savouries try and get in as its cheap booze see," George told them. George and Tina kissed and said their goodbyes. They closed the door behind them. Tina had said goodnight to Nicholas and he was blowing bubbles at her.

"He's still teething, Mel," Jean said.

"Yes I know, but have you felt his gums, Mum, they are starting to come through." Mel said, quite chuffed, at least there was some reward for all of his screaming lately. Nan brought out dinner not long after Tina and George left. Liver and onions, with mash and baked beans, Mel's favourite.

"Mel, are you sure you don't want to go out with Tina and George on Christmas eve?" Jean asked. "You know me and nan would look after him," Jean added.

"I know you would, Mum, and you, Nan, but I want to be here with Nicholas. As I said it's his first Christmas. Christmas is for the kids and new year is for the adults, maybe if there is something on for new year. I will do that and you both can look after Nicholas for me," Mel told them both.

Mel hadn't even thought about going out on New Year's Eve, but now it was a possibility and they were both eager to look after Nicholas. It's funny, Mel thought, how having a baby in the house can make you feel all young again. She took Nicholas up for his bath once dinner was over, then she put him down. She put the baby monitor on, then ran herself a bath. "I'm going in the bath, Mum," Mel shouted down the stairs.

"Where's Nicholas then?" Jean asked.

"He's already in bed and snoring his little head off," Mel shouted back down the stairs again. It was easier putting her head down towards her mum, rather than shout from the hallway and wake up Nicholas. Mel enjoyed a bubble bath in the evenings. She heard her bedroom door open and her mum checking in on Nicholas, close the door again and walk back down the stairs.

Mel had already washed her hair and body and was just relaxing. She thought she would stay for a few minutes then get out and sort herself out. When she had done that, she went to bed, having a relaxing bath can make you really sleepy.

***

Mel only had a couple of days left to Christmas. She took Nicholas with her to the shop. She wanted to see how business was going and also there was a lovely Christmas tree in the middle of the town centre. She wanted Nicholas to see. She had left him at home with Mum and nan lately, partly because it was rather bitter now.

All of their activities they did together, were now closed down for Christmas. Her mother and baby group had had a little Christmas party, where all the children loved Father Christmas had been there. Nicholas wasn't really interested in anything except his big red suit, because it was vibrant I suppose. He screamed when he was handed over to him to have his photo taken.

Nicholas got a Christmas book, that Mel helped him open. He just watched the other kids opening their presents. He looked at the paper and looked away again. They wouldn't be going back to the group until the 5 January, so Mel wouldn't have to rush around with it, but would be doing Christmas shopping instead.

Mel had bumped into a couple of the mums out from the group when she was doing her shopping, they had their kids with them. Mel was thankful that Nicholas was at home. She could whip in and out of the shops without much fuss. Anyway, she had just managed to open the florists door, Lesley came rushing over and pulled it open fully for her. "Cheers, Les. How are things here. Have you been busy?" Mel asked.

"Well, yes it's been really busy to be honest. How are things with you? Hello, Nicholas," called Lesley.

"Oh well, that's good. Are you managing all right though?" Mel enquired.

"Yes, we are just about, Mel, can I have a quick word?" Lesley asked.

"Yes OK, out the back?" Mel asked and Lesley nodded. "What is it, Les?" asked Mel.

"Well, I wanted to ask you two things really, Mel. One, are you coming back to work, and two, if not can we take on another member of staff?" Lesley asked, relieved she got the words out. She had been fretting about asking Mel both questions really and she hadn't wanted to sound like she's the boss.

"Les, I was thinking about that just the other day. Now you know I have always wanted to have a family, but I had also hoped that I would have a husband as well. Well, you know how that evaporated, so at the moment, I don't think I can come back just yet. I will one day, but I am not able to do that."

"I know I have Mum and nan who are both capable of looking after him, but I didn't have him for someone else look after him full time. So the answer to your next question is yes, you hire someone else. Were you looking for full or part time?" Mel asked.

Lesley was a little taken back by what Mel had said but was also pleased that Mel wasn't going to leave them in the lurch. "Les, I wasn't going to let you continue how you were, because I know how busy it gets and you're already doing two people's jobs. So yes, either put a sign on in the window asking people to 'Apply Within' or unless you want to go to the job centre. Whatever you decide is fine with me."

"Thanks, Mel. It's just it's been getting really busy and I am not getting out in the evening until at least 7pm."

"What?" Mel interrupted her. "How come, Les?"

"Well, it's just been so busy with orders, but also getting to the suppliers. I am so tired when I get home," Lesley told her, ending with a big sigh.

"Now why didn't you tell me before now, Lesley," Mel used a little harsh tone, not because she was angry with her friend and employee, but because she could see that Lesley looked like she was about to drop.

"Well, I wanted to, but you just seem to have so much going on with Nicholas, the books. I didn't want to worry you," replied Lesley.

"You silly mare, of course you should have told me before now. Is one member of staff going to be enough, even though its Christmas in a couple of days. I could get Tina in for a couple of days to give you a head start."

"She won't mind, and you can start sorting out for staff straightaway. Unless, would you like me to do that, as you have already said you have enough on your plate?" Mel suggested.

"Mel, that would be great and I wanted to know when did you want to close and re-open for the Christmas period?" Lesley asked. They hadn't got round to sorting that out yet.

"Well, we always close on Christmas eve, then normally open the day after boxing day, but that also depends on if it's a bank holiday. So as Christmas is on a Sunday, do you want to return on Thursday, that gives you an extra day off and I think you have earned it. You all have and don't worry, you will get paid for it."

"I do appreciate what you do for me, Les, and I am sorry I haven't been on the ball much lately. I didn't realise how much time would take up looking after a little one would take, and the time goes so quickly," Mel told her. Mel asked Lesley if that was everything.

Lesley said that was it, but she would drop the books round on Christmas eve. "No, you won't, missus. It's Christmas eve, give them to Tina before you leave. She can drop them over, she won't mind. I want you to close at 4pm. If it's on the door early enough the customers will see it."

"I don't want you running ragged, so is that settled then? Also I will pop in on Christmas Eve. Actually, I can get the books then, save me asking Tina. So I will see you later. Get some rest and get starting on the apply within notice on the window, that way they may be able to start straight away," Mel said.

She went back into the shop, Lesley looked like she had just lost ten years on her face. She was worn out but didn't want to let Mel down. She had known her since Mel took on the shop, but this was great. A new member or staff and Steve, her husband, would see more of Lesley.

When Mel came out, Nicholas who was now sitting in his pram rather than laying down was grabbing hold of the flowers Julie and Fiona were both serving. He didn't like some of them. He had touched a petal, that looked lovely very dull to look at, but he touched it and it felt like velvet, he soon whipped his hand away. Mel pulled out a wipe and cleaned his hand and fingers. He didn't like that either, but it had to be done.

Mel didn't want him to get pollen on his fingers, that would stain him, and she didn't know if it would do him any damage if he put his fingers in his mouth. After Mel had tidied him up, she said her goodbyes and left the shop.

She moved along and pressed the buzzer to the flat upstairs, where a cheerful "Hello," was said.

Tina buzzed the door and Mel pushed it open, made her way into the entrance and closed the door behind her. She took Nicholas out of his pram and headed upstairs to see Tina. "So would you be alright to work a couple of days up to Christmas Eve."

"I know the money will come in handy, but you will also get me, well Lesley, out of a tight spot, while she is recruiting for a full or part timer. I personally think a full timer would be better to tell you the truth," said Mel in a frenzied speech to Tina.

"Mel, will be fine. I have done all of my Christmas shopping. George will be working right up until Christmas Eve, so it saves me sitting here watching TV and eating food I shouldn't, like these lovely chocolates I bought the other day for Christmas. They are so yummy and as you say the extra money will come in handy."

"So yes tell Lesley I will see her tomorrow. Actually, when you go, I will pop my head around the door and tell her," said Tina handing Mel her cup of tea. "How's Nicholas doing. He seems a bit of a handful at the moment," asked Tina.

"Oh he's fine. Oh no, he's at your plants now. He was touching the petals of the flowers downstairs," Mel said as she went over to pick him up. It was funny, Mel hadn't seen him get over to the plant that quickly.

"Well, he just crawled over there, Mel" said Tina.

"But he hasn't crawled at all at home, Teen, so this is a first. Mum and nan are going to be sad that they missed it," commented Mel.

"How's the teething going?" Tina asked.

"Well, he seems to have got a tooth come through," Mel said as she was running her fingers over his gums. "Ouch," said Mel rather quickly. She withdrew her finger almost straight away.

"Wow, how many teeth does he have now then?" Tina asked.

"Well, I thought he had only two coming through, but it looks like there are six now!"

"SIX?" Tina replied. "When on earth did they come through?" Tina looked rather puzzled.

"I have no idea, but he has two up top at the front, two on the bottom front and one either side of his mouth, but further up. It's although, they have come through before the ones next to the two front ones at the top!" Mel told her.

"Mel, it seems he's doing things that you're not aware of. I thought he was just a little behind or slow," looking away from Mel as she said it, but Mel was thinking same thing. She hadn't seen him even attempt to crawl. He had already learnt how to pull himself up and roll over onto his back and was sitting nearly fully up in the pram, but not sitting up at home at all.

Or maybe he was, but maybe she was missing it. She thought that she may have a word with the health visitor about Nicholas' progress. Mel finished her drink, put her mug into the sink and then picked up her son. Tina went to kiss him and he turned his head, which also was a shock. He loved Tina, Mel couldn't understand it.

She took him downstairs to put him back in his pram, said goodbye to Tina and then left. True to her word, Tina popped down to see Lesley, who had a wave of relief wash over her face. Then she went back upstairs. Mel took Nicholas into town, so he could see the big Christmas tree with the pretty lights on it.

It sparkled so much, Nicholas's face was a picture. Mel always left her camera in her bag when she went out. She took a few of Nicholas looking at the tree, his eyes like saucers and the biggest smile she had ever seen him have. She didn't take it straight in front of him, but to the side, so he wasn't aware of the photo snapping and was just mesmerised by the flickering and sparkles of the lights.

When they finished there, she took him home. She realised that she hadn't changed him, she should have done it at Tina's, but she didn't think. She was more distracted with him crawling. She thought she had better get him home. She didn't want him to sit in a soiled nappy.

Chapter 8

"Merry Christmas," Jean called out as she opened the door to Mel and Nicholas' bedroom.

"Merry Christmas, Mum," replied Mel. Nicholas wasn't quite awake yet. Jean brought over a cup of tea and popped it onto her bedside cabinet. Jean leaned over and kissed her daughter on the cheek. "You getting up soon, Mel?" Jean asked.

"Yes, Mum. I'm just going to see how long it takes for Nicholas to wake up," Mel replied. As Mel had said that, Nicholas opened up his eyes and looked straight at his mother. Those big chocolate brown eyes, that were full of life and sparkle. "You ready to get up yet then, sleepy head?" Mel asked him.

He smiled in response. "Here, Mum, can you take my tea downstairs, while I bring Nicholas down. I don't want to burn him with the cup and I don't want to slip down the stairs. We don't want to be in A and E on Christmas day," Mel said, Jean then took the cup.

Mel got out of bed and then picked Nicholas up to her. "Boy, you're getting heavy now, son!" Mel exclaimed. They went downstairs. Nicholas smiled as he saw nan, Mel's nan, Marge. She put her arms out to take him, which he responded.

"Merry Christmas, my big lad!" Nan said to him, then she kissed him on the cheek.

"Is Tina here yet, Mum?" Mel asked.

"Not yet, Mel. I think George is dropping her off before he goes off to his mums. Anyway drink your tea, Mel, it will get cold," Jean said to her. Mel did as she was told.

"Mmmmm, that hits the spot, first drink of the day, Mum!" Mel said. Nan handed Nicholas back to her and they sat down. Mel thought that Nicholas was looking at the presents under the tree, but he was distracted by the lights, he loved to watch them twinkle.

Ten minutes later, there was a key in the door. "Bye, love. See you later on," said Tina, then she shut the front door and opened the sitting room one. She soon closed it, she didn't want the heat to escape from the open door. "Merry Christmas, everyone," called Tina. She in turn gave them all a kiss on the cheek. "Merry Christmas, little man!" Tina said to Nicholas, who smiled at Tina, but didn't take his eyes off the tree, well the lights.

"Mel, what are we going to do, when we have to take down the tree. He's not going to like it, he's quite attached to the lights you know?" Tina remarked.

"I know, Teen, I have no idea. Let's see how we get on when the time comes!" Mel replied.

"Tea, Teen?" Nan asked.

"Oh yes please, I didn't finish mine before I left home, so it got poured down the sink," Tina said aloud. Nan disappeared into the kitchen and then came back with four piping hot cups of tea.

"We aren't in any rush for the presents yet, are we?" Jean asked.

"Not yet, Mum. It's just nice to sit down after all the running around lately. Oh, Mel, I forgot to bring the books with me. I know you were going to collect them yesterday, then Lesley was going to drop them round, but we were so busy. I said I would bring them round this morning," said Tina a little upset.

"Tina, it's OK, don't worry. I can get them later on or even tomorrow, not to worry," Mel teased her. They drank down their drinks, nan returned their cups to the kitchen sink and then returned.

"Now let's make a start on these presents, shall we?" Jean said.

Nan stayed sitting on the sofa. "I can't get down there girls anymore, sorry," she told them.

"Don't worry, Nan, we can pass them up to you, and anything that looks exciting or a bit racy, we can keep, can't we?" Tina joked.

"You cheeky madam, whose going to send me racy things. Unless it's a bike that I would not be able to get my leg over..." Nan said. They all burst out laughing. Tina passed all of the relevant presents to nan and everyone else really, they had fun opening everything.

Nicholas on the other hand, wasn't too happy about the whole thing. "Mum, I'm going to sort out Nicholas' breakfast. He's normally eaten by now, maybe that's why he's a little grumpy," Mel said. She picked him up and took him to the kitchen.

She had a jar of food ready for him. Baby rice and a bottle of milk, not full as the baby rice would fill him up a bit as well. She warmed up his food and bottle, and went to put him in his chair, not a highchair. He wasn't able to sit up properly on his own yet, even though he was 8 months old. Mel made a note to tell the health visitor on her next visit the following month.

Nicholas did like his food though, he ate it with such gusto. Once he had eaten his food and drank his bottle, Mel changed him and then returned to the present opening. He still wasn't interested. "Well, Mel, he is only still a baby really, so he won't find it interesting," Mum told her.

"I know, Mum, but he's not even interested in the paper. How many babies his age love playing with the paper?" Mel asked her.

"I don't know, Mel, maybe he's just a little behind. He will catch up, they all do by the time they go to nursery you know and if not, definitely by school," said Mum.

"School? Mum, that's ages away, years in fact," retorted Mel.

"Well, yes, but no Mel, it soon comes round. Talk to the health visitor the next time you see her. When is that by the way?" Mum asked.

"Next month, I think I have a couple of things I need to ask her actually," Mel replied. They carried on with the rest of the presents, then tidied up. Nicholas got some new toys as well as clothes for Christmas. Well, what do you get a baby for its first year to 18 months, they grow out of everything, including their toys.

Mind you, thought Mel, Nicholas does seem to enjoy his baby toys. Hopefully he would get used to his new toys in no time. Just another thought though.

They had had a great day. A lovely turkey dinner with all of the trimmings. "Mel, Tina, anymore, love?" Mum asked.

"No, thanks, it was lovely though. I'm full. I mean really full, couldn't eat another bite," Mel said and Tina jumped in too.

Jean looked a little upset. "Mum, honestly dinner was lovely, but I didn't think we were feeding the whole town, how much food did you actually cook?" Tina laughed.

"Well, we can have it later, sandwiches and there's tomorrow, Boxing day lunch, bubble and squeak, with pickles, mmmmm," replied Tina, then she remembered. "Mum, will you save me some. I'm going to George's family tomorrow, I had forgotten," asked Tina.

"Of course, love. I know you both love my cooking. As you said, I think I bought a bit too much, but thankfully it will get eaten and hopefully next Christmas, Nicholas will be on our food too, so he can have some too," thought Mum, smiling to herself.

"Mel, this time last year, we were still waiting for him. Doesn't it come round rather quickly," said Nan. Mel thought to herself the same thing. They had a lovely evening, with a couple of sandwiches each. Then Mum brought in the Christmas pudding, mince pies, custard, cream and brandy butter. She put them on the table and told everyone to help themselves.

Which they did. Jean brought out the teapot and some clean cups and saucers. Tina got up and made the tea, and they all settled down to watch a bit of TV. In the evenings it was great, but the daytime, Mum didn't want the TV on, except for the Queen's speech. Otherwise they played a couple of games; nan would snooze in the chair, before they knew where they were, it was bedtime.

Tina was going back home. George was going to pick her up about 9, which he was there a little later on. He popped in to say Happy Christmas and then they headed off home. Mel had already put Nicholas to bed and he was sound asleep. He slept through the night now, so Mel had a little time to herself.

The next morning, was a bit more chilled. There wasn't any rush to get up and open presents, but Mum did make a fry up for everyone if they wanted it. Mel enjoyed the day just as she had done Christmas day. Nicholas still enjoyed looking at the twinkly lights. Mel knew that she wouldn't be seeing the health visitor until after the New Year. As soon as they were open, she was going to make an appointment. There was a few things she wanted to ask her.

"Oh, Mel, I forgot to ask you, Tina said that she may hit the sales and wanted to know if you wanted to go with her. I suggested that I look after little man here if you want to go," said Mum.

"Oh, Mum, there's nothing I actually want from the sales. I got everything I wanted and Nicholas got more than enough for Christmas, so I won't bother. But I think I may take him out to the park to feed the ducks. Would you like to come with us?" Mel asked her.

"Oh that would be lovely. The park down the bottom?" Mum asked. "I thought nan might want to come as well, it's not far and not too much walking for her what do you think?" Mum asked.

"Yes, that would be great," Mel replied. "Mum, Mum, we might go down to the park later on to feed the ducks. Would you like to come? It's not far and it would be good to get a bit of exercise after all of that rich food the last couple of days?" Jean asked her mum.

"Yes that sounds like fun, Jean. When are we going?" Nan asked.

"Mel, when are we going to the park?" Jean asked.

"Tomorrow when Tina goes to the sales. I can get Nicholas some fresh air, that ok with you both then?" She enquired.

"Yes," they both said. "So we can still relax a bit for the rest of the day then, good," replied Nan. Mel chuckled to herself. Her mum and nan make her laugh so much.

***

New year's eve had popped round so quickly. Mel had agreed to go with Tina and George. Mum and Nan had begged her to go really. They would look after Nicholas, which they both loved doing, especially as he was the only boy in the family, Well, not including George; him and Tina weren't married.

Well Marge had girls and Jean had girls, they wanted to make the most of their time with him. Elsie, Marge's other daughter, had died a few years before and she hadn't had any children. She hadn't married, but had lived over the other side of town. She had a boyfriend, but they weren't too keen on him.

He was a bit of a loser always chasing ways of making money get-rich-quick ideas without having a job. Once Elsie died, he had disappeared. Marge and Jean were pleased to be rid of him. Thing is Elsie had a good little job, but she paid for everything and Fred, her no-good boyfriend, used to sponge off her.

Marge couldn't understand it. She thought she taught her girls better, but both of her daughters came un-stuck, but Jean made a better job of hers, went back to her mum and continued to bring her girls up with her mum's support.

So Mel got herself glammed up and ready. Nicholas' food was already done for him. He had his bath and was already snuggled down in his Babygro. Mum and nan waved her off once Tina and George picked her up and off they went. It was only to the club, but Mel had enjoyed herself last time.

Tina and George went on Christmas Eve and had a blast. Mel had wanted to stay home with her boy for his first Christmas. Anyway, when they got there, George parked the car. The girls got out and made their way to the club entrance. Jim, Angela and Elaine, Angela's sister, were already there.

Jim made his way to the bar. "Hi, Mel, Tina, George, mate, how are you?" Jim asked him. They said their hellos and grabbed their drinks. Angela moved up so Tina could sit down. Mel pulled up a chair to sit next to Elaine. "Hi, Elaine, how are you? Good Christmas?" Mel asked.

Elaine had taken a sip of her drink, gulped then said, "Yes good, quiet. You, Mel?"

"Yes same, quiet. How's Todd doing?" Mel enquired.

"Yes, he's fine. Mum has him now. Well, actually, Mel, he's been a bit strange!" Elaine replied.

"Strange? Oh because of Christmas and the activity going on with it I suppose," suggested Mel.

"No, I thought that too, Mel. I thought he would enjoy it, you know the bright colours of the decorations, but he has had no interest, not even the Christmas lights. I suppose they are boring though they just are on, little coloured flowers. But no interest whatsoever. I can't understand it."

"My friend's little boy has wide eyes where the Christmas tree lights, especially where they are in town. That huge tree, nothing. How is Nicholas with Christmas?" Elaine asked.

"Well the only thing he does like is the tree lights, he's not bothered with anything else. Tina and George were blowing raspberries on his belly but he screamed the place down, but he likes the lights. I'm taking him to see the health visitor once the holidays are over," Mel remarked.

"Actually that's not a bad idea, think I will make an appointment too. I am a bit worried about it," said Elaine.

"Elaine, there isn't anything you can do about it tonight. Todd is in the best place with your mum, so why don't you stop worrying and try and enjoy yourself. We can both sort it out in the new year, but keep each other updated with progress," suggested Mel.

"Yes of course, Mel, and I would be interested how you get on with yours. Anyway, for the night, let's leave the babytalk at home with our folks, we are here to enjoy ourselves," Elaine suggested. Jim brought them over more drinks. They had a DJ on this evening rather than a band, to get everyone in the party mood.

The girls were up dancing, having a real good time. Mel couldn't remember the last time she had a good boogie. Thankfully, she didn't have to get up too early and if she did want a lie in, she had Mum and nan to take over. Mel knew she was really lucky, because some mums out there didn't have any help whatsoever.

***

Everyone was back at work now. The holidays were already over and it was business as usual. The florist was doing really well, with having two part timers, Lesley a manager now and advertising for a full timer. Mel knew that Lesley had her work cut out for her, but she was always up to the challenge.

She had a call from Sam. Her and Mike had now set a date for the wedding. They wanted August, but Sam's mum said that it might be too hot, but they had already discussed that. Mike had suggested a destination wedding, well his mum, but she wanted Mike to pass it off as his idea. Sam said "NO WAY." She wanted a wedding at home, in the local church and then maybe the hall behind it or there was a couple more she had in mind.

Mel had managed to get an appointment with the health visitor for the following week. She wasn't excited about it, but wanted to voice her concerns, even though the health visitor may think she is a neurotic mother, that wasn't the case. Mum and nan had enjoyed the Christmas break, but were well aware that the holidays were over.

The bin men hadn't been for at least a week before Christmas. They had their Christmas box but not overly keen on returning to work. Nan had a word with them on their return the following week. Lots of sickness, hence them not showing up…"More than likely too much of the Christmas spirit," she laughed.

Mel popped her head around the door to the florist. She had already had the books and was quite pleased that they were doing well. Mel had given the staff a good bonus each. She valued their work and they were all loyal. Lesley had taken on Andrea as Full Time.

Mel had met her, she seemed to know what she was doing. She also knew that Lesley knew her stuff. In the meantime, Mel was trying to write down everything she wanted to ask the health visitor about Nicholas. She knew there wasn't much that he wasn't doing but she was concerned.

Tuesday afternoon was soon here and Mel made sure she had everything she needed—nappies, bottle, teething rattle, wipes, oh and Nicholas's red book, with all of his medical information. She checked just one last time, put her baby bag onto the handle of the pram and then headed out the door. "Mel? Mel? Would you like me to come with you?" Jean called.

"No, Mum, I shall be fine. I shouldn't be long. Will you be in when I get back?" Mel asked her.

"Oh yes, me and nan are staying in today. There's a good film on later on, so see you when you get back," Jean replied.

Mel continued up the path. Once she closed the gate, she turned left away from town and her shop. It was a little while away, but it was January. Nicholas was wrapped up and she liked the fresh air. It definitely felt like winter, but not bitter cold. Mel opened the door. It was a bit stiff, but she got there. Someone from inside had held it open for her.

She said thank you and went to reception. "Hello, I'm here to see Eliza Frame, the Health Visitor, my appointment is at 2pm," Mel told the receptionist, Jill.

"Hello, Mel. Yes, I have found it. There is a lady in there now. You're next. How's Nicholas doing?" Jill asked.

"Yes, he's doing alright as far as I know really. I'll just sit down then!" Mel told her. She manoeuvred her pram to the empty row of seats. Nicholas was wide awake and was smiling up at her, oblivious to where he was and what was going to happen.

The other lady came out of the room, with her daughter in her arms. She had blonde curly hair, like a little cherub, and a beautiful smile on her face while looking at Mel. "Nicholas Shaw," called out the health visitor. Mel had then brought her pram into the medical room.

"Hello, Mel, how are we today?" Eliza asked.

"All good I think. I did have a couple of things I wanted to ask you if that's ok?" Mel quizzed. Mel took Nicholas out of his pram. He gave Eliza a big smile.

"Oooh look at those beautiful brown eyes and those eyelashes, Nicholas. You're going to break some hearts, little man," Eliza cooed. Mel sat Nicholas on her lap. "Would you like me to weigh him first and take it from there. Is that OK, Mel?" Eliza asked.

Mel nodded. She started to undress Nicholas down to his nappy. "Mel could you take off his nappy too please, it's just if it's full at all, that will change his weight," suggested Eliza.

"Sorry, Eliza, I forgot," Mel said, a little embarrassed.

"You must have stuff on your mind. Don't worry this won't take long!" She told her. Mel took Nicholas over to the weighing scales. He was so much bigger than when she went last time. "He's put on a whole pound, Mel," said Eliza with a big smile on her face.

"Is that good?" Mel asked.

"It's very good. It means he's enjoying his food and he's putting on weight as he should be. How is his appetite?" she asked.

"Nicholas does enjoy his food. He does have a bottle in the morning, but not full. He had baby rice or porridge, baby porridge that is. Occasionally, he has a rusk with milk. Then for lunch, a bottle but also a jar of food. I have tried him with our stuff, but he just turns his nose up at it. Maybe it's a little too early," said Mel.

"Mel put on a clean nappy, once you have wiped him down and get him dressed again, it's not that warm in here," Eliza suggested. Mel did as she was told. She's not normally this absent minded, but she had a lot she wanted to say. "So he now weighs 19lbs, which is very good for a boy his age. Now is he up to date with his jabs?" Eliza said this as she was looking down at his book.

"Yes I think he's up to date at the moment, not due anything for a few more months," said Eliza. She put in Nicholas's new data and handed back the red book. "So what's troubling you, Mel?" she asked. Mel took a deep breath and then she started to say what had got her worried.

"Eliza, he still can't sit up on his own. He doesn't hold his bottle. He's not even trying to crawl, he does roll over though. He still likes to play with his baby toys and hasn't touched what he got for Christmas. My sister and her boyfriend tried to blow raspberries on his belly at Christmas, he screamed the place down."

"He did like the Christmas lights and that did distract him. He didn't like the Christmas paper. He doesn't like his feet tickled…"

"Mel, please stop, at least draw breath," Eliza interrupted her. Mel sighed, not because she was told to stop, but because she felt like she had just done a marathon trying to get all of the information out. "First of all, Nicholas is a healthy baby, so he's a little late in doing somethings, he will catch up. Some babies are a little slower, it doesn't mean anything," said Eliza.

"That's what my nan said," replied Mel, now she had taken a couple of deep breaths.

"The tickling of the feet, well that's understandable, not all babies like that, and I don't blame them, not everyone likes tickles. The raspberries on his tummy, that could just be a bit of a shock. The rest of it, there's nothing really to worry about. As I said, he will catch up by the time he goes to nursery, but definitely by the time he goes to school," she told her.

"Nan said that too" Mel said.

"I tell you what, if you can, keep a diary. Oh not of everything, you will be tired after you write in every entry, but just some of the things, like the raspberry blowing, doesn't like Christmas paper etc. Things that you notice, other children or rather babies doing or not doing. Just to put your mind at rest, and when you come next time; when are you due again, let's say a month, just keep your eye out."

"You live with your mum and nan, ask them the same. Not to make a big deal out of it, but keep an eye on what he does, how he reacts. It's still too early to tell yet, Mel. He has lots of time to catchup," said Eliza. "Now is there anything else?" she asked and Mel shook her head.

"Well, make an appointment with Jill and I will see you both then. Otherwise Nicholas is doing extremely well and his weight gain is great. See you soon, Mel. Bye, Nicholas," said Eliza and she dismissed them both. Mel put on Nicholas's things in the waiting room. Was Mel overreacting about Nicholas? Maybe she was. Eliza didn't say that, she put her mind at rest a bit.

At least she could tell Mum and nan about it and a diary was a good idea. Not every day, but the different things he would or wouldn't do. They could all watch out, three pairs of eyes and ears are better than one and nan wouldn't miss a trick.

Mel braved the cold once she left the surgery. She was thankful that Nicholas had lots of blankets, well he was wrapped up. Mel walked rather quickly. She knew that Nicholas was due a mid-afternoon nap. He hadn't had it on time, as the appointment was smack bang in the middle of it.

So once she got home, she was going to put him down for a nap. He had his lunch before they went, then when he woke up, he would be due his dinner, then a bath, then bed. He wasn't having a late night bottle like he used to. His last one would be about nine, then that was it for the day until the following morning. Bottles and bums, that's all it seemed to be for the first year or so.

Mel got her key in the door. Nicholas had fallen asleep already with the motion of the pram. Thankfully it was just wet, no snow as of yet. She pushed the pram through the front door and parked him in the hall. She took off the top cover and one of the blankets. He had a thick jacket on, one he got for Christmas, but she didn't want him to overheat.

"Oooh, Mel, is that you?" Mum asked. Mel had her finger to her lips to let her mum know that Nicholas was asleep. "Want a cuppa?" she asked.

"Yes, please," Mel replied. She left the sitting room door open in case he stirred awake.

"How did you get on with the health visitor?" Mum asked her. Nan had popped her head around the kitchen door, she was just bringing in the tea.

"Same as nan really, that he still had lots of time to catch up, but because of some of the strange things he was doing, to keep a diary!" Mel said.

"A diary? What for?" Marge asked.

"Well, some of the things, are normal. Is that right to say normal, but the blowing of raspberries and that, she said it may have been a shock and maybe he didn't realise it was supposed to be fun. He's a baby, how is he supposed to know it's fun. Anyway, stuff out of the ordinary just to keep adding."

"I suppose it will be good to look back on and then we can add to it. Actually, I think she wanted to shut me up, you know neurotic new mother, hasn't really got a clue. I don't know, Mum," said Mel.

"Er, Mel, did you talk that fast to the health visitor. I mean did you come up for breath?" Nan asked.

"What? Oh yeah I did, Nan," Mel replied.

"I don't think she wanted to get rid of you, Mel, it's just Nicholas is a little bubba still. It's too early to say just yet, so be patient hmmm," suggested Nan. Mel gave her nan a big smile. She knew her nan meant well and she would have known best. They would have had to have dealt with all sorts of stuff when her nan was a mum. Her husband was at war, she had two girls to look after.

Mel sipped her tea and looked over at the pram where her young son slept, making deep breathing sounds, fast asleep in the land of nod.

Chapter 9

"Hello, yes oh hello, Elaine. Yes, he's fine. Erm yes, that's great, Elaine. What time? Yes, see you then, bye," said Mel.

"Who was that, Mel?" Jean asked.

"That was Elaine, Mum. You know Tina's friend, Angela, her sister? Well, she wants to meet up this afternoon. Nicholas doesn't have anything on today, no appointments for a change. So we are going to meet up in the cafe in town, you know the one we go to every once in a while. Well, I'm meeting her at 1pm, so that will be a nice change," Mel said as she went upstairs to get her and Nicholas' laundry out of the laundry bin.

When she did that, she got him up. As she had just told her mum, they didn't have much on, so she didn't always want to get him up too early. It had just gone 10 in the morning and he was still snuggled up in his cot, next to Mel's bed. She looked over at him fast asleep still.

She grabbed the washing and went back downstairs. She turned on the baby monitor, so she could hear him if he woke up. The one in her room was always turned on, but not the one in the living room. She put a load on and then went back upstairs. She wanted to have a shower and feel refreshed before she went out. She still had time to get Nicholas sorted and be out on time.

She grabbed her wash things; towels were already in the bathroom. She shut the door but not locked it, just in case she had to run out for Nicholas at all. Mel put her pyjamas and other items into the laundry bin she had just emptied. She would empty it again before she went downstairs.

She turned on the hot water, climbed into the shower and got out her shower gel, shampoo and conditioner and then continued to shower her hair and body. The hot water was lovely, therapeutic but also relaxing. When she finished, she wrapped her hair up in a turban in the towel. She went back into her bedroom, where Nicholas was wide awake.

He gave her a beaming smile and she returned it. She dried herself off, grabbed her dressing gown and then picked him up out of his cot. He cuddled into her, but when her hair started to fall out of the towel, he shuddered. He didn't like her wet hair on his skin.

She put him back down onto her bed and then put her hair up again tighter this time, so it wouldn't fall; at least until she could get it towel dried before she put any heat on it with the hairdryer. "Come on then, little man, let's get you downstairs so you can have some breakfast and a changed nappy. At least you will be a bit fresher. Then I can get you washed and changed, because we are going out with Elaine and her little boy, Todd, for a little while. We haven't met Todd yet, so that will be fun won't it?" Mel asked her little boy.

Not that he could answer her yet, he just made little grunting noises. She took Nicholas downstairs. "Morning, Nicholas," said nan.

Jean turned her head around, she was busy with something or other. "Morning, my big lad. How are you this morning? Here, Mel, let me take him," suggested Jean.

"Mum, he needs changing first," Mel told her.

"Well, I will sort out his breakfast, Jean, if you change him and you, Mel, get back upstairs and get that hair combed and dried before you catch your death. It's still winter you know," Nan told her a little sternly.

Mel smiled to herself. "Yes, Nan," Mel saluted, and legged it out of the room before she was told she would get a hundred lines.

She returned a little while later, with clean dry hair and completely dressed, except for her boots, who she was looking for. "In the hallway, Mel, where you left them," said Jean not looking up from what she was doing, who was feeding Nicholas.

"Thanks, Mum," Mel replied. "I was just going to give Nicholas a wash this morning rather than bath him, because as nan has said, it's still winter. I don't want to give him a cold or rather flu," Mel had said rather loudly without shouting.

"That's good thinking, Mel," replied nan. Mel had also brought down Nicholas's clothes. He had nappies and wipes both upstairs and downstairs.

Nan came in with a washing up bowl full of warm water. He could just about fit inside it, but Mel wanted to just wash him. Bath time was better at night, it would relax him into getting to sleep. Nicholas liked to splash with the water every chance he got. His cute little fingers used to love the feeling of the water through them.

"Right, you ready, mister?" Mel asked Nicholas.

"Have you got everything? He had a late breakfast, Mel, so he won't need much for lunch," stated Jean.

"Are you kidding, Mum, he would eat all day if I let him. I have a jar of food, a bottle and some little snacks that he can eat," said Mel. "You didn't put raisins in his bag, did you, Mel?" Jean asked.

"No, of course not, Mum, he's too little for raisins. I think he has to be about three to have them, because they are a choking hazard," Mel replied.

Mel had Nicholas settled in his pram, in a sitting position. Both nan and Jean came over and kissed him on either the cheek or the forehead. He squealed with delight. Mel had already put the cover on the pram and made sure he had enough blankets on him.

He didn't like mittens, but he wouldn't keep his hands on under the cover, but as he was facing her in the pram, she could stop and put them under the covers. "Have fun with your friend, Mel. Bye, Nicholas darling, see you later," Jean replied. Nan waved and Nicholas lifted his hand but put it back down again. Mel re-adjusted his covers, with his hands beneath them and as she thought, it was bitter cold outside.

Mel closed the door behind her and made her way towards town. She was glad that she had them both wrapped up and thankful there wasn't any snow. It didn't take long to get to the café. She opened the door, saw Jackie behind the counter and waved over to her.

Elaine was already seated and sorting out Todd. He was a sweet looking little boy; blonde haired and blue eyed, just like Elaine. "Hi, Mel, over here?" Elaine called to her. Mel navigated her way with her pram. Jackie had made space for their prams, so they weren't in anyone else's way.

"Hello, Elaine. Hello, Todd, well aren't you the cutest little boy," said Mel while Elaine was cooing away at Nicholas. They both had handsome boys and were proud of the fact. Mel took off her coat and hat, then picked up Nicholas and removed his outerwear. Mel smoothed down his tousled hair, his big chocolate brown eyes and brown hair, he was stunning.

"Mel, he's going to break some hearts when he is bigger. Well with those eyelashes most definitely," Elaine remarked. "Tea or coffee, Mel?" Elaine asked.

"Tea please and one of those iced bun things over there," Mel said.

"Thank you, Jackie," said Elaine, once she put the whole order in.

"So, how are things with you then, Elaine?" Mel asked.

"Err not too bad," replied Elaine.

"Elaine, you sounded a little worse this morning for…Err not too bad…" said Mel. "What's wrong, Elaine, come on you can tell me!" Mel said, not taking Elaine's explanation as good. Elaine took a swig of her coffee and then a big gulp.

"Ok, well, you know we were speaking on New Year's Eve before we started to get a little, well worse for wear. We were talking about the boys," Elaine told her.

"Yes, go on," prompted Mel.

"I made an appointment for Todd to see the health visitor."

"Oh yes and what did she say?" Mel interrupted.

"Well, they don't really start tests out on a baby Todd's age, Mel."

"Why not?" Mel interrupted her again.

"Well, Mel, he's really too young at this stage," Elaine replied.

Mel was scratching her head. "I don't understand, Elaine," replied Mel.

"You see, I hadn't really noticed too much about Todd, but things weren't starting to add up. So as I said at New Year, I wanted to see what was wrong with him," Elaine continued before Mel could interrupt her again. "I can put socks on him, just but not shoes, not even pram shoes. He curls his toes over, so I can't put his feet in them."

"Also, Mel, he should be sitting up on his own, he's one next month, but he just lays on the floor, like he has limp limbs. So he's like he's floppy. Also he has started having muscle spasms," Elaine said. When she had a moment to sigh and Mel had a space which to speak.

"So, what does the health visitor think it is at the moment then? If Todd can't have tests until he's older, how on earth are you supposed to know what to do, with him, for him and everything else?" Mel asked. Elaine put her head down. Mel had just noticed that Todd wasn't sitting up as straight as she first thought and his head was flopped to the right side.

Elaine started to weep, to cry. It sounded like this was the first time she had said this to someone who wasn't a professional or a family member. Mel put Nicholas back in his pram, strapped him in, so he didn't try and get out. Not that he did anyway, but she needed to be there for Elaine, she didn't know what Nicholas would do.

She sat next to her and held her. Elaine sobbed into Mel's shoulder. Once she had stopped, Todd looked no different, he didn't seem bothered about his mother's distress, so Mel knew what Elaine had been talking about. "Oh, Elaine, is there anything I can do?" Mel asked, she had tears in her eyes.

Jackie was watching them and then came over. "Everything alright, girls?" she asked them.

"No, not really, Jackie, but thanks for asking," Elaine smiled at her. "Don't worry it will be fine," added Elaine. Elaine wiped her tears and face.

"Jackie, can we have another coffee and tea and two sticky buns. Actually, Elaine, cheese or ham salad sandwich?" Mel asked.

"Er cheese please," added Elaine.

"Make that a cheese and ham salad sandwich and two sticky buns as well. Don't worry, Elaine, my treat," Mel told her. Elaine nodded.

"Thank you, Mel, and not just for the food and drink, for being there and listening to an old fuddy duddy like me," Elaine said.

"So, without upsetting you anymore, Elaine, did the health visitor have any idea what could be the problem with Todd?" Mel asked nervously.

"Well, she did say, or rather indicate, that it could be Cerebral Palsy, but until they can test him properly and not for at least another year. She said she can refer him to the GP and see what he says, but it could take a while. GPs don't actually specialise in anything particular, it may have to be when he can be referred, before we get anything concrete," Elaine finally finished.

"Elaine, what do your family say about it?" Mel asked.

"Well, the same as me really. Just thought that Todd was a little behind, but this, Mel, is going to shock them to the core, like it has me," added Elaine.

"Elaine, at least you have some support. Your family will be a great help to you," Mel said kindly.

"But, Mel, it's not their problem or their issues," said Elaine.

"Elaine, they are your family. They will understand and help with everything that they can and fully support you and Todd. I know I have only met Angela and Jim, but they look and sound like lovely people. You said also that your mum is very supportive and if they are anything like my family, they will be with you all the way."

"So don't worry, it will all turn out fine. You have me and Nicholas as well now. I can read up what info you need, if you want? Don't think you're on your own, because you're not," said Mel.

Elaine smiled at Mel, mouthed the words, thank you and then kissed Todd on the top of his head. Mel hugged Elaine and then went back to her seat and picked up Nicholas who looked blankly at both of them. She put her hands out to get him out of the pram again and he put his hands up a bit...

'Phew', she thought, 'at least he doesn't have limp like arms and legs'. Then she felt awful for thinking that after what Elaine had just told her. She picked him up, put his on her lap, grabbed his bottle and asked Jackie for a jug of hot water, to put the cold bottle of water in, so it would warm up enough but not too hot for Nicholas to drink it.

Elaine looked rather relieved once her tears had dried up and she was dealing with Todd. He seemed happy enough in himself, but Mel knew that Elaine had a tough time ahead of her. "Mel, I forgot to ask, did you make your appointment for Nicholas with the health visitor?" Elaine asked.

Mel thought she had told her that she had, but with what she had going on, she had probably forgot. "Yes, I went few days ago and yes, the health visitor suggested that I am a neurotic new mother. I should keep a diary of Nicholas's things he does out of the ordinary and see how he goes. Once I see her again, in I can't remember when to be honest, then take it back to her for her perusal. Fun and games, eh?" Mel said.

Elaine burst out laughing, "Trust us to get stupid health visitors," said Elaine.

"Oh, I don't think they are stupid, Elaine, but they do go by the book, all the time!" Mel laughed. The girls ate their food, the boys had their bottles. Nicholas didn't want his food, so Mel put it back into his bag. Mel paid and the women made their way out of the café and before they headed in different directions, Mel stopped.

"Elaine if you need me, anytime day or night, if you need to talk, please call me. I can't say I know how you're feeling, I don't, but I will always be here for you, ok?" Mel said to Elaine. Elaine hugged her and said thank you again to her and they parted ways for the time being.

Mel was pushing Nicholas on her way home. He was just staring up at the inside of his pram. She wondered how on earth she would cope if Nicholas had that sort of diagnosis. She was walking on distracted and found herself outside her shop.

She thought she would pop in, she did that once in a while. Mel never arranged to go in at a certain time, unless it was for something important. "Coooee," called Mel. The shop was empty of customers, but Lesley was out back with Fiona getting the orders ready.

"Well hello, Mel and Nicholas," said Lesley as she put her head into Nicholas' pram. He smiled at her and then continued looking at the inside of his pram.

"Cuppa, Mel?" Fiona asked.

"Oh erm, yes please. Tea please," added Mel.

"You OK, Mel?" Lesley asked.

"What, oh yes, sorry. I am a bit distracted," replied Mel.

"Well, I can see that," said Lesley.

"Sorry, Les. Yes, I have just heard something a little distressing, but it will be fine. How's business, is it picking up yet?" Mel asked.

"Well, it's Valentine's Day soon, so that will help," added Lesley. Lesley ran through the books with her and the orders. They were indeed getting busier, which was great stuff.

"How is it working out with Andrea?" Mel asked.

"Yes, good, she's slotted in well to our team. She's just out with a delivery at the moment" said Lesley, as she could see Mel looking round for her.

Mel stayed little while longer. Nicholas had nodded off to sleep. "Lesley, I will be off now, he's asleep. I can get in before he wakes up and it's getting colder out there," Mel said. Lesley held the door open for her and she manoeuvred Nicholas's pram out of the shop, said goodbye to everyone and continued home.

She automatically walked down the road towards home, but something on the other side of the road caught her eye. A couple, they looked familiar, but the day that Mel had, she couldn't think where from. He looked a little older, a little bit grey. She had longer hair and a huge bump in front of her.

He smiled over a weak smile, she looked a little stressed. Mel walked past them and looked down into her son's pram who was snoring slightly. What a weird sort of day she had had today—full of surprises, not all good, but shocking to say the least.

Mel turned into her path, opened the gate and went up the garden path. Put her key in the door, took Nicholas's pram inside and put her fingers to her lips to her mum and nan. "Good time out, love?" Jean asked.

"Er yeah, I think so," she said, reminding herself how lucky she was having the family and support that she needed and hoped that Elaine had that too.

***

Two weeks later, Elaine called Mel and wanted to know if she could pop round to her at home. Mel told her that was OK, they weren't going out that day and Mum and nan would be there but Elaine had said that was OK. Also Mel wanted to let her know she was quite distracted once she got in that day and had told both of them about her predicament. Elaine said that was quite all right, as she knew Mel would have to tell someone, as it was a shock to both of them really.

"Right, I will be about an hour, Mel," said Elaine.

"No problem, see you then," Mel replied. Mel had gone into the living room and told both Mum and nan to expect two visitors, a big one and a little one. They all had a little chuckle...

The doorbell went and Mel got up to answer it. She had already made space for Elaine's pram. "Hi, Elaine, come in out of the cold. How's Todd?" Mel enquired.

"He's fine, Mel, asleep at the moment though," replied Elaine. Elaine came in with the pram, Mel showed her there was space for it. She took off Todd's top cover and one of his blankets so he wouldn't get too hot. Elaine took her handbag off the pram and followed Mel into the living room.

"Mum, Nan, this is Elaine," said Mel introducing them to each other. "Elaine, Mum Jean and Nan Marge," said Mel. They all said their hellos.

"Tea Elaine? Mel? Jean?" Nan asked.

"Oh yes please," they all said together.

"Elaine, you, OK?" Mel asked, as Elaine was settling herself down on the sofa.

"Oh yes, Mel, rather good actually, better than last time saw you really," replied Elaine, with a big smile on her face.

"Elaine, I'm really sorry about your latest news. I hope you don't mind Mel told us," said Jean.

"Jean, it's ok really. I thought Mel must have been upset by it, but also how I balled all over her shoulders. Anyway it's OK, I do have good news and good news!" Elaine said. Marge came back into the living room from the kitchen. She went over to Elaine and gave her a big hug.

"You know, Elaine, if you ever need us, any of us we will be there for you and little Todd. It broke our hearts when Mel told us," said Marge. Jean came back with the tea and they all sat down.

"So let me tell you this good news and good news. Well I made an appointment with the GP the day after I saw you, Mel, for the day after. I told him my concerns that I told the Health Visitor, Helen. He asked me what made me come to the conclusions that Todd could have Cerebral Palsy, so I told him about what Helen had said and he hit the roof."

"He did apologise, he said it wasn't professional to lose his temper about another colleague. But it wasn't her place to say that especially without having tests done first. He also knows that they can't really do any tests on Todd yet, as he is too young. She should have put her concerns in a letter to him, because it could have and did, frighten the life out of me, as you saw."

"So, he is contacting the medical board of directors and she is to be suspended pending an inquiry to her use of sensitive and confidential information and diagnosis. He said she isn't qualified to give out this sort of information to parents without some direction from a doctor or consultant. So that's one piece of good news."

"The other is yes, Todd may have Cerebral Palsy, but even though he's showing symptoms, it is rather early to make a diagnosis. So, he is going to send me and Todd for some extra help. Just to keep an eye on him, but he has also asked me to keep a diary, like they did you Mel. I think the more information they have the better."

"So Todd may not be out of the woods yet. He may still have this condition, but I don't feel like it's just all on me and I have felt so guilty lately about it. Did I do something while I was pregnant for this to happen, but the GP assures me, it's just one of those things sadly. But now, I know there is help out there."

"I feel much better and my family have been brilliant, just as you guys have been. Thank you, it means the world to me!" Elaine finally stopped and had a breather and a sip of her hot tea.

"Oh, Elaine," Mel jumped up as she said it. "That's wonderful news, because either way, you get the help and support you need from the professionals and what sort of help with Todd get?" She added.

"Well, the doctor did say about some physio to start and some light work, to see how his brain works. I know, it sounds weird, but they have these fine light things on long clear leads of some sort. I think to see if it stimulates his brain. I am just so glad really that I got so upset, because it gave me the confidence and courage to contact the doctor. How many other patients has that health visitor said what she shouldn't have done," exclaimed Elaine.

"Actually, Elaine, I think she has done you a massive favour. You may not have had the doctor jump on it so quickly and that's a positive, and a way to move forward," said Jean. Marge nodded her head in agreement. They all drank their tea.

Nicholas was awake from his nap and it seemed also that Todd had woken up too. Mel went upstairs to get Nicholas, who gave his mum a big smile. Elaine had taken Todd out of his pram and was back in the living room by the time Mel went back in. Elaine was taking off Todd's outerwear.

He had one of those all-in-ones in navy blue. His blonde hair was all tousled from the heat from his hood. "Oh, love him," said Jean, once he had been sorted out. Nan and Jean sat down on the chair opposite him and Elaine. They were smiling at him, but he wasn't too bothered about returning it. He was looking all around him though, taking in everything.

"Elaine I'm going to feed Nicholas. Would you like a jar of something for Todd?" Mel asked.

"Oh no, Mel, thank you. I have something in his bag for him," replied Elaine. She got up, went back over to her pram, and picked up his bag. She sat back down and was rummaging through it for his food. She pulled out a Tupperware with some pieces of fruit, that was cut up into small chunks but not small enough for him to choke on. She opened it up and handed him one.

He took it, put it in his mouth and started to eat. He had his hand out for another one. Mel thought, that baby hasn't got much strength in his arms, but he can put something in his mouth, that's amazing. Elaine looked like she could read Mel's mind. "I know, Mel, weird isn't it. He can't hold anything, but where there is food about, he can manage it," said Elaine.

Todd didn't even need help putting the food to his lips or open his mouth, it was like automatic. Mel was giving Nicholas his food. Once Todd had finished his fruit, his body seemed to stiffen and then go limp again, all floppy. Mel had hoped that the doctors and professionals could help him and Elaine, because this all looked rather nuts, but Elaine just took it in her stride.

"Elaine, you're coping so well with him, Todd," remarked Marge.

"Well, you have to don't you. Nobody is going to do it for you. I don't mean that to sound rude, but if I don't do it, who will? Just because it's a bit difficult, doesn't mean I shouldn't give up on him. He's my baby and I love him with all my heart."

"So if it's a bit different, it's a challenge I am up for, even though it's a difficult one. As long as I have him and you guys, my family and support for him, to my best ability, I can't do more than that," said Elaine with a huge smile on her face.

"You're right there, Elaine," said nan. She had a long road ahead of her, but she was willing it on for her son and she knew it was going to be difficult, but with her attitude, bring it on. Mel thought that her friend had shown so much courage considering the battle she would have on her hands, but she was so proud of her.

When Elaine left them that day, they all felt a lot lighter in themselves than they had before she had arrived. She had taught them, that it was family, that stuck together no matter what, and in Mel's book, that was more important than anything else.

Chapter 10

Eye contact? Check. Responds to his name? Check. Look when trying to get his attention? Check. Cuddling? Check. Feet tickled? No, he doesn't do that. "Mum, can you come here please?" Mel asked.

"What is it, Mel, I'm just making lunch," answered Jean.

"I was going through this list of things to make sure that Nicholas is doing what he is supposed to and so far. He's doing everything, except the feet, but that doesn't matter, does it?" Mel asked, a little nervous.

"Mel, just write it all down, and don't forget to write the date and how old Nicholas is. He is nearly one, so this stuff is just what they want to see he's doing correctly," said Jean returning to the kitchen.

'Oh well', thought Mel, 'they seem to know what they are looking for'. She had been putting stuff down in a diary, and dating it. Elaine was doing the same with Todd, but it wasn't changing for her since the last time she saw her. Ring, ring—"Mel, get that, love," asked Jean.

"Hello, oh hello, Sam. Yes, I'm fine. Nicholas, Yes, he's in his bouncer, just lying there. He doesn't like bouncing in it or anything. Yes that's fine, what time, after work, cool. See you then. Do you have any ideas then? OK, see you later bye, Sam," said Mel putting down the receiver.

"Who was that, love?" Jean asked.

"Sam, Mum, she's popping round later to discuss flowers for the wedding. Is that ok?" Mel asked.

"Yes, of course. I take it then her and Mike had set a date and obviously for here than a destination wedding if she wants you to do the flowers," suggested Jean.

"Yes I would have thought so," replied Mel. She was glad, her and Mike had some struggles with the wedding already with Mike's mum, but hopefully that was all sorted now. She went to get Nicholas his lunch. He looked bored in his bouncer.

"Mum, I think I am going to get rid of Nicholas's bouncer. He doesn't seem to like it anymore, not that I think he did anyway, what do you think?" Mel asked.

"Who doesn't like what?" Nan asked as she came in from upstairs.

"Nicholas's bouncer, Nan. I don't think he likes it. I might take it down to the Mother and Baby group next time we go, see if anyone there wants it or unless they can donate it to someone who needs it. Yes that's a good idea," Mel said to herself. Nobody ever bothered to listen to her anymore over Nicholas' things that he had outgrown.

It's not like she was planning on having any more babies and it didn't look like Tina would be starting a family anytime soon. So that's what she would do. "Oh, who was on the phone, Mel?" Nan asked her.

"Oh, Sam. She's popping round later on to order some flowers!" Mel told her.

"But why wouldn't she do that at the shop, you don't really work there at the moment?" Nan suggested.

"I don't know, maybe she would like mates' rates you know," said Mel.

"What's Mates Rates?" Nan asked.

"Well, because she's a friend, she will want them cheaper!" Mel told nan.

"Well, I never heard of that before, eh, Jean. You learn something new every day," nan chuckled to herself. Sam came round just after they had their dinner. Mel had popped round to the shop to pick up the brochures of flowers and her order books.

Jean and nan as usual had Nicholas. Nan popped on the kettle. Nicholas as always wasn't really bothered what was going on.

Nan brought back tea for everyone; she put it down on the table, so it was away from Nicholas. "Tea up," said nan. Everyone took their cup. Mel left hers on the little table from the nest of tables. Sam popped hers on the other one next to her left.

"Sam, I went over to the shop. Do you have any sort of ideas you want for the wedding, like your colour?" Mel asked. "Oh hang on, where's your mum? I thought she was coming with you or is Mike coming?" Mel asked.

"Mum's coming. Mike's not really bothered about the flowers. He said I had a good sense of style, so I could choose," Sam added.

"So where's your mum then?" Nan asked.

"Oh she will be here in about ten or fifteen minutes," added Sam.

"Better get another cup then," suggested Nan. Just after they got comfortable, the doorbell went. Jean went to the front door, it was Sam's mum, Gladys.

"Hello, Gladys. Love, how are you?" Jean asked.

"I'm ok thank you, Jean, and yourself. You alright?" Gladys enquired.

"Yes, good," replied Jean. Jean showed her to the seat next to Sam.

"Tea, Gladys?" Nan asked.

"What? Oh yes, Marge, thank you," said Gladys. "So where have you got up to then girls?" Gladys asked.

"We have just started, Mum. Mel has just got her photos and books out to have a look," said Sam.

"Well, there is quite a lot of choice for August, Sam. It is the end of August, isn't it, Sam?" Mel asked.

"Er yes, the 29. Mike's mum, June, wanted us to have it the following week, but we put our foot down. So thankfully, she doesn't always get her way!" Sam commented.

"Well, it is his mum, Sam," remarked Gladys.

"Yes, I know, Mum, but she keeps trying to get us to postpone the wedding until a year or two later. I have told Mike that if we postpone it then that's it!" Sam said.

"Isn't that a bit drastic, Sam?" Marge asked.

"I know it sounds it, but since his dad died, Marge, she won't leave Mike alone. I'm surprised she lets him go to the loo on his own. So, I told him, if this doesn't happen this year, then I won't bother marrying him," said Sam.

"She's probably lonely, Sam, that's all."

"I know, Marge. She did everything for his dad and now she's lost. She doesn't know what to do with herself. Anyway, let's get on looking at these flowers. I don't want to talk about Mike's mum at the moment!" Sam told them. They started to go over the photos. Her mum wasn't too impressed.

"Sam, what colour theme are you going for, because that would help?" Jean asked.

"Oh sorry, Mel, I was thinking of a soft pink, with maybe a few darker shades of pink inline and the girl's bouquets. What do you think?" Sam asked, looking to Mel for approval.

"I think that would be lovely. What about the mums and other guests?" Mel asked.

"Well, I thought of deep pink roses buttonholes for Mum and June," Sam said smiling over at her mum.

"That sounds lovely" said Marge.

"What about everyone else though, Sam?" Mel asked. "What about the men in the bridal party? Red carnations?" Mel asked.

"Again I thought of maybe the soft pink rose buttonholes for Mike and his best man, and the rest of the men to wear red carnations, with the fern on them and the little silver bottoms, that end in a point, you know the sort?" Sam said. Mel nodded her head.

"What about everyone else then?" Gladys asked.

"White carnations are normally the best unless you want the women to wear pink?" Mel suggested.

"No, no, Mel. Now it's going too far. You are all going to look like you're going to a barn dance rather than a wedding," said Nan, quite shocked at what she was hearing.

"OK, so what if the bridal party, with the exception of the mums. Groom, best man with pink roses in their buttonholes, red carnations for the rest of the men in the bridal party. Then everyone else with white carnations in their button holes. Then it's just to sort out the bridal and bridesmaids' bouquets?" Mel asked.

"Yes, I like the sound of that," said Gladys.

"So what about the bouquets?"

"I was thinking of Calla lilies, spray carnations, cornflowers, hydrangeas and roses?" Sam asked.

"Sam, that is all a bit busy. Are you sure that's what you want. It won't look very nice you know and far too much colour. It will look all of a mismatch," said Mel.

"What would you suggest then, Mel?" Sam asked.

"Look, I know you love all of those flowers, Sam, so what if I said to you, pale pink roses, pale pink carnations with an accent of about three deeper pink roses or carnations, whatever you prefer to break it up, with some small spray carnations in maybe a white again, just to break it up and then maybe some Gypsophilia, added here and there, just to make it that more delicate," suggested Mel.

"Mel, what's Gypsophilia?" Nan asked.

"Nan, it can be shorted to gyp or baby's breath, so it's not difficult to pronounce. Oh, Nan, it's beautiful. It's tiny little flowers, but it looks so lovely. I will bring some home from the shop. Lesley has been using it for a little while now and she said it's so soft, so subtle and makes such a difference. So, what about your bridesmaids' bouquets then?" Mel asked, glad that she got that out of the way.

"What about the same as mine, but smaller, more rounded," suggested Sam.

"Do you want your bouquet rounded or hanging to a point or something, Sam?" Mel asked.

"Oh rounded I think, just bigger than the girl's ones," Sam said.

"Oh, Sam, how many bouquets for the girls?" Mel asked.

Sam looked at her mum. "Is it four, Mum, or five, I can't remember now?" Sam prompted her mum.

"Four. You're having a flower girl, so you will need a basket with flower petals in them, Sam," Gladys told Mel.

"So, Sam how many red carnation buttonholes?" Mel asked.

Sam started counting on her fingers silently. "Six red carnations. Two rose buttonholes for the ladies and two for the groom and best man, one bridal bouquet, four bridesmaids' posies, a basket full of flower petals. Is that it?" Sam asked.

"What about everyone else? How many white carnations do you need?" Mel enquired.

"Oh I hadn't thought. Mel, can I get back to you on that one, because I need a final count from Mike for his side, is that ok?" Sam asked.

"Yes, of course, but don't leave it too long. Now I have a couple of other weddings that Lesley is doing for June. What if you pop into the shop with me, then we can see what they look like to give you more of an idea. It's fine looking in books at flowers, but seeing the real thing, then you can let me know how many then?" Mel asked.

"Yes, that's great. Thanks, Mel. I didn't think of that. Now, Mum, we should get along. Mel has to get Nicholas sorted out for his bath or something," said Sam.

"Oh yes I didn't see him there, Mel. Sorry, he's really quiet. You wouldn't know he was there, would you," Gladys said, looking over at him. "Is he ok? He looks rather still. Do you have to poke him to check?" Gladys asked.

"No, he's fine, Gladys, just a quiet baby," replied Mel.

Both Sam and her mum got up. Gladys handed the empty cups to Marge. "Thank you for the tea, Marge, and see you both soon," said Gladys.

Jean let them both out, came back into the room. "Wow. Mel, that's a lot they have to deal with. I mean Sam had some very strange ideas about flowers. I thought she said she had a sense of style," said nan, chuckling away to herself.

Mel thought the same actually. Sam had no idea about what suits and what doesn't; but never mind, Mel would keep her on the right track.

***

Mel had a couple of weeks until it was Nicholas's first birthday. She wanted to just do something little at home. She had gone to the Mother and Baby group. Some of the children she had met had already left, as they had places for nursery. She had dropped the baby bouncer and a few other things when she went the last time. "Somebody would be grateful for it," she was sure.

Mel had asked Elaine to come over with Todd, not that him and Nicholas really notice the other there really, but it would be nice for them both to come over and give her a bit of a break for a couple of hours. Tina, George, Lesley, Sam, Paula and Jodie came over. His birthday was in the week, but Mel decided to have the party at the weekend.

She knew it wouldn't make any difference to Nicholas, but it was the best time everyone would be able to make it. She had been to the shops and picked up some streamers. Tina managed to get some stringy lights that needed batteries, that she was going to put up, some balloons, garlands and a big happy 1st birthday banner.

Mel had picked up the food shopping. She knew there would be lots of adults there, so wanted to make sure there was enough food for everyone. George and Tina picked her up from town laden down with shopping bags. Nicholas as always was at home with Mum and nan getting lots of cuddles.

On the morning of the party, Mel, Jean and nan were all up early. Nicholas slept in. Mel got his clothes out ready for him, once he had had his bath, but this was still early, so Jean made the tea and nan made the breakfast. Mel got Nicholas up from his cot. He was still bleary-eyed, but had a small slight smile for his mum.

She kissed him on his cheek and grabbed his bottle that was empty and took him downstairs. She was always careful with him down the stairs, but thankfully he wasn't a wriggly baby or little tot as he was growing into. Nan came in and gave him a big wet kiss on his forehead and excitedly told him he was having a birthday party later on that day.

On his actual birthday, they made a fuss of him. Gave him a couple of presents, not that he was interested in them at all. Mum came in with the tea, nan put the breakfast down, but gave Mel a three quarters full bottle of milk and a bowl of porridge for Nicholas to eat.

Mel put him in his highchair and started to feed him. She had already handed nan the dirty but empty bottle of milk that she brought down with her. Nan liked to clean and wash Nicholas' things; whether it was his clothes, toys or his dishes or bottles. It definitely felt good to have a little one in the house again, chuckled nan to herself.

Even though it was bottles and bums, she didn't care. He was worth every bit of it, was their Nicholas. Once Nicholas was sorted out and clean for now, until he had a bath, Mel enjoyed her breakfast and cuppa. Even though Mel had gotten rid of the baby bouncer, it got replaced with a baby playpen, so he could play with his toys in there and was still safe.

Nicholas still hadn't managed to start walking just yet, but he was pulling himself up to stand. He could sit up by himself; like it was just overnight, he seemed to change all at once. Mel was pleased that he was making progress, but she was still filling in that diary. If anything to prove the health visitor wrong.

Mel put Nicholas in the bath first, then into a Babygro. They still made them to fit him. She didn't want to put him into clean clothes in case he got his outfit dirty. Mel went and had a bath, then got changed.

Nan just changed her pinny, she wasn't dirty, there wasn't a bit of dirt in that house anywhere, it wouldn't dare sit there. Once Tina and George arrived, Mel had already got changed. Nicholas was being re-dressed into his new outfit of a check shirt and navy dungarees, little navy socks. He still didn't like shoes at all even pram ones.

Tina and George put up the decorations. George blew up the balloons, one popped and Nicholas jumped out of his skin, so George went into the garden to blow them up and put them together, he didn't want to upset Nicholas. Only came back in when it was all done. Mel took Nicholas upstairs so George could put the balloons up and she shut the sitting room door on her way upstairs.

Once he was ready and the coast was clear, Mel brought him back down. The sitting room looked lovely. Nicholas was mesmerised with the twinkly little lights, he wouldn't look at anything else. Tina was admiring hers and George's work, she was chuffed what she had done.

Mel checked her watch, it was nearly 2, the others would start arriving soon. Mum and nan had been working since the day before on the food, chicken drumsticks cooked, salad, potato salad, coleslaw, cheese pineapple and little onions on those cocktail sticks, some crudites, dips, sandwiches, cheesecake, gateau and a birthday cake in blue and white icing saying 'Happy 1st Birthday Nicholas'.

Mel couldn't believe how quick this last year had gone. She kept pinching herself. Everyone turned up on time. It was nice to see everyone. Jean and Marge were the perfect hosts, making sure everyone had a drink, plenty of food to eat, topping up glasses and plates.

Nicholas, on the other hand, was just smiling to himself whilst looking at the sparkly twinkly lights. Elaine had come with Todd and he was just the same. Even though the birthday party was for Nicholas, it seemed like an adult party, because the boys weren't really interested in what was going on around them.

When everyone was sitting down, Lesley turned to talk to Mel, who was trying to get around all of her guests. "Mel, are you letting Nicholas have that MMR jab?" Lesley asked.

"What MMR jab? Nicholas has had all of his jabs. He's totally up to date with them. Elaine, will you be giving Todd that MMR jab?" Mel asked a little concerned, because she hadn't really heard much about it.

"What oh yes, I was told a few months ago that Todd would need it at 18 months old, but then I got a call from the GP to book Todd in for it at 13 months. He was going to get the health visitor to call me, then thought better of it. So yes, I gave it to Todd a couple of months ago," Elaine said.

"So what is the MMR jab?" Mel asked but directing her question to Elaine.

"They replaced the measles, mumps and rubella into one jab, rather than have three. The medical people thought it would be a good idea to combine them, as the little ones would have a lot going into their system one month after another, but not it's in one jab, they had to have a booster though just before they go to nursery. You know what children are like, pick up everything that's going," said Elaine.

"Elaine, did you have any concerns about it. I mean giving it to Todd?" Mel asked.

"No, not at all. I just want to make sure he's protected. We don't know what struggles he would have, so I wanted to get everything covered. Mel, I am glad he's had it and like Nicholas, Todd is up to date with all of his jabs too," Elaine told her.

Mel put it to the back of her head. She wasn't going to worry about that now, but she would ask the next time she took Nicholas to the clinic to be weighed and just check he is up to date with everything. Nicholas had enjoyed himself, well the best that he could. He wasn't interested in any of the presents either, but he did hold onto a piece of the wrapping paper, which Mel managed to prise off him later on in the evening, before he went to bed.

"Well, I think that was a success!" Mum exclaimed.

"Yes, it went very well and I think Nicholas liked the party," said nan.

"He liked the sparkly twinkly lights, Nan, but I'm not sure about anything else," said Mel. "Mum, what do you think about that MMR jab? Do you think I should give it to Nicholas?" Mel asked.

"Mel, why would you ask something like that. You have given him all of his vaccinations, why would you be thinking about this one?" Jean asked.

"It's combined. It's three vaccinations in one injection. What if it's too much for him? What if he doesn't like it?" Mel asked.

"Mel, how was Nicholas with his other injections. He cried like all of the other babies do, he's no different to all of the other babies having their jabs. This one is a bit bigger that's all. If you're worried, talk to the health visitor or doctor. He doesn't have to have it just yet, so you have time to think about it," said Mum, tidying up the last of the birthday celebrations.

"Todd looks well, doesn't he. He doesn't seem to be moving much, but he looks healthy," said nan.

"Yes, he does. Like me, Nan, Elaine is keeping a diary to just make sure she has covered everything."

***

Mel got Nicholas ready. She checked her bag already to make sure that she had his red book with all of his detail's vaccinations, weight etc. "Mel, are you leaving yet?" Jean asked.

"Not yet but in a few minutes though. Why? Did you want to come with me?" Mel replied.

"No, love, I just wanted to nip into town so would walk some of the way with you. Is that alright?" Jean asked.

"Of course it is. It's nice to talk to someone who can talk back," laughed Mel. Jean chuckled also. "Right all done. See you later on, Nan."

"Yes, see you in a while, Mum," added Jean, locking the front door.

"Mum, you have just locked nan in!" Mel remarked.

"Oh, dear, force of habit. When me and your nan go to town. Let me just unlock her and we can go. Are you still on time for your appointment?" Jean asked.

"Yes, we have tons of time. I just wanted to make sure we were early," suggested Mel. Jean walked ahead of Mel, so she could hold the gate open, so Mel didn't have to struggle with the pram trying manoeuvre it out of the way and onto the path. Mel turned left and Mum walked next to hers.

The doctors was only a few minutes away and Mel knew she had a lot to ask, so hoped her appointment would be long enough and she wouldn't have to make another. Mel turned into the doctor's surgery and waved bye to her mum. "Good luck, Mel. It will all be OK, don't you worry," called Jean.

Mel opened the double doors to the doctors and a kind gentleman held the door open for her. Mel said thank you to him and continued into reception and gave the lady there Nicholas's details. And she was told to sit down and wait, as they were a little early.

Nicholas was wide awake in his pram. He loved to look around; he was very observant but held little interest in what he saw. Mel had already checked her bag twice to make sure she hadn't left anything behind. "Nicholas Shaw?" The receptionist called.

Mel gathered her things and pushed Nicholas into the doctor's room. "Why hello, Mel and hello, little Nicholas, or should I say not so, little Nicholas," chuckled the doctor. "Mel, he has grown so much since I last saw you both. How are you?" The doctor enquired.

"We are both fine, Doctor Jones. I brought Nicholas's red book with me. He is up to date with his vaccinations and his weight is slowly gaining, but I don't think to a bad level!" Mel said. She handed the book over to Doctor Jones. He had a look at it and was pleased with the results in there.

"Mel, he's doing rather well, but I think you had some concerns about his development?" He asked her.

"Well, yes, I was. I had told the health visitor and she said to keep a diary, with what I thought would be out of the ordinary," Mel said. She looked in her bag and gave also gave it to the doctor. He had a quick look at it.

"Mel, by what you have put in here, it seems that Nicholas is progressing just as any other baby child his age. Yes, I know that some babies progress rather quickly with things," he said wanting to reassure her as she looked a little concerned.

"Nicholas is doing beautifully. I expect you are up to date with everything. Does he go to childcare or any baby groups or anything?" Doctor Jones asked.

"Yes we go to a Mother and Baby group once a week, but we haven't been in a little while with Christmas and then Nicholas's first birthday," Mel said, then she remembered. "Doctor Jones, may I ask you something?" She quizzed.

"Yes, Mel, what is it?" he replied.

"Well, someone at Nicholas' birthday asked me about the MMR jab? What is it and does Nicholas have to have it?" Mel said a little flustered. She had wanted to ask as soon as she got there, but now she had her chance.

"Mel, have you been worrying about the MMR?" Doctor Jones asked.

"Well, yes, I have really, because I didn't know anything about it! Does Nicholas have to have it and why is it more than one jab?" Mel asked.

Doctor Jones cleared his throat. "Well, Mel, it seems a lot to have to give a child one injection at a time, three times, but because of how the MMR is administered, it's three jabs in one that can be given once the child turns 18 months, or sorry 13 months old. They will then get a further booster before they go to school or nursery. I think it is, aged 3 years 4 months because the school age has been brought down."

"It's just to make sure that they are covered. Once they start to engage with lots of other children at once."

"I know…"

Doctor Jones put up his hand, so he could finish and he didn't want to lose his train of thought. "Mel, the medical board and the NHS didn't come up with this to mess with your heads, as it might seem to be the case. They thought they would trial it out a few years ago and was very susceptive."

"People thought it was a good idea, but as any vaccination, especially new ones, people aren't always keen, because they don't like change or because they don't know what's in it. It's nothing harmful, otherwise it wouldn't pass the checks it needs and be able to be out there to be used as a validated vaccination. I do have some pamphlets if you would like to have a read, but as you know, Nicholas is now of the age to have his first MMR jab."

"We can book you in today for the first free appointment if you want? Even though time is of the essence. If you want to look over the pamphlets first, if you have any queries or questions, we can re-schedule?" Doctor Jones asked Mel.

"No, no, I think if we make an appointment, then as you say I can come back if I have any doubts about it. You think what I have wrote with the diary is ok? Should I continue to do it?" Mel asked.

"Mel, I think it would be a good idea. I will tell you why. Partly it's great to be able to look back, because you do start to forget stuff and it's great way to compare and see how far he has come in his young life," he told her. Mel sorted Nicholas out, got together his stuff. Doctor Jones handed her back his red book, his diary and an *MMR for all: general guide* and *MMR for all: general leaflet*.

"Mel, these pamphlets with give you the signs and symptoms for measles, mumps and rubella. Also who is eligible for the vaccine. The importance of having the correct complete doses of MMR. You can get MMR vaccination at any age especially if you're not sure if you have had it. The importance of calling ahead to the GP or clinic if you suspect you have measles."

'My my', thought Mel, 'there is so much to read, but I will give it a go'. "So if I make an appointment outside then for Nicholas to have this MMR jab, and see you then, Doctor Jones, thank you," said Mel.

"Bye, Mel and bye, Nicholas. See you soon," said Doctor Jones, pulling a little face to Nicholas, who smiled back. Mel made the appointment and then left the doctors and then headed home with her homework to do. She put her key in the door and found that Mum had got back from the shops before her.

"How did it go, Mel?" Jean asked and nan looked a bit apprehensive.

"Yes, fine. I have some leaflets to read through, but it doesn't seem to be as bad as I first thought. We have an appointment for next week for Nicholas to have them MMR jab."

Chapter 11

"There, all done. Now make sure if he starts to get a fever, give him the regulated dosage of paracetamol or Calpol Mel if you have any. Or if he gets any swelling of his arm, if he can't use it or hurts him, bring him back. He may be a bit grizzly for a day or so, but he should be alright. Any questions?" Doctor Jones asked.

"No, none, I am glad I brought him here today. After I read through the pamphlets, I knew it was the right thing to do to protect him. The last thing I need is for him to get either measles, mumps or rubella, because they said in that leaflet, that getting either of them, could make them seriously ill or even die."

"So I know have done the right thing. Thank you, Doctor, for your help and support. Right, young man, shall we be off home?" Mel said. She got Nicholas's coat on him, being very careful with his arm. She said her goodbyes to the doctor and then the receptionist and headed off home.

Nicholas was sitting up in his pram. He could sit up, stand and even took a few steps this very week. Mel was delighted, even though she had continued with the diary. She now thought that she should stop, but her mum and nan encouraged her to carry on with it.

As the doctor has suggested, it would be great to look back on later on when he was much older. Mel put her key in the door. "Is that you, Mel?" Jean asked.

"Yes, who do you think it would be? Who else has a key to the front door, Mum? Mel Gibson by any chance?" Mel suggested laughing out loud.

"Well, you never know anymore. Anyway, Tina still has a key," Jean said.

"How did you get on at the doctors?" Nan asked coming in from the kitchen. "Yes, good. Nicholas was a little lamb as good as gold!" Mel told them both.

"What no crying, no tears at all?" Nan asked.

"Nope, he was as good as gold. He used to scream when he first had injections, but not now. Doctor Jones said that he may get a temperature and to make sure he has paracetamol."

Nan interrupted. "Yes, we know about vaccinations, don't we, little lad," nan added.

"Mel, have you heard anymore from Sam and her wedding at all?" Jean asked.

"Er no, Mum, I haven't. Why?" Mel asked.

"Well, don't you think you need to sort out these flowers for her?" Jean asked again.

"I have already told Lesley about Sam's flowers and what she wanted and when. Yes, her mates' rates too, so the price won't be dropping any more than I have already dropped it. Have you seen anything of Tina lately, Mum. I haven't seen her in a couple of weeks," Mel quizzed.

"No, I haven't. She called yesterday, she's been really busy with work, same as George, but that's nothing new with those two," Jean added.

"Tea anyone?" Nan asked.

"Yes please," came the reply from the sitting room. Mel got Nicholas out of his pram, took off his coat gently then put him in his chair. Nan came out with a bottle for him, which he pushed away, he didn't want it. 'Funny', thought nan, but she paid it no never mind.

She brought the tea in and Mel put Nicholas in his playpen. He didn't seem to want to do anything, but that was the usual nowadays. Mel went up for a bath and asked Mum and nan to keep an eye on him. He wasn't able to have bath for twenty-four hours.

So she had already bathed him in the morning but made sure he was completely dry and his hair too. She didn't want him to get a cold. Nan picked up Nicholas' red book and yes it was down about his MMR jab and the date. Nan made a mental note of this date, just in case things did change.

***

Talk of the devil and he or she appears. Tina popped in after work. George was going to meet her there, then they were going out for dinner. He had done lots of overtime recently and wanted to treat his girlfriend. Mel had her bath, but brought Nicholas' pyjamas down with her, so she could change him.

She was already in her night things and even though the clocks had already gone forward, it still was a bit cold, even though it was the beginning of May. So, by the time George had got there, both Mel and Nicholas were in their pyjamas, Jean had just made tea for everyone.

Tina and George left, so nan grabbed George's tea, as he liked sugar in his, and Jean grabbed for Tina's mug as she didn't like sugar like Mel. Tina and George were only out a couple of hours, when Tina opened the door and both of them walked in the sitting room with big smiles on their faces, grinning like Cheshire cats. Tina was waving her left hand all over the place, then Mel caught on and grabbed her hand.

On her third finger, there was a huge diamond sparkler that was making lights on the ceiling. Nicholas loved it and was following the sparkles. Nan and Mum came running over. "Oh my giddy aunt," said nan.

"Would you look at the size of that thing!" Mum replied. "Well, let's have a proper look at it then, missus," asked Mum. "Oh, Tina, that's a beauty. That's absolutely gorgeous. Can I try it on?" Mum asked.

"Jean, that ring will not fit you. Look at Tina's dainty fingers to your sausage fingers. Sorry, love, but it's true," said nan, not wanting to hurt her daughter's fingers. "So come on, how did he do it?" Nan asked.

"Well, we had our starters, then the main meal came…"

"What did you have?" Nan interrupted.

"We had steak and chips, Nan, and it was on one of the steak chips. Oh they were huge, big thick steak chips, Nan. Then George took it off the chip, then held it in between his fingers."

"What the chip?" Nan asked.

"No, Nan, the ring. Then held my hand and asked me to marry him, right in the middle of the restaurant…"

"Did he get down on one knee then, you know do it proper like?" Nan interrupted again.

"No, he just held my hand and then put the ring on my finger, when I replied…"

"You replied yes though?" Nan nudged.

"Of course I said yes, Nan, and now we are engaged. An engaged couple, so this now is my fiancé," replied Tina, as if they had never met George before. There were lots of hugs and cuddles and kisses. "So, Mel, you know when we set the date for the wedding, would you do the flowers for me?" Tina asked.

"What mates rates?" Mel teased.

"No sister and auntie rates, Mel," replied Tina, still admiring her ring.

"We have to go now I'm afraid. You see we haven't told my folks yet. We wanted you three to be the first to know, so see you later," said George, having a last hug from everyone and the congratulating them again. Tina and George both left.

"Well, another wedding soon then. Oh, Mel, did Tina say it was this year or next year the wedding. Did she say they had set a date yet?" Mum asked. "I couldn't quite take it all in," said Jean.

"No, Mum, she never said about a date, but she did ask if I would do the flowers as sister and auntie rates," Mel told them both. They all three of them burst out laughing.

"Trust our Tina, eh?" Nan replied.

***

Nicholas's arm was fine. There was no swelling after his jab, which Mel was pleased about. He did get a bit hot, but she gave him some paracetamol just to be on the safe side. Mel had spoken to Elaine after Nicholas had his jab, to see really how her and Todd were doing.

She asked if he had had any reaction to the jab. Even though he was a couple of months older than Nicholas, he had his jab a couple of months before and Elaine said he was ok with it. She was keeping a diary still just to make up-to-date notes if needed. As she said before, she wasn't sure if Todd had Cerebral Palsy or not, but the more information she could give the doctor the better.

Mel asked Elaine if she still took Todd to the local Mother and Baby group that they attended, on the other side of town, but Elaine had said that they found a different group, which was geared up towards more special needs as such. She knew that Todd was different to most of the children that she knew of that age, so she had sought out another parent support group rather than a new mother and baby group. "Mel, would you like to come with me this week?" Elaine asked.

"Where to Elaine?" Mel replied.

"Building Bridges!" Elaine told her.

"What's Building Bridges? Is it some kind of construction company or something? Are you looking for a job then?" Mel asked.

"No, Mel, it's a support group. Would you come along with me, for moral support?" Elaine asked her again.

"Elaine, why would you want me to come to a support group with you for moral support, because isn't that what they are there for?" Mel piped up.

"Yes, I know it is, but I have only been once. You can bring Nicholas with you. I'm bringing Todd, just as support," pleaded Elaine.

"Oh, OK then, what time do you have to be there for?" Mel asked.

"10am on Thursday. It's once a week. They have toys for the little ones to play with," suggested Elaine.

"Where is it then?" Mel quizzed.

"What if I meet you and we can go in together?" Elaine said.

"So where do you want to meet up then, before 10am I take it?" Mel asked.

"Yes about 9.30am outside that big Boots, the one on the corner. Then we can walk, it's only a little way," Elaine told her.

"OK, we will come. See you on Thursday outside Boots, bye," said Mel. Elaine said goodbye too. Even though Elaine hadn't seen much of Mel lately, partly because they both had so much on. When Elaine had been to Building Bridges before, she had noticed some babies and a couple of tots, that seemed different.

One of the little boys was just like Nicholas, but he was a little older. Elaine wanted Mel to see a different side to these places, rather than just going to a normal Mother and Baby Group. Even though they say you shouldn't compare children, but these few children she had seen, were too much like Nicholas and Todd.

Not to notice that they didn't really fit into Mother and Baby groups. Thankfully, Mel had agreed. Elaine hadn't wanted to frighten her but make her a little bit aware of Nicholas and his behaviours. Even though she was completing a diary at every change, she could see what others are like to.

***

Thursday morning quickly came round and even though Mel was nervous, she wanted to be there for her friend. Elaine had popped round a few times and they got on really well. Elaine's sister, Angela, was a wife of George's friend,

Jim. They all got on great, but Elaine and Mel found they had quite a connection and Mel had been there for Elaine when she was told by the health visitor that Todd could have Cerebral Palsy.

Mel was the first person outside of her family she went too. Mel waved over to Elaine who was indeed waiting at Boots. Both of them pushed their prams down the road together in unison, "You OK, Elaine?" Mel asked.

"Yes, fine, just looking forward to you meeting everyone," replied Elaine.

"So what do they do at this support group then?" Mel quizzed.

"They support each other, you know!" Elaine replied.

"Yes, I get that, but what sort of support group is it?" Mel asked again.

"Well, you know that Todd has erm…problems. We don't know what yet, but this is a support group for families who have children who are different. It's just a time for parents who are in similar situations as me, and not everyone has good families and their support like we do. Also, a lot of these people have already been in the system so they know their way around and what help we can expect to get." Elaine explained.

"Oh, that sounds interesting," said Mel, not sure what she was supposed to say or think really. They stood outside the building, it was a big building, but they only had the ground floor. Elaine opened the door and they moved to the right of the lobby, that's where they could put their prams.

Nicholas was awake, but a little grouchy, which wasn't like him. Mel grabbed his bag and his bottle, he was getting used to having his bottle when he felt like it rather than every few hours. So if Nicholas was getting a little grouchy like he had been lately, Mel had taken to bring an extra bottle to help pacify him.

Elaine took Todd out of his pram and grabbed his stuff also. Mel followed her to the end of the corridor and then opened the door. There were a few parents with only a couple of children. Some were at school or hadn't started nursery just yet. A nice friendly lady came over to greet Elaine and Mel and see the boys. She introduced herself as Helen and she was one of the directors of 'Building Bridges'.

She had started it with her partner a few years before, because as she said, "There wasn't much around for children and families like ours, so we started our own and it's growing now." She offered both of the ladies a cup of tea or coffee, which they both accepted. Mel went to get her purse, "Oh no, Mel, you don't have to pay for it. We do a kitty once a month for a couple of pounds.

Everyone puts in, but not until at the end of the month. So how do you know, Elaine?" Helen asked.

"Her sister, Angela, is a friend of my sisters and we met socially and hit it off," replied Mel.

Helen smiled. "And who do we have here? I know Todd of course but this little fella?" she asked.

"This is Nicholas and I am sorry, he isn't normally this grouchy. It's only started recently," Mel said.

"Well, welcome, Nicholas, and to you too, Mel. You will soon meet everyone, this is a drop in. We start at 10am and end around 12–12.30 once a week. Elaine has been coming for a couple of weeks now. She said she wanted to bring a friend along for a bit of moral support, so it's lovely to meet you both." Helen said.

Mel had taken Nicholas's coat off and put it down on one of the comfy chairs which she sat on. She put him down on the floor to play, but he didn't seem to want to, which was also nothing new. She had put a couple of new things in the diary, but she had put how grouchy Nicholas had become.

Mel's mind was wandering, she didn't hear another mum called Tanya say hello. "Oh, I am so sorry. I was miles away, sorry what was your name again?" Mel asked, feeling a bit rude after that encounter.

"My name is Tanya and this little one here is Poppy. She's just turned 2, my other little one is William, and he is 6. He goes to the local primary school down the road Hilt Top Grange. He's only been there a little over two years, but I still don't know if it's the right setting for him."

"You see he has autism and he seems to cope, but it's hard to tell at this stage, especially as he isn't really talking yet," Tanya told Mel, who was a little dumbfounded at hearing this.

"So, if you don't mind me asking, is that the setting for autism children's mainstream schools?" Mel enquired.

"Oh no," said Tanya, "but it was difficult to know where to put him, because of his non speech. Me and his dad will see how he gets on at Hilt Top Grange. If we need to change him, it will need to before the next school year starts, otherwise it might be difficult to get him settled," Tanya told Mel. "How old is your little lad, Mel?" Tanya asked.

"He's not long turned 1, so now he's 14 months old," Mel said.

"He's a little darling, Mel. Is he your only one or do you have more?" Tanya asked.

"No, Tanya, he's my one and only," replied Mel.

Elaine came back over to sit down and join them. "They have a toy library here, Mel, so you could check out some toys for Nicholas to play with," suggested Elaine.

"Play with; Elaine he doesn't play with what he's got at home, let alone anywhere else," she replied. Mel was starting to wonder if she did the right thing coming today. Even though everyone she had met was lovely, she thought she was out of her depth being there. Talking about special schools, non-verbal children, she thought that Elaine had done well before her being there, so why bring her along today.

Suddenly, a couple more people had turned up and Helen was getting them to sign in, just for security purposes, in case of a fire. There was Christine who was Mum to Jonathan, who was 2 years old and into everything, and then Rachel who was Mum to Paul who was 6 and at the local special school Longridge Creek Academy. He had been there since he was 3 years old, he also had Autism, but was non-verbal.

She came over and spoke to Mel and Elaine. She kept looking at Mel, and Mel felt uncomfortable with what she was hearing. She stood up and said to Elaine, "I'm sorry, Elaine, but I don't think this place is for me and Nicholas, sorry." She didn't give Elaine time to speak but grabbed Nicholas' and her things and made a dart for the place where the prams were.

She hurriedly put Nicholas in his pram and legged it out of there as quickly as she could. She must have nearly run home, because she was home in under ten minutes. "Mel, is that you already?" Mum asked.

"Er yes, it's me, Mum. Just me and Nicholas." She put the pram in the hallway. Nicholas had fallen asleep, so she took off his coat and let him sleeping in the pram.

"How come you're back so early. It's only just 11am. I thought you weren't going to be home before 1 at least, because you and Elaine normally go on for coffee. Mel, what is it, love?" Jean asked, looking a little puzzled at her daughter.

"You are not going to believe what sort of place Elaine took me to, Mum. It's all kids who have autism. I didn't stay there long enough to find out about any other disabilities, Mum. Why did she take me there?" Mel asked.

"Mel, I thought it was for you to support Elaine, not the other way round?" Jean asked.

"What do you mean the other way round, Mum? I was there for Elaine, but all of these other people. Hang on what did you say, that Elaine was there to support me? Why would she be supporting me, Mum? I don't have a child like that. Nicholas is not autism."

"He's just a little boy who has had some difficulties and he's growing out of that now. I admit he has become rather grouchy these last few weeks, but he's a little boy, still a baby. We all have our off days," Mel told her mum.

"Hey what's all this shouting for? You will wake up Nicholas and he's fast asleep right now. So come on what's up?" Nan asked.

"Nan, you know I was going with Elaine today to this support group, to be moral support for her. Well, it seems like she already has the support she needed, so Mum suggested that maybe Elaine wanted me to go there, so I, ME, can be supported. What am I supposed to be supported for eh? Nicholas is a good little boy."

"Yes, he was delayed with a lot of stuff, but he's picking up now and his behaviour is fine. He doesn't lash out, but he's also become grouchy, but that's nothing really. So why is Mum saying that Elaine is supporting me and not the other way round? Do YOU think there is something wrong with my son?" Mel quizzed once she stopped to draw breath.

"Now you're asking ME if I think there is something wrong with our boy? No, I don't. Nothing that can't be sorted out over time and help if that's what he needs," said nan, but Mel jumped in.

"What do you mean? NOTHING THAT CAN'T BE SORTED? So, you do think there is something wrong with him or do you mean ME; that there's something wrong with my parenting?" Mel demanded. She had never been so furious with her family. The fact that they thought there was something wrong with her son. He was getting to his milestones, his doctor was pleased with his progress.

Mel looked at both her nan and Mum and left the room, slamming the door shut; thankfully not waking up Nicholas. Jean and Marge both looked at each other and Jean shrugged her shoulders. "I don't know, Mum. What do you think? Do you think Mel's right? Has Elaine seen something that none of us have?"

"Maybe Mel's right. Maybe she does think that we think that there's something wrong with Nicholas. He's an unassuming little boy; he likes the twinkles on the lights, but he doesn't really like toys, does he, Jean?" Jean nodded in agreement. She knew her girl was hurting, but this time she had to give her time to cool down. She opened the door of the living room and checked on her grandson who was sleeping and snoring lightly, completely unaware of what had just unfolded.

Two days later, Mel had calmed down. She wasn't really talking to her mum or nan, she was still very angry over the last days events. She brought Nicholas down from his sleep that morning. She had just put him in his highchair to give him his breakfast, when the doorbell rang. Jean hurried over to open it, she gasped.

It was Elaine, she wanted to talk to Mel. Jean left her on the doorstep. She would normally have asked her in, but with what went on a couple of days before, she couldn't risk it. But she left the door open, went over to Mel to tell her who was at the door. "Fine, I will talk to her, but not in here. Please could you give Nicholas his breakfast, thank you," Mel said, just as matter-of-factly.

"Yes, Elaine, what do you want?" Mel snapped.

"Mel, I am truly very sorry about what happened on Thursday. You have every right to be mad at me. I only thought I was helping you, by bringing you to the group so you could meet everyone," Elaine said.

But without getting a chance to say another word Mel jumped in with, "Why? Elaine. Why?" Mel again demanded. She had never spoke to any of her friends or family like this, but she felt they had all crossed the line.

"Er well, I thought it would be nice to get to know some new people…"

"Not good enough, I'm afraid. So you like my mother and nan in there thought there is something wrong with my son, but didn't have the decency to tell me yourself. You drag me to this group so I could meet some new nice people, who were staring at me and then my son, telling me their stories of tales of woe, and about autism and mainstream and special schools."

"What the hell do you think I am thinking when I am around all of these nice new people. Which is why I got out of there. You were out of order not telling me first, at least your concerns about Nicholas to me before. I didn't once go against you at all when you were told that Todd could have Cerebral Palsy, I supported you the best way I could. I didn't know what I was doing, but let you speak, cry when you needed to, but just to be there for you."

"But no you take a different approach and I am supposed to be thankful for it; thank you but no I am not. So goodbye, have a good day," Mel said as she closed the door on her friend. Now she was angry again. She went back inside the sitting room.

"Well, I suppose you both heard that then, did you? Happy with yourselves for making me feel like a shit mother. That my parenting skills are not up to your standards; then I am rather sorry for both of you!" Mel snapped at both of them.

"Now wait a minute, young lady, who the hell do you think you're talking to? We are your family and we love you and we love Nicholas too. Now you have not had anything diagnosed for your boy. Your friend in her wisdom, who got it wrong, tried to help you, there's nothing wrong with that."

"But how you spoke to her just now, I am ashamed to say that you're my granddaughter. I would never have expected you to speak to her, let alone us, Mel, like this. Now you have to get yourself together. Maybe Elaine did see something in Nicholas that she saw at the group before."

"She asked you to accompany her there, but she didn't want to upset you by saying anything to you but thought you might see it with your own eyes. That way she is subtly telling you to get him checked out." Mel opened her mouth to say something but Marge put up her hand to silence her.

Marge continued, "First of you I expect an apology to your mum and me, because we don't deserve this behaviour. We love Nicholas just as much as you do and we love you just as much. You know we will help with anything you need or want, babysitting shopping, the occasional treat for you both."

"Mel, this isn't you. This isn't your normal behaviour. Do YOU actually think there is anything wrong with Nicholas and this just hit a sore spot? And that's why you're taking this attitude?" Marge had finished a rant, that she had wanted to do for a little while but had held it in. Even though she was pleased with how her girl was coping, she could see she was struggling.

Mel burst into tears. "I don't know; maybe Elaine was right. Maybe you all are and I know you all have our backs, know you're there for more than just support, but since Nicholas has had that jab, I am starting to wonder if I did the right thing?" Mel agonised. She looked at both her mum and nan, who both came over and gave her a big hug.

"Listen, Mel, you said yourself, it would be better to have that jab rather than have the measles, mumps or rubella. They can cause lots of problems, becoming sterile, going blind, you can't take that chance for him," said Jean.

"I know, Mum, but Nicholas is changing. He has become moody and grouchy. His food tastes have changed and even though it's only recently, when you call him, it's like he's ignoring you. He gives no eye contact. Maybe I should take him to the doctor again and see what he says," Mel suggested.

"Mel, to be honest, I would hold off for now. Have you been adding this stuff to your diary? Then leave it a month or so, he's still young enough for things to change and he maybe just having one of those phases and see what happens. If it continues or he gets worse, I would then take him back. Don't leave it like 6 months, but just another month or so, monitor his behaviour," suggested Jean, giving Mel a hug.

"Now I think you need to go and find Elaine. You owe her an apology too, Mel. You didn't speak very nice to her and she was only trying to help. Get ready, leave Nicholas here with us and go and talk to her, yes?" Marge asked. Mel nodded, then left the room to go and get ready.

Mel found Elaine in the coffee shop where they go quite frequently and considering it was a Saturday, it wasn't very busy. Elaine was sitting down drinking a cup of coffee with Todd still in his pram playing with the toys across his front. Mel came over. "Can I join you?" Mel asked.

"Only if you're not going to shout at me again!" Elaine said smiling.

"Jackie, can I have a cup of tea please and a coffee for Elaine, and two apple Danishes please?" Mel asked.

"Oo treats, this is good," smiled Elaine.

"Look, Elaine, I am really sorry about what I said to you earlier today and what happened on Thursday. I felt overwhelmed. You obviously saw something in Nicholas that you had seen there before, am I right?" Mel asked.

"Yes you're right, Mel. There was a lady, she hadn't actually got there on time on Thursday. She got there half an hour after you left. Her son, Arthur, is exactly like Nicholas. I wanted you to meet her, but some of the other families go to you first."

"I am really sorry. I didn't want to tell you what I thought, because exactly of the reaction you had on Thursday and then again today. What made you change your mind to come and find me?" Elaine quizzed.

"Nan and Mum," replied Mel.

"Ok, that says it all! I suppose they have been giving you a hard time too then?" Elaine asked quite intriguingly.

"No actually the opposite, it wasn't until I blew up on Thursday that they both said that they have noticed a slight change in Nicholas and if there was anything wrong, it would get sorted and we would all deal with it," said Mel.

"Well, at least you have their support, Mel. There are some families that don't have that kind of family support. Once they found out the child isn't perfect and has real issues, they abandoned them, to fend for themselves."

"Another parent at the group?" Mel asked.

"Yep. Cor Elaine."

"This sounds like a whole lot of fun, to have to be dealing with for these people," Mel replied.

"So, will you come back next week or do you want to leave it for a few weeks?" Elaine asked.

"Elaine, do you mind if I leave it a few weeks. I want to see how Nicholas progresses or not as the case seems to be. I have to keep updating that diary, both nan and Mum have said. It would be best, that way if there are significant changes. I have already made a note of it and it will be easier to check on before and after the jab."

"I know it's not definitely the jab that is the cause of this as yet, but I have to go on what has been happening since he had it. It's like he's a different child to what I had, and it happened practically overnight these changes. Anyway, enough about me. How are you and Todd getting on?" Mel enquired.

Elaine updated Mel on what's been going on at her end and this group that she found, seemed to really help her, which is why she wanted Mel to go in the first place. They had another drink but no cakes this time. Mel and Elaine said their goodbyes and went their own way, with a promise to give the group another try in a few weeks. Mel put her key in the door and was happier than when she went out anyway.

"Hi, Mum, Nan, I'm back. How has this little monkey been while I have been gone?" Mel asked.

"Mel, he has been fine, no tantrums or grumps. He's had a bath and about to have his lunch. I gave him some yoghurt earlier, you know the ones he likes with fruit in it; he spat it out and refused to eat it. Mel, you have to write this in your diary. His changes are subtle, but they are there. How was Elaine?" Mum asked.

"She's fine. She's had a lot on and has found this group very supportive towards her and Todd. Don't forget she can't get any sort of diagnosis for him yet; they have done a couple of blood tests, but not much else. She also said to say thank you to you both, for talking to me. She did ask if I would go again to the group."

"Apparently, there is another mum there whose son is just like Nicholas in his ways. She wanted me to meet her, but she wasn't there until after I had left. I told her that I would return in a few weeks, because I had to get my head around what's going on with Nicholas myself and keep an eye out for any changes. She was fine with that. So, what's Nicholas having for lunch now then?" Mel asked.

"I made shepherd's pie. I am hoping he will be with that?" Nan said with her fingers crossed. Nicholas ate up all of his lunch and was looking for more. 'Well that's better I suppose', thought Mel.

***

It was now July. It wasn't long before Sam and Mike's wedding. Mel had been to the shop to talk to Lesley and Sam about the flowers wanted for the wedding. The church had already budgeted for the flowers there, so it was for the buttonholes, posies for the bridesmaids and the bride and a couple of baskets of petals for the flower girls, they were having two. Gladys had another of the great nieces to be one; she was forceful when she wanted.

Sam had asked Mel if Nicholas could be a page boy, but Mel said he was too young, also he was acting out a lot more than he used to. But when she saw the look on Sam's face of disappointment, she suggested putting him in a suit, giving him a buttonhole and put him in the photos, if she wanted that instead, Sam agreed.

Paula and Jodie were both coming to the wedding and Mel really couldn't remember the last time she saw them both socially. They had popped over to her mums for Nicholas' 1st birthday party but hadn't really seen them since. Mel had chosen a nice lemon suit for the wedding. She put Nicholas in a cream suit.

He looked divine, with his chocolate brown eyes and hair, which was very thick. Mel had trouble getting it cut, he wouldn't sit still.

Before she knew it, the wedding was here. Mel had declined Sam's invitation to the hen do. They were going away for a few days to Amsterdam and she didn't want to leave Nicholas as he was becoming a bit more of a handful. Mel had made an appointment to see the doctor, but it kept getting cancelled.

She was going to see him on Monday, providing it didn't get cancelled again. She needed this sorted out. Nicholas had started to stop speaking but would point for what he wanted. Mel looked like she was nearly at the end of the tether. Not today though.

Mum and nan were also invited, so Mel had extra help and she brought along Nicholas' buggy; he was too big for the pram now. That was in the shed at home, waiting for Tina to use it, because Mel knew she would not be having any more children. Tina and George had set a date for 24 June the following year.

Tina was working as much as she could, and George was working all of the overtime, he could get his hands on. They didn't really want a flash do, but they did want a good honeymoon. They were paying for it mostly themselves. Nan and Mum had clubbed together and gave them a thousand pounds, and so had George's parents, so that was a huge start. Mel was going to give them the flowers as her and Nicholas's wedding gift to them.

Back to today's events though, Sam had ordered her dress from a wedding boutique that she went with her mum to Paris. It got delivered just over a week ago and thankfully it fit her perfectly, so she was very happy with that. Also her mum was pleased that nobody else had a dress from Paris.

Mike was quite tall, so he could wear top hat and tails. He had his best man, his friend Colin, from work. June was happily sitting up the front of the church behind Mike and Colin. She only had one sister and they didn't get on too well, always sniping at each other; but her sister, Enid, made sure she was there. She wanted to see how this wedding was compared to her son and his wife's, Ted and Julie.

They had an extravagant affair, horse and cart, reception in a hotel and ten bridesmaids, not like Sam and Mike's. With that the bridal march started and the doors opened, and in walked Sam with her dad, Edward. She drifted down the aisle with her dad close to her. Sam looked lovely but her dress was a little posh, for most of the guests, and Enid turned her nose up when she saw her at the altar.

Once the hymns were finished and the vicar had married them, June left to follow as did Sam's mum and dad. Once they all returned, the wedding march began again and they walked back down the aisle as Mr and Mrs Dixon. Once everyone was out of the church, there were some lovely grounds with a couple of trees, for a lovely backdrop for photos.

Sam had photos with Mike, with her friends and Mike, Mike and his buddies, family photos, one with just the bridesmaids and flower girls, Mel and Nicholas. Enid kept looking at Mel and Nicholas, with her turned up nose. Once the photos were taken, the cars took them to the reception venue.

"Well, it seems to be going rather well. Did you see Mike's mum and her sister sniping at each other. I knew them both at school you know, a lot younger than me though, Mel, but they have always been like that towards each other. Jealousy I suppose," said nan.

Once they got a cab to the venue, Nicholas was getting all fidgety. Mel had brought a spare or two pairs of clothes just in case he needed to change. She could tell he didn't like his suit anymore. So Mel took him to the toilet, to change him. Enid came in and saw Mel changing Nicholas, his nappy as well as his clothes. "Erm, are you supposed to do that in here?" Enid demanded.

"Where else do you think I would change my baby, out on the top table?" Mel retorted.

With that, Marge walked in. "You OK, Mel? Do you need a hand?" Nan asked.

"Oh is this your grandson then?" Enid asked.

"No, he's my great grandson actually, Enid," said nan.

Enid didn't realise that Marge knew her name. "Oh I just wondered, how long has he been Mongrel then?" Enid asked.

"Excuse me?" Mel said.

"For your information, Enid, he isn't Down Syndrome, as the word is now. He has issues, but not that it's any of your business. So why the hell don't you get out of here before I give you a knuckle sandwich!" Marge suggested. "Don't look down your nose at me, Missus, think I am all it. I remember you from school, you nasty little bitch," nan shouted. Mike and Sam came running in.

"Did you hear what this witch has just called me?" Enid asked.

"Yes, I have and yes, you deserve it, you ignorant witch," said Mike, with that June came running into the toilets.

"HOW DARE YOU COME HERE AND INSULT MY FAMILIES FRIENDS AND THEIR CHILDREN, YOU WICKED WITCH. I WANT YOU TO LEAVE RIGHT NOW. YOU'RE NOT WELCOME HERE WITH YOUR TURNED UP NOSE LOOKING DOWN ON EVERYONE!" June screamed, and with that she threw her hand back and slapped her sister straight across the face.

"NOW LEAVE, BEFORE I THROW YOU OUT. OH AND DON'T COME BACK EITHER!" June said. Enid left.

"Wow that felt good. Sixty years I have been wanting to do that!" June exclaimed. "Now, Mel, Marge, please do not take any notice of what that witch has said about your Nicholas. He's a darling boy, my Sam and Mike have both said so. They also said that you're having a few problems, confidentially."

"I haven't said anything it's not my place, but you have my full support. My husband would never have stood for it and neither do I. So, when you're ready, you change Nicholas, come back into the wedding. You are all welcome and I do apologise for my behaviour, but not for my words," commanded June.

"Wow," said Marge. "This is better than the soaps, Mel. Well, shall we?" They left the toilets, and returned to a standing ovation and an applause, which June had instigated. Mike and Sam were happy with that, even though the focus was off them, they were glad why.

"Come on everyone let's get this party going!" June shouted. And they did. Everyone enjoyed the food, the drink and most definitely the dancing; everyone danced until late. Nicholas had fell asleep. He had seemed to enjoy himself though Mel couldn't work out why, maybe it was the disco lights all around the room. Her, Mum, Nan and Nicholas went over to say goodbye to Sam, Mike and June, Mike's mum.

Marge also thanked her for her words. "It's long overdue, Marge, I can tell you. Anyway have a safe journey home and see you all again soon, and Mel thank you for the beautiful flowers. Sam is giving me her bridal bouquet to put on Mike's dad's grave, so thank you once again. Night," she said giving Mel a hug and then a kiss on the cheek.

A great day and night had been enjoyed by all who attended except for Enid. Marge chuckled to herself. "As June had said, Mel, it was a long time coming. Enid was always sniping at her and her family. June didn't want to take it anymore and you can see why. I am proud of that lady, I really am. Now let's get home it's getting a bit chilly and it's not good for Nicholas."

They got in and sorted themselves out. Nicholas was put to bed. Mel changed and then went downstairs. Nan came in with a hot drink for them all. "You know, I can't remember the last wedding that I enjoyed so much since your wedding, Mel, that was great fun," said nan.

Mel hadn't even thought of her wedding; it was such a long time ago. Thank goodness she had nan, Mum and now even June on her side. She could imagine if anything did happen with Nicholas, she has more than enough support including her family and friends.

***

"Mel, you can go in now," said Kay, the new receptionist, at the doctors. She was lovely, warm and calm, not like the last one who was there for all of two weeks; she was too rude to the patients.

"Hi, Mel, what can I do for you or rather Nicholas?" Doctor Jones asked. "I am sorry I have had to cancel your appointments, it wasn't anything personal. I had a death in the family and times were quite strained, but all back to normal now though. What can I do for you?" He asked again.

"Well, you did say to come back if I noticed any sort of change in Nicholas and there has been quite a significant change in him. I have kept up his diary, which am really glad that I have because it's quite noticeable the changes in him," Mel told him. As she handed the doctor the diary, which had a lot of recent entries lately. It was a lot thicker than it was the last time he saw her.

"Ok, Mel, start at the beginning, if you can," he said.

"A couple of weeks or so after Nicholas had his MMR jab, he became rather grouchy, grumpy. It was like he was a different child that what I had before. His eating habits have changed, he won't eat fruit yoghurt or anything with bits in it. He loves shepherd's pie and cottage pie."

"He used to eat sausage and scrambled egg for breakfast at the weekends sometimes, now he won't touch it, turns his nose up at it. I tried to give him Weetabix. Even got it into his mouth and he spat it straight out. He's getting rather fidgety and certain things he used to like, he no longer does."

"He doesn't have much interest in toys at all, but he likes playing with paper; well he used to, he doesn't like the texture anymore. He never ever liked his feet touched, now I can't even get socks on him anymore. Also, he was

172

saying Mum, nan, cat, dog, the usual you know, now he won't speak and points at everything. I am actually at my wits end," she finally finished.

Doctor Jones looked at her and then at Nicholas asleep in his buggy. "Hmmm," he said while he was looking at Mel. "It sounds like he has sensory issues, Mel. Material, foods. How is he with loud noises or high-pitched noises like the emergency services, ambulance etc?" He asked her this to hopefully confirm what he was thinking.

"He goes absolutely nuts, Doctor, he screams the place down, but I didn't make the connection of the sirens. Oh my goodness, am I bad mother?" Mel asked imploringly.

"No, Mel, you're not a bad mother. You just don't know what you're looking for. Whereas I do, here's what I am going to do, I want to refer Nicholas for some blood tests. Do you have his name down for nursery or anything yet? Does he still go to that mother and baby group?" He asked Mel.

"No, to all of that. My friend tried to take me to one and I sort of freaked out. She could see what was going on with him, but I poo pooed it. As you said I didn't see the signs or really know what I was looking for but the word Autism did come up," she told him.

"Ah ok that makes sense then. Listen I will put these recommendations for these tests for urgent, only because we need to get some answers and quickly. I will fax them to the blood testing centre, so we can get these done and then when the results come back, I will call you back in. Is that ok?"

"Please, Mel, don't worry. It's not going to be anything serious. We just have to know that's all, then we take the next chapter, ok?" He told her. "Mel, are you alright?" He asked.

"Sorry, yes, it's just been a lot to deal with and now take in. I look forward to hearing from you with an appointment. Is that everything, Doctor, for now?" Mel asked him.

"Yes for now. I will see you both soon. Oh and Mel take someone with you for the blood tests, you're going to need it. Nicholas is going to not want it to happen, he may scream. Also make sure you have paracetamol just to be on the safe side, because it could make him anxious," he told her.

Mel thanked him and went outside to sort herself out. Nicholas thankfully was asleep still, so she didn't have to worry about him being examined. When Mel got in, she told both her nan and mum what the doctor had said and they both had their mouths open wide.

"I will go with you, Mel; I will hold Nicholas and you can distract him," said nan. Nan never went anywhere like that, but she knew that Mel was starting to fall apart at the seams and needed her this time, rather than her mum, who was great as a nan, but stuff like this, she wouldn't be able to handle.

A week later, Mel got the appointment through for Nicholas's blood tests for the following week, which she did attend with nan, who was brilliant with Nicholas. Mel tried to distract him, but he wasn't having none of it. He was trying to wriggle, but nan held him fast, but not too strong handed with him, but firm. He cried a bit, then bawled his eyes out. "I thought they were going to put Magic cream on him, Nan?" said Mel.

"They would have done, but he's too young, needs to be 2 or 3. I can't remember what the nurse said to be honest. Anyway, that's done now, so let's take him for a treat, to make up for what he has just had to have," suggested Nan. "Oh and I will call your mum and let her know that we have gone for a treat, so she doesn't worry."

They went into the café got him a sticky bun, but he wouldn't touch it. Nan had it instead. "Nicholas, I can't keep eating your treats, my waistline isn't liking this one bit," she chuckled. He just laughed at her, something he hadn't done in a while. She gave him an iced finger, while she ordered apple Danishes and tea for them both.

Mel returned to her seat, she looked like she wanted to cry. "What's up, Mel?" Nan asked.

"It's just all of this, Nan. I never thought I would have a child that would have difficulties and issues," said Mel.

"Mel, none of us do. We think when we have these babies that everything is going to be perfect, but it's not the case, they say, 'What doesn't kill you makes you stronger'. I mean it's kind of true really. We all have our boundaries and sometimes they are pushed to the limit. We just get on with it or give up and most people just get on with it, the very few give up."

"So, don't you worry, you have a great support network, is that what they call it these days? I can't keep up with it anymore. That must be worth its weight in gold, Mel. You're doing a great job. You have just been given a different deck of cards to work with that's all, and you know we are all with you, behind you and in front of you if you like."

"Don't worry, it will all turn out right I promise you," Nan said. She hadn't been that vocal before. Then their drinks and cakes came, and they all tucked in, even Nicholas. They had their treats and then went home where Jean was frantic with worry. Marge explained to them and now all they had to do was wait.

Three weeks later, Mel got a call from the doctor to come in and see him. She could leave Nicholas with her mum if she wanted to come on her own. Which she did; she got a little early as she was so nervous. "Mel," said Kay. Mel left the reception and went along to the doctor's room.

"Come in," he called. "Oh hello, Mel. I'm glad you came on your own, so you can hopefully digest what I have to tell you," he said as he ushered her to sit down. "Well, your concerns and mine were right, Mel. I'm afraid to say that Nicholas has Autism. He has a mild form of it, that can change over time," he said, but Mel interrupted him.

"So he can get better or worse?" she asked, with her eyes boring into his for every shred of information she can get at this stage.

"It can go either way, but I'm not really an expert in this field. With what you had told me and the changes he has made in his progression and development, pointed towards Autism. I will of course refer you to specialists in this field. I will be doing that today, but I wanted to talk to you first, will that be ok?" He asked Mel rather delicately.

Mel nodded her head, whilst she had tears in her eyes, she couldn't hold back. Doctor Jones let her carry on and handed her a tissue or two. "Mel, sadly it's just the way it is, I'm afraid. Now this is going to take some time to digest and I suggest you start thinking of nursery places for Nicholas, which means you need to get the local authority involved."

"My letter will go to them directly, so you may get a call from social services. Now don't worry, Mel. They are not going to take Nicholas away from you, but they have a great support system for these reasons," Doctor Jones said.

"I have a great support network actually, but I suppose it can't hurt, can it? I mean I can't be selfish here and try and do it without support, plus that's no good to Nicholas. Me sticking my head in the sand like an ostrich, is it, so I will do what I have to for my boy. Just because he can't speak, it doesn't mean I can't be his voice," said Mel wiping her tears and sniffing into her tissues.

"Thank you, Doctor Jones, for all of your help and support throughout this. Is there any leaflets you have here at all that I can read up on?" Mel asked him.

"Not here, but the specialist will have lots of information for you and there is also the Early Bird Course, that I have heard is very informative. You can ask about it when you hear from them. Mel, don't forget I am here if you need or want my help or advice, even though this isn't my field of expertise. I can help with referrals if you want anything. You know where I am, just call OK," he told her.

Mel blew her nose, said thank you to Doctor Jones and then left and went home. She put her key in the door. Her mum and nan got up from the sofa and went to the door to see Mel. "Well, Mel, what did he say?" Jean asked.

She nodded, "It's Autism."

Chapter 12

"Autism? Are you sure, Mel?" Mum asked.

"Yes, Mum, it's definite. All the blood tests comeback and the conclusion is that Nicholas has mild autism!" Mel told them both.

"Well that's good news then, Mel. Mild Autism, that means he can get better eh?" Jean suggested.

"But it also means Mum that he can get worse too. He could change so drastically, or he could stay how he is, but as this isn't Doctor Jones field of expertise, his words, Nan, but he is referring Nicholas to a specialist who can hopefully help us. He has suggested that we get in extra help or support from the local authority, because that can probably hold more weight I suppose. Oh don't worry, Nan, it doesn't mean they are taking him away. But it also means that this was inevitable," said Mel.

"What does that mean, Mel?" Nan asked.

"Well, it doesn't always mean it's the MMR jab that's responsible for this, but it could have triggered it or kickstarted this," Mel told them.

"Mel would you come and sit down for a moment?" Nan asked.

"Mum, do you think when I was pregnant, I had a couple of drinks. Do you think that this is what it was. Nicholas was still being formed maybe that's what did it?" Mel asked, trying to make sense of it. "Where is Nicholas by the way, Mum?" Mel asked.

"He's in his cot, because he fell asleep just before you got it. Here, we have his baby monitor on," said Mum in reply. "Mel, what drink? What are you talking about?" Jean asked.

"Do you remember when I was going to court to see Terry about the divorce and he didn't turn up, well I went and had a few glasses of wine to block it out, but I didn't know then that I was pregnant. My goodness that seems like a lifetime ago now," Mel asked.

"Mel, it wouldn't have anything to do with a few glasses of wine. Now please would you both come and sit-down. I want to talk to you about something important," said nan.

"More important than this, Nan. I don't think so," Mel was nearly shouting, but nan had to get Mel to be quiet.

"MEL, PLEASE, THIS IS IMPORTANT AND DEFINIETLY RELEVANT!" Nan shouted. Now she had both of their attentions. "Please sit down and I will begin. Now I don't know if you have ever heard of me talking about my great aunt, Mary. She died long before you were born, Jean, but she had a daughter, Nancy, she was a sweet thing. She worked up in the bullet factory when the war had started. As you know, the men had to fight a war, so the women had to stay behind and become the men. As such, do their jobs and that, driving lorries, making ammunition for our boys out in the thick of it…"

"You're talking about World War One or Two, Mum?" Jean interrupted.

"Well both, but the one I am talking about is World War Two. So anyway, where was I? Oh yes, so about Nancy. She was married to a man called Walter and he had to go to war, where sadly he didn't come back because he was killed. Anyway what Nancy didn't know when he had gone was that she was pregnant and had a little girl called, Jill, she said she had always liked that name."

"Don't worry I am getting to the point. Nancy had the baby and she was doing fine, but like you she felt something wasn't right, something was off. Now Jill was a sweet little thing, we loved seeing her. She had gotten sick and had a really bad ear infection, which they couldn't really clear up and once she was better, Mel, she had changed."

"Now she hadn't had any MMR jab because it wasn't invented then, but they tried warm oil, that had worked in the past before, but it wasn't touching the sides, Mel, so they had given her penicillin, you know anti-biotics. Well that's how it cleared up and as far as I know, she never had an ear infection ever again. Now as I said she changed, she wasn't the sweet little thing we knew, she changed."

"Oh not like Nicholas getting grouchy and grumpy, but she started to get violent with Nancy, her mum, and other relatives and she had to go to into erm…an asylum, like an institution. It was all above board and everything, but it meant that she didn't mix with now, I don't like that word, normal, because who of us are normal. So I will use the term everyday folk, I know it's not the best, but I don't know another way to put it," said Nan, glad for a breather for a minute.

"So where does that bring Nicholas into all this? Oh, Nan, she was autism" Mel said.

"Yes, Mel, she's autistic and her family couldn't help her. Not that they didn't want to understand, but she was too strong for all of them. She knocked me out one day, I was unconscious for about 5 minutes. It really wasn't her fault, but there was no alternative for her."

"Thankfully nowadays, they try and keep the families together with support, so I understand when Doctor Jones said you might hear from Social Services. I knew you had nothing to worry about because it shows they want to change things from how they used to be, to a different time where these children adults can possibly live as independently as they can. Now not all of them can, but they have help put in place for those individuals."

"So please don't worry about Nicholas. I know we can get him sorted to whatever he needs and he will get, I promise you," said nan, a little relieved to get that off her chest finally.

"Nan, where is Jill now then?" Mel asked.

"She's still in some sort of care, but they shut them institutions down years ago, Mel, because it gave such bad press about them. I am still in contact with her friend who visits her. I go and see her once every so often. She sort of remembers me. She's happy enough, she's on some sort of medication."

"So, listen here, Mel, this was nothing you did or didn't do. You had one drink or five, it's just what it is, that jab may have just kickstarted this all, we don't know, we may never know. As long as Nicholas knows he's loved and that's all that matters, yes?" Nan said, a little upset now.

Mel hugged her and then Jean joined in. All of a sudden, they could hear Nicholas on the baby monitor, wide awake and wanting to get up.

***

Mel was still trying to come to terms with what she had been told a few days previous, but she was still getting on with it as usual. Marge though looked like she had a weight lifted from her shoulders. "Mum, how long had nan been sitting on this information about cousin Jill, did you know?" Mel asked.

"I had heard of Jill, but I didn't know whatsoever about what had happened to her. I think it's great that Mum still has contact. It's a shame that we haven't all met her before. I wonder if it's worth seeing if we can go and visit her. We would have done before now if we had known about her."

"Anyway, Mel, we can't dwell on it, love, it will only make it more difficult for you to deal with Nicholas and we all still have a long road ahead, especially Nicholas. After all, Mel. this is about him, isn't it?" Jean said.

A few weeks later, it all seemed to happen at once; the specialist's letter came, Social Services had called them to arrange a visit to see the family unit and also see about getting some assessments done for Nicholas, really to see what they could offer him.

In the meantime, Mel had bitten her tongue and gone back to the support group, full of apologies, which they told her were not necessary. Elaine had explained the situation, so they definitely weren't judging her, but they did say that they could also help her, to make sure she was getting the correct support and what else information about nurseries and schools she could look into. Also Nicholas would need a Statement of Educational Needs report.

Before Mel could ask any questions, Helen told her that is was for Nicholas to get extra funding for his education and that they could definitely help with forms and that, Mel was delighted. Elaine was right, these were the right people who could help her and Nicholas. When they told her that, she sat down and burst into tears, really long tears, ones that make your body start to shake.

This is all she needed, massive arms around her and Nicholas to get them all that they needed. She was feeling overwhelmed but for the right reasons this time.

Mel went to her appointment with Nicholas, where she met her consultant, Mr Roger Whitehead. He was really lovely with both of them, very calm. He also had a couple of his staff with him—a clinical psychologist, speech and language therapist, who he introduced. Mel couldn't remember all of their names, but it would be on her letter once this visit was over, so she could make a proper note of it.

They had some toys for him to play with, which he had no interest in, but he did pick up the magazines on the table and put them in a line like a train track. The staff were taking notes. Mr Whitehead explained that he knew what Doctor Jones had put in his letter. It's not normal practise for the GP to give the diagnosis of Autism, but Doctor Jones had already spoken and met with him, before he called Mel into his office.

Mel was quite relieved because she had thought that this wasn't common practise for this to happen, but in these circumstances, Mr Whitehead had agreed with Doctor Jones for this information to come from him. Mel sighed a big sigh. "Relieved?" The speech and language lady asked, who had now introduced herself as Janice. "Is Nicholas having any speech and language therapy at all, Mel?" she asked.

"No, I'm afraid he's not," Mel replied feeling a bit stupid with her response.

"Is Nicholas in nursery at all?" The clinical psychologist asked, who told Mel she was Tracy. Again the response was no.

"Well, we have to get that sorted for you. You need help and support, even if you have a great support network, you need a break. So we will talk to your local authority and see what they can offer you. Also Nicholas has stopped speaking, so if we can speak to the SEN dept at your LA, then we can suggest a special school for him."

"Don't worry, Mel, it takes ages, but we do suggest you put Nicholas in nursery. The LA will have all of the information on the best ones for him to go to, and don't worry, you have the last say. So don't just go with what they say. When you have a look at them, schools included, don't go on your own, take someone who knows Nicholas, they will be looking for the same things as you."

"Now Nicholas is looking a bit tired, so I suggest that we leave this here for today and arrange a follow up meeting, in a couple of months or so, that gives us time to sort out what we need to at this end. Unless there is anything else or would like to ask us questions?" Mr Whitehead asked.

"Er no, just thank you. Yes, thank you. You seem to know all about what's needed for Nicholas, how come I didn't?" Mel asked rather sheepishly.

"Mel, this is our job. What we have been trained for. I don't want to doubt your intelligence by saying you're just his mum. You're Nicholas' expert, you're the one who can tell us what's going on. We take it to the next level and this is how it will be."

"You get to one stage, then it can change, you both adapt until you need to change again. We are all here to help and support you and if we are no longer able to help you. Later on down the line, there are other professionals who will take our place and take you to the next stage. That's how it works and hopefully it works well, so anything else?" He asked her.

"No just thank you and see you again soon? Oh, before I forget, Doctor Jones did mention something about an Earlier birding course or something?" Mel said wanting to sound like she knew what she was talking about.

"The Early Bird course is a course that gives lots of information about Autism and different levels. Autism is a huge spectrum, that's like one shoe doesn't fit all. We can put your name forward if you want us to. There isn't any spaces at the moment as one course has just started, but there will be another one soon after Christmas. So, thank you for coming today and see you in a couple of months," Dr Whitehead said. Mel said her goodbyes, got Nicholas ready then back into his buggy and then they left and went home.

"Mel, how did you get on with the specialists?" Jean asked as soon as she heard her key in the door. Mel brought Nicholas in and she took him out of his pram, and he went into the sitting room. He was steady on his feet now, as he had been walking for months.

"There was a lot of information, Mum. I mean really a lot. They are going to put us in touch with the education dept because Nicholas should already be in nursery, but they are going to help with that. Then they are going to look at schools, because they want to put him in a special school, because he's not talking anymore and they think it will be beneficial for him. They did also suggest that I take you or nan," Mel said, but nan interrupted her.

"What about nan?" Nan asked.

"Would you come with me and Mum to look at schools for Nicholas when we have to go looking. Because they want to put him in a special school and after what you told us the other day, I think you will need to see how this all works. Will you come with us?" Mel asked rather nervously.

"Of course I will come, I want to see where our boy is going and to make sure it's up to scratch. So when do we go looking?" Nan asked rather intrigued now.

"Not yet, we have to get him in a nursery if there's a place for him," said Mel.

"Maybe not until January. These nurseries do an intake in January as well as Easter, so we have plenty of time, Mel," encouraged nan.

Mel had a letter from the council with recommendations for nurseries. Sadly there were no special nurseries, but mainstream. Nicholas could have a

1:1. He was nearly two so Mel, Mum and nan had gone to look at a couple. The first one, they didn't really like, so said they would think about it, just in case they couldn't get anything else.

They went the following day to look at another one, that looked quite promising. They had been there for a little while, saw two of the rooms, then they went into the other one where the little tots were. A room where Nicholas would be playing in, there was lots of toys and tons of books. He hadn't really shown any interest in books but maybe they would be able to encourage him.

Mel liked the look at this nursery, the staff seemed to engage with the children well. Yes, Mel was impressed with this one. She spoke to the manager of the nursery, Kim. Kim was already aware of Nicholas and his issues as such. Kim told her that there was another little boy who had autism who had been there for a few months and would she like to meet the other mother so they could have a chat, because she could ask her when she comes in next time.

Mel was grateful that everyone she was dealing with was so helpful. Mum and nan were just as impressed as Mel. Now Mel was aware of a distant cousin on the spectrum and as nan had a bit of experience with this, she wanted her approval as such, as she was more aware than the rest of them. Mel had asked Kim if there was a place for Nicholas.

She said that there was, but she wanted her to bring Nicholas first to see how he would cope in this setting, as he had only been to Mother and Baby, and didn't really have many children around him. As it was a Tuesday, Kim had suggested bringing him in for the next three days, just for a little while. He wasn't quite two yet, but she thought it would be good for him.

"But the only thing is, that you will be on the premises, but not in the room after the first half an hour. Otherwise he might not want to leave you. He may be more inclined to play with toys and stuff if you're not here. You see with all the will in the world, children tend to do more for the people looking after them rather than mums and dads, because there's no emotional connection."

"We are doing a job, but your mum and you love them, which is how it should be. Do you get what I mean?" Kim said, trying not to sound patronising at all.

Mel nodded in agreement. "I know what you mean. We can't really get him to engage with anything at all. So yes, you do what you have to," said Mel.

"Don't worry, Mel, we will look after him. We won't let anything happen to him, ok?" Kim replied.

"Ok, Kim, thank you," said Mel.

"So see you at 10am then?" Kim told her.

"10am? I thought nursery started like school at 9am?" Mel quizzed.

"No, this nursery runs from 10am until 6pm for parents who work, otherwise once Nicholas is settled, he can do until 4pm. That way, he gets used to the hours of school, but school does start for 9am as you have said. But this week, he will do a couple of hours and once he has settled down, he can come four days a week. That way everyone gets a fair chance at childcare," said Kim.

"So see you tomorrow at 10am. It was lovely to meet you, bye," Kim said as she was already leaving them, she had to go for a phone call.

"Well, I like this place, Mel. When can Nicholas start then?" Nan asked.

"Tomorrow at 10am" Mel replied.

"10? Blimey, oh well early to bed tonight. I hope he will be ok getting up?" Nan chuckled.

Mel got Nicholas up at 8am, which he wasn't quite used to, so he was a bit grumpy for a little while. Mel got Jean to give him his breakfast while she got his clothes out. "Mel, don't put him in anything too good, you don't want it ruined. You know with paint and that," suggested Jean.

"Oh heck, I didn't think of that, better put him in something else," Mel thought as she put away his cream dungarees. She grabbed something dark for him—a pair of navy cords and a navy lightweight top, long sleeves. Grabbed his shoes and everything else he needed then she ran back downstairs. Armful of clothes and his shoes.

She dumped them on the sofa and ran back upstairs to get herself washed and dressed, then ran back down again, to get him sorted out as well. Nan brought her in a cup of tea. "Hold on a minute, my girl, you need something inside of you. You're going to be out at least until lunchtime," said nan.

"Nan, I will take a piece of toast with me, to have on the run, so to speak," said Mel, that's exactly what she did. She put Nicholas in his buggy and then off they went to nursery. She put her buggy in the buggy park with the other ones already there. Picked Nicholas up and went into nursery. Kim showed Mel where Nicholas peg was for his coat and bag, nappies etc.

She asked what he had for breakfast, then told her that he would go home just before lunch today, but tomorrow he would have dinner. Also if she could bring in anything specific that he eats say a particular snack as such. Mel said she would. Kim took them both to the room they were in yesterday.

Mel put Nicholas down and he went off wandering. Mel couldn't believe her eyes. He didn't do anything at home. He went straight for the books. Mel was standing there with her mouth opened wide. She was struggling at home and this help was a stone's throw away and her son just walked away from her, she couldn't believe it.

Kim told her to just observe for now, then in a little while, she would take her to the parent's room, where she could have a coffee or tea and just have bit of time to herself until it was time to take him home. Mel was watching Nicholas just off on his own, she still couldn't believe her eyes. Then it was time to go and leave him there. He didn't bat an eyelid. She was taken there by Teresa who came back with a cup of tea for Mel and said she would pop back in a little while and just let Mel know how Nicholas was doing.

Mel was there, they had a few magazines so she had a look at them, something to while away the time. Teresa came back half an hour or so later to say that he was engaging in a story about trains. She said he was mesmerised, was smiling and his eyes were wide like saucers.

Mel burst into tears at hearing this. They tried everything at home to engage with him, it just wasn't happening. Teresa sat with her, she reiterated what Kim had said that they often don't play ball with Mum and Dad, but do for others that just look after them. She also said, they only have them a few hours, where Mum and Dad have them for twenty four hours a day. That seemed to calm Mel down a bit.

Teresa checked that Mel was OK, before leaving her. Mel knew that she had chosen the right place for Nicholas; they were so understanding and caring. Soon it was time for Mel to come and collect Nicholas. When she went into the classroom, his eyes were bright and he ran up to her and put his arms up for her to pick him up. She burst into tears again and then kissed Nicholas on the cheek, which he hated, but most boys hate being kissed on their faces.

She got his coat and things. He only needed his nappy changed once and he had snacks. Mel made a note of what they were, so he could have them at home. She thanked everyone and then they went home. Mel opened the front door and Jean and Marge darted for the door.

"Well Mel, how did it go today?" Mum asked. Mel burst into tears again. Nicholas was looking at her, not knowing what was going on again. Nan picked up Nicholas, she had got his lunch ready and put him in his highchair to feed him. Mel started to tell her mum and nan what had happened; how

Nicholas went up to look at the books, was mesmerized by the book of trains as being told to him.

She couldn't understand it. "Mel, there will always be a time where he does things at school and not at home and vice versa, that doesn't mean you're a bad mother, a bad parent. Kids have their little boxes, you, me, his nan, nursery; he will be different with different people who he comes into contact with."

"There's nothing wrong with that. I think you need to adjust the same as Nicholas does, that doesn't mean anything bad by the way, but it's life, love, it's what happens. So let me put the kettle on and make you a cuppa and a sandwich. Your nan is feeding your son, so let me wait on you for a change," said Jean.

"What do you mean for a change, since I moved back with Nicholas, you haven't let me lift a finger," retorted Mel.

"No, because you have enough with little man here. We know, Mel, we have all done it. Your nan, with no help, me with your nan's help and now you with both our help. You're not on your own and we would be very disappointed if you did do it on your own. So now, take your shoes off and enjoy being waited on," said Jean.

"That's her told love," Chipped in nan.

Nicholas enjoyed going to nursery and he settled in very well. It wasn't long before Mel was contacted by the Local Authority (LA) regarding special schools, because they had now started the process for Nicholas' Statement of Education Needs, which was a long process; with Nicholas settled into nursery, with their reports and then the educational psychologist who would be assigned to Mel, who was Debbie Longhorn. She was going to meet Mel at the nursery first. She was dealing with children from there for quite a little while.

Also, Juliet, the other mother, with an autistic child was going to meet with Mel on Wednesday that week, so they could have a chat. There was so much to do and so much going on constantly. Mel thought she had it hard enough before now and was wondering how she was going to manage it all, but as nan said, they will get there and it will be alright in the end.

Wednesday came and Juliet who was often late, due to her son, Arthur, not wanting to move in the morning, Mel had been told to wait for Juliet in the parent's room for her to arrive. Kim had already given her a cup of tea and said that she shouldn't be long. Bang on 10.30am the door opened and Juliet said hello and introduced herself.

"So, Mel, how long have you had Nicholas' diagnosis?" Juliet enquired.

"It came through about six weeks or so," replied Mel.

"How old is Nicholas then?" Juliet asked her.

"Nearly 20 months old," Mel told Juliet.

"Wow, that is really quick. They don't normally diagnose until 2 upwards, because of the milestones and targets they aim for them to reach. How come you got yours so early?" Juliet asked.

"Well, Nicholas wasn't doing anything he was supposed to at the right times or afterwards. He started crawling one day and a few days later, he starting standing and then walking. It was nuts. All he used to do before was lay on the floor. It was very difficult knowing what to do about it. Anyway my friend took me to this support group 'Building Bridges', just past the high street. Do you know it?" Mel asked.

"Yes I do, I frequent it often. They are great for support and brilliant on doing and helping with various paperwork," said Juliet. "I think I missed you that day, I was rather late," added Juliet.

"OH you must be the lady my friend, Elaine, wanted me to meet, but I sort of kicked off before you got there. You see these other parents were talking about autism, mainstream schools and special schools and they kept directing their questions and answers to me. I didn't even know Nicholas had autism, not because I was being ignorant or arrogant, I just didn't know."

"I think Elaine had spoken to you and saw your little boy and saw the same things as she had done in Nicholas. Oh I'm not saying she meant anything bad, but she wanted me to see for myself rather than tell me. As I said, she wasn't saying anything about you or your son. But Kim had suggested that I speak to you, as we are today. Anyway, how long has Arthur had his diagnosis and how long has he been here for?" Mel asked a little out of breath after that.

"Well, Arthur got diagnosed about 3 months ago. He's not long turned 3, so you understand my surprise that Nicholas got his diagnosis early, but obviously his symptoms showed early. Anyway, I'm a single mum. My parents aren't really interested in Arthur. I have siblings who have their own lives and are too busy and they don't live in town but moved around the country.

"So, without 'Building Bridges', I would have been totally lost. A friend of mine, Lorraine, who has now moved away, introduced me to Building Bridges, because she saw what your friend, Elaine, did with you. She saw in Arthur. Her son is Autistic. He's now 7 and goes to a special school. She said it was the best thing she could have done."

"He didn't speak, but now with help and support he's getting there and she's no longer pulling her hair out. So yes, it does help, now I'm not full of information as of yet, because it all takes a long time, but you do pick stuff up along the way. What you're not sure of just ask. The other mums or dads, building bridges' professionals, get as much information, Mel, as you can, but don't overload yourself with it."

"It can drive you nuts; get a folder a lever arch something, or a boxed folder might be better. When you get leaflets and stuff put it in there, then you can always read it later on when you're ready. Also you do know about the National Autistic Society? They are a mindful of information and great help finding your way about stuff."

"They can help with info for schools and such, but sometimes just like Building Bridges can just listen. Not everyone likes dealing with them, not because they don't know their stuff because they do. But because some parents are in denial about their children and sometimes the older generation, they just think that the kids are naughty, or need a slap as they would have done in the olden days," Juliet said.

Mel looked horrified at this clarification. How people can do that to their kids. "No, Mel, I'm not saying do that, but that's how some of the older generation can be. Also they think when our kids have meltdowns, they are just having a tantrum because they are spoilt. When you tell them, they look at you as if you're from outer space. You will know what to say when the time comes when you have to, because sadly it will," Juliet told her.

Mel was quite lucky, so far Nicholas hadn't had any meltdowns or temper tantrums. He just got grouchy and grumpy. "Juliet, can I ask you what you're doing about school for Arthur?" Mel asked, eager to know where she would even think about sending Nicholas.

"Well, yes, I am in the process of doing that right now. I have a meeting later on today, to see what they have come up with. Have you started your Statement of Educational Needs yet? That's fun and games and it can take ages, but you can't get Nicholas into a school without it I'm afraid," Juliet told Mel.

"Yes, I gathered that. How long can it take, Juliet?" Mel enquired.

"Well it can depend. If the information goes in without a hitch, because once you have you Ed Psych, put their piece in. Who do you have by the way?" Juliet quizzed.

"Debbie Longhorn," replied Mel.

"Oh I hear she's quite good, so that shouldn't be too bad. So once everyone puts in their bit, you have to do some as well, it's on one of the Appendix's too. I can't remember now sorry, my heads full of information. Yes, Arthur, school. I am hoping to send him to Forrester Greenwood Special School."

"It's supposed to be good. That is what I am waiting to hear today, if I can go and have a look at it, if it will be suitable for Arthur. I can then name it as his Named School, which is in the statement, Statement of Educational Needs. Everyone calls it their statement otherwise it gets nuts. So, if he gets that one, I will be pleased."

"Oh, Mel, there is a Forrest Green that's a Mainstream school, please don't get them mixed up or you will be sending Nicholas to it. If Nicholas is non-verbal, sorry is he non-verbal?" Juliet asked and Mel nodded in response. "Well, he won't get the sufficient help he will need, because mainstream schools can sometimes be beneficial but not all shoes fit the same size. So it would be a mistake to put him somewhere he won't get the right help."

"I'm not saying the mainstream schools are bad. It's just there aren't all geared up for our kids and to be honest, they want a few disabled kids with statements, it bumps up their budgets, but not all the kids get the right support. Oh, sorry I don't want to worry you, you have plenty of time still."

"Thankfully Nicholas has been spotted and diagnosed very early, which is the best thing. It means they can jump on it so quickly. Now I know I have told you a lot today and you won't really remember it all until about 3am this morning. If you're not sure, make notes, take a pad and pen to bed. If you wake up and remember something write it down, it's the best way."

"Now I am really sorry, but I have to go for this meeting. Let me have your number and I will give you mine, but don't forget I go to the support group every week. It's great to get people's updates and feedbacks where they are in their lives and the support or not, they are getting," said Juliet in a bit of a frenzy.

Mel handed her number to her and Juliet handed hers to her and they both said goodbye. Juliet had definitely given Mel food for thought. How was she going to break this all down. These parents deal with this stuff every day.

Mel got up took her cup to the kitchen and then she left the nursery. She was going to pop into the stationers on the way home for a couple of folders or so and a couple of notepads and pens. She had to take all of this stuff seriously because this is what she had to do for her boy. She headed home, found Mum and nan at the table enjoying a cuppa.

"Like one, Mel, or do you need something stronger?" Nan asked.

"No, Nan, tea will be fine," Mel replied.

"What have you got there, Mel?" Mum asked.

"Well, I met this other mum. Oh my goodness the things you have to do and go through, the paperwork, there is so much. This lady, Juliet, is a single mum, no family support. She only has this support group that Elaine took me to, which she finds really helpful. Mum, she may as well be a speaker as a commentator, she said so much. Some of it sunk it the rest forget it."

"She did suggest though that I write everything down that I need to know, keep leaflets and that store them away and read them when I can. It just goes on and on. The one thing though that she said will go in Nicholas's favour, his diagnosis came through really early. Normally it's not until 2 or 3 years old. Now I will put this lot away, once I hear from the council about this statement thing," Mel said.

"What statement thing?" Nan asked.

"Oh it's what they call the Statement of Educational Needs, or it's too much of a mouthful. Anyway, until I hear from them the few leaflets I have will go in there, but for now, we have to start getting ready for Christmas. With all of this stuff with doctors and hospitals, it's now time to put it away, until I need to deal with it again, agreed?" Mel asked, looking at both her mum and nan.

"Agreed," they said in unison.

Chapter 13

It was a few days into the new year and the children had gone back to school and nursery. Nicholas seemed to enjoy or rather engage with Christmas a bit more this year. Tina and George had come over. They had got him some children's book on trains and he actually sat in George's lap mesmerised. Mum and nan couldn't believe it when they saw it.

Mel had been known to take various photos of these monumental times happened. Thankfully, she had a digital camera and she had started to get her photos printed and started to make a scrapbook with as much information— when the photo was taken, date, year and how old Nicholas was, because it was all good progress for him and great to look back on later on.

They had rather a chilled and relaxed Christmas. They didn't go too mad really once Nicholas came along, but they all enjoyed themselves. Tina wanted to talk to Mel once Christmas was over with nan and Mum to start making preparations for the wedding in June. They had already booked their church and their venue as they were booked up a year in advance; it was just everything else.

They had decided on only a hundred people. Both of the places they had booked would have ample room, so it wasn't a problem.

Anyway, Mel had heard from the education dept and the council about the next stages. Debbie Longhorn had been observing Nicholas at nursery. She saw Mel and the family at home just before Christmas, and that went well, so they were nearly at the stage to start looking for a school. They had recommended though as Nicholas was non-verbal, a special school would be a better setting for him.

Mel was relieved. They had sent her the relevant information about the nearest schools, including a couple of mainstream, just because these were able to meet his needs. But Mel remembered what Juliet said about some of them NOT being able to meet all of the kid's needs. She had remembered Forrester

Greenwood. She did ask the lady at the council, does she just call the schools to make an appointment or does it have to go through them.

They told her she can call and make an appointment as it would be easier for the school and her diaries, to make it available to suit both parties. So, Mel called the school. They gave her a day on the following Friday. She said she could make the appointment, could she bring someone with her, they said yes. They would need to meet Nicholas if she wanted him to go there, just so he would become familiar with them and him.

She put the phone down. "Mum, Nan, can you make next Friday at 11.30am? We are going to see Forrester Greenwood special school." They both looked at her and nodded in agreement. She knew he wouldn't be starting yet, if anything he would go into the nursery, if they had a place for the following September.

He would be two and a half, but if they were willing and they all liked the place, the earlier the better, nan had told her.

The week had flown by and they were already into the second week. Mel had been going every week to Building Bridges. Once she relaxed, she realised that it wasn't a bad place and the people who went there loved going there, she just went initially at the wrong time for her. Anyway, the staff were hot on all the latest information from the council.

What was going on in the system and other general stuff like benefits these families were not getting but should have been. Mel actually enjoyed going there and she saw Juliet a lot. She was able to help with information and yes Arthur got into Forrester Greenwood Special school. Mel was so pleased for Juliet.

"You know what, Mel, you seem to get bombarded with stuff for months and months, then it all falls into place. When Arthur got diagnosed with Autism, all I could think of was what did I do in my pregnancy for this to happen. Did I have too many drinks, did I smoke too much, hold on I don't smoke. I don't do substances whatsoever, so how on earth did my son end up like this, with this condition."

"Then I thought, I didn't do anything wrong and neither did my son. It's just what it is and we either deal with it and get on with it for them and our peace of mind or we stick our heads in the sand like ostriches and hope it goes away, which it won't so why bother trying. It's nobody's fault it's just life. It's the cards that we are dealt and sink or swim."

"Me, I would rather swim. Yes, don't get me wrong, when they told me, I took Arthur home. He went for a sleep in his cot and I bawled my eyes out for about two hours straight, it helped a bit. I then realised that I can mope about or try and do the best for my boy and every time good stuff happens, make memories, take photos, because it's a great way to look back on and see how much progress they make," Juliet told her.

Mel thought that she was full of wisdom, but really it was common sense and having a grip on reality. She knew Juliet had no illusions about what could happen or not, but she knew that she was on the ball and had to be. "The only thing about this is, Mel, sadly it's an isolating time. Not everyone can see you, meet up with you or have the time."

"So when you get the chance of a bit of respite, babysitters so you can go out, grab it with both hands and if you can have it regular, then grab that too, for your mental health and wellbeing more than anything. To help you feel like a human being rather than a walking zombie sometimes. If you have the time to get your hair done or nails or just a massage," said Juliet with her eyes glazing over.

"Then you do it. Take every opportunity that comes your way, but also for you and Nicholas. There may be trips he can do later on. Let him fly, let him spread his wings and fly and I mean take a chance, like don't throw him into the air to fly," added Juliet, but Mel knew what she was talking about. Mel was glad she came every week; it really was a breath of fresh air.

***

"Weddings, weddings, how many weddings do you have so far for this year, Lesley?" Mel asked.

"I think we have about six at the moment. I know it's January, Mel, but these were booked from last year," replied Lesley.

"I'm not complaining, Les, you have another one now though end of June. Our Tina is getting married and we don't have to worry about the church, they are laying on their own. But I need to go and see her venue what we can do. Now Nicholas is at nursery full time and soon hopefully going to big school."

"I should have some time on my hands. Don't worry, Lesley, I'm not taking over here, just want to help out once in a while, because I have so much going on with Nicholas but it's a welcome break. So once I know what Tina's preferences are, I will sort out her wedding order. Ok?" Mel told her.

Lesley looked relieved on more than one count. Partly because of her coming back, but also Mel doing the wedding flowers for Tina as she has another wedding that same day. If Mel was doing it, she wouldn't have to but could focus on the other lady's wedding.

Tina and Mel had already sat down and discussed the colour scheme which Mel said was adorable colour, lilac and cream. She could have lilac dresses and cream shoes and flowers, with a hint of purple if she didn't want what was available. Tina had popped into the shop to look at the books. Julie, Fiona and Andrea still all worked for Mel and they didn't see her often but they all still loved their jobs.

As long as the work got done, Lesley was quite good with the girls. "You looking forward to seeing the new school tomorrow, Mel?" Tina asked.

"Yes, but a bit nervous too though. I think it would be, OK? Did nan tell you about our cousin, Jill?" Mel whispered.

"Yes, she did," Tina replied.

Mel took her out to the back, so they could talk about it freely. "Were you surprised, Tina?" Mel asked.

"Yes, I was, but at least now we know where Nicholas had got it from. I know it's not a disease, Mel, but it is in the family. So please don't be beating yourself up again about it. It's what it is," Tina replied.

"Yes, I know, I have been told that lots. It doesn't change that I do feel guilty even though I'm not to blame. But how many people out there do blame themselves and probably for many years. They can't accept it wasn't their fault, and this MMR stuff just adds more anxiety about it."

"It makes people scared to vaccinate their children. Nobody should feel scared or pressured into doing something they aren't sure about, but on the other hand, we all want our kids protected. So, it's not an easy one, Teen," said Mel. "So, how's the wedding guest list going? How many hundreds do you have on it?" Mel laughed.

"Oh, Mel, don't. Was it this difficult when you and Terry got married? It seems never ending. I just don't know what to do sometimes. You know we didn't want anything big, a hundred people would be OK, but George's dad wants to invite his entire family."

"There are tons of them and they don't all live here. Some emigrated to Australia and even New Zealand, we can't afford that, which is why we said average wedding-big honeymoon. I mean it's not like we have kids, so why not before we have kids. We were thinking of Barbados or somewhere exotic like that, but if they keep adding to the numbers, we will be lucky with a week in Blackpool," said Tina sighing.

"Tina, don't worry, as nan always says," Mel and Tina both said at the same time.

"It will always work out in the end." They both laughed. "Teen, it will sort itself out, but don't get stressed about it. It's not worth it. I know it's both your big day, but the stress is not worth it," said Mel, relived she was able to recover with Tina getting offended.

The next day, Marge, Jean and Mel went down the path once the front door was locked, headed to the school. It was a little bit away and too much walking for nan, so they jumped bus, it was only a couple of stops. They got off the bus, walked down a little lane and saw lovely red brick building with double doors at the front. A path with trees either side of it, a big sign saying 'Forrester Greenwood Special School', 'for children with Autism and learning difficulties' underneath it in smaller writing.

Mrs Deidre Fellows as Head. They walked up the path and pressed the buzzer. A lady asked who they were, Mel told them and she let them into the building. On entering the building, they were in reception. They had two receptionists, Gail and Emily.

Gail looked like she was in her forties and Emily looked like she had not long left school, but hey ho everyone has to start somewhere. Gail introduced themselves and had already told them that Mrs Fellows was on her way down to greet them. She was a nice lady. Tall blonde hair cut into a short bob, this made her look severe in her appearance, but she was a lovely lady who made all three of them feel at ease at once.

"Are you OK, if we go around the school for a tour of the building and then we can have a cup of something and you can ask as many questions as you like," suggested Mrs Fellows.

"Yes, that sounds great, Mrs Fellows," replied Mel.

"Oh Deidre please. We are really informal here, it makes it easier for our children you see. Everyone is on first name terms. Shall we go then?" she asked. They all nodded. "Well, as you can see this is our reception. Oh don't worry, Gail would have signed you in the book."

"Oh did you read the sign by the book. No course you didn't. If you wouldn't mind, you will understand when you read it." Deirdre took them back to reception. "Gail, it's not your fault, I didn't give the ladies the chance to sign in, but can they have a look at the A4 laminate. Yes, here you are, ladies, it reads.

Dear all, this school is for children with disabilities, autism and learning difficulties. We try to be as calm as we can in the school for the children who attend here. It is their place of safety and where they feel comfortable. So if you could please be considerate and accept these terms, you can continue to visit the school.

Marge teared up a bit after reading that. She didn't realise how much of an impact these children and their surroundings have on their life or their school life. Deirdre took them to the left of the building. All of the walls had a cobalt or royal blue width wise across the building, just where they would have pictures of the children's work or photographs of different activities.

Mel noticed this blue followed all through the building. They went into a couple of classrooms. There were little dividers that they had in call centres, to divide their workspaces. They had schedules of the day with various symbols on them with the word underneath them. Deirdre explained that the class had their schedules regarding what was going on for the day.

Once they get here, every lesson they did, which was quite extensive—soft play, body work, boxwork, circle time, snack time, trampolining. 'My my', thought Mel, 'this is great, school wasn't like this when I went?' Deirdre, took them to another class, which was full of all of this big spongey stuff. It was waterproof, so could be wiped down. It was like foam with a covering that you would find in jungle gyms.

"Oh, the soft play. I could take you in there, as it's empty at the moment," said Mrs Fellows. She opened the door; it was empty of people but full of soft stuff to play with. "This is where the children do soft play. They can run, jump, throw themselves onto it."

"They can't hurt themselves and it's all cleaned after every class in here uses it. Got to think of hygiene. Some children younger children are in nappies, so we don't take any chances." When everyone had a good look inside, Deirdre closed the door.

They went along to another class, that was full of children, well about six, but they were busy. Mrs Fellows knocked on the door and the teacher beckoned her to come in. "Hello, Jules, we just wanted to have a quick look around." The children were sitting at the circular table and had bells in front of them.

Instead of picking them up to ring them, they just pressed the button on the top and it make a noise. The child who was doing it, gave a huge smile. All of the bells were different colours. The children seemed to be enjoying themselves. Mel, Mum and nan were looking at everything.

"Come on, let's let them get on with their lesson," said Deirdre. Mel, nan and Mum waved to the teacher who nodded in response. Mrs Fellows closed the door. As they were walking down the corridor a classroom of children, came out of the classroom. Some had one to ones, some on their own.

They didn't all wear school uniform, but as Mrs Fellows had said they try to have a calm time at school. So if a child would come to school, but wouldn't let their mothers dress them in uniform, then they came in their normal clothes. They did what was best for the child, but that didn't always mean that the child would get away with being badly behaved.

The child would have to conform to the world, not the other way round. They just made it as easy as possible for the child and then young person to adapt as they got older, with the routine and structure.

They had been through most of the building. Mrs Fellows took them to the dining room, and the children they had seen in the corridor was already seated and waiting for their food. They had a big table to sit at with the staff to assist. There was quite a selection of food and the staff knew what each child would eat, because some of them were sensory eaters and would only stick to one thing.

One child they said would only eat toast, so the staff would go to the kitchen when they knew they were having lunch, ask for the toast to be made so the children would all eat at the same time. So they didn't think they were being left out, it also showed them patience. They went through the dining room and out onto the playground, which was out through another door.

They had a few little apparatuses that the little children could go on. A thing you could jump on and a couple of ride things, what you find in a playground. There wasn't hopscotch or snakes and ladders on the ground, but some tarmacked area so they could run and not hurt themselves if they fell over. They went over to the other side of the playground, up a few stairs.

"This is where the nursery is, Mel. This is where Nicholas would be playing, learning, eating his snacks etc."

"Excuse me, Mrs Fellows, sorry, Deirdre, why are there two bean bags over there? Is that for rest time or something?" Marge enquired.

"Well, not really, sort of, a couple of the children in nursery have epilepsy, so if they have an episode, then they can rest on the bean bags and we cover them over so they are warm when they recover from it," said Mrs Fellows. "It doesn't happen often, but we need to be ready for any eventuality," she replied.

Marge was in awe of it all, she wondered if this was how it was for Jill. She thought Jill would have been lucky if she had people like this caring for her. They left the nursery and went back across the playground through a different door. They were now going into the hall, where they had the trampoline at one side of the room.

"As you may have seen in one of the classrooms, the children do trampolining, once a week. We have staff supervision with them on the trampoline. As you can see this is an Olympic size one, which the children love, because it gives them the freedom when they jump and for some of them, it really helps with their balance."

"It makes everything right in their head. What I mean is they can have problems with their ears, but jumping on here can help that regulate. Do you know what I mean? It's all very technical, but it's something we have found that works for the children and young people," said Mrs Fellows.

They went back out; the staff were getting ready for a class of 4 to come in for their session. They went through another door. They had a small library that the children would go once a week for a term, so they could all get a chance to look at and read the books. Mel, Marge and Jean were so impressed with this school, Mel knew that she had done the right thing looking at this school. In fact, she didn't really want to look anywhere else.

When the tour of the building came to an end, Mrs Fellows took them to her office. She made drinks for everyone, and then asked them if they had any questions, where they had many. "Mrs Fellows, Deirdre, how come there is a deep blue throughout the whole building?" Mel asked.

"Ah, well that is because that blue is a very calming low arousal colour. So the children are calm and feel grounded and safe and we can get the most out of them while and when they feel calm. When the children get here in the morning, every class, the staff play classical music for about 15 mins to half an hour, whilst the children are working. It calms them right down from their journey into school, which sometimes can be a bit traumatic."

"Most of the children live in borough but need school transport for the children to arrive safely. Some families have more than one child, but sorry, I digress. Is there anything else you would like to ask?" she asked them.

"Yes, I would like to ask something," asked Nan. "We have seen the school and I might add, I am very impressed. We saw where the children eat, do soft play, I even spotted horse riding on one of them schedule things. Does Mel have to pay for that separately, when they go out and I do like that soft play stuff. I would have loved that as a kid," said nan, now a little embarrassed.

"Mrs?" Deirdre said.

"Call me Marge," Marge told her.

"Well, Marge, as you know all the children who attend Forrester Greenwood, will have a statement, so that in itself is a legal document. Which means that your local authority will have to pay so much towards Nicholas' education. Now once in a while they have trips, like to the seaside or a theme park and sometimes we want the children to bring money with them, but that's for spending, not for anything else."

"So once all of that paperwork, which I think you're in the middle of, Mel?" Deirdre said looking at Mel. Mel nodded back. "That will all be included. So please don't worry. One lady, love her, said she would scrub our floors if it meant her son could go to this school, even though he had a full statement, which is what they all have here. She was so delighted that he could come here, but she thought she would have to pay."

"Sadly it's not made very known to the families beforehand. Anyway, it will all be fine, I am sure," she told them. Mel didn't know what else to ask. Mrs Fellows gave them her direct number. "Mel, if you have any queries, issues or are worried about anything, just call me. Even if you're unsure about something on Nicholas' statement, then please don't hesitate to call me."

"Leave a message on the answerphone if you can't get me though and I will call you straight back. Please don't worry, Mel, it will be fine. The nursery and the council did send me over some information about Nicholas, so I was already aware, and of his age, we have taken children at three before and I think we have a place for him, but if you could hold on a couple more months. I will confirm then you can put Forrester Greenwood as your named school, that is if you want to," suggested Deidre.

Mel nodded her head. "I didn't know what to think or expect, but you have exceeded my expectations a hundred-fold. Thank you, Mrs Fellows, Deirdre," said Mel.

"Thank you, I will let you go now. Sadly I have a meeting in about ten minutes. This is one of my perks of the job, but I wouldn't have it any other way. Goodbye to you all. See you soon," she said taking them back down to reception.

They said goodbye to Gail and Emily. They buzzed the door for them and they walked down the path. They opened the gate and then closed it, safety for the children. They walked to the bus stop. "Well, I think that was a great success Mum, Nan. I think I would love to send Nicholas there. I think he would love it and I know he would come on leaps and bounds. I just know it."

They got the bus home and when they opened the door, Jean went into the kitchen and put the kettle on. "Mel, do you think that Jill would have had that kind of care where she is and if she had been born now?" Nan asked, who had teared up again.

"Yes, Nan, I do. I think she would have been well looked after and cared for," Mel said giving her nan a hug.

Chapter 14

Nicholas was making slow progress, but nevertheless he was making progress. Mel was chuffed to bits because she didn't know how he was going to cope, so far so good. Tina was getting a bit bogged down with the wedding preparations, but thankfully George stood up to his relatives who wanted to invite the whole world and his wife to their wedding. So they backed off reluctantly, but George got it sorted in the end.

Mel hadn't seen Elaine in a while. She had so much on and she hadn't made it to the support group in a while either. Mel had managed to meet up with Juliet a couple of times and let her know how Nicholas was doing. Arthur was going to start school in September, which she was chuffed with and if the local authority or council got their fingers out, then hopefully Nicholas would be going too; but in the nursery, so at least they would be under the same roof so to speak.

January was over really quickly, Mel hadn't even noticed with meetings and stuff going on all the time. Nan had mentioned it to her and Jean, because they hardly saw her. She was either running around to this meeting or that or with speech and language.

Nan couldn't work out what was going on next. She kept thinking is that what Nancy had to do for Jill, but maybe not, because nowadays it was very different to when the war was over. There wasn't the funds for all of the care and attention. Nicholas second birthday was in a weeks' time. She had hardly any chance to get him much for his birthday and how far had she come in a year.

She asked at nursery apart from books what he liked to play with so she could get the same. He was doing so well at nursery, she wanted to make it a great experience for him at home. She picked up a cake from Marks and Sparks, it was chocolate and was in the shape of a caterpillar, she thought it would be fun.

Tina was terrified of putting on any weight. She had already chosen her dress straight after Christmas, so it was being made from a boutique. She didn't want anything from Paris like Sam did, but she loved it and looked beautiful in it. She didn't have any nieces at all, she only had Nicholas and that would be tricky to ask him to be a page boy.

But she did her best and asked Mel, if she would let him wear a suit and walk down the aisle with him as her Maid of Honour. Mel was delighted. She knew that Tina had wanted to have the bridesmaids in lilac. George did have a couple of nieces, but also Jim and Angela had two little girls, so Tina asked them if they would like to be bridesmaids.

Of course, they both said yes. The chance to dress up and wear pretty dresses, so that was four bridesmaids and one page boy and her sister as Maid of Honour. She had wanted to ask Elaine as well, if she would be a bridesmaid, but also have Todd in a suit like Nicholas. Elaine wasn't sure at first, but Mel and Tina encouraged her. Even though Todd was a bit older than Nicholas, he could still be part of the wedding.

Elaine was grateful to Tina for asking for both of them. Also, Todd was now too big for his normal pram, but had to get a disabled pushchair for him, which fitted him better. He wasn't more or less all over the place and uncomfortable. Elaine had called Mel to meet up. She did while Nicholas was at nursery. She still hadn't got Todd into nursery yet.

They were still trying to find something suitable because of his needs and now extra. So, Mel met her in the café. Todd was in his pram, not doing too much but mesmerised by something Elaine had bought him from the support group toy library. "Mel, can I ask you something?" Elaine asked.

"Yes, of course, what is it?" Mel asked.

"Have they said anything to you at the hospital about Nicholas having seizures at all?" Elaine asked rather sheepishly. She always did look rather sheepishly if she was worried about something.

"No, why? Should they have done?" Mel asked a little nervous now.

"No, of course not. I just wondered. I had heard the last time I was at the hospital saying that if your child has autism, there's a fair chance that they will have epilepsy," said Elaine. "It's just that Todd has been diagnosed as having Temporal lobe epilepsy."

"The right side of his brain shuts down for seconds, sometimes a couple of minutes. They have put him on medication. Hang on, I have it in my bag; it's called Lamotrigine, he has to have 25ml twice a day then it gets increased by 25ml every two weeks until he's up to 100ml twice a day," Elaine said to her.

"Oh, Elaine, I am so sorry. You seem to get more bad news every time you go to the doctors or hospital," said Mel.

"Well, these things were happening quite lot, so I had to get him checked out. He would be looking at something that he's enjoying then he would stiff up and his eyes would look like there was nothing behind them. Anyway they are getting him sorted out and he doesn't seem to have them as much, but without the medication, it would definitely get worse."

"Oh, Elaine, at least you had the foresight to get him sorted out as soon as you could. How long has he been on the medication?" Mel asked.

"Only two weeks. He's due to start his evening one tonight," Elaine replied.

"Is it liquid, Elaine?" Mel enquired.

"No, it's soluble. Apparently, the medical companies don't make a lot of money out of it that way, but it's OK, he seems to take it OK, " Elaine told her.

"How do you get it into him?" Mel asked.

"I have to make it up, with the water, then put it into a syringe and then it into his mouth. You know like the ones they give babies," Elaine said to Mel.

"Thank goodness, I thought you might have had to put it in his arm or something. That's how had to give Nicholas his anti-biotics when he was a baby. So, what's next for you and Todd then?" Mel asked.

"I have no idea. Well, we have the wedding to look forward. What colour suit is Nicholas wearing then?" Elaine quizzed.

"I think it's a light grey. I'm not sure if she's having cream or lilac buttonholes yet though. Poor Tina, doesn't know whether she is coming or going at the moment, love her," Mel told Elaine. They finished up their drinks and Danishes. "Oh yes, we have a fitting for our dresses next week, to make sure they fit us and suit us, otherwise I have no idea," Mel said.

"What are the dresses like, Mel?" Elaine enquired.

"Again I have no idea, as it's a June wedding, more than likely strapless, but who knows. Anyway on Thursday, we have to miss bridges though, but can go the following week. That ok with you?" Mel asked.

"Yeah, no problem. See you then. What time on Thursday?" Elaine asked.

"10.30am, but should be done in a couple of hours. Mum and nan are both coming too, so it should be fun. Don't worry lots of people to fuss over Todd. Love him, bye, Elaine," said Mel.

Mel went back home; Mum and nan were in the kitchen making tea. "Lunch, Mel?" Nan asked.

"Oh no thanks. I have just had something with Elaine. I reminded her about next Thursday though, about the dress fittings. We are having ours done and then in a couple of weeks' time. The little ones are having theirs done, makes it easier, so the girls aren't running around the shop while we are trying on dresses and Tina is trying to decide. Mum, I wasn't this nuts when I got married, was I?" Mel asked, hoping she would the reply she wanted.

"No, you were worse. You would bite our heads off all the time, when we were trying to help you and oh my goodness Terry's mum, what a pain in the butt. She kept changing her outfit colour, kept changing her mind about what Terry's dad, he was just as annoying," said Nan.

"Oh what Billy big potatoes. Who wouldn't keep his mouth shut, going on and on all the time about what it was costing him and he didn't put his hand in his pocket once, but he was up at the bar the whole time, checking on what everyone else was drinking," Mel replied.

"Anyway, it should be fun," said Nan.

"What the wedding?" Mel asked.

"No, trying on those beautiful dresses next week. I wish I could wear a beautiful dress," stated Nan.

"Nan, you will look like a million dollars. Now what are you going to wear? Did you wear peach at Sam and Mike's wedding last year, I can't remember," asked Jean.

"Yes, I was going to get something in pink if I can. I looked through my wardrobe, when you are as sociable as I am, you can't wear the same thing twice. I saw a lovely little purple dress that I was going to get to wear for Nicholas' christening, but that never happened, did it?" Nan said looking disapprovingly at Mel.

"Nan, we did talk about this. I will get him christened, but too much else was going on with him and I didn't think it was fair on him. He can do it standing up," replied Mel.

"Yes, but he can't wear that beautiful christening gown I had for you," Nan replied.

"Nan, it doesn't matter as long as he gets done and he's not scared of the water. Maybe later on this year, we will see," said Mel, with a look of now that's the end of it.

"As you say, Mel," nan said rather quietly.

Thursday came around. Jean and Marge left to meet Mel. She had already dropped Nicholas off and she had to walk down to the high street to meet Tina and nan and Mum were on their ways. Tina was standing outside the shop when Mel got there. Mum and nan were a few minutes behind her and then they saw Elaine coming up with Todd in his new pushchair.

Everyone said hello to Elaine and especially Todd, who was full of smiles. Mum and nan made a big thing about how nice his pushchair was and how he looked so comfortable. Did it have a rain cover. They were full of praise and Elaine looked rather pleased, rather than embarrassed as she thought she would.

Tina suggested that they go into the shop. They were a little late and didn't want to annoy the lady showing them the dresses. She had opened the door and let them all in. Elaine struggled a bit at first because it was a little higher step than she thought. She managed to get the pushchair in with Jean's help.

So the assistant asked who was the bride and who were the bridesmaids, maid of honour. Tina told her who was who. Tina asked her what dresses they had in lilac and what styles and what if they saw a dress that wasn't lilac, would they be able to get them in lilac? "So how many more appointments do you have? Do you have any little ones at all or midsized bridesmaids?" The lady asked who said her name was Sandy.

"I have another appointment with the four smaller bridesmaids, there are two who are twelve and one is five and the other seven," said Tina.

"Oh a lovely selection of ages and sizes, so will you be having any page boys?" Sandy asked.

"Yes, I am having Todd here and my…"

Before Tina could continue Sandy said, "Pardon, this boy is a page boy?"

"Yes, is there anything wrong with that, missus?" Nan asked. "This darling boy is going to be a page boy and so is my grandson who is autistic. Is that a problem to you because, my love, we can always go somewhere else that would be happy to have our custom, eh?" Nan said, angry but calm at the same time.

Elaine was close to tears. Jean ran over to her to comfort her. "Now, missus Sandy, you owe this lady an apology or we are leaving. Don't think we won't spread it around the area, don't go to this shop if you have anyone disabled as they aren't welcome. I'm sure the bridal shop just off the high street would be happy to have us in their shop and would be much more welcoming," said Nan.

"Er I am so sorry. I apologise for my behaviour. I didn't realise, of course you're more than welcome in my shop. Everybody is welcome, no exclusions for anybody. Miss, do you have your suits for these young men already?" Sandy asked.

"Er no, not yet. We wanted to see what shade of Lilac that would go with the suits," replied Tina.

"Well, miss, I would like you to choose two for this young man and your nephew, free of charge, including shirts and ties. I fully apologise for my disrespect to you, madam, and your beautiful son. I will go now and get the dresses for you to choose from!" Sandy said leaving rather red in the face.

"Thank you, Jean, and you too, Marge. I really appreciate it. I haven't had anyone stand up for me and Todd before," said Elaine.

"Well get used to it, love, because we aren't going to have anyone say anything about your little lad and ours," said nan. With that Sandy came back with about six dresses, long, short to the knee, a couple of short sleeved, capped sleeve and a couple of strapless for Mel and Elaine.

Elaine left Todd in the capable hands of Marge and Jean, went up with Tina to have a look at the dresses. Tina wasn't too keen on a couple of them and poo pooed them straight away. Mel liked one of the strapless and Elaine liked the capped sleeve, they both grabbed one of each and went to try them on. They fit both of them nicely but it was up to Tina to which one she preferred.

They then went back into the changing room and tried on the other one. Elaine came out first, then Mel. They both looked great in the strapless, but the capped sleeve on Mel looked awful. They looked against the other dresses, even those that weren't in lilac to see if any of those were any good.

"No, looks like a cocktail dress, no looks like we should be in the funeral parlour, no this one look like I'm out for a night on the town. No, I'm not sure about these. Oh, actually, Sandy, is it ok to have a look at what you have in lilac for the younger ones. I will help you put these back on the rails," asked Tina. Sandy disappeared for a little while and came back with dresses in the relevant ages and styles.

There also were two that they narrowed down to, but she asked if she could make a note of which dresses that she had chosen, so when she brought the other girls in, they could try them on in the right sizes. Sandy said that was possible. Tina also said she would have a look at the suits when she came with the other bridesmaids.

Sandy said that was fine, then she could see how well the colour went with the girl's dresses. Tina had picked the two strapless dresses for Mel and Elaine and paid for them. They all said their goodbyes, nan and Jean both shook her hand. Sandy apologised to Marge again.

They all left and then went to the café for a treat. It was just after 12.30pm and they were hungry; dress shopping makes you hungry. When they had finished the food and drinks, they all said their goodbyes. Tina was going home in one direction. Elaine was going the opposite way, and Mel, was still too early to pick up Nicholas, went home with nan and Mum.

"Well, Mel, what did you think of that sales assistant? She was rather rude, wasn't she?" Jean asked.

"Yes, she was, but I soon put her in her place, Jean. I'm not having it. Poor little Todd, it's not his fault. Love him," said nan.

"What if she doesn't give those suits to Tina, Mum, like she promised. She may have just said that to get herself out of a sticky situation?" Mel asked.

"I don't think she will go back on it, Mel, because if she does, I will give her a bunch of fives and then I will tell everyone that she goes back on her word and is awful with disabled children. She won't have much left in the way of a business, because nobody will want to go to her, and the other bridal shop the other side of the high street will get everyone's business. Where did Tina get her dress, Mel?" Nan asked.

"I think she got it at the other dress shop, but I'm not a hundred percent on that, so don't quote me, Nan," said Mel.

"I just wondered that's all, just in case. Don't want her to ruin our Tina's dress." They got in, Mum put on the kettle for tea. They weren't hungry as they had already eaten at the café.

"Poor Elaine though, it's not fair, is it?" Jean said.

"At least she has us fighting her corner as well as her family. She got really teary. Love her. Some people don't know how to act around others, their mouths get into gear before their brains engage," said nan. Mum and Mel burst out laughing.

***

Nicholas had been doing ok at nursery. Sometimes if there were too many kids in, he couldn't cope with it, so they would let him play on the computer in the office for a little while. Watching the children's channels, lots of characters, big furry ones, dancing around the screen, singing their hearts out. He loved it. It was fast moving. He used to get excited when they singing, he would bounce up and down whoever's lap he was sitting on.

It was coming up to April, so everything was going a bit nuts trying to get everything sorted out by the end of the tax year. Mel was sorting out the taxes for the shop, but also everything was coming in from the council. Mel had to have a look and check the appendix for her part of the statement. She read through it again and again just to make sure she hadn't missed anything, added what she thought would be needed.

She re-read it and was pleased with it. She handed it back to Debbie. "Now, Mel, it shouldn't take too long. Did you put your named school on?" Debbie asked.

"Oh yes, I have. I put Forrester Greenwood Special School, because I looked at it and decided that's where I wanted to put Nicholas," said Mel.

"So you didn't look at anything else, Mel?" Debbie asked.

"No, I saw Forrester and knew that's where I wanted to send him. I didn't need to look at anything else," Mel replied.

"Oh well, if you're sure," Debbie told her.

"Yes, I am really sure. It is a good school, both my nan and Mum liked it too. So that's our choice, well my choice for Nicholas," Mel told her as she had handed back the statement, to be finalised.

"This should be done soon. Once the paperwork is finished and you have said yes, then the education dept will contact the school. I do know that they have a place for Nicholas, but it's just dotting the I's and crossing the ts. Then you should get a letter from them offering him a place. Don't worry, Mel, it's just procedure."

Mel was happy that this part of the statementing process was nearly done and there hadn't really been any hiccups. Once Mel had got home with Nicholas, she was telling Mum and nan about what Debbie had said. "But you were happy with Forrester Greenwood, weren't you, Mel?" Mum asked.

"Oh yes, that's why I didn't want to look at anything else and I told her that," replied Mel.

"That's my girl, you tell them. Our boy will go where his mum and only his mum sees fit, not these professionals," retorted nan. Mel was pleased when she had nan and Mum on her side. She knew it was difficult and get more difficult as time wore on, but she could only do her best as any mother, father, parents, extended family members.

She did have Tina's wedding to look forward and even though it was a bit stressful, it was a different stress to what she was going through dealing with the stuff for Nicholas. She wasn't complaining whatsoever, it was just making sure she had got it right. Time was going really fast. It was nearly the beginning of June and even though everything was sorted for the wedding, Tina had popped back to the shop with the bridesmaids, their mums and of course nan and Mum, ready; just in case Sandy got a bit too big for her boots, nan would put her right.

Tina chose a lovely dress for the other four girls and she paid for them. She was going to collect everything for the girls and boys at the same time. Mel was going to give her a hand, "Oh and before I forget, Mel, me and all the bridesmaids will be getting ready at mum's the day of the wedding. As it's not until 2pm, we're getting the girls and mums round early, hair, make-ups will be done, then to get ready," Tina told her.

"Oh but I won't be there first thing, Teen, I will be at your venue," Mel said and Tina looked at her funny.

"Why?" Tina asked.

"Don't you want your flowers delivered and arranged all nicely. I can't send Lesley as she is doing another wedding the other side of town, or don't you want nice flowers at your wedding anymore?" Mel joked.

"Oh, Mel, I am so sorry, I forgot. What about Nicholas?" Tina asked.

"Well, I was hoping Mum and nan would fuss over him a bit in between getting themselves ready. Tina, I was going over there at 8am, but just in case I overrun, don't worry I have checked this all out with the venue. They know I am supplying your flowers, most of the arrangements will be made and just need to be taken over, but there will be some I have to do from scratch, if I remember how actually. I haven't done flowers, ooh for a couple or so years now!" Mel teased.

"Sorry, Mel, I forgot. I am sure it will be fine," Tina told her. She was getting a bit nervous now the time wasn't far away.

"Oi missus, have you decided on a hen night yet? Because you're leaving it a bit late you know!" Mel informed her.

"Yes, I am sorting it out this week. You're coming, aren't you?" asked Tina a lot nervous now.

"Of course I am coming. Nan was going to look after Nicholas, so Mum could come. What are you doing actually? You know for your hen night?" Mel quizzed.

"Well, I thought we could go for a meal and a couple of drinks and see where we end up. What do you think?" Tina suggested.

"I think that would be great, but I don't think Mum would appreciate going to a nightclub. They don't play the sort of music that her and nan like," chuckled Mel.

"I think that maybe the only thing that gives everyone a chance," Tina added. They carried on what they were doing, then Tina had to go and make tracks. "Oh yes, Mel, George's mum is coming on the hen night, so at least Mum will have someone to talk to, ta ta," Tina laughed on her way out.

A week before the wedding, two A4 envelopes popped through the letterbox. One had the council post frank on it and the other had the school post frank on it. Which one should she open first? "Mum, nan, can you come down here please?" Mel asked. Both of the ladies came down the stairs as fast as they could.

"What's up Mel, where's the fire?" Nan asked.

"It's just these have come and I wanted you to both be here when I open them. I think I should open the one from the council first, then I will be a bit prepared for the schools one, what do you think?" Mel asked them both.

"Good thinking, Mel. Well, come on then open them up," said Mum. She tore open the letter, she pulled it out with another tons of paperwork. She read through it and then looked up. "This is Nicholas Statement of Educational needs, he got it, Mum, Nan. HE GOT IT. AFTER ALL THAT WORK HE GOT IT," Mel screamed, she was so chuffed.

Now the other one, she couldn't wait for this one, she read it then put her head back up. "He's got a place to start in September, Mum, Nan. It's his confirmation letter, I am going to frame it, no I'm not. I'm going to put it in his file with all of his important paperwork, but I will frame it. I will photocopy it and frame it."

She was so excited, all of their well her hard work had paid off. Next thing Mel was crying, really crying. She felt so relived. She and Nicholas had done it. Whatever happened now, she was over one of the first big hurdles in Nicholas' life. She couldn't have been more pleased.

Mum and nan read the letter, they were crying too. They knew Mel had been through so much and always wanted to do her best by Nicholas and she had done it, she had achieved it. This is one of the first goals and milestones that they both had reached.

***

The next day was Tina's Hen night. George was going out with his mates and a couple of his cousins. They were doing the local area, but Tina was going up to the main high street. There were going to be about twelve of them or so, her friends from work, Mel and Elaine, her mum and George's mum was going as well.

They had arranged to meet about 8, go to a restaurant; Tina's friends had encouraged her to go for a Greek Restaurant, because they did the Greek dancing and broke the plates. The Italian and Spanish restaurants didn't do that, and they were quite a feisty bunch. So that's what they arranged for her, then off to have a few cocktails, then off to a club to dance the night away.

Everyone was on time. They met at the local pub for a first drink, then head over the other side of the high street to the restaurant. Jean and Elsie were a little uncomfortable at first, but they enjoyed themselves. Mel and Elaine both helped them with the menu. they could have Meze which was a bit of everything, or they could have Moussaka, stuffed vine leaves, kleftiko which was lamb cooked very slowly.

Jean and Elsie had that with seasonal vegetables. Some of Tina's friends had the Meze. Mel and Elaine both had the Moussaka. They had ordered some wine with the meal, which Tina's friends lapped up; they all enjoyed the food too. Jean and Elsie were having a few drinks as well, so they loosened up a bit.

Once all of the food were eaten and the tables cleared of the decent crockery, the waiters put on the Greek music and started to dance and on occasion they smashed plates in time and beat with the music. Tina was having a great time. Everyone could tell she was the bride, because she was the most drunk, not quite falling over at this stage, but Jean hoped that someone would be able to keep her in check and make sure she got home alright.

Mel and Elaine were going home, because even though they had someone to look after their boys, they wanted to get home to rest. These party nights out and the party girls, Mel felt as though she was too old for these sort of nights out now, even though she wasn't quite 35 yet, she still felt like the oldest there, even thought that wasn't the case, that's how she felt.

They had all eaten plenty, so the drink was soaked up, but they all still had plenty of space for some more. "Tina, Tina?" Mel called. "Do you have enough money to get home once you go to this club?" she asked.

"Yes, I still have quite a lot on me, Mel, but don't worry I have Kerry helping me home afterwards. George is going back to his mums afterwards, so she's coming back with me to mine. Don't worry, Mel, I won't wake the neighbours," Tina replied.

"Well that was news to me," said Elsie. "I thought George was going home, but never mind, I am glad that we still have his room ready and didn't rent it out, like his dad wanted to," she joked. Mel, Elaine, Jean and Elsie, were still at the restaurant finishing up, while the girls left for the nightclub.

"Tina, please be careful getting home," said Jean.

"Don't worry, Mum, I'll call you," she said smiling as she was going out the door.

"Don't you dare, we need sleep, not like you young ones!" Jean replied. Elsie nearly choked on her drink. When they had all finished, the bill had already been paid. The waiters were clearing the tables.

One of them came over to talk to Mel, he enquired about Tina, said she was a pretty girl and that her future husband was a very lucky man. He wanted to know how these women left from the party would be getting home? "Mini cab I think? Actually would it be possible to call one from here?" The waiter said that wouldn't be a problem, and went to call for one.

He came back a couple of minutes later to tell them, one was on the way. He also asked Mel for her number. She was quite shocked at this. She hadn't had her number asked for a long time. She wasn't sure whether to or not, so gave him her mobile number. He said his name was Andreas; his father owned the restaurant and had only been open a couple of years.

He thanked Mel, after he asked her name and then kissed her hand, all in front of Jean, who looked very surprised. They all got up, said thank you to

Andreas and his staff and then left and got into the cab. "Ooooh, Mel, he was alright," said Jean.

"Alright, don't you mean dishy, Jean?" Elaine said. "I wouldn't say no, oh sorry, Mel," Elaine added. Mel who was quiet was still in a bit of shock. She hadn't been around a man since Andy and that was a couple of years or so ago now and Terry before that.

She wasn't they type that men really went for, but she was pleased that she got his attention, even though that wasn't her intention. They dropped off Elaine, then Elsie, then Mum and Mel pulled up outside the house. The curtains were all drawn, but the sitting room lights were still on.

Nan peered out of the curtains, then a few minutes later she opened the door. She had already put the kettle on for tea. These two ladies needed something, just about holding each other up coming down the path or up the path. "Good time, ladies?" Nan asked.

"Yes, Nan, we had a great time," said Mel.

"Yes, and Mel pulled," Mum said matter-of-factly.

"Oh yes," nan interjected. They both got inside. Nan closed the door behind them.

"Nan, how has Nicholas been?" Mel asked.

"He's fine, fast asleep, which is where I should be. I will make tea, then I am off to bed, staying up for you too. I'm not a teenager anymore and neither are you two," said Nan, scowling a little.

"Well, we could have gone to the nightclub with Tina and her friends but thought we should be grown up and come back," Mel replied to nan.

"Too blooming old you mean!" Nan laughed. "You two in a nightclub. I would pay to see that though. Hang on did your mum say that you pulled?" Nan asked again, thinking maybe she had imagined it.

"No, mum was right. The waiter, the owner's son, Andreas. He was gorgeous, Nan and he kissed my hand when we were leaving. I don't think I will wash it again, ever again," Mel told her nan.

"Well you will when Nicholas has a dirty nappy and it goes on your hand, as it sometimes does, my girl," pulling her down a peg or two. "Night you two, see you in the morning. Oh look, it is the morning," said Nan. Mel looked at her watch and then the clock, it was only just after midnight. Nan made it sound like they were out all night.

Mel drank her tea that nan had made her and then said goodnight to her mum who drained her cup, took them both into the kitchen; she could wash them up in the morning. "Night, Mel. Night, Mum," they both said.

Jean turned off the lights, shut the sitting room door, went upstairs, checked on Mel, then turned off the hall light, before she went into her own room. She had a great night tonight. She was glad she went and she really did enjoy the food there. Maybe her, Mel, Tina and Mum could go again and maybe take Nicholas with them, but that was for another time. Now she was going to bed in the land of nod.

Chapter 15

"Mel, can you get that, I'm up to my shoulders in water," asked Jean. Nan was upstairs with Nicholas getting his bath ready.

"Hello," Mel said as she picked up the receiver.

"Hello, is that, Mel?" The voice asked at the other end of the phone.

"Yes, it's Mel, whose calling please?" she asked.

"It's Andreas from The Greek God. You know the restaurant you were at the other evening?" Andreas said, trying to jog Mel's memory.

"Oh hello, Andreas. How are you?" Mel asked.

"I am very well, thank you. I was wondering if you were free this evening to come out with me for a drink or something to eat, if you haven't already eaten?" He asked Mel.

"Er, Andreas, can you give me a second?" Mel said covering her hand over the voice part of the phone. "Mum, it's Andreas from the restaurant the other night. He wants me to go out with him for a drink or something to eat. What do you think?" Mel asked.

"Go, Mel, we will watch Nicholas. What time does he want you to meet?" Jean asked her.

"I have no idea. I wanted to ask you first," Mel replied. "Er yes, Andreas, sorry my mother just asked me a question. Yes, I am free for a drink as I have had an early dinner, that would be lovely."

"Yes, yes, I could meet you outside the restaurant and yes you would like to go to a bar, that would be great. In half an hour, yes that should be OK. See you then. Yes, bye," Mel said hanging up the phone.

"So I take it you're going and your meeting at his restaurant? So is it going to be a late one? It's short notice though, Mel. Well, you know me and nan will look after little un, so go and get ready and have a great time. Do you have enough money? Go on or you're not going to make it," said Jean.

Mel legged it upstairs. Thankfully she had not long had a shower. She just had to quickly dry her hair and then put on something decent to wear, put on some make-up so she didn't look like the living dead. Twenty minutes later, she re-appeared, popped her head round the sitting room door and gave Nicholas a kiss on his forehead and then Mum and nan. Thanked them again for doing this for her at short notice then she flew out the door.

On the way to meet Andreas, Mel was trying to remember the last time she had a date. She hadn't since she had met Terry. She was out of the dating game once her marriage was over and Andy well, he was just a one-night stand that she never saw or heard from again. She was soon at the restaurant. Andreas was standing outside waiting for her.

He looked different from the other night, mind you she was a little tipsy. He looked a bit shorter than she had remembered, but he was still turned out quite nicely. He had dark jeans on a pale green shirt, a blazer, nice polished shoes. His dark curly hair was very nice to look at and I suppose feel as Mel was thinking as she was walking up to him.

"Hello again, Mel. I am sorry for the short notice, but I only found out an hour ago I had the night off. My father came in and told me to enjoy myself, so I thought I would give you a call. I know a lovely little wine bar just around the corner," he told her. Mel was expecting him to say his cousin or uncle owned it, but he didn't.

"Did your sister get home safely? She was a bit out of it when she left the restaurant?" He asked her.

"Yes, she did. One of her friends went back with her to make sure, she's her friend from work," Mel told him. Andreas opened the door of the wine bar. It really was around the corner from the restaurant. He found them a table and then ordered white wine for each of them. He seemed really keen on Mel and wanted to know everything about her.

She told him she owned a florist and had four staff working for her. His eyes seemed to light up. So she was a business woman and she wouldn't be wanting to spend his money as she had her own, that was a plus, Andreas thought. So, was she married, he wanted to ask her, but thought he would let her talk and then hopefully she would drop it into conversation.

He could already see that she had a wedding ring mark on her finger, but no ring of any sign. But that could also be that she doesn't wear jewellery for work, so it won't get lost in the water or flowers or plants, or whatever it is they do at a florist. These were two pluses in her favour. He asked her what she did at the weekends and does she get out much. She knew the inevitable was going to come up, she couldn't really avoid it anymore.

"Andreas, I have a child. He is two and two months old and no, his father isn't in the picture. I do get out every so often and I have a great network support and also babysitters, so if you wanted to go out with me again, it won't be a problem," Mel said, what Andreas was wanting to ask but couldn't find the words. Thank goodness Mel had found her confidence again.

It had taken her a long time and to be honest. She didn't have the time and energy for time wasters, it took too much of her energy and she needed that for Nicholas. He had asked a couple of things about Nicholas, like his name and does he go to nursery, but Mel wasn't going to talk about anything else about him. It wasn't anyone else's business and certainly not someone she had only just met.

They had a few drinks, but Mel was tired. She had been planning and sorting out the flowers for Tina's wedding in a couple of days' time. Before she left Andreas, he asked her to come to the restaurant for a meal with her mum, nan and Nicholas, once the wedding was over. She thanked him for that and he kissed her softly on the lips.

He had offered to walk her home, but she said it was fine, she was getting a cab. He eventually let her go, and she got into her cab. "Hi, Mum, it's just me," said Mel, as closed the door.

"Didn't you want to bring him in then, Mel? Nan wanted to meet him," said Mum.

"Oh no, I got a cab back," Mel told her.

"So how did it go then? Is it going to be wedding bells again in this house sometime soon then, young lady?" Nan asked.

"Nan, give me a chance, it's far too early you know," Mel said to them both, as they both looked as eager as each other.

"So, what did you talk about? Did you tell him about Nicholas?" Nan asked.

"We talked about a lot of different things, but he didn't mention much about himself a part from the restaurant. He let me talk. He would say a word and then it would be a full-blown conversation," Mel told them.

"So he didn't really ask you any questions then?" Mum asked.

"He kept looking at my left hand. I suppose to see if there was a ring there, but he would have been disappointed as it was empty. I did tell him about Nicholas, just that he was a tot and no, his father wasn't in the picture. But he didn't ask too much," Mel added.

"He probably was letting you do all the talking, Mel, because that way it looks as if he's a good listener, but also you're not realising how much he's actually taking in. Be careful, Mel," Nan encouraged.

"So you didn't tell him that Nicholas is autistic then?" Mum asked.

"No, Mum, it's none of anyone's business, especially a man I have only met twice. Not because of frightening him off, but because I don't want to meet a man and then introduce him to Nicholas and it doesn't work out. It's not fair on Nicholas and it's not fair on me, thinking I could have a potential relationship."

"No, I am not blaming Nicholas. I meet a man, he has to adapt to us, we won't be adapting to him, but there is also a compromise, which could be met, but not this early. It's too early," Mel said flatly.

They both knew not to push it, but they were proud of their girl. She wasn't going to just date and bring anyone into their or more importantly Nicholas' life. Nan thought, that their girl had grown so much in the last few years since Terry and her split, and Nicholas was such a blessing to their lives. She knew Mel was going to protect that for as long as she could.

***

Mel woke early the day of the wedding. Tina had stayed at theirs for the night. They had a lively night of chatting drinking a couple of glasses of wine. Nicholas was loving getting lots of cuddles from Tina, he wasn't as grouchy and grumpy as he had been these last few months. Nursery had really settled him down. He was still having problems, but it was taking it a step and a day at a time.

Mel had to be at the venue early, she had grabbed Julie as well. Mel and Lesley had sorted out that Lesley would take the flowers to the venue with Julie in the van, unload it, then go onto the other wedding where Fiona was going to be. It just meant Andrea was in the shop on her own for the time being, but these things were never all day.

Just get everything ready and head over to wherever the bride was going to be, drop-off her flowers, buttonholes and then when they get to their reception venue, all of the arrangements would have already been done. But this time for Mel, time was of the essence. Thankfully she had Julie there as well. Also Julie had worked for Mel for a few years now, so she knew how it worked and had often come along with Lesley to sort out the flowers.

Mel was already there and had started on sorting out chairs and stuff. Tina and George had to do a seating plan to make sure this one didn't sit with that one and that, mainly on George's side. Julie came in with boxes of flowers. "Mel, Lesley has already taken the bouquets and buttonholes to yours once she dropped me off, so it's just these ones too."

Mel had already been to the church earlier and they had done lovely arrangements, so it was only the venue to do. Tina had some lovely lilac, purple and cream flowers. Mel had done her best for her sister. They put various arrangements on the tables. She had also had the balloon people in, for lilac and cream, balloons, so you either got a balloon arrangement on your table or a flower arrangement, which made a lot of sense and also a bit less work for Mel and Julie.

She had made a beautiful running garland across the whole top table, which was full of flowers, but she also used ivy as well, to help it trail where she wanted, it was easier to work with. Three massive table arrangements with drops of pearls on them. They looked beautiful. Mel stood back to admire her handiwork and so did Julie.

"You have done her proud, Mel. The flowers are beautiful." Over the top table, was balloons, but also some twinkly lights that Nicholas would love if he was laying in his pram or pushchair.

"Right, missus, we had better get going. We have the hair stylists and make-up artists at ours in half an hour and I am still here, but I think we did a good job. Now can I drop you home, Julie?" Mel asked.

"No, Ted, is picking me up, then I am heading home to get ready. See you at the church, Mel," said Julie as she picked up her cardigan.

"Bye, Julie. Yes, see you at the church," Mel replied, who now had to dash home. She jumped in the car and off she went. When Mel got in, it was chaos. There were kids running up and down the stairs; nan was trying to make tea; all of the bridesmaids were there with their mums, who were already ready. Mel climbed over the two sitting on the floor.

Elaine had just got there with Todd and she was trying to stay out of the way of the other kids. Tina was upstairs having her hair done. Mum was running around just as nutty, trying to keep things under control. Mel went upstairs to see Tina. Nicholas was in his cot, happy to see her. She put her arms out and he grabbed them and tried to get out of the cot. He could hear all of the commotion but wasn't sure if he liked it or not.

So Mel went into her mum's room to see her sister, in her dressing gown, with her hair up. Her hair was different to Mel's. While Mel was a brunette, Tina was blonde and her hair looked lovely, whatever style she had. She had a tiara, so had it raised at the front to give volume also to help hold the tiara in place. Then she had the back up to a really old-fashioned style but it really suited her and a few cascading curls at the sides.

With the veil on, it would look really classy. The bridesmaid dresses were all up in nan's room, but she didn't want the little girls in their just yet, they would be ready too early and then up to too much mischief. The bridesmaids' mums had all left now. Nan had said that they would manage with the girls and if they could go straight to the church, that would be great.

"Phew, they were much harder to deal with than the kids," said nan.

"I need to get in the shower. Can someone look after Nicholas, I don't want to put him back into his cot. Also has he had a wash or bath yet?" Mel asked.

"Not yet, Mel. As you can see, it was a bit of a circus when you came in," said nan.

"Tina, do I have time to get Nicholas bathed and get ready before your photographer gets here?" Mel asked a little nervous.

"Oh, Mel, what do the flowers look like, I forgot to ask you?" Mum asked.

"Oh, Mum, they are beautiful, so are the balloons, missus," said Mel to Tina.

"I thought the kids would like them!" Tina said. "I know that Nicholas doesn't really but..."

Mel interrupted, "He will at the top table though, thanks, Teen," giving her a kiss.

"What?" Nan asked.

"Wait and see, Nan. It's really beautiful," said Mel. "Now I need to get me and Nicholas sorted. See you in a little while," Mel said as she exited the room. She had grabbed her things and Nicholas'. There were always towels in the bathroom.

She thought if she bathed him first, it wouldn't take long, no playing today though. Then she would quickly shower, she could watch him at the same time. He was a good boy, he wouldn't try and move or leave the room. She got his bath on, stripped him and then tested the water.

She still did that, she didn't want to take a chance on him being scalded. No, the temperature was fine. She popped him in, washed his hair, washed his body down, rinsed him and then took him out of the bath, popped him in his towel and dried him. She put on a nappy and let him sit on a dry warm towel, where she could see him.

She wouldn't be long, it's amazing what you can do in a few short minutes. There done. Nicholas hadn't moved thankfully and she popped a towel round her and picked up Nicholas and then went into their bedroom. Elaine was in with Tina. The older bridesmaids had their dresses on and were having their hairs done.

Tina had gone for a few curls, with some gyp into their hair, so it looked plaited, but wasn't and the flowers were exposed on the top. They all looked lovely. The flower girls had their baskets, but nan wouldn't let them hold them until they were getting into the car. So, once they were downstairs, they had to sit down on the sofa until the photographer came.

By the time Mel had dried off, it was time for her to have her hair and make-up done. Thankfully her hair was clean. Everyone else had been done and Mel was last. The middle bridesmaids had gyp also in their hairs but on side clips, Mel had managed to sort all of these out. Also Tina had gyp in her hair at the back, so when she was at the aisle there was something for everyone to see in her hair.

Mel had her hair up, similar to Tina's, but she like the middle ones had gyp clips. Mel had those in her hair about three of them, they looked lovely. Elaine had shorter hair, so she had gyp clips at the side of her hair. She had thick curly hair so they sat well. Once Elaine was finished, she went downstairs to get Todd ready into his suit.

Nicholas's was downstairs as well, so they would get ready at the last minute. They both weren't too keen on suits, but as long as it looked alright when the photographer came. Tina wasn't too bothered for them, because she understood what it was like for them both. Nan and Mum were getting ready in Mel's room, because there wasn't any more room otherwise.

Nan wore Royal Blue and Jean wore a soft pink. George's mum had changed her mind about the pink. She was going for the tangerine, a bit bright, but she wanted to make an impact. Both the ladies came out a few minutes later with their hair, make-up and outfits on. It was lovely to get ready to go and celebrate and it seemed like they were doing that a bit now.

They went to see Tina, but she wouldn't let them come in. She had called for Mel. Elaine watched Nicholas for her. Nan and Mum came downstairs a little upset, they had wanted to see Tina before she came down, but Tina wanted to surprise them downstairs. Mel went into her room, she looked absolutely stunning.

Her bouquet was downstairs in the kitchen with all of the rest. Mel helped her with her dress and train, then they made their way downstairs. Mel told Tina to stay on the step, so she could get the door, then come down slowly, to stand in front of the door. Mel opened it and Tina walked in. Mum and nan both gasped, they were stuck for words, for once.

"Oh, Tina, you look so beautiful. Her dress, hair, it just all looked beautiful," said nan, tearing up and probably not for the first time that day.

"Tina, you look absolutely amazing. I am so proud of you, to call you, my daughter!" Jean said also tidying up her make-up because of the tears. Everyone was getting tears, happy tears though. Ding dong, ding dong, went the front door bell. Elaine was closest so she opened the door, it was the photographer.

They stopped crying and wiped their eyes and waited for the photo guy to put them where he wanted. He took the photos they had asked for. He had already been to George's mum's. He took about forty five minutes, then the two white Rolls-Royces pulled up. "Oh wow, Tina, look at those cars, talk about going in style. Now will we all fit in there?" Nan asked.

"Of course we will. Mum's coming with me, the rest of you in the other one. I think actually you lot had better get to the church," said Tina. Mel had brought the flowers, posies and buttonholes in, gave everyone theirs, put nan's and mum's on, then Nicholas and Todd's on. Well popped them into the holes for buttonholes rather than put pins in their suits. Not because of holes they would make, but in case they hurt themselves with them.

Elaine and Mel took the boys pushchairs, which they gave to Angela and Julie, when they got to the church. They knew once they walked down the aisle, the boys could go in them. So, they all bundled into the cars, Mum and Tina were left for a few minutes before they got into their car.

Jean made sure she had everything, also the keys, so they could get back in once the celebrations were over. Jean opened the door and the neighbours were outside waiting to get a glimpse of the bride. When they saw her, it was lots of 'aahhs and oohs', some wishes of congratulations. They made their way down the path and the driver had opened the door for Tina to climb into the back seat. Jean helped with her dress, then gave her bouquet.

Mel had really done a great job with the flowers they were beautiful. The driver shut the door. Once they were both in, then they made their way to the church. It was a slow drive, the photographer was there had wanted a group photo of the bridesmaids before the bride got there. He took a few, because the girls were acting up little, they couldn't wait to get down the aisle, so everyone would look at them in their pretty dresses, well the little ones did.

Tina and Jean's car pulled up. The girls went over to where she was, getting out of the car, but the photographer wanted another photo of her getting out of the car with her veil over her face. Once he had finished, Tina got out of the car. Jean got out from the other door, then they straightened themselves up, sorted out Tina's dress and train.

Then they started to go towards the entrance of the church, but the photographer wanted another photo just like that before they entered the church. Then he let them move on. Jean was giving her daughter away. They walked into the church and the music started, they had the wedding march going in.

The walk seemed to take forever, with the bridesmaids, especially the little ones, but they got there. Everyone was looking at them and smiling. George had a beaming smile on his face from ear to ear, when he saw Tina. She did look beautiful. Mel helped her remove her veil over her face to behind her tiara, so she could see clearly and George could see her face properly.

The music started for the first hymn. *All things bright and beautiful,* they sang. Once the singing had stopped, the vicar had started his sermon of the wedding. Once he asked, "If anyone had any lawful reason that these two people couldn't marry?" Nobody looked round or said anything, he continued and asked Tina and George to look at each other and say their vows.

They were both word Perfect, not a mistake at all. Then they sang again; this time, *Amazing Grace.* Then they had to go into the area at the side of the church to sign the wedding register. The wedding party followed and everybody else of the congregation then sang the 23rd psalm, the lord is my shepherd. Once it had finished, Tina and George were now married.

Jean had the marriage certificate in her handbag as it's given to the bride. So now with her bouquet back in her hand and George on her right-hand side. Their exit music started Signed, sealed, delivered, *I'm yours* from Stevie Wonder. They didn't quite walk back down the aisle, but had a little dance as they were going. Nan thought it was hilarious, the bridesmaids followed in the same style and so did Nicholas and Todd in their pushchairs.

Everyone filed outside for their photos. The photographer asked for everyone to let Tina and George stand in the doorway of the church, with the hint ready to throw their confetti at them, so he could catch the photo. "One, two, three, go," he shouted, every hand in the air threw the confetti, it was everywhere, "Got it" said the photographer, then he got everyone into the photos he wanted.

Tina, George, his mum and dad; Tina, George, her mum and nan, then with Mel and Nicholas; then with his side and her side. It was never ending photographs. Thankfully Elaine and Mel had brought with them bottles of drinks for the boys, including spares, just in case, because it was hot out; it was the end of June.

Thankfully the vicar's verger came out with water for everyone to drink. Thankfully it had been in the fridge for a while, so was a welcome sight to everyone.

The photos went on for about another half hour or so, then everyone made their way to the reception. The photographer got a few photos of Tina and George at the entrance of the car with the door open. Then he had a bright idea, to make it look like the groom was pushing the car from the back and the bride was trying to hail a lift, the car had its bonnet up. A great sight to see if you didn't know what was what.

Then they got a couple of them at the bus stop, then outside a police station, where two policemen had put the Tina in handcuffs and George was telling her off. The policemen thought it was really funny. Thankfully they had the key to the handcuffs, but it made some great photos for later on. They then headed to the reception, and as tradition goes, nobody was allowed into the wedding breakfast room until the bride and groom arrived.

They pulled up outside, had a quick kiss and a hug, then they made their way out of the car, with George's help, Tina managed it. He also held her bouquet, because he didn't want his bride to fall over because of her holding it and trying to get out of the car. He helped her with her dress once she was out of the car.

They walked towards the entrance and two men opened the double doors for them. They walked into cheers from the crowd of family and friends. They made their way to the room, Tina had look round. She loved what Mel and the balloon lady had done.

It looked stunning and she asked the photographer if he would get a few photos of the room, with them both standing at the front of the top table. It looked absolutely stunning. Tina had tears down her face when Mel saw her a few minutes later. "Oh, Tina, you don't like it?" Mel said.

"No, Mel, I love it. You have done an absolutely amazing job on the flowers. Thank you so much," she said hugging her older sister. Mum and nan had got into the room now and so had George's mum and dad, so they could get ready for the line-up to welcome their guests to their wedding breakfast. First it was Tina, George, Mum, nan, George's mum then his dad.

Nicholas was at the top table with Mel, Elaine and Todd. Tina said it was ok for them both to be seated before everyone else, because she didn't know how the boys would deal with it, but so far so good. Once the good wishes were done, everyone took their seats and sat down waiting for Tina and George to sit down.

Angela and Jim sat near the top table, so they could be by their daughters to two younger bridesmaids and also the other parents of the other girls. But other than that, Tina decided to mix up the tables a bit. That way people who didn't know each other would then make new friends or at least acquaintances for the rest of the day or even longer if they got on well.

The food was then served. Tina had arranged for prawn cocktails or clear soup to start, followed by a roast chicken dinner, then raspberry cheesecake with a raspberry coulis or Lemon tarte with lemon drizzle all over with touch of icing, or chocolate profiteroles with extra chocolate sauce. Tina had tried to cater for everyone. After that if anyone had any room, there was cheese and crackers and then coffee. That was just the meal, not including the evening buffet, but that was a couple of hours away.

Once everyone had eaten their meal, then came the speeches. Jean got up to speak for Tina's side, then Jim, George's best man, got up and said a couple of funny stories about George over the years. Then mentioned Jonathan, Jim's brother, who when George first met him, didn't realise he was Jim's brother but thought he was the waiter taking their order for their food. They all had a laugh about that. Mel hadn't known that Jim had a brother, who was rather dishy.

Then they toasted the bride and groom and the bridesmaids and maid of honour, then gave out gifts. Jonathan didn't realise either that Tina had a sister and a pretty one at that, with a very good figure. Tina handed Elaine and Mel something for both of the boys.

She wanted to get them some sort of jewellery, but didn't think it fitting for them. They would never wear them and they would be stuck in a drawer forever, so she got them both books that they both liked. Nicholas got trains and planes. Todd got ones on caterpillars and butterflies. Tina and George got kisses from both of the mums; nobody really took much notice except the people who knew what was what.

Elaine's mum had been invited, so Elaine had a bit of help with Todd at the wedding if she wanted to dance at all. Not that Jean and Marge wouldn't have jumped in if they needed to be, they had both become rather fond of Todd and Elaine. They both knew that that could have been Mel, with not many people to help her.

There was some background music on. Some of the children were up dancing, but people were mostly chatting. Some catching up on their lives, people were busy and sometimes the only time they get to catch up is as events as this. The staff at the venue pushed some of the tables towards the wall, as to give more space for dancing.

It was time for the first dance now. Tina and George had chosen *Can't help falling in love* by Elvis Presley. They shuffled round the dance floor looking at each other's eyes. They looked madly in love and Jean and Marge were slowly tearing up now, thank goodness they had lots of tissues ready to hand. Once the first dance was done, now it was time to get the disco up and ready, thank goodness he was all set up and raring to go.

The music flowed, the drinks flowed and everyone was enjoying themselves. Mel had picked Nicholas up and was going to dance with him. Elaine did the same, Tina and George were so pleased to see the children up with their mums dancing. Nicholas had spotted the lights on the balloons over the top table and he was mesmerised.

Jonathan was watching Mel from one of the tables. He was hooked, she was so beautiful, and her boy was an absolute darling. Thing is with Jonathan, he was shyer than Jim. Jim, Angela and their girls were up dancing on the dance floor, they loved to dance.

The other little boys on the dance floors, were playing at being planes. Zooming in and out of everyone. A couple got told off and told to sit down for a little while and have a drink as they were getting hot.

Mel had picked Nicholas up, and was dancing nicely while he was watching the lights, while being twirled round by his mum. "It's now or never, Jonathan," he said to himself. He got the courage up to ask Mel and Nicholas to dance. Mel said yes and away they were. Nicholas was still looking at the lights, so Mum came over and took Nicholas back to the table so he could see them and Mel could dance with Jonathan in peace.

It wasn't a slow dance as such, but still an enjoyable experience for them both. Jonathan wasn't a bad dancer, at least he didn't have two left feet like Terry did. They moved around the dance floor quite nicely. They had put on a couple of slow ones, so the couples could have some nice quiet times.

It also gave a chance for Jonathan and Mel to talk. He asked Mel what she did before she had Nicholas. She told him about the flowers at the wedding and that she had her own shop etc. Then he told her about himself; he was 36, single for a little while, had his own flat and worked on the other side of town, in a special school for disabled kids.

Mel's heart was in her mouth. "No kidding, which one? Do I know it? Do you enjoy your work?" Mel asked. She was full of questions, she hadn't spoke as much all day. She had found someone she could talk to about Nicholas without frightening them off. Jonathan answered all of her questions.

He wasn't at the same school that Nicholas would be going to and he had heard of it. He said it was a very good school and that she had chosen well. "What made you go into that profession, if you don't mind me asking you, Jonathan?" she asked him.

"Well, I always wanted to teach children, and when I was doing my experience, I had to work in a special school and I absolutely loved it, so that was my chosen field," he replied. Jonathan was a lovely quiet man, he had a great sense of humour and Mel seemed to like his company. Nan and Mum were watching them both like hawks and nan had seen something, she hadn't seen in Mel in a long time, she looked happy.

She hadn't been there at Tina's night out, but Jean had said that the guy seemed nice enough, but she wasn't sure if it would lead to anything. Nan nudged Jean. "Hey, Jean, have a look over there," she told her.

"Over where?" Jean didn't know where she was looking towards.

"Not over there, Jean, but over that way," she said pointing in the direction of Mel and Jonathan.

"Oh, well that's a turn up for the books," said Jean.

"Jean, did Mel look that happy around that guy at the restaurant as she does now?" Nan asked.

"No, she didn't, but saying that, she was only talking to him for a little while, not dancing round on a dance floor for what three songs so far. Good job we have Nicholas!" Jean said.

"Oh, come now, Jean. When on earth does Mel get a chance to dance with a tall dark and handsome sort of stranger," suggested Nan.

"Not ever really, let her enjoy herself. Anyway, this little one needs changing, so I will take him to the loos," said Jean. Taking Nicholas to the toilet to change his nappy, he seemed a bit happier in his suit. Well, they took his jacket off and that was on the back of Mel's seat. Mel was busy dancing, so was Tina and George.

Then the DJ changed the dynamics of the music and put on tons of dance staff, to get the party really going and everyone up on the floor. Mel wanted to sit down. She invited Jonathan to sit with her and meet Nicholas, but when she go to the table she noticed that he wasn't there. "Mel, don't worry, your mum has taken him to get his nappy changed. He's fine. Now who is this young man?" Nan asked.

"Jonathan, this is my nan and mentor I suppose, Marge," Mel told him.

"Nice to meet you, Marge," he said.

"Nice to meet you too Jonathan, so I take it your Jim's brother, older or younger?" Nan asked.

"Older, but just by two years. He has the brains, I got the looks?" Jonathan chuckled, but so did nan. She liked this man and thought that he would be great for Mel. Mum came back with Nicholas, who was wide awake. Mel introduced Jonathan and he said hello and shook her by the hand, then kissed her on the cheek.

He bent down to say hello to Nicholas, who looked at him and then continued to look back at the twinkly lights. "Nicholas, would you like to see what I have in my pocket?" Jonathan asked. Mel, nan and Mum all looked. He pulled out this weird thing, it looked spongy, it was long and thin, but a bit springy.

"Oh, don't worry, Mel, it's a chew stick, not like what dogs have, but it's a great distraction for children who can't sit still for long. It won't hurt him," Jonathan added. He handed it to Nicholas who took it straight away and put it straight into his mouth.

"Oh, Mel, don't worry, its brand new, nobody has had it. I normally put a couple in my pocket just in case. You never know with some children, some take them, some push them away." He handed one also to Elaine for Todd, who did exactly the same thing. His was blue and both of the mum's were astounded with what they both saw, but happy that the boys were comfortable with Jonathan and also that they knew what to do with it, or was it just that babies of all ages, put things straight into their mouth.

Jean and Marge were talking to Elaine, asking her how things were going, they had stopped doing tests for now, just waiting for the results to come back, but her and Todd were doing OK. She was still going to building bridges. "Elaine, why is it called Building Bridges?" Nan asked.

"Because it builds bridges between special and mainstream, so everyone gets a fair bite of the cherry. You see some of the kids who have issues who go to mainstream school, don't seem to get the same help, so they help with that, but they aren't miracle workers. They can only do what they can, sometimes the social workers can help, but not all of the time."

"So parents are referred to Building Bridges, who are a great help. Well, you know what Mel has told you about them."

"Yes, I have heard of Building Bridges. they are a great charity. Sadly there isn't enough of those sorts of charities around," interrupted Jonathan.

"He seems to know his stuff, Jean," said Marge.

"Oh yes, he does," added Elaine. "He's very good at information and what's going on with the system. He's seen it for years, but he said small steps can make big changes," Elaine told them both.

The wedding was already in full swing, but it was getting late, some people had already left the party. Mel and Jonathan were dancing some more, they were getting on really well. Mel could see where she was dancing from that Nicholas had fell asleep. She wondered if they should make a move.

"Mel, if you want to take him home, it's ok with me. I can drive you if you want. I promise I won't make a move, but just want to make sure you both get home, ok?" Jonathan offered. Mel thought it would be a good idea. Jean and Marge were going to stay for a bit longer, didn't want it to look like to Tina that they were all going at once.

Mel went over to Tina and George and said she was going to take Nicholas home. They said that was fine, they loved the flowers and thanked her again for doing them for them. "So how are you getting home then?" George asked.

"Jonathan has offered, you know Jim's brother," said Mel.

"Oh OK, well then, we will talk tomorrow and you can let me know all of the juicy details, missus big sister," said Tina with a huge grin across her face.

"Oh, stop it. Thank you both for a beautiful day and a wonderful do. It was fantastic and you look absolutely stunning, both of you," she added so George didn't get upset. "Mum and Nan are staying a while yet," added Mel.

She went back over to her seat, got Nicholas's all sorted, made sure she had his stuff and Jonathan helped her with it all. He said goodnight to Jean and Marge, also to Tina and George and then all three of them left the party. His car was just outside, and up the road a little bit. His car was a Mondeo and there was room for Mel and Nicholas in the back.

He didn't have a car seat, but Mel felt confident with him on her lap. She couldn't do the seatbelt up over the two of them, but she took her chance. She knew she shouldn't have done, but what else could they do, her car seat was at home. Jonathan drove very carefully. They were home in no time.

Jonathan opened the door, also the boot and took out Nicholas' buggy. Mel just carried him inside; Jonathan took the buggy and Nicholas's bag. Thankfully she had her keys in her little bag, she had left her posy at the reception, but she knew her mum or nan would pick that up. Mel opened the door and stepped inside.

She put Nicholas down on the sofa safely, so he wouldn't roll off, then went to collect what Jonathan had. She thanked him and kissed him on the cheek. He left his number, so Mel could call him, when she was ready. He knew she had a lot on her plate, but he also didn't want to rush her.

She waved him off when he got to his car and she then closed the door and went to put Nicholas pyjamas on him, so he would be comfortable when he was in his cot. Mel was getting him a new bed this week, this cot was getting too small for him. She sorted him out and put him to bed, then went downstairs, leaving the night light on, so he wouldn't get scared in the dark.

Mel went into the kitchen and put the kettle on. She also went back upstairs to take off her bridesmaid dress, thankfully she could reach the top of the zip, put on her pyjamas, then went back down to make her tea. She had a great day and Tina looked like she was so happy, even happier than when Mel married Terry. So she knew she would be with George for a very long time. She downed her tea, then put the cup in the kitchen.

The front door opened and it was nan and Mum, holding Mel's posy. "I didn't think you would be back so soon," Mel said.

"Well, once you had left all of a sudden, a lot of people did the same thing. So Tina and George are still there with a few of their friends, so we made tracks home. Tina is going to pop in tomorrow, with one of the flower arrangements from the table. She was trying to give them away, but everyone said the same thing, they couldn't carry it. You did a great job on those, Mel," said Mum.

"Yes, you did," chirped in nan.

"So Tina will be over sometime tomorrow, she said she's leaving a few for the venue as a thank you, but she wanted us to have a couple and the balloons with the lights too, but that's all going to be done tomorrow," said Jean. With that they all headed upstairs to go to bed, they were all shattered.

Nan turned off the lights downstairs and then walked upstairs to bed. She checked they all had their night lights on, before she turned the hallway stairs off. Mel checked on Nicholas, he was fast asleep, obviously worn out from the day's events. Mel got into bed and snuggled down under the covers, thinking about Jonathan.

He was a really nice man. She had a great conversation with him, so it was quite nice to see how this was going to blossom. She turned over and turned out the night lamp. Jonathan had just got into bed and he was already thinking of Mel. He hoped she would call him in a few days, especially as the holidays were upon them soon.

***

The next day, everyone was up bright and breezy and they were all in great moods. The doorbell went and it was George and Tina, fully loaded up with their arms as full as they could be. Mel let them both in. "Hi you two, how are you both since last night?" Mel asked.

"We are fine, been busy though, getting what we needed from the wedding venue. They had already cleaned everything up, love them. They put the flower arrangements and balloons to one side, so we could pick them up this morning. Actually the place wasn't as bad as they had both thought it would be."

"So how many of these did you get then?" Jean asked.

"Well most of them. I left four there for the staff to take home and a couple of balloon ones also, so we are going to drop two off for George's mum and aunt, one for us at home. Then the rest here for you, oh and we got the twinkly lights off for Nicholas. You can put them round one of these branch tree things, that way it can be up all year round, rather than just at Christmas," said Tina.

"So what are you doing now?" Jean asked.

"Well, we were going to George's parents then back here, before we get ready to go to Barbados tonight," said Tina.

"Do you have time for a quick cuppa?" Nan asked, looking as though she wanted them to stay a little while.

"Yes, OK, Nan," said George.

"Cheeky," said nan.

"Let me lock up the car and make sure we have everything we need, then we can head over to mums after," George said as he left to lock the car.

"Oh, how did it go with Jonathan then, Mel?" Tina asked. "He's really stuck on you, you know" said Tina.

"How do you know that?" Mel asked.

"He told George last night, before he took you home," said Tina with an even bigger grin than she had before. They had their tea. Mel took the flowers out to the kitchen, so she could change the water. She heard Mum and nan talking about Jonathan.

"Yes but what about the one from the restaurant, Mum?" Jean asked.

"I thought about that one, what if me, you, Mel and Nicholas go there for dinner one night and see what happens. If I am right he will see us all and bolt out of the door. But don't say anything to Mel just yet. I think this Jonathan is a better bet for our Mel. This Greek guy seems a bit too good if you know what I mean," said Nan, shushing Jean when Mel returned to the sitting room.

"Mel, I was thinking about something," suggested Nan.

"Hmmm, what's that, Nan?" Mel asked.

"I was wondering, Mel, if we could go to that restaurant that you went to for Tina's hen, and I have always fancied that Greek food. What do you think? We could go in the week. I mean Tina and George will be away eating lovely exotic food in Barba dados," nan said.

"Nan, it's called Barbados, not Barba dados," Mel corrected her. "And yes, I think it would be nice to try something else and you can meet Andreas and let me know what you think of him," said Mel.

"But what about Jonathan?" Jean asked.

"I like Jonathan, Mum. I like Andreas too, but I don't know what I am going to do. Jonathan was great with Nicholas, Andreas hasn't met him yet. Anyway, what day did you want to go out then or rather evening I take it?" Mel suggested.

"Oh, what about Thursday? Nothing much happens on a Thursday. Do you want me to book a table?" Mel asked.

"Yes, please for four, no five," added nan.

"Five?" Mel enquired.

"Yes, we can't leave Nicholas behind," said nan.

"But nan that still makes four, you, me, Mum and Nicholas," said Mel.

"Do you know what, I was including our Tina in that number. Silly woman I am," said nan.

"No you're not, but its fine. I will book it for what about 8pm?" Mel asked.

"Yes, of course," said Mum.

Thursday evening was here in no time. Mel, Mum and nan had all got dressed up. Mel wore lovely black dress, Mum wore a blue dress and cardigan and Nan wore green, a light green. Nicholas always looked lovely in Navy blue too, so Mel had put him in a check shirt with red and navy going through it and navy cotton dungarees.

Mel drove them all there. Nan sat in the back with Nicholas, he was always good going out in the car. Mel pulled up and got out. Mum got out and opened the door for Mel to get Nicholas out of his car seat, and straight into his buggy, which nan had grabbed hold of the handles. Mel locked up the car and walked up to the restaurant. Mel saw Andreas inside.

He was a little towards the back. One of his staff opened the door for Mel. Andreas saw Mel with her family and then spotted Nicholas. He went round the back so he could watch, but not be seen. Mel, nan and Mum walked up to the table, they moved a chair so to get the buggy in, Mel didn't want to be any trouble.

Nan and Mum were at the table. Nan had seen a man move around slowly but watching their group, but not noticing he was being watched. Nan whispered to Mum and Mum looked in the direction of Andreas and nodded her head. He was watching Mel but mainly Nicholas. Edging his way out of sight, until he was gone, but one of the other waiters came over to take their order.

Mel had a soft drink and so did Mum and nan for the time being. She had brought Nicholas's drinks with her already. The waiter brought over their drinks. Mel made her excuses and took Nicholas to the bathroom to change his wet nappy. It was great that he was drinking lots of fluids mainly water, but if it went in at one end, it had to come out at the other.

She picked him up, his nappy bag, with wipes etc, asked the waiter where the toilets were and made her way there. She had spotted or thought she spotted Andreas in the kitchen, but she wasn't sure. She sorted Nicholas out, now he was fresh and clean. On her way, back, she noticed that it was Andreas and she went to wave to him. He put his head down and tried to ignore her.

Thankfully her mum and nan, didn't see this. She was going to enjoy her night out, but she now had no illusions about Andreas anymore. At least with Jonathan, she knew he was a genuine guy who made a beeline for her little boy, because he could see he was special.

They ordered their food. Mel never said anything to her mum and nan about Andreas. When it came, she made the same fuss of Nicholas as she would have done anywhere else. The funny thing was the rest of the waiters were really lovely. They asked if he needed anything particular to eat or to be cooked.

He had some bread with olive oil, also pitta bread, which they broke up for him, which he really seemed to enjoy. They didn't really have much on the menu that he would eat, so they made him a big plate of chips, the steak ones, so he wouldn't get them stuck in his throat. Nan had the Moussaka. Mum had the Kleftiko, so did Mel but she also had stuff vine leaves as well as Taramasalata Tzatziki, humus with pitta bread or bread sticks, to start with.

They all enjoyed their food; the waiters brought a bottle of Greek wine for them complimentary. By the time they had their starters and main meal, they couldn't eat another thing. Mel was really pleased with how the waiters were with Nicholas but the fact that Andreas didn't even come out to say hello, knowing that he was there and hiding. Mel thought that she would love to come back, but only if Andreas wasn't working.

Mind you she thought as soon as he would see her, he would hide again. They thanked the staff for their lovely service and said they would come back again. Mel left them a great tip, said goodbye and then they left, with one of the waiters opening the doors for her. She walked over to her mum and nan and then unlocked the car to go home.

Once they got in, nan said, "Well, we never saw your young man, Mel, did we?"

"Oh, he was there, Nan," said Mel, matter of factly. Nan and Mum looked at each other, they hadn't told her that they saw him when they got there. "Because he was hiding in the kitchen, the whole time. When I gave him eye contact, he put his head down. Funny though because his staff were really lovely with Nicholas."

"Now you know why I didn't want to tell him, not because I wanted to trick or trap him, but I had to wait until the time was right. Now I didn't know whether he would be there or not tonight, but look how he acted. Now Jonathan, look how he was with Nicholas. Completely different but definitely genuine. So am I going to see Andreas again? No. Will I call Jonathan, most definitely," Mel told them both.

They both had their mouths open. Every day, their girl surprises them.

Chapter 16

The next day, Mel knew that she liked Andreas, but not enough to start seeing him regularly, but when she met Jonathan, she liked him a lot, enough to call him, as he left her his number. So, she did. It was already July, and the summer holidays were going to start. Sometimes he worked over the holidays with projects and stuff, but not this year.

For some reason, he had some time off for himself. So, Mel asked to meet up with him and Nicholas, because Nicholas was still going to be at nursery. It was still a Monday-Friday thing. Well, Nicholas didn't do Thursdays. Anyway, they had arranged to meet up on Saturday and go to the park for a picnic and maybe feed the ducks.

Mel normally wouldn't have introduced Nicholas straight away but they met at the same time, and as Jonathan was already working with special needs children, it was already a start and definitely a talking point of conversation. So, Saturday came. Mel got Nicholas up a little later than normal. It was Saturday, so no rushing in the morning.

They were meeting Jonathan about lunchtime. She had made some sandwiches and brought pork pies, sausage rolls, some crisps for them and some softish ones for Nicholas. He couldn't eat normal crisps just yet, because they were still too sharp for him and he could choke on them. Mel also packed some squash and a couple of cans of fizzy drink, just in case he liked his caffeine.

As it was still summer, Mel put shorts and t-shirt on Nicholas with some ankle socks and sandals. On men it looks awful, but on little tots, well they can get away with it, but not for too long. She wore a summer dress, and sandals. She put a hat on Nicholas and brought sun cream with her. The highest factor she could get for Nicholas and about thirty for her.

She had good skin colouring and would tan, but she still wanted to protect herself. Tina, on the other hand, was fair skinned and blonde, so would have to have a high factor of sun cream, which Mum and nan had commented on, when they realised how hot it could get in Barbados.

With everything all packed, a sun umbrella on Nicholas' buggy, they were all set to go. The park wasn't far away, about a ten-minute walk. It was lovely and sunny out. Nicholas had his fisherman's hat on, that covered his neck at the back.

Nan always fussed to make sure he had everything he needed, enough water to drink, a blanket just in case it got cold. Nan meant well and Mel knew she wouldn't probably be in this position if she didn't have Mum and nan's total support. Not everyone was as lucky, as she had met at Building Bridges.

Mel turned round the corner and there was Jonathan standing there in his summer slacks in a soft beige and a cool blue short sleeved shirt, his dark curly hair. He looked so handsome. Mel was glad she went with her heart on this one. "Hiya, Mel, hiya, Nicholas," he said to them both, but bending down to Nicholas' level when he said hello.

Nicholas wasn't really talking much, so he just smiled at Jonathan. "That kid's going to break hearts with that smile and those eyes and eyelashes. Any girl wouldn't be proud to have those eyelashes of his," Jonathan told her. "How are you, Mel. Have you had a good week?" He asked.

"Yes, it's been great, busy. We went out for dinner at the restaurant where Tina had the hen do. Food was lovely. Nan wanted to go really, I think she felt she missed out by looking after Nicholas. Not that she would admit to that, but she did want to try some exotic food as she said," Mel replied.

"Then Nicholas had nursery. I went to Building Bridges on Thursday. Nicholas comes with me sometimes now, but that will stop once he starts school, but that's great, to enjoy more time with him. They have some great toys there, that he is now looking at. Also he's enjoying the books that we read there," Mel said.

They reached a lovely patch of grass. Mel pulled out the picnic blanket and put it down. She grabbed her cooling bag and started to take out the food. Nan had packed some paper plates for them and a couple of plastic cups for their drinks. Nicholas at the moment was still in the buggy.

Mel wanted to get the food sorted out before she got him out, because even though he hadn't done in the past, she didn't want him to run. She had seen it with a couple of the other children at Building Bridges and talking to some of the other parents, their children had started doing it. Once she had finished, she got him out and sat him on her lap. Well, partly, so he could sit a little bit independently.

Mel hadn't noticed but Jonathan also had a bag, he pulled out somethings for Nicholas to play with. "Oh, Jonathan, that's a thoughtful thing to do, thank you!" Mel said.

"It's fine, I wanted to bring a couple of things that may help with distraction, they are in my pocket," he whispered. "Just in case" he laughed. They had a lovely afternoon. Mel was finding out quite a bit about Jonathan. He liked to go out for walks and stuff; he liked holidays away in this country and sometimes abroad.

"Do you know what, Jonathan, I hadn't even thought about taking Nicholas abroad to a hot country. I don't know how he would cope with flying and the heat abroad is different to here. I have been away a few times, really just to Spain and Portugal, never anywhere as far as Barbados like Tina and George have, but good luck to them. I had actually wanted to go to the USA but that hasn't happened," Mel said.

"How come?" Jonathan asked.

"Life got in the way, with the business, then my marriage breaking down, then not being able to have a baby to having a baby but being on my own. Oh don't worry, it's what it is. I don't mind it. I do have a great support network and thank goodness that I have, but holidays since Nicholas has come along, hasn't really happened."

"Trying to get on with day-to-day stuff, then all of this extra stuff that has come along has sometimes been a challenge. But you rise up to it and then move onto the next one, because it hits you in the face like the obstacles on a course, get over one, there's another just right there. So maybe even thinking of a holiday, would be great. I mean we don't live near the sea, but I suppose we have only really had days out as such."

"Well, that's settled then!" Jonathan said. "We will have a holiday every year, even if it's a caravan site, or camping out and looking at the stars in the sky at night, while sleeping under canvas. Mel, it will be great and when you think you and Nicholas are ready, we can go on a plane somewhere. Even if it's a plane on the Isle of Wight, they used to do the little plane rides."

"You know however much for like twenty minutes up in the air, well they used to. If you both like it, we can try for something else further afield. You know start with France, Spain, Germany, Portugal, and then if you feel a bit more confident, then we could try for the USA, Disneyworld or Disneyland. I can't remember which one is in Florida, but you know what it will all be great," he told her.

Even though Mel had only met Jonathan, she felt that this is what she has been missing a man who could understand her and Nicholas. Now she wasn't that gullible to think that they were going up the aisle just yet, but it was possible to have something, to aim for a goal as such, but these were dreams for the future, for when Nicholas was a bit bigger.

They had been out for a few hours, and even though Nicholas was asleep, he was still napping in the afternoon, he had loved the couple of toys that Jonathan had brought with him. He had them one in each hand. They walked back slowly, talking constantly about different things. Mel didn't realise that she and Jonathan had so much in common.

They both liked the arts, walks out and about, nice food, talking about faraway places, that Mel had only read about but never really had an opportunity to go to. Jonathan walked them both back home. Mel had offered for him to come in for a cuppa but he said, maybe next time. They had arranged to meet again the next Saturday. He had some stuff too the following day, for work, but would make time for both of them then.

"Mel, have you thought where you would like to go on Saturday, there is a fete in town if you would like to go. See if Nicholas likes it and how he deals with crowds," Jonathan told her. They said goodbye. Jonathan leaned in and kissed Mel on the cheek, and also now he had her number, he could call her.

Mel took Nicholas indoors. "Well?" Mum asked, with nan nudging her.

"Well, what?" Mel asked, a bit coyly.

"How did it go with Jonathan?" They both asked.

"OH, Mum, Nan, he's such a darling. We have been talking lots today. He asked if we had been on holiday. I said since Nicholas, no, not really. He said well, we will have to do that every year," she said to them both.

"Do what?" Nan asked.

"Have a holiday every year, whether it's a caravan site or camping and then even maybe abroad if Nicholas can deal with it. Not all autistic children can, you know," she said. Mum and nan looked at each other and smiled.

"Well that's good then. It sounds like he's looking into the future a bit though, Mel," Nan admitted.

"Yes, I know. I was thinking the same thing, then I thought, when have I had a man think of holidays and stuff for the future but also the present at the same time? I haven't, Nan, Mum. Terry left me. Andy, well that's different, but meeting Andreas last week, look how that turned out. He couldn't look me in the eye because my son is different."

"To actually find a man nan, who puts my needs, my son's needs, thinking about him with crowded places, would he be able to fly. Yes, I think if this works out, this guy is a keeper. He's also very good looking!" Mel added, both nan and Mum agreed with her there.

"Well, I wouldn't kick him out of bed," remarked nan.

"Nan, I am shocked," said Mel, with her arms folded across her chest, laughing. They all burst out laughing.

"Mum, I have never been so shocked in all of my life," said Jean, holding back the laughter tears, but not doing it very well. They went into the living room. "Mel I have just made some lemonade, want some?" Nan asked.

"Oh yes please, it's really hot outside," she said.

"Mel what's that in Nicholas' hands?" Mum asked.

"Oh that is a couple of special need toys that Jonathan thought that Nicholas might like," Mel replied.

"Jean, I think we need to get new hats and outfits!" They giggled together.

"What are you pair like?" Mel quizzed.

"Well, Mel, he does seem like a keeper, bringing stuff for your son, that he knows will help him. You want to hold onto him and don't let him bloody go. You have definitely got a good one here," Mel agreed, she thought the same. With that she heard Nicholas stirring, so she got up to see him. He was smiling and held his hands up in the air with his new toys in them.

"Mum, I think I will get a box or a container of some sort," said Mel.

"Why, love?" Jean asked.

"Well, if Jonathan does see a lot more of Nicholas', it would be great to have his special toys all together. What do you think?" Mel asked.

"Good idea and that way, if he does get distressed at all or anxious, his stuff will be altogether and at hand," Mum replied. Mel nodded her head in reply.

***

Over the next few weeks, Mel and Jonathan went out rather a lot. Nicholas came along too. They went to the fete, but they went when it first opened, so it wouldn't be busy. When it did start to fill up more than half, Nicholas was starting to get anxious, with Jonathan's help, Mel had noticed a pattern with Nicholas. She would have noticed it herself, but not the pattern of it happening. Sometimes these things can slip passed without you realising it, so was grateful for Jonathan's help.

He actually was more help than he realised. Mel was still keeping a diary for this sort of thing, because she would be able to look back later on and see how far Nicholas had come. This was more for herself than the doctor, who was always supportive when she went to see him, about some ailment or other. So, when Mel got back from the fete, she documented everything, for how Nicholas was when they got there.

She noticed he was getting a bit ratty, when more people were arriving, but when it was over half full, she knew it was time to take him away from the situation. Thankfully, Jonathan was also watching Nicholas's behaviour, not that he was being naughty, but how this situation could quickly arise to something much bigger escalating, before it got to a meltdown. Jonathan had told her about these things and how quickly it can change and happen.

She had told him about the Early Bird Course. He had said to her, that it gets full up quickly and can have a big waiting list, which is probably why she hadn't been contacted about it as of yet. "But don't worry, Mel. If they have suggested it and they know you're interested, then it shouldn't be a problem. Just the waiting game, I'm afraid" he told her.

He knew so much about the system, but as Jonathan had told her, sometimes they change a lot of it and you have to start again. If there are new courses, they want to trial out first, but it depended on where you lived and how much there was of a need of it at that time. Nan and Mum were always on hand to look after Nicholas for Mel if her and Jonathan wanted to go out, he was becoming a bit more of a fixture at home as well as George.

Tina and George had a great honeymoon. Nan had suggested if they were thinking about the patter of tiny feet yet. "Not a chance, Nan, not just yet. We want to enjoy our married life for a little while and have a few big holidays. Oh my days, Nan, you would have loved the Caribbean. It was great," said Tina. "I thought you went to Barbadadosdos?" Nan said a bit confused.

"Nan, Barbados is in the Caribbean you know," replied George. He was taken to calling them Mum and nan now rather than Jean and Marge, and the ladies liked it very much.

"Eh, Jean, I think we are starting to be a bit outnumbered now," she said to her daughter.

"What do you mean, Mum?" Jean enquired a bit puzzled.

"Well, George, our Nicholas and now Jonathan. What if Tina and George have boys and no girls," said nan. "Well, it has rather been a lot of women and poor George coming into this lot until Nicholas came along. I'm surprised he wasn't a bit intimidated by us all," said nan.

"Who said I wasn't?" George suggested. They all started laughing.

"Er, so when did this all start then. I mean with Jonathan?" Tina asked rather nosily. Mel had explained what happened with Andreas but out of earshot of the men.

"Please don't say anything to George, Tina, I don't want Jonathan to think he was second best," begged Mel.

"I won't say anything, you silly mare. I think Jonathan is the best thing that's happened to you. Well since Nicholas, and you deserve to be happy, Mel, with what you have been through with Terry and then a single mum. Grab it with both hands and this conversation never happened, ok?" Tina added.

Tina and George went back to work, so they could save up for a couple of more big holidays. Then they had decided that even though they loved the flat, they actually wanted to buy a house, but they were going to try the other bank in town as they didn't want to have to ask Terry for a mortgage, but they were going to do that in a couple of years or so.

So while Tina and George were getting on with married life, Mel and Jonathan were starting to blossom. They had a couple of days out down the seaside. On the third occasion, he asked Mum and nan if they would like to come along as well. "There's nothing like dipping your toes in the sea, Marge," Jonathan told her.

They both said yes. They hadn't been to the seaside for years, with so much going on with the girls. They don't know what they did before Mel moved back home and Tina moved out to live with George, but they both knew that their girls had now finally landed on their feet.

***

"Nan, Mum, are you ready, we want to get on the motorway before it gets too busy," said Mel.

"Yes, we are coming don't worry. I was just making a flask of tea," said nan.

"Why?" Mel asked.

"Because we are going to the seaside and their might not be anywhere to stop," said Nan. Mel and Jonathan laughed. "What's the matter, have I said something wrong then?" Nan asked a bit puzzled.

"Nan, there are places there to eat, there are services along the motorway," said Mel.

"Oh, I didn't know that. Shall I leave it behind then?" Nan asked.

"Don't worry, Marge, we can have it in the car if you want, but…" said Jonathan.

"Yes, I know, I wouldn't have any near Nicholas, because he might try and grab the cup. Also we don't want to spend the whole day in A and E, now do we?" Nan asked. "No, we don't," she said to Nicholas.

Nan thought it was quite funny. Not funny ha ha but funny how quickly Jonathan has taken his role and place in the family. Him and Mel had only been together for a few weeks and it was like he had always been there.

They got to the seaside in record time. Even though it was in the holidays, so far it wasn't very busy. Once they parked in the car park, and all locked up. "So where do you want to go first?" Jonathan asked. He didn't want to feel like he was taking over.

He had just slotted in well with them and Mel knew that he had her and Nicholas's best at heart, also Mum and nan. "What about going down the front, then we can see what they have here. I know, Mel, that most seaside's are roughly the same, but some have different things to others."

"That's where we will start then!" Mel said.

"Let's have a walk along the promenade, then we can really see what they have here," suggested Mum. So that's what they did. Mel pushed Nicholas, whose eyes were like saucers. He liked all of the bright lights, but he didn't like the loud and high pitched noises that came from the arcades and some of the rides. He put his hands straight to his ears.

Jonathan was watching him really closely, to see his reaction to various things. "Mel, Nicholas needs ear defenders!" Jonathan told her.

"How do you? Never mind, where can we get them from?" Mel asked.

"Well, I don't think that they will have them here. It's more specialised but I can get him some if you want. At the moment, they only come in a lime green/yellow colour, which is great because you will be able to see him in the dark with then," said Jonathan.

"How come, do I need to see him in the dark?" Mel enquired.

"No, not because of infrared, but because they look a bit neon that's all. Your silly billy," Jonathan laughed.

"I will never be able to remember all of this stuff, Jonathan," Mel told him.

"Yes you will, it won't take long. The more that happens the more you will notice it and then you will see it coming before he does, so you will be more prepared," he told her. They went all along the promenade.

"Shall we take Nicholas down to the beach and let him dip his toes in the water, saying that, I wouldn't mind a little paddle," said nan. They headed down to the beach, there were some stones or rather big pebbles and some sand. Mel took Nicholas out of his buggy. Jonathan picked it up and carried it over. Jean found a nice spot to sit down.

Mel pulled off her sandals, she took Nicholas' sandals off, so did nan. Nicholas was watching what everyone was doing and was a little anxious. Mel put him down onto the sand so he could stand up, but he wouldn't stand up. He let his legs open as wide as they could so when she tried to lower him; his nappy nearly hit the sand and his legs and feet were either side of him. Mel knew this couldn't continue, so she picked him up and carried him.

Mel went to put him down so he could touch his toes in the water, but he spread his legs again. Nan started to laugh. "They do the funniest things, don't they?" She said. She had already taken her sandals off and was walking into the water.

Nicholas was watching her like a hawk, but wasn't moving yet. Once he looked around and saw other people in the water and watching nan, he was then a little curious, he lowered his legs a bit. "That's it, my boy, put your feet in. It's fun, you like a bath, well this is a bigger bath!" Nan told him.

He pulled his legs down a bit more, so that in the end, his feet or toes were just above the water. He dipped his toe in and let out a squeal, he pulled his feet up again, then lowered them a bit more. He had shorts on, so he didn't have to have his bottoms rolled up.

He again lifted his feet then lowered them again, he was starting to have fun. Nan was splashing her feet a little bit. "See, Nicholas, it's lovely and cool now, as it's a hot day," Nan told him. He smiled at her and then dunked his whole feet into the water. He loved it and then started splashing at it.

"Well, at least you know he likes the water, Mel," said Jonathan.

"He always has. He loves a bath, but this is a bit bigger, well a lot bigger than a bath. So I am glad he liked it," said Mel. "I just hope he likes the sand as much," she whispered. She didn't want him to hear her and go and put his legs up again. He was already heavier because he started to eat more food since he started nursery.

When Nicholas had enough, Mel had him by his hand and Jonathan had the other hand. They started to walk on the sand and Nicholas screamed. He didn't like it, he was trying to climb up Mel's leg. "Well, then, that's something else to add to the list," Mel had said to the group.

"Mel, it's the only way, its trial and error. You won't know if he likes something or not unless you do it. Try it, take him or let him try new things and also new foods and drinks, then you can eliminate them and try and re-introduce it later on," Jonathan also told the group. Nan and Mum knew that Mel had hit the jackpot with Jonathan, for all of his mindful knowledge, techniques of stuff, sensory expertise and sensory problems.

So now this was something for the pros and cons list. Pros—He likes the sea, cons—he doesn't like sand. After their trip down to the beach, everyone was starting to get hungry. "Fish and chips everyone?" Jonathan asked. Nan, Mum and Mel all nodded their head, they were hungry; it was all the sea air.

"What about Nicholas? Does he like fish and chips or we could get him something else or just chips if you want?" Jonathan asked. He was always tentative when he would speak to Mel about her or Nicholas. You wouldn't have thought they had only known each other a couple of months or so.

"I think chips, but let's see how big they are. I don't want him to choke on them," she said to him. They went into a fish and chip shop. They were able to sit down. Marge and Jean were both pleased, they didn't want to eat their food back down on the beach.

"What would everybody like to eat then?" Jonathan asked. They were all looking at the menu.

"I think I will have cod and chips, if that's OK, Jonathan?" Nan said. She went to get her purse.

"No, Marge, I'm getting this," Jonathan told her.

"Thank you, Jonathan, but I am getting this. You have paid for the fuel to get here today. Mel wouldn't let me give you any money towards it, so this here is on me for everyone. So have what you want, it's OK, honestly but thank you, " she said giving him a kiss on the cheek. Jonathan went a little bit red.

Jean and Mel also chose cod and chips. Nicholas had chips. Then Mel spotted the sausages in batter, but then she saw the saveloys. She thought that Nicholas might want to try one or a bit of one, it couldn't hurt could it. So, she ordered one of those for him and Jonathan ordered Rock and chips.

Tea all round, Nicholas had some juice in his bag and a couple of spares. Mel asked the lady if she could rinse out his cup, as it was a little dirty. Somehow, she got sand on it, goodness knows how.

Once they had finished eating, and had a second cup of tea, they had a walk into the town. On the way, they pass the funfair, nobody wanted to go on anything, Nicholas had already put his hands up to his ears again, it must have been hurting them. "Jonathan, why does Nicholas put his hands up to his ears?" Jean asked.

"It must hurt him. You see some sounds they can manage and some they can't. You hear a siren police, fire truck or an ambulance, they can have high pitched noises, which we can filter out but Nicholas can't. It can hurt his ears," he said. Nan looked horrified.

"Marge, it can hurt his ears, but it can't do any damage to his ears. On a sensory level, it's too much for him to deal with. So, he covers his ears. I will get him some ear defenders on Monday, it will help him I promise. It will also make him less anxious with the noise levels being lower," he told them.

"But do they work though?" Nan asked.

"Well, yes, they filter out the noise. It's like everything is slightly muffled, but you can still hear. You know when you have the workmen digging up the roads, they have to wear them. Not because of the high-pitched noise, but because of the vibrating sound and noise levels which are quite high. Those men would have hearing problems for the rest of their life if they didn't use them," said Jonathan.

"Oh OK, it makes more sense now. Can we get a couple of pairs of ear defenders then, just so we have a spare. I will pay for them," said Nan.

"Oh, Nan, don't worry, I will pay for them," said Mel.

"No, Mel, I might need to wear a pair once in a while. If Gladys keeps knocking on the window or when I am out in the garden and I don't want to talk to her, she can go on and on," she told them, with that they all burst out laughing. Nicholas was looking at them all with a weird expression on his face. They had walked to the town, but wasn't very impressed with it, so they took a different walk back.

"Hey Mum should we get some candyfloss to take home and some rocks and also a few souvenirs?" Mel asked.

"Great thinking batman," said Jonathan. They went into a little rock shop and had a look round. They all picked up what they wanted and then went to the till to pay. They all seemed to be having great time today.

"Anyone fancy another cuppa?" Nan asked.

"Yes please," they all agreed. They walked along this road and found a lovely little café, Mel had the apple pie and custard with her tea, so did Jean and nan. Nicholas had a soft gooey iced finger, Jonathan just had a coffee. They were chatting happily. They were all pleased with how the day had gone.

Nan and Jean were laughing with Nicholas. "Well at least now, when he wants one, we can get him a paddling pool, but no sand pit," said nan. They all burst out laughing. Nicholas was getting used to these outbursts of laughter; he didn't understand it, but he didn't need to. It was grown up chatter and laughter.

Once they finished their drinks and dessert, they made their way back towards the fun fair. Nicholas looked a bit more interested. "Shall we have a walk through, not to go on anything unless you want to," suggested Mel. They all agreed and had a slow walk back.

Nicholas loved all of the lights on the rides, but he did have his hands over his ears, just in case of the noise. They walked past the Waltzer, the ghost train, the dodgems, the swings, the big wheel and other various rides. They walked right through it. "Is there anything else you would like to do or do you want to start making tracks home?" Jonathan asked.

They all looked at each other. "Is there anything you would like to do then, Mel?" Mum asked. Nan nodded.

"No, unless you both want to?" she asked them.

"No, to be honest, I'm knackered and worn out, that sea air does get to you, doesn't it," said nan. So, they headed back to the car park and unloaded Nicholas' buggy, put everything in the boot of the car.

"Marge, did you want me to go and get your flask filled up with tea from that little café over the road there?" Jonathan asked.

"No, sweetheart, if I have any more tea, I will need the loo more than once on the way back. Let's wait until we get home, shall we?" she replied.

Chapter 17

Mel, Nicholas and Jonathan, were going out most of the summer holidays. Before they packed up, she had headed over to the school to pick up Nicholas' school uniform. You could still get it from the school—a Polo shirt with the school Logo and also the sweatshirt with the school logo. Mel couldn't believe how cheap it was. £3 for a polo shirt and £5 for a sweatshirt.

This was really because it was the smallest size, but even once it was washed, it still fit Nicholas with room for him to grow or chance to shrink it. They had gone out together on their own when Nicholas was at nursery, but Mel was told that the week before he was due to start school, he would finish nursery as it gave him time to forget the worker who was assigned to him. So he would be home with them for the last of the holidays, so Mel, Nicholas and Jonathan could spend some time together.

Mel and Jonathan were getting quite close. He told her that he felt like the luckiest man alive finding both her and Nicholas. Mel thought it was the other way round, her and Nicholas were lucky to find Jonathan. Anyway, it was getting near to the time where Nicholas would be leaving. He knew a party, because they had had them for other children for their birthdays.

So even though it was a bit loud, Nicholas did have ear defenders with his name on them. All of the other children in his class were aware that he was different, but they still tried to communicate with him with PECS—Picture Exchange Communication System. They had used A4 sized paper to get him used to it. He did really well with it, so they made them than half the size and on A5 paper. They left the ones already because they didn't know if they would have an autistic child coming their way again.

He had his party. Mel was invited to it, which the staff were pleased. "Now, Nicholas, this is the end of one chapter by leaving here and you will be starting a new chapter at Forrester Greenwood. We know you will love it there, but we will miss you. So, this is a little something from us at nursery," said Trudy, the lady in charge of his class.

She handed Mel a bag, with a book of photos of his classmates and the staff, a couple with him included. A bag with his name on it and a little case for his ear defenders, so they don't get lost. "We thought of practical presents, Mel, that way he wouldn't forget us. Put it in his baby box you have at home and then when he's a bit older, then show it to him. Also it shows you how far he has come," she added.

Mel had tears in her eyes. She didn't realise how much they had loved Nicholas. "Don't cry, Mel, it's the next step for you and him on your journey together," Trudy said. "Anyway, you will start me off," she added. Mel was overcome with emotion and felt overwhelmed by this beautiful gift to her boy.

When the party had wrapped up, she took him home. She still had tears in her eyes, but she was fine, they were all right. This was his next chapter for him and it was going to be a positive one. She was so chuffed, who would have thought how far they would have both come.

Who knew five years ago, her husband would walk out on her and she would have to start this new life without him. They had been together over fifteen years, but now that seemed a lifetime ago. Her and Nicholas had come so far, but they still had a long way to go. She got to the front door. She opened it and saw that Elaine was sitting down on the sofa with Mum and nan.

"Hi, Mel, how are you? Where have you just come from, because you look like you have been crying," asked Elaine.

Jean jumped up. "Mel, you OK, love?" she asked.

"Oh yes, Mum, I'm fine," she said picking Nicholas out of his buggy. "Hi, Elaine, how are you and how's young Todd here?" Mel asked.

"We are both fine, Mel, what about you?" Elaine asked.

"We have just come back from Nicholas' leaving party from nursery. Oh, Mum, you want to see what they got him," said Mel handing her mum the bag. There were oohs and aahhs. Nan came over to have a look. "Don't you think we should go into the living room rather than hang out here in the hallway?" Mel suggested.

They all walked into the living room. Nan disappeared into the kitchen to put the kettle on. She hadn't quite made the tea, but now she got Mel a cup out too. "So, what have you been up to, Elaine?" Mel asked again.

"Not much, getting on with it day at a time. You know what it's like, Mel," Elaine said. Mel nodded in agreement. "But I do have news now though," Elaine said.

"Oh come on then, Elaine, don't keep us in suspense," said nan, bringing in the tea, she put it on the table. Thankfully the boys never went near the tea.

"Well, I got Todd into a nursery. It's run by the council and there is extra help for him and he's to have physio twice a week there. His arms and legs don't have too much strength in them and they want to build him up. Physio is the first thing they offered, if that doesn't work then they will think again."

"But, Mel, it's a start. I have been pulling my hair out, now knowing what to do," Elaine told them. But was looking at Mel, maybe for reassurance.

"Are you still moving nearer to your mum's or staying where you are?" Mel asked.

"Yes, we are moving in a couple of weeks, so I need to start getting a wiggle on," Elaine said looking a little concerned.

"Well, we will help you of course, Elaine. Yes, and I am sure Tina and George will want to help," said Mel. "I can ask Jonathan. All the extra pair of hands will be making it a lot easier. Do you have a removal company or can you just get a van?" Mel asked.

"I think I have to get a van. I can't afford a removal company. I was going to ask George if he knew about vans and hiring them, but I haven't seen either Tina or George since they came back from their honeymoon," Elaine had suggested.

"They have both been working really hard. We haven't seen much of them either, but we can have a word with George if you like?" Nan asked.

"Yes, that would be great," Elaine sighed. They knew Elaine worried about stuff like that.

"Leave it with us, Elaine. Now what about boxes or tea chests do you have any?" Jean asked.

"No, I don't have anything yet," Elaine added.

"Don't worry, we will sort that out for you too. Maybe bring some boxes over in a day or two so you can get started. I'm sure I have permanent pens around somewhere," said nan rushing back to the kitchen. She returned with about five different coloured pens, black, blue and red. "These OK, Elaine? Take them and pop them in your bag. We can pick up some brown tape. We can go in the morning, can't we, Jean?" Nan nudged Jean.

Jean was thinking. "You know the Co-op up the road are always having deliveries. I am going to pop up there now and have a look. Mum watch Nicholas, come on, Mel, you can come with me," said Jean, grabbing her coat. Mel did as she was told. Elaine felt overwhelmed by how much this family have taken to her and Todd. She was so grateful.

"Er, young man, please can you tell me where you manager is please?" Jean asked. The man pointed her in the right direction. "Excuse me, are you the manager?" she asked a tall, sandy haired man, who looked rather dashing in his suit.

"Yes, madam, I am the manager. How can I help you today?" He asked Jean.

"I was wondering, you have deliveries most days I take it. What do you do with all of your boxes once you unload your deliveries?" she asked him.

"Well, we normally destroy them, why?" The manager asked her intrigued.

"I have a lady who has a disabled boy who is moving soon and she doesn't have any boxes. I was wondering if you wouldn't mind and be so kind to let us have whatever you had left," Jean said pleadingly.

"Hang on a minute," he told her. "Gary, do you have any boxes left or are they already in the crusher?" The manager asked.

"No, boss, I was about to do it," Gary replied.

"Good, how many do you have?" He asked.

Gary started counting, "Three, four, nine, ten, we have fifteen boxes. What do you want me to do with them?" Gary asked his boss.

"Do you have your knife? Could you open every slit on the box top and bottom, flatten them, then string them up so they look like a bundle," the manager told him.

"But they are different sizes," said Gary.

"How many different sizes?" He asked Gary.

"Three, I could put the three sizes together and make three bundles if that OK. Do we have string though?" Gary asked the manager.

"Yes, we do. I will help you. Excuse me, ladies, if you wouldn't mind waiting for a few minutes and we will see what we can do for you," he told them both.

"Mr Manager, how many deliveries do you get a week?" Jean asked quick thinking.

"Three, the next one is due in tomorrow then again on Tuesday. Would you like me to save those boxes for you too?" He asked.

"Not if it's too much trouble," said Jean rather coyly. Mel couldn't believe the cheek of her mum and nan sometimes, but you have to do what you need to do to get what you need, people were very kind and that helps. Nobody wants to see someone less fortunate than them struggle.

They came back about ten minutes later with the boxes tied up and a carrier bag. "You said the lady needs them for moving, so we have put string and some brown boxed tape in there. When we get the next lot, we will do the same and let us know if you still want boxes on Tuesday," said the manager.

He couldn't get anything else out, Jean had hugged him so tight. "Hang on a bit, missus, a thank you would have sufficed you know," said the manager.

"Thank you, Mr Manager, and yes we will need boxes tomorrow and Tuesday. I will let you know when we pick up the Tuesday boxes if we need anymore. Thank you again. You don't realise what you have done for our friend," said Jean. "See you tomorrow," she added.

Jean and Mel struggled a bit with the boxes. Mel had taken the big boxes and there were two bundles of smaller ones. Jean knocked on the front door, she had her hands full. Nan answered. "Well, I never," said Nan, who moved out of the way so her and Mel could get in the door.

"Leave them in the hallway, Mel, we can get George to drop these off later on," said Jean. "Now, Elaine, they are having another delivery tomorrow and again on Tuesday. Do you think this will be enough boxes? Don't worry, we will help you pack and sort what you need, but this will get you started. Now when you're ready to go home, I'm not kicking you out, but I want to make sure these boxes get to you this evening."

"Once you get Todd sorted out, we can give you a hand. It's a shame Todd doesn't have nursery, because you could really get stuck in. Hang on, Mel, what are you doing tomorrow?" Jean asked rounding on her.

"Nothing. Why? Oh, yes that will be fine. Todd will be fine here with me and Nicholas. They both know each other and we can put a video on if you want, maybe the train one or something," said Mel rather excited that she could help and still look after the boys. She had been around Todd enough.

Elaine looked really relieved, she burst into tears. "Jean, Marge, and Mel, I didn't expect all of this. How can I thank you?" she asked.

"Don't worry about that, my love, we just want to get you sorted. So is your family helping at all?" Nan asked.

"Yes, Angela has been great, having Todd on the occasion so I can go and get stuff done. Jim said he would help with moving, but it's just been a bit nuts. With dealing with the council about Todd's nursery place and then the physio and trying to get some more help from the doctor and health visitor," Elaine said.

With that, nan went over to the phone. She called Tina and George, who came over straight away, they both said they would help. George called Jim, who also came over with Angela. "Right now we have a bit of a plan then," said Jean.

"We have boxes, tape, string, permanent pens to write on the boxes, more boxes coming tomorrow and more on Tuesday, so what we now need is a van. At the moment, we need to get Elaine and Todd packed up, but so they can still sort of live there, because once you know you're moving and start packing, it's no longer your home but your place to get ready for the new one. It's just storage to put your stuff. So, when Elaine do you get the keys to the new place?" Jean asked.

"I get them next Friday, so we can do a lot of moving over the weekend," Elaine said.

"That's plenty of time. Do you need to have Todd's cot or bed dismantled then. What about your bed and furniture?" Jean asked at a hundred miles an hour.

"Ok, so if I get them in the morning, we can take some stuff over and work it from there!" Elaine said.

"Oh hold on, does it need decorating and carpeting then?" Nan asked.

"It's being done now, painting this week, so it can dry out and so it doesn't smell of paint for Todd's chest. Next week, it's being carpeted on Monday and Tuesday, so by Friday, nice and fresh and no paint smell," Elaine told them.

"Right, so if we can get vans from work. We could hopefully do it in two drops. Would you be ready to move in on Friday, Elaine, if we got this all done?" George asked.

"Yes, I think we could, if we get packing as much as possible. We could always come back on Saturday for any stuff we can't manage on Friday, so we aren't totally knackered," said George. Tina and Angela were going to go the following day and make a start on the packing up of stuff.

As nan had suggested, to give Elaine a chance to get Todd settled for the night and make a start on what she was taking and what she wanted packing the following morning. It wasn't worth her struggling tonight, when they had more hands tomorrow. "So, more boxes tomorrow. Angela, Tina, Mum and me go and help pack. Is there anything you need taking down that the boys could do tomorrow, Elaine?" Nan asked.

Elaine started to cry. She couldn't believe it, she came over to tell Mel her good news about Todd and his nursery place and they had sorted all of this out. "I can't thank you enough, all of you," Elaine said, she couldn't get any more words out.

"Now listen here, little sister, you should have said how stuck you were, but never mind it's all being sorted out now. So let's get you and little man here sorted. Mel will watch him tomorrow," said Angela.

"And on moving day," added Mel.

"Ok, thank you, Mel."

"It takes out the stress of it. I remember when I came back from having Nicholas, but that's for another day," said Mel.

"Mel, if we make a move with the boxes and take Elaine and Todd home," said Angela.

"Hang on, where did you get those boxes from, Elaine?" George asked.

"Jean and Mel got them from the Co-op. They are getting more tomorrow and then again on Tuesday, why?" Elaine asked.

"Well, there are more supermarkets. We can go round and see what else we can get. We might get some of those really big ones, you know like the ones they get the nappies in, the really huge ones. Come on Teen, let's see what we can get. We will pop over later with what we get, ok?" George asked.

Elaine nodded. "Thanks everyone," Elaine said again. Mum and nan sorted her out, got her stuff together, gave Jim the boxes and bags. Nan had put the pens into the bag as well, that way her and Angela could have a look at what they needed sorting out this evening.

Elaine went home with Jim and Angela and they sorted out Todd. Then Elaine started to have a sort through her stuff, most of it was ready to be packed. She didn't really need to get rid of anything, so her and Angela made up the boxes ready, but out of the way so Todd didn't hurt himself. She put the bag with the tape, string and pens up high.

Tina and George went along to the other two supermarkets, to see if they could also get some boxes. They were in luck, two out of the other three had a dozen or so. They took what they had and they gave them string and tape as well. It wasn't too late, so they popped them round to Elaine, who was already filling them up.

Angela was taping them up and writing what was inside each box, so they knew where it would go once it was at the other end. Jim and George started to stack them, but not high, because even though Todd wasn't walking, they didn't want him pulling even one over himself; it would do him a lot of damage or even kill him. So, they took them into Elaine's bedroom and stacked them up against the wall instead, that way Todd wouldn't be anywhere near them.

Angela was making up the boxes and Elaine was filling them up nearly as quickly. They had finished with the boxes. Elaine didn't realise how much stuff that her and Todd had, but that's the thing with having children, they need a lot of stuff. It was nearly midnight before they finished. Todd was already in his cot fast asleep. Elaine was shattered.

"Don't forget, Elaine, Mum and Nan will be over tomorrow with more boxes and they will help you fill them too. Mind you make sure you leave yourselves some clothes to wear otherwise you will be emptying them all again," laughed Tina. They hugged. Elaine said thank you again for the hundredth time. She couldn't believe how kind people could be.

Elaine very rarely asked for help, unless it was truly necessary. She waved them goodbye and then closed the door, as Jean or Marge had said she couldn't remember who, when you're moving, your home becomes the storage place for all of your belongings to go to the next place and they were right.

Marge and Jean were over at Elaine's very early; well early for Elaine, about 11am. She hadn't forgotten they were coming, she just realised the time. She had been up for a little while and she was giving Todd his breakfast. They put the boxes and more tape and string over by the sofa.

"Oh my goodness, you lot are like the SAS. I couldn't believe how much we got done last night. There is still a lot to do, but I am so grateful and thankful to you all. Let me finish with Todd and we can get started," said Elaine.

"No, Elaine, you finish with Todd, take your time. We can make up these boxes, just show me where you put the last lot," said Marge. Elaine handed

Todd's breakfast to Jean, so she could continue feeding him, then she took Marge into the bedroom.

"Oh my goodness, they did get lots done, are these all full or empty?" Marge asked.

"All full," Elaine stated.

"Well, do you have much stuff to go then?" Marge asked her.

"Yes, a fair bit, but the clothes, Todd's toys and most of his clothes. I have left clothes out for the following week, but have packed most of them now, so it's really just the kitchen stuff, bathroom stuff won't take five minutes, also the bedding. I managed to sort out we didn't need to use, so I wanted to get started on that today, but I thought Mel was going to have Todd for me?" asked Elaine.

"Oh yes, she is. Tina is going to look after Nicholas, so she can come and get Todd. She said she would be here in half an hour or so. If you can get a bag ready for him and some clothes on him, so he will be ready in time."

"You see she only has one car seat, so she couldn't bring Nicholas, and then when she gets back, Tina is coming over to help us. Not that I think that there's much to do now. I know there will be as the week goes on, but if you have done most of it," said Marge.

A little while later, there was a knock at the door, it was Mel ready to take Todd. "Mel, thank you for this. I know we got a lot done, but there's still so much to do," Elaine said.

"Elaine, don't worry. Nan and Mum will help until you don't need them," said Mel. Mel took Todd, he waved to Elaine. She kissed him on his cheek, said goodbye and then Mel and Todd were gone. Marge and Jean were making a start on making up the boxes.

Elaine had gone into the bedroom. She remembered she had a couple of suitcases and those laundry bags in the bottom of her wardrobe, cases on top of it. She got the little ladder and called Marge, who was very willing to help with what she could. Elaine handed her the cases and then half a dozen or so laundry bags, those big ones that you would take to the launderette, they had big zips on them, so you didn't lose your washing.

"Well, these will be a big help, Elaine. Do you have many more clothes to put in the cases? Maybe put your coats and coat hangers or something into the laundry bags," said Marge. Elaine hadn't even thought of that. Three heads and pairs of hands were definitely better than one. They made a start on filling up the laundry bags and suitcases.

There was a knock at the door, it was George and Jim. "Hi, Elaine, Jean and Marge. Look what we found round the back of the high street, the guy was throwing them out, so we thought they would help with the move!" George said. It was about five tea chests.

"Great, that's the kitchen stuff to go in there then," said Marge. Jean was doing what she was told. Marge was in charge of this, but she did look to Elaine for approval. Elaine was grateful for all of this extra help.

"Now Elaine, what's happening with your cooker and washing machine?" George asked.

"Well, the cooker is electric, so that just needs unplugging, but the washing machine needs to be emptied with a great spin and drain, then it needs to be unplumbed," Elaine told them.

"Well, I can do the washing machine if you want. I did ours at home when we moved to this side of town, so if that's ok?" George asked.

Elaine was thrilled. "It's all coming together, I don't know how to thank you all." She told them all.

"Now we just need newspapers to wrap your kitchen stuff," said Jean.

"Er Elaine, you haven't packed the kettle yet, have you?" Jim asked.

"No, Jim. Would you like some tea. Would you all like a cuppa, then we can get started," said Elaine.

"Elaine, show me the way, I will do the tea, so you can sort out what you need to," said Marge. She was the best tea maker though.

Marge made her way to the kitchen. Then Elaine went in, so she could see what she needed to pack that she wasn't going to use or need until they got to the other end. "Oh, Elaine, the guy threw these in, I have just found them. He said there was a couple of newspapers, but I think I found about a dozen of them so that should help," said Jim.

Marge made the tea. She wanted to get a move on, they didn't want to take up much of her day doing this. But it did have to be done. Tea drank and they all cracked on. Tina had got there and helped with whatever could be done, mainly making tea, not as good as Marge, but it was wet and that was all they needed.

A couple of hours later, they had packed up most of the flat. The only things left were the essentials, or the big furniture. So about 3pm, they all left.

Jim and Angela took Elaine to pick up Todd. She had missed him, but knew she had to get this done and thankfully with all of their help it was going to get done.

Jim, George and Jonathan were going to move the big stuff with the vans, then take it all up to the next place. So when they did this all again, they all helped sort Elaine out. Once they had moved her in, they put the stuff out of the boxes and would let her put it where she wanted. They just wanted to get the boxes out of the way, so Todd wouldn't hurt himself.

They had all had a busy week. Elaine had already picked up new curtains and that for the new flat. So when she picked up the keys on Friday, it was all systems go. Jim, George and Jonathan made their way to Elaine's old place to start sorting everything out. Marge and Jean were watching the boys at home, so the adults could do all the moving for the time being, but Mel was going to have them.

So once all of Elaine and Todd's stuff was in there, they would help her unpack everything. She didn't have to do it all on her own. Angela and Tina helped too. The women came back home about 6pm absolutely shattered. The men followed. They had to take the vans back in the morning, so had to make sure everything was done.

"Right, we are having a take away tonight. Chinese? Indian? What do you fancy?" Mel asked. They were hungry with all of the physical work they had done today.

"Not fussed, Mel, just food."

Elaine was going to leave. "Where do you think you're going, missus?" Marge asked.

"Well, you're all going to eat, I just thought I would leave you to it," said Elaine.

"Now you have worked just as much as the rest of us, but you have had all of the stress, we have just sorted out the chaos. So have some dinner with us, we can still sort Todd out. Now don't think you're ungrateful for what we have done today and this last week. But if we can make sure you eat something and Todd, we wouldn't leave him out."

"Don't worry, we won't give him curry or anything. There is loads in the fridge for him and Nicholas. Then George and Tina can drop you home when you're ready. Your bed and Todd's cot are already made up, so you can just slip back into it, when you get in fully clothed or not, that's up to you."

"But please stay even if it's just an hour. I know you dying to get into your new home tonight, but have some food then you have the rest of the weekend before everyone goes back to work. If you need any help, just ask, eh?" Marge asked. She was great at taking control of the situation without taking over.

Elaine nodded. "Sorry, I just didn't want to being the way, that's all!" She said.

"We know, but you know you're part of the family. Yes, we know you have your own family too, but this is your extended family. When you need us, we will be there. So, Elaine, do you fancy Chinese or Indian?" Marge asked.

"Chinese please," she said.

"Right then, Chinese it is. George, my love, can you order it and collect it?" Nan asked him.

"Of course, Nan," he replied. That was settled then. Elaine didn't have to drop the keys back of her old place until the Monday morning, so it gave her the rest of the weekend to put what was left where she wanted it. She said that she had never seen a group of people work so hard and so together like a team before.

***

Thankfully, Elaine had moved the week before, they wouldn't have managed to get it all done with the boys going to nursery now. Nicholas was going to Forrester Greenwood and Todd was going to Hampton Barge nursery for special children. There wasn't any way that Todd could go to a mainstream nursery, he needed too much care. They were geared up for it at his nursery and it was only around the corner from Elaine and Todd's new home.

Mel was excited but sad, because Nicholas would be at nursery/school Monday to Friday every week, except for the holidays, he would now be home with her. So, she was really pleased about that. Nicholas' eating was slowly getting better. He would be having school meals. He was able to use a spoon, but not the rest of the cutlery.

The school said not to worry, as he would soon pick it up when he needed to. On his first day, he looked rather smart, so Mel took a few photos. Well a lot of photos, of Nicholas on his own, with her, with nan, with Mum, with nan and. Mum together with him, then with nan, Mel and Nicholas, and then the same with Mum as well.

His transport turned up at 8.30 sharp. Mel was able to go with him for the first morning, to get him settled on the school bus and also to his class. He would be coming back with his peers and the driver and escort, who were Betty and June, they were both older ladies, but they had great patience with the children in their care on the bus. They seated Nicholas, put his seatbelt on and then told Mel she could sit at the back.

Nicholas was oblivious to her even being there after a few minutes, same as when they got to school. The staff came out to greet the children and take them to class. Mel followed, but a little behind, she didn't want to stress Nicholas out. She walked up to the classroom. Nicola, his teacher, said that she could stay if she wanted to, or she could go home.

She wasn't being horrible, it's just they wanted to get Nicholas into a routine and he hadn't really spotted her on the bus. It would just upset him to see her again and would get confused. Mel agreed. She was glad that he had settled down on the bus so easily, she thought he might fret a bit. Betty called Mel over.

"Mel, we are going back if you would like lift home. We are going past your place," she said.

"Is that alright? I mean you won't get in trouble or anything?" Mel asked her.

"We shouldn't really, but as its Nicholas' first day and you can't really stay, you may as well get a lift home, but don't tell the office," June added. Mel laughed, she wouldn't get them into trouble, because they are doing her a favour. She hopped onto the bus and they waited until all of the children were in the school then the school keeper or caretaker, Alan, Mel didn't know what he was, then let the buses and cars go.

Mel was home in minutes. "Mel, is that you love?" Jean asked, when she heard the key go in the door.

"Yes, Mum, it's me," she said.

"You're early back. I thought you were going to stay for the day," Mum replied.

"Well, his teacher, Nicola, thought as though Nicholas was fine on the bus. He didn't even realise I was there. They didn't want to upset him, by me just turning up or so he would think. It will be fine, Mum, honestly. I wonder how Elaine has got on with Todd starting today as well?" Mel said out loud.

Mel looked at the clock, she heard a toot outside. It was the bus. "Blimey, it's that time already," she said as she darted out of the door. "Hi, Betty and June," Mel said to them.

"Hi, Mel, he's been a little darling today. They said he had a great day, but look in his book bag. They have like a diary, so you can tell them how he was. If he had a good night as such and they do the same, say what day he had. So off you come, poppet," said June undoing Nicholas' seatbelt. Mel put her hands up to Nicholas and he gave her a huge smile.

"Thanks, ladies," Mel said.

"See you tomorrow, bye, Nicholas," June said.

"Ta ta" said Betty as she looked behind her to make sure it was safe before she pulled away. Mel waved them off and then took Nicholas inside.

"Hello, little man, how was nursery today?" Jean asked.

Marge came running out of the kitchen. "Sorry, I didn't hear him pull up. Hello, Nicholas, did you have a good day?" Nan asked. Nicholas was pulling some strange faces, then he smiled. "I have his dinner on, Mel, do you want to change him out of his uniform or do you want to bath him first?" Nan asked.

"You know what, Nan, I don't know. He hasn't been to nursery for a week, so he might be tired. I will give him a quick bath and see how he goes. So what's for dinner then?" Mel asked.

"Shepherd's pie," came the reply.

The rest of the week went in a whirlwind, Mel couldn't believe how fast it went. Jonathan popped round that evening; he had also been really busy that week. "Hi, Jonathan, want a cuppa?" Nan asked.

"Yes, please, Marge. So Mel how has Nicholas got on this week with nursery well school?" He asked.

"He's loved it from what I have heard from his driver and escort. Also he gets a home/school book, which is excellent. So we put in how he has done at home, sleep etc, then they do the same back," replied Mel. "Oh, one thing though, he keeps making these faces we don't know what he wants," Mel told him.

Jonathan had a look at what Nicholas was doing. He was pulling some faces, but Jonathan wasn't concentrating on his face but his mouth. "Mel, he's had speech and language therapy and if you look at his mouth. He's trying to make an O, now look he's making an E. They teach them the vowels first, because it's easier," he said.

"Oh my goodness, we thought something was wrong with him. At least now we know, thank goodness we have you around, Jonathan, when we are stuck," said Jean. Nan brought in the tea. Nicholas was having his tea, he was having his bath a little later on as it was Friday, so he could have a lie in, in the morning.

Now Nicholas was at full time nursery, Mel wasn't sure what to do with her time anymore. She had wanted to go to Building Bridges a bit more to help out and talk with other parents which was always full of information and to get other people's insight on their situations. Mel was also going to have a word with Lesley about coming back in maybe part time, because she was going to be bored.

Mel was never one for lazing around even when she was pregnant for Nicholas. She worked up as late as she could.

She had arranged to see Lesley on Tuesday morning. All three of the women were busy when she walked in the door; Lesley was taking orders, Andrea was sorting out what had to be delivered, and Fiona was serving a lady some flowers and plants, she had her van outside. Mel took herself out the back and put the kettle on for everyone.

Lesley popped her head in. "Hi, Mel, you ok for a couple of minutes?" she asked.

"Yes, fine. Making a cuppa for everyone. What does Andrea drink?" Mel asked.

"Tea, 2 sugars," replied Lesley going back into the shop. Lesley returned when she had finished. Mel heard the door close and Andrea had left to do the deliveries. "So how can I help you today, Mel?" Lesley asked.

Mel took a deep breath. "Well, I know it may sound like a bit of a cheek, Lesley, but how would you feel me coming back part time?" Mel asked a little nervous, but she didn't really know why, this was after all her shop. But she had been out of it for so long, that she didn't even know if there would be any work for her to do anymore.

"Well, to be honest, Mel, we only just have enough for all four of us to do, it's steady enough. Don't get me wrong, but for another person, you may end up cleaning the windows and washing the floor and I don't really think that would be fair. It's up to you of course," added Lesley.

"No, Lesley, you're right. It's just I feel a bit redundant now Nicholas has gone to full time nursery. I suppose it was naughty of me really to just expect there to be enough for everyone and me as well. Maybe I need to try something else, maybe a course or something, but thanks, Lesley. Don't worry I wasn't suggesting letting anyone go, so I could come back. I just thought, well you know," Mel said.

"Mel, I understand, I was the same when the girls went to school, it's what happens to all mothers. You could you know, have another baby!" Lesley suggested.

Mel burst out laughing, "Definitely not. Nicholas is hard enough. Oh, Lesley, what am I saying. I would have killed to have a baby. Now I have one, I don't want anymore. I didn't realise how hard it would be," Mel added.

"Yes, and now you can have some time off from doing anything. As you said try a course or if not, take up knitting," suggested Lesley.

"It's not that bad yet, anyway I leave that sort of stuff up to nan and Mum," said Mel.

"How are they both? I haven't had chance to pop in. Mel, you still do the books. Why don't you go on a refresher course, just so you're not out of the loop?" Lesley suggested again.

"I will think about it. It's one thing doing it because you have to, but not to get tip top on it. I can manage and if not, I can always get another accountant," Mel then suggested. She finished her tea, said goodbye to the ladies and then left to make her way home.

'What on earth was she going to do with all of her free time? Have another baby? It was hard enough for her to get this one', she laughed to herself.

Chapter 18

"Mel, is that the post, love?" Jean asked.

"Er yes, I think so," Mel replied. Mel bent down to pick it up. Nicholas had already left for school, nan and Mum were in the kitchen sorting out their drinks. They had eaten their breakfasts. Nan would make a mean fry up, which George and Jonathan were very partial to.

Mel brought the post in and handed the relevant post to the relevant recipient. Nan had a couple, Mum had a couple and Mel had about three letters, all about Nicholas; one was from the local authority, one from the school and the other from Building Bridges, the support group. Jean opened her letters and Mel noticed that nan was rather engrossed in one of her letters.

"Nan, are you ok? You have gone a funny colour?" Mel asked. Jean stopped reading her letter and looked at her mother. "Nan?" Mel repeated.

"What? Oh yes, sorry, you remember my cousin, Jill, who's in that…"

"Yes, Nan, is everything OK?" Mel knew who nan was referring to, but didn't want to upset her.

"It says here that Jill is rather poorly and they think I should come and see her as soon as possible really, Mel," nan told them.

"How poorly, Nan?" Mel asked.

"They don't say, but it doesn't sound great. I haven't seen her in a while and she was always perky when I visited her. I think I will give them a call and see what's happening with her," nan said. She left the room. Jean went into the kitchen to finish making the drinks.

Nan had closed the sitting room door behind her, she wanted a bit of privacy whilst making the call. She knew her family loved her, but this was her cousin. She had been keeping an eye on her for years, but hadn't had much chance to see her in a little while.

"Yes, thank you for letting me know. Yes, on Friday, what time? Yes, that should be OK. Well, I will see you then. Thank you again, Mrs Hammond," said nan, putting down the phone. Nan returned to the sitting room.

"Well, Nan, is Jill ok? What did they say was wrong with her?" Mel asked. Jean looked at Mel, then she stopped.

"It seems that Jill is getting on like the rest of us, but they don't think she has very long left and I was the only living relative who give a damn about her. They wanted me to know that she had been asking after me, so I'm going on Friday morning. Jean, Mel, would you both come with me please? Nicholas will be at school already by then," said Nan, hoping that Mel would agree to come.

Mel got up from her chair and hugged her nan. "Of course I will come with you to see your cousin. By the way, you were with that letter and the way you told me about her, when I was so blind to everything about autism. She's our family, but she only knows you. So I would be honoured to go with you," said Mel.

"Me too, Mum, I want to meet her," said Jean.

"Er well, you did, Jean, but a long time ago. You were only little and you loved to see Jill, but you got really upset when they got a bit rough with her. You see, it's not like now where they take really good care. They don't punish them anymore, but try to helping every way they can."

"Yes, some of them had to be restrained, but it's done properly, not any old how. Anyway, as I said you got really scared when they manhandled her a bit. Oh don't you worry, I had a go at them, but you started to cry when you saw how they were with Jill. So, I told myself I wouldn't take you there again until you were older."

"Then they moved her somewhere else, but you were still upset about it and I never did take you back. I am sorry, Jean, but it was hard enough seeing Jill there, but for you as well. You were only a little girl, but this time, it will be different."

"Nan, if you don't mind me asking, how often did you go and see Jill?" Mel asked.

"Once a week on the Greenline. It was a long way then but now she's just the other side of town, on the outskirts. So, it's a bit easier now. I haven't been in a while though, just so much else going on. The thing is, you can get so caught up with your own lives, sometimes you forget to look out for others," nan told them.

On Friday, Jean, Marge and Mel got themselves together once Nicholas had gone to school on his bus. Mel was going to be driving them instead of going on the bus as nan normally did. It was a bit further away than Mel had thought. She knew her area like the back of her hand, but this place she had no idea.

They drove down this road and then, "This is the place," said nan.

Mel was looking at a fish and chip shop. "Surely not, Nan?" Mel said looking rather alarmed.

"Not this side of the road, Mel, the other side," nan told her.

"Hold on then, let me park outside. Are you sure this is the right place. It looks a bit grim, Nan," Mel said,

"Yes, I know, never mind, so come on," said Nan. Mel turned off the engine. They all got out and Mel locked up. Nan went to the main entrance and pushed open the gate. Mel closed it behind her, didn't want anyone to get out who shouldn't, Mel thought to herself, though she would never say that to Nan.

"Here we are," she said. Nan buzzed the door and a lady answered it. She had jeans on, a blue tee shirt, trainers on with a navy tabard. 'Practical', Mel thought again.

"Hello yes, can I help you?" The lady asked, whose name was Jane.

"Hello, Jane, I'm Mrs Marge Johnson. We are here to see my cousin, Jill Coombes. We are expected," said nan very official.

"Oh yes, I remember Mrs White did tell me. Won't you follow me to the day room," said Jane.

"The day room, I thought that Jill would be in her room?" Nan said.

They were shown in the day room. "Mrs White would like a word with you before you see Jill," commented Jane.

"Oh OK," said nan a little taken back by this. A lady in a rather casual outfit of blouse, slacks and loafers came into greet the women.

"Mrs Johnson?" Mrs White asked, looking at Jean.

"No, I'm Mrs Johnson, Marge Johnson, and it's Jill Coombes we're here to see. Is she alright?" Marge asked a little nervous.

"Sorry Mrs Johnson, Marge, I didn't mean to worry you. I just wanted a word with you before you see Jill. You see she is on some new medication and it's still kicking in, but that's not for her autism. It's to make her more comfortable and in less pain," said Mrs White.

"Oh is she in pain then?" Marge asked. "Is there anything I can do?"

"It's quite strong pain relief. She's actually on Morphine. We tried the tablets we couldn't get them down her. Oh don't worry, we didn't try to force them down her. We tried to coax her into having them, but she wasn't having none of it. So you know Jill is quite a character, but she is on liquid form, now it is chilling her out…"

"It's not making her zombie like, is it?" Marge interrupted.

"Oh no nothing like that. We know you have been to see her frequently, Marge. We just didn't want you to have a bit of a shock if she wasn't her normal happy self," Mrs White told them. Marge sighed a sigh of relief.

"Would you like to come and see her now? She is in her room, which is quite large and there are enough seats for all of you. Do you have any questions at all before I show you to her room?" Mrs White asked.

Everyone shook their heads. "OK, then let's go and see Jill," said Mrs White. She opened the door and they met another resident, David.

"Hello, David, how are you today?" Mrs White asked.

"I'm fine, Mrs White, where are you going?" David asked.

"We are going to see Jill. These good people are her relatives."

"Hello, Jill's relatives. How are you today?" David asked. All three of them stopped and said that they were fine then Mel asked him.

"David, how are you today? Are you doing anything nice today?" Mel asked.

"I am going to watch some TV my favourite programme is on, it's a wildlife programme about lions and tigers. I'm going now, bye, Jill's relatives," he said and left them.

"Bye, David" they all said.

"He's such a sweetheart. He loves his wildlife and nature programmes, it calms him down a lot, if he's having a bit of a rough day." Mel made a mental note of that. It could be something she could try for Nicholas, after all it was all trial and error. They walked down the corridor and came to a room with the door halfway closed.

Mrs White knocked softly, "Jill, is it ok to come in?" Mrs White asked. "I have some people who want to see you," she added. Jill looked at her and nodded her head. Mrs White went in first, Jill was sitting up at a table. She was just finishing a cup of tea and having a light snack, it was elevenses.

"Hello, Marge." She got up slowly and made her way over to her and hugged her tightly. "Jean, cousin Jean, I remember when you used to come and see me when you were a little girl, and this must be Mel. Marge has told me lots about you and your little boy, Nicholas."

"He has autism just like me. He will be fine. He's the light of your life. Marge showed me his picture, was that alright, Mel?" Jill asked, looking rather unsure that she had said the wrong thing.

"No, Jill, it's OK. I have a couple of spares with me if you like to have to keep?" Mel said.

"Oh can I? Has he grown much, Mel? He's coming up for three Marge said and he has started nursery school," said Jill. Oh my, Mel had no idea how much her nan had told her cousin about her and Nicholas. Mel wanted to cry but held very hard to keep the tears at bay.

"Oh, Mel, he's gorgeous. He looks like you," she said as she kissed the photograph. "Oh, do you want tea. They will make you tea. I just had one, but I can't have too many, I wee too much," she said matter of flatly. "It's a shame I haven't seen you before but you're here now, and, Mel, can you bring Nicholas next time you come? I would love to meet him properly," asked Jill.

"Yes of course, Jill, I can bring him at the weekend as he has nursery in the week. Would that be, OK?" Mel asked.

"I will have to ask Mrs White, the visiting times at the weekends. I don't normally get visitors at the weekend, but only in the week," said Jill so innocently.

"We can ask her on the way-out, Jill. How have you been? Mrs White said that you have been poorly, but they didn't say what was wrong?" Marge asked.

"I have got cancer and its spread, but they can't do anything except give me this medication," she pointed to a tube that was attached to the top of her breast. She pulled her top down. She didn't show them everything, just the tube. Marge couldn't believe what she was hearing. She felt like the stuffing had been kicked out of her.

"Jill, why didn't they let me know before? About you not being poorly," asked Marge.

"Because I didn't want them to tell you just yet, I wanted to keep it to myself until I was ready for you to be allowed to know," Jill told them all. They didn't know what to say. "Where's Jane, she will bring you some tea," said Jill.

She opened the door and called for Jane, who came running, "Are you ok Jill?" Jane asked.

"Oh yes, Jane, but could you bring some tea please for my family?" she asked, Mel had to wipe her eyes very quickly before Jill could see them.

"Ok, milk and sugar everyone?" Jane asked.

"Just milk please," they all said at the same time.

"Just like me, milk no sugar, because I am sweet enough!" Jill remarked. Jane came back a few minutes later with a tray of tea and biscuits for everyone, but on plate not as a packet. "How come you didn't bring the packet, Jane?" Jill asked.

"You know very well, Jill, it's so they only eat what's on the plate, if they see visually what's there, they don't ask for more. No, don't worry, we aren't starving her or the others, but if there is a packet brought, they will eat every one of them. It's how they see it. That's how we know they eat their dinner, they clear their plates."

"Oh some of the residents are fussy, but that's autism, it can be…"

"Sensory," Mel interrupted. Jane nodded. She knew that Mel knew about autism. "My son has been diagnosed not that long ago," said Mel because she knew what Jane was thinking.

"How are you coping?" Jane enquired.

"Yes, OK, it takes time and with care and support. I have joined a support group with other parents with families, also some other disabilities and it helps to have family," said Mel.

Marge looked at Jill, she took her hand. "I'm sorry about the cancer, Jill, you should have told me, but never mind, that was your choice. How do you feel?" Marge asked, trying to hold it together.

"I'm fine, Marge. I just feel a bit sick with this tube thing. They put me on some liquid medication as well, they said it's to help with the pain, but it doesn't bother me. I am just glad you came. I told Mrs White I was ready to tell you, but I wanted to tell you, not the staff. You have been there for me all of the time, Marge, I owed you that," Jill said.

"Jill, you owe me nothing, my darling, my family and I want to help if I can," said Marge.

"But you can't, Marge, and I know you have things going on with your own family, my family. It's the way it is, there's no point looking backwards only forwards," said Jill. Considering Jill had autism, she was as sharp as a button. They drank their tea and Jill sneaked a couple of biscuits to have later on.

"Now, Mel, will you bring Nicholas to see me on the weekend, this weekend?" Jill asked.

"If Mrs White will let me bring him on Sunday, would that be alright?" Mel asked.

"Ooh yes please, I can't wait to meet him," she replied rather excitedly. "I'm getting tired now. I think I will have a lie down. Now don't forget, Mel, ask Mrs White and I will see you all then," said Jill. Marge bent over to give her a kiss on the forehead. Jean kissed her on the cheek and Mel kissed the other cheek.

"See you on Sunday, Jill," said Mel. Jill waved and then closed her eyes. They left the room, they found Jane.

"You all ok?" Jane asked.

"Er yes, we were wondering if we could back on maybe Sunday this week, because Jill wants to meet my great-grandson, would that be ok?" Marge asked.

"Give me a minute," said Jane. She returned a couple of minutes later. "Mrs White said you can come after 4pm but I am afraid you have to leave by 7pm. That way the residents have time to wind down then for the evening, they can get rather excited," said Jane.

"Thank you, Jane," said Marge.

"Jane, may I ask you something? We know what's wrong with Jill, she told us, she seems happy enough. Will she be able to stay here or will she have to go to hospital?" Mel asked.

"She can stay here as long as she wants. If she gets into too much pain and she feels that she wants to go to hospital then that's her choice. Jill can't function like most normal. I hate that word normal, but she can still function and even though she's autistic. She knows what she likes and dislikes, also what she wants and what she doesn't want."

"But yes, she is happy here. We wouldn't want her to stay if she wasn't happy. I'm sorry I have to go, but see you on Sunday," said Jane as she left the group. They then went down the main corridor and out of the building. They walked to the car in silence.

Mel unlocked it and they all got in. Mel didn't put the key in though. Marge who was so level headed, burst into tears. Jean, her daughter, held her tight.

Mel couldn't contain her feelings and tears also; they were just streaming down her face.

"Why didn't she tell me, Jean? It must have been so hard for her," said Marge through sobs. None of them could stop the tears, they were all crying uncontrollably. Mel's shoulders were going up and down with her sobbing. They let the tears and feelings just flow, there was no point trying to stop.

Once they all composed themselves several minutes later. "She must have known, well as much as she could have known that she had cancer," said Marge. "Nan, for someone who has condition that she does, and her difficulties. It's amazing that for one. She could keep a lid on it, but for two make that decision to tell when she wanted to, not because she had to but because she wanted to tell you herself, rather than let the staff tell you now or at worst even later, you know," said Mel, she didn't want to say the words.

"Right are we ready to go home, we can talk when we get in. I think we need a stiff drink, but not until we get home or I will end up getting pulled over," said Mel.

"Yes, love, let's go," said Jean still holding onto her mum tightly. When they got in, Mel put the kettle on and Marge went to the drink's cabinet. "Brandy or Whisky?" she asked.

"Brandy will warm us up," said Mel.

"But so will whisky," said nan. Nan poured Brandy into the teacups, once Mel brought them in.

"I think we need this for the shock more than anything. Mind you, I don't want to smell of drink when they bring Nicholas home, that would be all I needed today," said Mel. They nodded in agreement, but had their drink up to their lips taking big gulps.

Nicholas came home as he always did in a great mood. They had done some painting. He got it all between his fingers, he liked the sensation it gave him. Mel put him in the bath, while nan was making dinner. "Ham, egg and Chips ok for tonight?" Nan asked.

"Perfect," replied Mel. Jonathan was coming round. Nan, Mum and Mel all wanted to talk to him about Jill and ask his professional opinion. He got there around 7pm. Nicholas had already gone to bed.

His cot went to the Mother and Baby group clinic for someone who needed a cot but didn't have the money for a brand new one. Nicholas' was in great condition, Mel kept his stuff nice and clean. So, they got him a bed that went up against the wall, but with a bed guard so he wouldn't fall out. He wasn't quite three yet, but it was ok for him.

"Jonathan, can I ask you something?" Marge asked.

"Yes go ahead, Marge," said Jonathan, not prepared for what he was going to hear. Marge explained the situation, and then asked what he thought.

"Well, I would definitely go again on Sunday and yes, take Nicholas. It will help Jill to meet him, even though she knows a lot about him. It would be lovely I think for both of them. You said you left her a couple of photos, well that's great too. So when you go on Sunday, she will recognise him straight away," Jonathan told them.

Marge burst into tears again. "I can't believe that she has held onto this information for all of this time, but didn't say anything," said Marge.

"Well, Marge, it's her right, isn't it? I don't mean that awful and I don't want to sound like I am being mean. For autistic people, they hardly get the chance to make decisions for themselves. Look at Mel, she has to do everything she can for Nicholas, but when he grows up, there will be someone else to make those decisions for him. Can you imagine how exhilarating that would be for him, for Jill."

"That's the thing isn't it? Society thinks that they can't make decisions for themselves, but Jill, she has done. She's made the biggest decision of her life and it's her choice. Marge, that is really big, if the timings had been better and she was born years later, could you imagine the life she could have lived with you guys here in this house for example."

"Please don't feel sorry for her, because she doesn't. She probably doesn't even realise the seriousness of this situation, but she has made a choice, and in my book that's the best thing. She's having treatment and she is on pain relief; she's choosing to stay in the home that she has known for years, rather than going into hospital."

"I know you probably are already, from what you have said this evening, but I would be very proud of her. She sounds like an amazing lady," said Jonathan. Marge said nothing but went up to Jonathan and hugged him.

"I knew Mel had done the right thing in meeting you," she said to him. Jonathan went rather red, but he knew this was a good thing. Mel went over and hugged him and so did Jean. It had been a very hard emotional day, but there was a light at the end of the tunnel.

On Sunday, Mel, Nicholas, Jean and Marge all got into the car. Marge had brought her some flowers, Jean brought her a couple of magazines, she had seen some on her table, just the new editions for the week. Mel brought Nicholas, with a couple of his sensory things, but made sure he had drinks and a couple of snacks.

They had already had their dinner, so when they did get home, they could have a light tea in the evening or early supper. Nicholas was making noise in his car seat but he was happy enough. Marge and Jean were talking, but not to distract Mel from her driving. They pulled up outside the home, the right side this time,

Mel turned off the engine and opened her door. She went to the boot and got Nicholas's buggy. She knew he was getting a bit big for it and had spoken to someone at Building Bridges. She said that Mel could get him a special needs one. A company had been making them for years, but they had recently overhauled them, so they looked like the smaller pushchairs, but were bigger, only slightly, but you would only just notice it.

She unfolded the buggy and took Nicholas out of his car seat and into his pushchair. Marge had got herself out of the front seat and Jean then got out of the other side from Nicholas. Once she had him settled and everyone was out of the car, she locked it. Marge and Jean, both brushed themselves down.

Nicholas was looking at one to the other and smiled. Marge walked up to the gate and opened it holding it open for Mel and Nicholas, Jean followed up behind. Marge pushed forward and pressed on the buzzer. Jane had let them all in. They all said hello and then she spotted Nicholas.

"Hello, little lad, you're absolutely gorgeous, aren't you. You're going to break all of the girls' hearts when you get older!" Jane exclaimed.

"He already does," replied Jean. Both of them laughed.

"Is Jill in her room again today?" Marge asked.

"No, she's in the day room. No, she's not sorry, she's out in the garden. She's wrapped up. Please don't worry, she likes to go into the garden," said Jane. "Please follow me," she said to them. They did so, they went into the day room which led out into the garden.

Jill was sitting with another member of staff, but also a couple of her friends. "Marge, Jean, Mel and little Nicholas," she squealed, like a little girl. "Oh I am so happy to see you all, and especially you, Nicholas," she said bending down to give him a kiss on his forehead.

Nicholas also squealed. "Jill, are you ok out here, it's a bit nippy," Suggested Jane. Marge nodded.

"Oh yes, let's go inside then. Do you want to come into my room rather than be with everyone else and their families?" Jill asked.

"Yes, Jill, if that's what you want," said Jean.

"Yes, I do want. I don't want to share my family with anyone else!" She retorted, she laughed a little. She wasn't being rude, just protective of her family she has only really just met. They all walked into Jill's room. Nicholas looked with big eyes, it was a big bright room.

Mel didn't really take much notice of Jill's room. I suppose it was because of the news that they had been blown. It had a huge bay window, she had some garden to look out onto, there was a field over the back of the boundaries. Jill had a bird table, which was empty except for a few seeds.

"I like to look out of the window, especially when the birds come and eat their food. Sometimes, Mel, they fight. Come, Nicholas, let's see if we can see a bird," said Jill, taking his hand. He went with her no problem, which the other three women were stunned at. Nicholas didn't really go with anyone.

Jill picked him up and showed him the bird feeding table. "ooooo," replied Nicholas. Mel was stunned. He reacted how a child would, not because he had special needs. 'Wow', thought Mel.

"Nicholas, I am your cousin Jill and I am very happy to meet you," she said. Mel could feel her eyes stinging again. Nicholas looked straight at her and put his arms around her neck and kissed her very lightly on the cheek. Mel, Jean and Marge were stunned. There is nothing this boy does that doesn't surprise them on a daily basis.

Jill was showing Nicholas the bird that had just landed on the edge of the table and Jill said to him, "Look, Nicholas, a bird, I think it's a sparrow," said Jill.

"Bird," replied Nicholas. He looked back at his mum.

"Good boy, Nicholas," she said. 'You're getting there', she thought.

"Jill, I brought some tea and biscuits for you and your family. I thought this shortcake might be nice for your little boy, Mel, is that ok?" Jane asked.

"Yes, Jane. thank you, that was very thoughtful," said Mel. Jane had only just looked up and saw Jill holding Nicholas and them both pointing out at the window. 'Wow', thought Jane, 'they are both so engaged and really connected'. She had never seen Jill like this before. She was glad that Jill had asked for her family to visit.

It's a shame she didn't ask for this earlier, this would have been some real quality of life for her; but Jill's Jill, she still has had a happy life. "Right, Nicholas, we can have a look again in a little while. The bird is going to fly away again in a minute. Let's have some tea. Do you have anything for Nicholas to drink, Mel?" Jill asked.

"Yes, Jill, I have brought him some juice. Come, Nicholas, let's get your juice," said Mel.

"Bring him back over here to sit with us though, won't you, Mel?" Jill asked.

"Yes of course, Jill," Mel replied. She thought that was a bit abrupt, but she didn't let it bother her. Mel got Nicholas' juice and brought him back to the table. Marge sorted out the tea.

"Can Nicholas sit on my lap? I will move the tea, so he doesn't hurt himself?" Jill asked.

"Yes, as long as he isn't too heavy for you?" Mel suggested.

"Of course not, he's as light as a feather. Aren't you, Nicholas," commented Jill. They all sat around the table and began to drink their tea. "It's lovely to see you all again so soon. I am glad you came and I am glad to meet this little fella," said Jill.

Marge didn't want to dwell on Jill's condition, but she was concerned. "Jill, how have you been since we last saw you?" Marge asked.

"I'm OK, but this medicine is rather strong and it makes me feel sick a bit, not all the time, but normally before I go to bed," she told the group. "Oh, Mel, could you please get something for me, it's in my bedside cabinet?" she asked. "Thank you," she replied. Mel went over to her bedside cabinet.

"It should be in the bottom drawer," said Jill. Mel opened the drawer, she pulled out a pad and pen, also underneath was a present wrapped up.

"Is this it Jill, the pad and pen?" Mel asked.

"Oh yes, but also the present, that's for Nicholas. Jane helped me pick it out and she got it for me," said Jill. Mel handed both of the items to Jill. She put the pen and pad on the table and then gave Nicholas the present, which they both unwrapped. Mel's eyes were as wide as saucers. Nicholas never opened anything at all.

They both unwrapped the present and then there it was in the box. "Look, Nicholas, it's a handheld firework," said Jill.

"Pardon?" Mel said.

"Yes, what you do, you hold it and it and press the button, the things at the top all spin round and it makes fireworks, not real ones, silly. Mel, it's not dangerous, its sensory, as I said Jane helped me pick it out. Do you like it?" Jill asked looking for Mel's approval.

"It's lovely, Jill," said Mel. "Thank you" she added.

"It needs batteries, but Jane has them for safe keeping, somebody keeps pinching them," Jill added. "Jane, can you come here please," said Jill, expecting Jane to be sitting right outside the door, but the next thing Jane was there.

"Yes, Jill, is everything ok?" asked Jane.

"Yes, but you know the batteries I gave you the other day. Can I have them please. They are for Nicholas's new sensory toy we got him," she said, smiling as she said it. Jane disappeared then returned a few minutes later, she handed the batteries to Jill, who opened them, but struggled with the new toy.

She gave it to Jean to open who did, put the batteries in. She handed it back to Jill, so she could show Nicholas. Nicholas' eyes were like saucers, it was great to see, something so simple could be enlightening for him to watch. "Nan, did you tell Jill about Nicholas and the twinkly lights?" Mel asked.

"No, darling, you're forgetting who you're talking to and what sort of things I have liked over the years, that's why I knew darling little Nicholas would like it too. You see, I see a lot of me in him and that's a compliment by the way. You have done brilliantly with him and will continue to do so."

"I am so glad you brought him to see me today, Mel, it means such a lot," she said, placing her hand over Mel's. Mel was tearing up again but fought the tears back. Once they had tea, Jill put Nicholas back down on the floor and then she joined him. "So, Marge, what have you been doing since I last saw you?" Jill asked.

"Not much really, Jill, just the normal. Keeping the place clean and tidy, looking after Nicholas," said Marge.

"How's Tina and George then? Did they have a good wedding?" she asked.

"Yes, Jill, it was lovely. We should have brought some of the photos you know, Mum" said Jean, then realising that Jill wasn't at the wedding. How can you show someone photos who didn't attend the wedding, thought Jean. All of a sudden, Jean felt absolutely awful, not because she felt ill, but she didn't realise how little Jill was part of their lives.

She was their cousin, she knew all about them, but she had been stuck away in this place for years, even though it was a nice place. Jean all of a sudden felt very guilty.

"Jean, please don't worry, its fine. I only asked if she had a good wedding. I didn't mean to upset you, it doesn't bother me at all that I live here. I am happy here. You all have your lives, I have mine here. I am just grateful that I got to meet you all again, apart from Nicholas who I have just met, but I have already met you all including Tina."

"She has lovely long blonde hair with blue eyes. Your nan brought her to see me when she was about Nicholas' age. I have good life here, yes, I get a bit confused sometimes and this autism does feel like it gets in the way, but it's me. I can't change it and I wouldn't want to. I have had a safe happy life."

"I have my memories and now I have made some new ones. If Tina and George get some time, would you bring them over to see me as well?" Jill asked. Marge and Jean nodded. Mel could hardly keep it together. "I'm sorry but I am getting a bit tired, do you mind if I go to bed?" Jill asked.

"We will leave you then, Jill," said Marge.

Jill nodded. "Don't forget Nicholas' toy," said Jill.

Nicholas said, "Bye, Jill, Bird." Marge, Jean, Mel and then Nicholas, all gave her a kiss on either the cheek or forehead. She then got into bed and said night night to them. Mel picked up Nicholas and then closed the door to, so the staff could still see her.

Mel caught hold of Jane when they left the room. "She said she's tired and has gone to bed, so we left her alone, but I left her door open ajar," said Mel.

"Thank you, Mel, see you again soon," said Jane.

"Could we come back in the week, when little fella here is at nursery. Then maybe again at the weekend?" Mel asked.

"Yes, I don't see why not," replied Jane.

"Thank you, Jane, see you again in a few days then," said Mel, waving as they were already at the door. Mel put Nicholas back in the car in his car seat, everyone got in. Marge sat in the front again with Mel, she had a hanky at her nose.

"You OK, Nan?" Mel asked. Marge nodded and sniffed at the same time, so did Jean on the backseat. Nicholas was looking at his nan rather confused. "Are we ready then to go home I mean?" Mel asked.

"Yes please, Mel," replied Nan. Mel drove back in silence apart from Nicholas gurgling. Next thing Mel pulled up outside home. Jean and Marge got out of the car as quickly as they could. Mel got Nicholas out of his car seat and into his buggy, then she closed the boot and then locked the car. She put Nicholas' things on top of the buggy hood. He was still holding onto his sensory toy from Jill.

"Hey hold on, you two!" Mel said. They had already gone indoors, but left the door open for Mel and Nicholas. "What's up?" Mel asked. She knew that Jill was full of beans and rather excitable but she was confused with what was going on with her nan and her mum.

"Mel, in all of the times I have seen Jill, she has never gone to bed before anyone else. She, even though autistic, was quite a live wire. You didn't know her before, her going to bed before her visitors isn't right. There's something wrong I know it," said Marge.

"Nan, she has cancer, she's on chemotherapy, she's on morphine. She's probably worn out and us being there for that short time, has probably knackered her out. You saw how she was with Nicholas, she probably hasn't had that much excitement in a long time. Don't forget she has seen us on Friday and then now again today."

"She's an older lady and no I am not saying you're old, but she's very ill. I'm surprised she was able to hold Nicholas as long as she did watching those birds with him. She's a strong lady but she probably doesn't have a lot of time left and wants to cram as much as she can in before her time comes, but it's still wearing her out," said Mel.

Marge knew her girl was right, but even when you have information about something, it's not until you see the person, before you know how bad or good they are. Marge hugged Mel and Jean joined in. This group hug thing was becoming a regular thing now, Mel thought.

Jonathan popped in that evening. He knew they were going to see Jill. "How did it go then?" He asked Mel when they were upstairs sorting out Nicholas.

"It was fine. She's a tough cookie to be honest. I feel sad though because we could have had her in our lives for much longer, not because she doesn't have much time left, but because we could have met her earlier. Does that make sense, Jonathan?" Mel asked him.

"Yes it does, but you have to remember, Jill liked living at the home she is now in. This may not have been up to your nan, but Jill herself. Don't forget she didn't live with her own mum for very long, maybe this is what she wanted, Mel, don't beat yourself up about it, eh?" Jonathan said.

He always seemed to know the right thing to say at the right time. "Do you think your mum and nan would mind if we went out for a drink for a couple of hours and they watch Nicholas?" Jonathan asked.

"I don't know until I try, wait here I will be back in a minute," suggested Mel.

"No problem. Let me just get a jacket and then bring Nicholas back down again, he still has a bit of time before he goes to bed." Mel told him. Nan took hold of Nicholas; Mum was busy doing something in the kitchen.

"We won't be long, Marge," said Jonathan.

"Take your time, you know he's in good hands and, Mel, thank you for today it means a lot," said Nan. They both said goodbye as they closed the front door. Mel and Jonathan walked hand in hand towards the pub. She hadn't been to this pub in a very long time.

She went to get a table and then she thought she saw something that made her jump. It was the blonde hair, slicked back. Then she looked again and thought she must have imagined it.

Jonathan came back with their drinks. "Are you OK, Mel? You look like you have just seen a ghost?" Jonathan asked.

"Oh no, I was just thinking about today. You know Jill has been in that place for a long time, many years. Apparently, where she was before wasn't very nice, they manhandled her a bit too roughly nan said."

"Mel, not all of those places were nice. I have heard some awful stories, but let's not talk about that, Apart from tired how was Jill?" he asked.

"She seemed really happy to see us, especially Nicholas; she loved him, you could see it. It's a shame we haven't met her before now. I know it's more than likely what she wanted, as you said before they like routine and structure, if she saw us at home, it may have thrown her and done her some damage. The more I spend with you and now Jill, I see and I think I understand Autism more, not completely, but just more. It's a difficult one and I have noticed over time it can also be an isolated situation for the families."

"Juliet told me at a meeting a while ago, that she doesn't really have much to do with her family. They have actually had parties, birthday parties, christenings and even the odd wedding and then her and Arthur haven't been invited, she said. 'What he's never had, he will never miss!' which I suppose is a good way to look at it."

"I thought everyone was like me, a great support network, but it's not the case is it, Jonathan?" Mel asked finally when she stopped talking. They chatted for a couple of hours and Mel was quite glad to be out of the house. She looked at her watch. "Oh Jonathan, it's getting late. I have to be up early in the morning, we have to go." She told him.

As Mel looked to get her coat, she noticed the blonde hair again, but this time chose to ignore it. She put her coat on, Jonathan had his on already. They then left, without looking back to double check. They were outside, it was getting cold. It had just turned into October. Mel put her arm through Jonathan's. "You ok Mel?" Jonathan asked.

"Yes just a bit chilly, it's really starting to bite now that wind. I think I need to change over the summer clothes to the winter wardrobe," she told him.

All of a sudden, Jonathan stopped walking. He held Mel in his arms and said, "Mel, I am sorry but I don't often get a chance to see and talk to you on your own. I know we have had a few dates and this evening was lovely, I think I am falling in love with you and of course Nicholas, if you know what I mean," he said. With that, he pulled her close and gave her a very passionate kiss, which nearly took her breath away.

When they finished and pulled slightly apart, Jonathan still had his arm around Mel, who in turn was a bit in shock. They hadn't really had many dates, but she felt an awful lot of Jonathan. Actually she thought that she too had fallen for him, but with everything else going on, she didn't give it much thought.

"Jonathan, I think I am falling for you too, with so much else going on," she said, but headed. "I know what you mean, we never seem to find time for us to be alone. I think which is why we missed the signs."

"I know it's rather difficult, I love spending time with you, Nicholas and Marge and Jean, but when do we get to have time together, Mel, I'm not suggesting you abandoning your family and I don't mean Nicholas, but maybe we could find compromise. Maybe me move in for a while and see how it goes. What do you think?" He asked her.

"If you don't mind, I will have a word with nan and Mum, because it's actually nan's house and I don't want her thinking I am taking liberties. What if we take it slowly, like you stay over once a week. I know just to get the ball rolling and we take it from there, sort of like a trial, to see if it works."

"I know it's not ideal, but a start, but I will have a word with them. Do you mind?" she asked him.

"No of course not, I hadn't even thought of that. You know staying over first, see how it goes. So have a word with both of them and let me know what they say and think about it?" Jonathan added. Jonathan seemed happy with that. He walked Mel home and kissed her at the front door. She put the key in and he waited for her to close it the other side, then he left.

"Did you have a good time, Mel?" Nan asked.

"Yes, it was really lovely, though I thought I had a bit of a shock though!" Mel said. "Is Nicholas in bed then?" Mel asked, forgetting what she was saying.

"Yes fast asleep, I just checked on him a couple of minutes ago," replied Jean. "Who had a shock?" Jean asked.

"When Jonathan was getting the drinks in, I spotted well someone," said Mel.

"Who?" Nan asked. "Well, I wasn't sure but I thought it was Andy," said Mel.

"Whose Andy?" Mum and nan asked together.

"Nicholas' dad, you remember the blonde guy?" Mel reminded them both.

"Oh, Mel, what did he say?" Nan asked.

"Oh don't worry, I don't think he saw me. I did see him again, before we left but I ignored him. I'm not going down that road. He didn't call me back and he doesn't know about Nicholas and it's going to stay that way. Now I have something I want to talk to you both about," said Mel.

"Oh, go on, Mel, this sounds juicy!" Jean said.

"Me and Jonathan have been talking. We both said it was nice to get out on our own, so thank you for that this evening. I know it's been a bit of a nuts day, anyway, what I wanted to ask you was…" Mel took a deep breath then continued. "If Jonathan could stayover say maybe at the weekends? I know this is your house, Nan, but if we don't spend time together, how on earth are we going to make this work?" Mel went to continue but Marge held up her hand to stop Mel.

"Now, Mel, listen to me, you're not a child anymore. You are a divorced single parent to a challenging young man and we know you can't do this on your own and you do need a bit of a life as well. So yes, if you want Jonathan to stay at the weekends with it to become more permanent at a later date, because I think this is where this is going, then it's fine by me, and it's not just my house, but your house; home whatever you want to call it."

"I know you had to give up the flat to Tina and George, well they decided that one, but when you had Nicholas, you couldn't really stay up there on your own, even if we were there every day, it would have still been hard. Now we all know that Tina and George want to get a house soon. So once you and Jonathan try it out and if it works out for you both, which I hope, then you can move back to the flat if you want."

"That's your flat, you do what you want with it, and you're an adult, but thank you for being respectful and asking first," said nan. She got up and gave Mel a big hug.

"And we all love Jonathan. He's been very full of information when you have needed it, Mel. I think you have hit the jackpot and don't you go worrying about Andy or whatever his name is. He's probably here for a flying visit," Nan said, trying to convince herself more than anyone else.

**

Nan, Mum, Mel and Tina were all set to go and see Jill at home today. The home knew they were going in in the week but without Nicholas when the phone rang. Nan picked it up. "Hello, oh yes, hello again, yes OK, I am sitting down, now, Mrs White…" nan dropped the receiver which Mel picked up.

"Hello, Mrs White, yes, it's me Mel. I'm sorry but my nan had dropped the phone. Yes OK, oh dear. It was peaceful, OK. Can we still come over? No ok another time. Thank you. Yes, we will be in touch, thank you for letting us know," said Mel putting the phone down.

"Nan, Nan, are you ok?" Mel asked. Marge had legged it into the sitting room and was rocking back and forth on the sofa holding a cushion. "Nan, did she tell you?" Mel asked. Mel knew the answer. Marge was trying to speak, but couldn't find the words, so Mel told the others.

"Jill died in her sleep last night, it was peaceful. She wasn't in any pain at all, she was doped up with painkillers. Mrs White said that we can't go over today but in the next couple of days, to go through her room and help ourselves to what we want," said Mel, with those words, Mel couldn't contain herself any longer. She, nan, Mum and Tina all burst into tears and were holding each other for comfort.

Thankfully, Nicholas was at school. Nicholas, Jill only saw him the once, but it really made her day. She loved showing him the birds. How on earth was she going to explain to a little boy whose only two and a half that the lady he just met, had died. They spent the whole day together. Jonathan called later on that day, he knew something was wrong. He knew she needed to be with her family, so he said he would call again the next day.

Mel was grateful for that. She didn't know how she managed getting Nicholas sorted out. They were all on autopilot for the next couple of days. The four of them all went a few days later to the home.

Mrs White greeted them at the door and gave them her condolences. They had told Marge that the other residents were aware of Jill's passing and that they had made them a card that they had all signed for the family. Mrs White took them to Jill's room. When she opened the door, they didn't smell death but Jill, as if she was still in the room with them. She had like Lily of the Valley scent and that's what they could smell.

"Now we have put her most precious belongings on the table for you to have a look at and see if you would like any of them. Please they are yours to have on Jill's wishes. We have taken the liberty I'm afraid of choosing three items of clothes that Jill particularly liked and wanted you to choose which you prefer for her to wear, you know?" Mrs White said.

Mel couldn't believe how peaceful the room felt, but she too felt that Jill was with them watching them choose her outfit and what they liked the best for them to keep. Mel walked over to the table and saw about a dozen different things—a couple of brooches, some nice pearls, a couple of pins you would wear on your coat, like the heart on your sleeve, a poppy she liked, it wasn't paper but made of some sort of resin, not plastic.

Tina and Mel had a look, but they both felt uneasy with it. They both sat on the chairs at the table and were talking softly. Nan was going through the bedside cabinet, just to make sure it was empty. The first drawer where she had her pad and pen and then Nicholas present, was empty, but the second drawer, had four envelopes in it.

Obviously nobody had looked in there or they had but left it alone. There was one for Marge, Jean, Mel and Tina; in Mel's there was a smaller one with Nicholas's name on it.

Jane walked into Jill's room. "Jane, these were in Jill's bedside cabinet. They have our names on them. Were we supposed to take them or are they meant to be given at a later date?" Jean asked.

"No, they are yours and you're supposed to take them with you today when you leave, to be opened up at home. Sorry but Jill's instructions. Have you chosen an outfit for Jill to wear, because we need to take it to the funeral home. I know it's up to you for sorting out the funeral arrangements, but as she died here, we are able to get hold of the death certificate unless you would like to collect it?" Jane asked.

"No, Jane, that will be fine. We don't want to take over the arrangements, but would like to help with them if that's ok?" Marge asked.

"But of course, you're her family," said Jane.

"Not just us, Jane, you all were here her family too. She often spoke of the happy times she had here for the last twenty years of so. So, if you don't mind can we do them together?" Marge asked.

"Yes, we can, so we can get the death certificate. Do you know if she has any other family who need to be told at all, because she hasn't ever mentioned anyone else to us," commented Jane.

"No, it's just us, oh and Nicholas, but also George and now Jonathan, Mel's new man as well," said Marge. Jane left them to it. "Do any of you want any of those things on the table?" Marge asked.

"Yes, I think we should each take one piece to remember Jill by and then give them to the staff to see if they would like a piece. What do you think?" Marge asked.

"I think that's a great idea," said Jean, So they all went back up to the table and had another look. Mel chose a brooch, Jean chose the pearls, Tina chose the other brooch, then Marge hadn't spotted it before but a rather delicate necklace that had an 'N' on it for Nancy, Jill's mum. She took that, there was some other sorts of costume jewellery, but they each decided on one piece.

"Right let's see these outfits for her to wear." Marge opened the wardrobe, everything in their looked fun. There was a lovely peach and white dress patterned, with a pair of tights to match in a soft tan colour, which would have suited well. Then there was a pink and white dress, with a pretty white cardigan and again, soft coloured tights.

Then there was a snazzy purple, lilac and white dress, with a lilac cardigan, with soft cream tights. "Do you think Jill would have worn the snazzy or the pretty pink or peach dress?" Tina asked.

"I think any of those would have suited her great, but I think Jill had a great summer playful attitude, even though the snazzy one would look lovely, I prefer the pink and white with the pretty white cardigan. So, I had better get Jane so she can take it with her," said Marge. Marge returned with Jane and showed her the dress and cardigan.

"I am glad you chose that pretty pink one, that was Jill's favourite," commented Jane.

"Jane, what will happen to the other clothes and the rest of her things?" Jean asked.

"Well, what we have done is bagged it all up for you to take home. Everything has been washed, that way if you would like to keep something you can, if you don't know what else to do with it, then you can take it to your local charity shop. Once someone has left us in these circumstances, we don't really want to keep them on the premises, not because of any reason apart from we don't want to upset our other residents, they were all fond of Jill. So, you do with them what you wish," Jane told them.

"I suppose it's because also nobody would want to wear a dead ladies' clothes," said Tina.

"More than likely, but what about an old people's home, sometimes they need stuff," suggested Mel. "I don't suppose they would mind really," Mel added.

"It's better than throwing it in the bin, let it go to a good home," said Tina.

"Jane, is that it or do we need to do anything else?" Marge asked.

"Well as we will be sorting out the death certificate, we will get you multiple copies just in case, then you need to talk to the undertakers, that's Winters in town. Then you can arrange with your local church. Do you know if Jill is going to be buried or cremated yet?" Jane asked.

"I don't know yet, we haven't spoken about it, but we will do later on today. Thank you, Jane, for all of your help and the staff who have been brilliant with Jill and for everything you have done for her," said Marge.

Jane handed Mel Jill's suitcase and they left. "Do we need to come back for anything at all, Nan?" Tina asked.

"I have no idea at the moment, Tina. Let's see when we get home," nan said. She now wanted to get out of there as quickly as they could. Mel opened the door and Tina closed it behind them. They got to the car and put Jill's suitcase in the boot until they got home.

Mel got them home rather quickly, there wasn't much traffic. They pulled up outside home. Mel popped the boot open and Tina took the case inside, nan and Mum followed. Mel locked up the car and shut the front door behind her.

They put the case down for now. Marge went into the kitchen to make some tea. They had managed to sort out what they needed for the funeral. Mel took to making a lot of the arrangements. Nan was in bits, it was starting to hit her hard. She had already spoken to Lesley about doing the flowers for the funeral.

It wasn't going to be a big affair, but she was paying for it herself. It was going to be mainly family, but also staff from the home and a few residents if they wanted to go. Mel had arranged a small gathering at the local pub, they were letting them have a room, so they could have some privacy.

It was the day of the funeral. Mel had sent Nicholas to school. School was aware of the situation as Mel had already told them. She had to be back by 3.30 at the latest. The bus driver and escort also knew. They gave Mel their good wishes for the funeral, because what do you say at a funeral, just hoping it can go as well as can be.

Once Nicholas left on his bus, Mel started to get herself ready. Jonathan couldn't get the day off, because him and Mel weren't married and it was her side of the family. But George was there for Tina, well, the family really. Everyone had congregated at Marge's for 11am. They did have a cup of tea beforehand, but Marge couldn't drink hers.

The funeral cars were going to the home first, so the ones who couldn't attend today would be able to say farewell and goodbye. Then it was going to Marge's for the family and the family cars to collect them and take them to the church. The ones who were coming from the home, Marge had laid on a car for them. They were the last two cars, there were three in total as well as the hearse.

When it pulled up, Marge took one look and had to compose herself. Mel had done a beautiful display of flowers, her name JILL was in white carnations round the edge and pink roses in the middle all the way down to each letter. They didn't want to put daughter, but they did do COUSIN because that's what she was to all of them. Mel did those in peach and white flowers, and then a big spray from Nicholas with purple, lilac and white flowers, the same colours as her favourite dresses.

They all had handkerchiefs and tissues, which they were already using. Marge walked out the door first and the undertaker opened the door for her to get in. Jean sat next to her, then Mel, Tina and George sat in the back. When everyone was seated, they checked it was safe to drive off. The hearse went first, then the family then her other family from the home.

The church wasn't very far away, so it didn't take long. Thankfully no other cars tried to cut in, when they got to the church, everyone got out and made their way inside the church. The pall bearers took Jill out and they carried her inside to *The Wind Beneath My Wings* by Bette Midler. That's how Marge had felt. She started crying openly, she couldn't hold it in anymore.

Jean was holding onto her mother. Tina, George and Mel were seated behind them. The home staff were seated on the other side so it looked like there were people from both sides. The vicar did his eulogy, he was very respectful. They only had a couple of hymns and then it was over. Jill was being carried out again, this time to *You Are My Sunshine* by Jasmine Thompson.

It was very moving, but people were trying to compose themselves this time. Jill was put back into the hearse and they drove to the cemetery which was only down the road. They got out of the cars again and went along to the graveside, the vicar was there also. He said the words he needed to, then they were handed a pot of soil, that they took some to put on the coffin before it was lowered into the ground.

Jill had been buried with her mum, Nancy, so she would be added to the headstone when the time came. That gave Marge and now the other family members some comfort. They left the graveside. Marge looked back and blew Jill a kiss and told her that she had loved her, then she carried on with her family to go to the wake.

When they got to the pub, the landlady had done a great job for them. The staff and residents of the home came for a little while. They had some food and soft drinks, then Mel ordered them their cabs and she paid for them. "Make sure they all get back safely. Thank you, Jane, and Mrs White, for coming today," said Mel.

"Mel, thank you for this and the other cars," said Mrs White.

"Mrs White, we were one side of Jill's family and you were all the other. Take care and maybe see you soon," said Mel waving them off.

She returned to the room, to see how everyone was. Marge was talking to a well-dressed man, it turned out he was Jill's solicitor. "Pardon?" Mel asked. "Jill had a solicitor?" Mel said, quite shocked.

"Well, I worked for Nancy and then Jill. You see when Nancy knew that she didn't have long for this world, she made provision for both herself and her only daughter, so once the home let me know that sadly Jill had passed, I got my paperwork together and made my way over here. I was at the church service but I sat at the back and then the cemetery, now here. If you all have a few minutes, I would like to speak to you all?" Jill's solicitor asked.

Everyone sat down, he cleared his throat. "Hello, everyone. I am Mister Rockwood and I am here on behalf and for Jill Coombes. Now as you all know that Jill resided in a care home for most of her life. But there has been provision for her in the way of what her mother had left her. There was monies due to an inheritance which Nancy had due to her husband's family's side, which went directly to Jill on the death of her mother, which is now to be divided up between her family," he said.

"Mr Rockwood, why didn't you do this whilst the staff from the home were here and now that they are gone?" Marge asked.

"Marge, the home know what they have been left by Jill and her mother before, it was always sorted out. They are to get the total sum of £20,000," he said to them. Marge, Jean, Tina, Mel and George had their mouths wide open. Mr Rockwood continued. "Marge, for you there is a total of £30,000. Jean Shaw for you there is a total sum for £10,000. For both Melanie and Tina, they will also get the sum of £10,000 each and also a footnote," said Mr Rockwood.

"A footnote, what's that?" Jean asked.

"That is an added extra entry for Master Nicholas Antony Shaw, who will get the sum of £25,000 once he is 18 years old. If he needs it for education of whatever he wants to spend it on, but only Nicholas, but with the guidance of his mother, Melanie Shaw. There is also a couple of charities that both Jill and Nancy wanted to add to and that is The National Autistic Society and Building Bridges Support Group," he said.

Mel's mouth fell completely open, she couldn't believe it. She had only mentioned about Building Bridges to her mum and nan. 'How did Jill know about it?' thought Mel. What Mel wasn't aware of, they had been helping her for a while with various stuff, so she and her mum before her, knew there would be a charity for Autism at some stage. So asked her solicitor to help her with it and then Jill when she was gone.

"That just about sums up Jill Coombes Last Will and Testament. If there is nothing else, may I go?" Mr Rockwood asked. Marge, Jean, Mel and Tina were still dumbstruck with what they had just heard.

"Oh yes, Mr Rockwood, thank you for everything," said Marge. He told Marge that he would be in contact in the next few days to finalise the details of everything. She shook him warmly by the hands, then he left. Mel had a quick bite to eat, then looked at the time, there was still a bit of food left.

Mel asked nan if she could give it to the bar staff to put on the bar. Marge said that was fine, she also wanted to go home, they all did. They had had a huge shock today, well since the last couple of weeks. Also, Nicholas was due home soon and she wanted to change out of the black.

Mel had ordered two cabs, they wouldn't all get into one. They came practically straightaway. Mel's cab pulled up after nan and mum's cab. She paid him and he drove off, leaving all of the group standing on the pavement.

Mel looked over the road and saw Terry pushing a buggy with a little tot in it and then spotted Clare looking very heavily pregnant. He looked shocked to see her, especially in black. 'Who had died he thought?' Mel looked away and then went inside with her family.

Chapter 19

Christmas was a little bit more sombre that the one before. Jill's death had hit nan a lot harder than they had all expected, but that was to be expected nan had known Jill all of her life. They rallied round the best way they could for Nicholas to have a good Christmas. He didn't really realise the mood had changed at all, around him they were all as cheerful as they could be.

Marge had also had to decide what to do with the money that Jill had left her. Mel was putting hers aside for the time being, but Tina had mentioned to George, that they could put it towards their deposit for their house. They had already saved about four thousand pounds, so this would be an extra bonus. They had planned to save for a year and see how they got on, so by the June that year, would determine how much they would have saved, but this gave them a huge injection to their savings.

Jean also was trying to decide what to do with her share, but for now, like Mel, was going to sit on it for a while. Jonathan had started to stay over at weekends. He waited a few weeks after the funeral, to give everyone time to grieve and then adjust to having another male in the house. So now they were into the new year, they only had a couple of days left of the holidays.

Nicholas was lost at the holidays, he had gotten into a great routine at school and home and the weekends, but the holidays completely threw him. Mel was actually glad they were into the new year and the holidays were coming to an end, not because of any reason. It was just that the back end of the year had become so awful—first meeting Jill, then her dying and having her funeral, yes been given some money, well a lot of money from Jill's estate.

Then bumping into Terry and Clare on the way back from the funeral, with a tot in the buggy and another one on the way. Mel thought that Terry definitely had his work cut out, considering he didn't want any kids with Mel in the end. But hey, sometimes that's how it goes.

It was Nicholas's first day back at school. Jonathan had left the night before so she and Nicholas could be up without any distractions and get him ready for school. Nicholas was enjoying having Jonathan around. When he wasn't there, he would always look for him. Jonathan liked the holidays, but like the kids at school, he liked the routine and structure of school life.

So, Mel and Jonathan were getting on rather well, and Mum and nan had got used to him being around. Thankfully once in the week the two of them would go out and Mum and nan would babysit, so they could have some time on their own, even if it meant going out for a meal or just a drink.

Tina and George used to see a lot of Angela and Jim, so they would keep them updated with how things were going with the newly involved couple, which Mel and Jonathan didn't mind. Actually they thought it was funny, being in their late thirties, referred to as if they were a couple of teenagers. Slowly, nan started to come back to her old self.

She asked Mel if she had seen Elaine. Mel had seen her quite frequently at Building Bridges, her and Todd were doing well. Todd was enjoying nursery, also his physio and Elaine was getting more of a grip on things as well. They had settled well into their new home a few months ago, so everyone was going OK.

***

A few months later, Mel had already decided to volunteer at Building Bridges support group. Well, she wasn't really able to go back to work even though she had the time. There wasn't enough to do, without letting someone go and Mel didn't want to do that. They had worked excellently since she couldn't work because of having Nicholas, but she was also grateful for them.

She was a good boss and paid them well enough. They got a bonus at Christmas and the staff didn't want to leave, they had been with her for a few years, just like she had with the woman who owned the florist before her. It was already June, Tina and George were at home with the family, not their flat they were renting from Mel.

They had discussed their finances together and decided to see how much they could get from a bank with the help of a mortgage, then once they knew their price range, they could start house hunting. "Mel, we have loved being at the flat, but we want to move on and buy our own home. You're not disappointed, are you?" Tina asked.

"No, of course not. I am just glad you had a stop gap before you brought your own home. Also it gave you a chance to save as much as you can," replied Mel. "So what are you going to do with the flat now? Rent it out again?" Tina asked rather nosily.

"Well, me and Jonathan have been talking as well, and I think we may try living together at the flat and see how we get on. You know we can't carry on at nan's forever," said Mel.

"But Mel, Mum and nan are going to be gutted if you move out. They love spending so much time with you and Nicholas," replied Tina rather shocked at what her big sister had just said to her.

"Look, I know it's not the best, but for us to stand chance as a couple wanting to get on in the world, we have to make decisions sometimes, not always good or nice ones, but don't say anything to them just yet, Tina. Because we have only just spoken about it and I don't want to upset, Nan. She's been through enough already these past few months," said Mel rather sternly.

"Don't worry, I won't but you know they are both going to take it hard," Tina told her.

"Yes, I know," Mel said.

Tina and George went to the bank at the other end of town. They still didn't want to go where Terry was and for him to get any commission on their mortgage. The guy they saw was very nice and very good to them as first time buyers. He said because they already had a good deposit, which was now £20,000 and considering both of their salaries, they could get at least an £80,000 mortgage, but could purchase a house up to a £100,000.

They were both delighted. The guy, Malcolm, said that he would be happy to lend them that much and when they had found a house to return and sort out the paperwork. They started looking straightaway, they were looking in estate agent windows and also the local paper; there wasn't much in the paper, but they had found a couple they had liked.

One looked awfully familiar to Tina, but couldn't remember why. They had made an appointment to see both houses on the same day. One was a few streets away, but the other one was the other side of town, but they could both get to work, so it wasn't a problem. They met the estate agent, Alistair, at 10am on Friday morning.

He took them to the one the other side of town first. It was a nice three bedroom house, with a utility room, a good sized garden, but Tina wanted to see the other house before she made up her mind. Alistair was fine with that, so he drove them over to the other house, not too far from Mum and nan. They pulled up and Tina recognised it straight away. She didn't say anything to George or Alistair at the time, she wanted to be nosey and have a good look round.

Alistair opened the front door and they walked in, there had been a few changes obviously—the decoration inside had been done, the kitchen was the same, but the units looked different, it wasn't the colour of them but the doors and drawer fronts had been changed. 'Oh well', thought Tina. The sitting room hadn't changed but the furniture was definitely different of course. Tina headed straight upstairs.

"Tina, you do seem to know your way around this property," said George still not clocking on to it. When they got to the master bedroom, George was looking a bit worried. "Tina, you have been in this house before, haven't you?" He asked her in a weird tone.

"Of course I have and so have you!" Tina replied.

"Me, I haven't been in this house before," he told her.

"Oh yes you have, didn't you recognise the address?" she asked him, "Think about it, George," she told him this time.

"Oh bloody hell," he replied. "Tina, do you think this is a good idea?" George asked her.

"Yes, I do. I don't think she would be worried about it, do you?" Tina asked George.

"Well, I think you should run it past her first, now we have seen it," George said.

"Why? She would be happy for us to have this house. It will be decorated differently and our furniture will be different. So I don't see a problem, unless she doesn't want us to take it," said Tina matter-of-factly. Once they had finished looking round, they asked Alistair if they could think about it over the weekend and then let him know.

They didn't want to look at anymore, they were both in their price range. He said that was fine, shook both of their hands and he had offered them a lift back, but they declined.

They were only around the corner as such, so they walked back to nan's and talked about the houses, they liked both of them. Tina was more interested in the second one of course. George liked both of them, but as always, he left the decision up to Tina to make the final yes or no. They knocked on the door, as they didn't have keys anymore.

Nan answered it. "Well, you two, how did it go? Did you like them?" Nan asked.

"Nan, at least let us in first!" Tina exclaimed. Nan moved out of the way so they could come in, she closed the door behind them. Tina and George went into the sitting room and there was Mum and Mel. Nicholas of course was at nursery. Tina and George had big grins on their faces, but Tina didn't know if that was the right expression to have when she would have to tell them about the houses.

"Tea, George, Tina?" Nan asked.

"Oh yes please, Nan" said George, wanting to take his time with the conversation, that he was actually dreading now. Nan disappeared into the kitchen, then came straight back in. Mel and Mum were sitting at the table, nan joined them.

"Well, come on did you like them?" Nan asked impatiently.

"Yes we did we liked both of them, but there is a bit of a problem," said Tina.

"Oh what kind of problem? Is it fixable, George?" Nan asked.

"Well, it is but it does depend on the conversation now really!" he replied, looking very nervous.

"Will you two stop talking in riddles and explain," said Mum.

"The first house we looked at was lovely; it has a utility room a massive garden and its huge and it is within out budget, but!" Tina said.

"Well, spit it out then, Teen," said Mel.

"The second house is beautiful, Mel. It's been really well decorated, its spacious, but we don't know whether to take it or not. Out of the two, it's the better one I think," said Tina, looking at George.

George continued "Mel, it's your old house I'm afraid. If you don't want us to buy it we won't. We wanted to run it past you first," he said looking at Tina.

"Oh, Tina, George, if you want to buy it, then buy it, if you don't then someone else will. Did they say how long the house has been on the market for though?" Mel asked.

"He said only a couple of months, Mel. It looks like it has been taken care of and well loved," Tina added.

"If you both want it, then you have my blessing to buy it. As I said, I would rather someone I know buy it than someone I don't. Is there anything the owners are leaving for you?" Mel asked.

"We don't know yet. We asked him if we could think about it over the weekend," said Tina.

"Why if you don't jump on it, Teen, someone else may get it," said Jean.

"Are you sure you don't want the other house, have you definitely ruled it out then?" Mel asked.

"They are both lovely, Nan, but Mel's house has the edge," said Tina.

"Well, then, either call up the estate agent or better go back and tell him you have decided which house you want. Hang on, can you still both get to work from Mel's house. Sorry, Mel, it's just what we are used to calling it," said nan.

"Yes, we can both get to work from either house. So, Tina, do you want to go back and tell Alistair we want the house?" George asked.

Mel threw her car keys to George. "Go on, get going before he takes someone else to buy it!" Mel said, rather excited that her sister and her husband will have her old house. Tina and George left straight away.

"Er you don't think it's unlucky to buy a relative's old house, especially that the relative's marriage broke up and they had to sell the house to pay off the mortgage and then leave that house?" Nan asked.

"No, Nan, because it's being brought with love and I can't see Tina and George breaking up because George has a wandering eye, do you?" Mel asked her.

"He had better not," said nan. "He will get my rolling pin over his head. We can't go through that again, sorry, Mel," said nan.

"Nan, look at what has happened since I sold that house, I met someone else, I had a baby boy who is growing up to be a very lovely little person. Why would I want to live in a house that ended up being with my heart broken? It's already had someone else live in it as I sold it."

"So any sort of bad luck will have gone and just think how the owner now is thinking, that they can fly high now, they can move on to their next home, their new project. It's all about closing one chapter and staring another one," Mel said.

"I think there's some truth and wisdom in that, Mel" said Mum.

Tina and George returned about an hour later. "We have put in an offer and it's been accepted, Mum, Nan, Mel," said Tina, who looked like she was about to burst with happiness.

"How long does it take to Exchange contracts then?" Mum asked.

"Well, it can depend on how long your survey comeback and if the other person is in a chain and if it needs to be done quickly or not. There are tons of reasons. If it's straight forward it could take 3 months altogether, I suppose. But don't worry, you will get there, so speak to whoever you need to at the agents and ask if they can recommend a surveyor or do you know anyone already?" Mel asked.

Tina and George jumped on it straight away. They found a surveyor pretty quickly and his report didn't take long. They also went to the bank and saw the same man, Malcolm, who they really liked. He told them about the terms and conditions to the mortgage and if they had any questions.

They said that they hadn't so far it was going rather smoothly. George was a little worried, it was going a little too smoothly but Tina told him it was nerves more than anything else.

They got the keys to the house on 1 September. Mel was delighted for them, she really was. Her and Jonathan had spoken again about moving in together with Nicholas at the flat. When Tina and George were packing up their stuff, including their furniture, there was still a bit of Mel's there.

Mel had another look at the flat. She got Jonathan over so he could have a look at it. "Mel, it's great, how come you didn't live here after you had Nicholas?" He asked, he had forgotten.

"I had a C-section and I couldn't really go up and down the stairs with anything heavy. Everyone sorted it out for me, while I was in hospital. Didn't I tell you this before?" she asked.

"I can't remember, maybe, so if this is our room, where is Nicholas's room? Oh I see it next door. It's a lovely size room. Do you think he would like it here, Mel?" Jonathan asked.

"I think so, as I said before even though they would love it. We can't really live there forever. I have to spread my wings again too you know!" Mel told him.

"Now Tina and George are leaving. Are they taking all of the furniture with them then?" Jonathan asked.

"Oh no, some of its mine, what I bought and paid for, they have kept it all in good condition though. We only need to get some new things, but we can choose that together if you want?" Mel suggested.

"Mel, will this place be big enough for us, you know, me, you and Nicholas and anyone who else comes along?" Jonathan asked.

"What did you want your mum to come and live with us?" Mel asked, about to burst out laughing.

"No well," he started to say, then he saw Mel's face. "Oh I see, missus clever, no I meant if we had any more children," indicated Jonathan. Mel hadn't thought of having any more children, but she didn't know she would have any more. "Do you want any more children Mel?" Jonathan asked nervously.

"To tell you the truth, Jonathan, I hadn't really thought about it. After having Nicholas, I didn't think I would meet anyone else and look how that turned out, eh?" She said with a little giggle.

"Mel, by the way, I wanted to ask you something?" Jonathan asked.

Mel was distracted with something in the kitchen, Jonathan hadn't noticed her going into the kitchen. "What was that, love?" Mel asked.

"Erm her herm," he said clearing his throat. "I was wondering what you would be doing for the next fifty years or so, Mel?" He said holding out a little box.

Mel gasped. "Is this what I think it is?" Mel asked.

"What do you think it is? Anyhow, you won't know until you open it up, will you?" Jonathan suggested, who had opened the lid of the box. Inside it stood a beautiful big white diamond on a beautiful white gold band. "So, Melanie Shaw, would you do me the honour of becoming my wife, Mrs Melanie Bradshaw?" Jonathan asked her, by now he had gotten down on one knee.

Mel couldn't believe her eyes or her ears. "Well, Mel, don't leave me hanging here!" Jonathan told her.

"Of course I would say yes, why would I say anything else," she replied, holding her left hand. He took the ring out of the box and put it onto Mel's ring finger. "It's beautiful, Jonathan, thank you for choosing such a perfect ring."

She told him as she brought him close and kissed him, rather passionately. He let out a huge sigh. "Wow, that was a big sigh. Did you think I would say no?" she asked him.

"No, it's just I didn't know if you would like the ring, but I am delighted that you have. Now do you have the keys to lock up this place and we can go and tell Mum and nan," said Jonathan. Mel did that, she was so excited. Nicholas was still at school but due home soon.

Mel and Jonathan would also break the news, that once Tina and George move into their new house, they would be moving into the flat, until they decided to buy something as well. They just wanted to save up some more money before they went for a mortgage too, then she could start renting the flat out again.

Mel and Jonathan opened the door at nan's. "Hi, we're home," said Mel. Nan was upstairs she came down and Mum was sitting at the table.

"Tea, Mel, Jonathan?" she asked them.

"Is there one in there for me too, Jean?" Nan asked.

"Of course, you two OK? You look a bit stiff standing there," said Mum.

"Me and Jonathan have something to tell you!" said Mel, but she didn't have to. Nan had spotted the sparkle on Mel's left hand.

"Oh my goodness, Jean, look at that, it's beautiful," nan said jumping off her chair. For a lady in her seventies, she was very swift when she wanted to be. "Oh, Mel, it's beautiful. Have you named a date yet then?" Nan asked.

"Er no not yet, but we did want to talk to you about something," said Mel. Nan and Mum both looked at her tummy. "No, it's not that, well I don't think so. No, what we wanted to say, we want you to give us your blessing though. When Tina and George move into their new house, we want to move into the flat, the three of us," Mel said, but was now wishing she hadn't both of the ladies mouths had dropped.

"Oh, Nan, Mum, we don't want to hurt you and you will see Nicholas every day. I'm not taking him out of your lives, but we need to move on and make a life for ourselves as we hoped you would want us to," said Mel.

Nan had started crying. "Of course you must. We didn't think you would live with us forever, Mel. We would have wanted you both to, but it's not very realistic for you ours really. As you said, we will still see you both, we are only up the road. It's how it would have been I suppose once you had him, if you hadn't had a C-section, you would have gone straight there. So yes, you have my blessing," said nan looking at her daughter.

"Of course you have my blessing, both of you. You're good to my girl, Jonathan, and we love you very much. We know you have both of their interests at heart and foremost I know you will make them both very happy," said Mum, coming over to both of them, hugging them, nan joined in as well. Once the tears were over, it was time for Nicholas to come home.

Mel went out to the bus, he was speaking now, not a lot, but he was more inclined to ask for help if he got stuck and his pronunciation wasn't great, but he was getting there. Mel didn't want to say anything to him just yet. She was going to ask the school if they could do him a social story, so he would understand, but she wasn't going to wait too long, the more notice that, Nicholas had the better he would be prepared for it. He noticed the ring on Mel's hand though. She took him inside and he saw Jonathan and put his arms out to him. "Jonphon," called out Nicholas.

"Well, it was near enough," he laughed, not at Nicholas, the fact he's trying to say his name. He held onto him, tightly. But kept looking at Mel's ring, it sparkled and Nicholas liked sparkles.

"Are you hungry, Nicholas?" Nan asked. Nicholas nodded in reply. "Toad in the hole for dinner, Mel, Jonathan, that ok?" Nan asked.

"Of course, Marge," said Jonathan. "Now none of this Marge lark now, you're part of the family. It's nan, same as the girls and Nicholas," said nan.

"And the same for me too now, Jonathan, it's Mum OK," said Jean. Nan made dinner and then plated it up. Thank goodness for the table extended so big. Even though they already had the keys to the flat, they wanted to decorate it and get it how they wanted it. So once they were in, they didn't have to do anything, except keep it clean and tidy.

So that also gave Mel some time to get herself sorted out with Nicholas, school, transportation etc. Plus her and Jonathan wanted to go and pick their furniture out that they wanted, they didn't have to get a lot. Nicholas' social story come back the day after Mel asked for it. She was delighted, she told everyone who needed to know, also the girls downstairs, just in case they wondered who was in there as they knew that Tina and George were moving out.

"Don't worry, girls, I won't be checking up on you!" Mel told them. Moving day was here for everyone. Mel didn't want to leave the flat empty. George had a couple of friends from work help them. The place had all been decorated and new carpet laid, so it was just a case of getting their stuff from the flat to the house. Mel did the same.

She had her personal stuff—her bed, she loved that bed, all of Nicholas's stuff. She did ask her mum if she could leave his pram there also his buggy, they did have a shed out the back. Just in case she or Tina needed either of them in the future. Nan laughed and said it was OK.

George and his mates helped Mel and Jonathan with their bits of stuff. Jonathan only had his clothes and personal stuff. The new furniture was coming on Monday. Mel was going to be in for it. It was all going swimmingly. Tina and George were delighted and so were Mel and Jonathan.

Once they had moved everything, Mel took Nicholas over to the flat. He had been there lots of times, but not he was living there, with his mum and her future husband.

***

A few months later, Nicholas was 4 years old. Mel and Jonathan had lived together properly since mid-September last year. They were visiting Mum and Nan, they had all been busy. Tina was 3 months pregnant with her and George's first baby. Nan was a little concerned as they only had their house for a few months and how would they pay the mortgage.

Tina and George had given her piece of mind, because they still had savings they hadn't touched just in case this happened. Tina would be off work for so long and then she would have to return but nan and Mum had already jumped in wanting to look after the baby. So then they were fine with it, as most parents and grandparents do worry about their children and finances.

Anyway, they were all sitting down drinking their tea. Nicholas was on the floor watching a DVD Mel had brought for him to watch and when they got everyone's attention. Mel and Jonathan had wanted to say something.

"Right now, so as you know we got engaged last year in September? Well, we have named the day, 19 August this year. We are going to have a small wedding about fifty or so people. We don't think Nicholas will cope otherwise, so what we have decided to do, is have it down the hotel the outside of town."

"So we can get married there and have the reception there and if we really want to treat ourselves then we can stay overnight, and no, Nan, you and Mum will not be doing the catering. We want you both to enjoy it, not running around like headless chickens. So what do you think?" Mel asked them.

"Well congratulations you two," said George holding out his hand to shake Jonathan's.

"Yes, congratulations to you both," nan said getting up, she could no longer jump up, she was starting to feel the effects of getting older now.

"Mel, Jonathan, how come you're not getting married in church?" Jean asked.

"Well, as I am a divorcee, they don't always agree on you getting married more than once in a church; some people do, but also Mum, because it will be too long and we don't think Nicholas would cope with a long ceremony," Mel told her.

"Fair enough!" Mum stated, she wasn't bothered really, but if upset Nicholas, that was a different thing.

"Have you booked it yet then?" Nan asked.

"Yes, well we had to as it gets booked up really quickly," said Jonathan.

"Where are you getting married then?" Tina asked.

"The Beaumont just past the high street, at the other end of town," said Mel.

"Oh I know it, Mel, its lovely there," said Tina.

"Now, Teen, I'm not having any bridesmaids, but would you be my witness or maid of honour whatever you call it. You can wear whatever you want as long as it isn't cream or ivory," said Mel.

"Oh OK, yes, I would be delighted and it will be fun to have a brother at long last!" Tina laughed. They all laughed at that one.

"Oh and yes, we forgot, we have put a deposit on house too," Jonathan told them all.

"What? My goodness, you two have been busy. You don't hang about, do you. Where is the house then?" Nan asked.

"Minster Way," said Mel.

"What number?" Mum asked.

"26!" Mel replied. Tina and George burst out laughing. "It's not that funny, Tina," said Mel.

"Oh yes it is. Mel, that's the house, we let go because we wanted your house," said Tina and George both laughing again, then the whole house burst out laughing, except Nicholas who was very engrossed in his DVD. He was quite upset that they were making so much noise, even with his ear defenders on.

***

The wedding preparations were in full swing. Mel and Jonathan had made their list and it was just over fifty people, with family and few friends. Mel had asked Elaine if Todd could be a page boy with Nicholas, and Angela and Jim if their two girls, Bonnie and Trudie, would be bridesmaids. Mel knew she said she didn't want to have bridesmaids, but changed her mind.

It wasn't going to be a grand affair but she wanted to have her friends and they were going to be her brother and sister in law, so in a roundabout way, so would Elaine and Todd. Elaine, Bonnie and Trudie were all delighted. Mel didn't know what colour to choose. She knew where not to go for the dresses, but a new boutique had opened up. She wanted to sort out Tina first, then take the colour from that.

Tina had gone out with her mum, nan and Mel to look at dresses. Thankfully she was only having the two little, well they were getting bigger girls now and Tina, Todd and Nicholas. The men were going to wear morning suits, with black jackets and black pin stripe trousers with either the colour cravat or waistcoat, they hadn't decided yet.

Tina tried a watermelon colour, the pink part, but it didn't look right with her skin tone and her blonde hair. She chose a softer pink, it looked like a Grecian dress, flowy and she would still be able to breathe and if she grew any bigger the dress would still fit. She chose a lovely long dress, with capped sleeves for the girls within ivory sash round the middle where the gathers were. The boys wore a pale grey, the black was too dark for both of them, but they still had the same buttonholes as the men did.

Sam, Mike and June were coming as well. Sam, like Tina, was pregnant but not as far as Tina. She hadn't really seen them in a little while, with so much going on, it seemed they only seemed to catch up at parties or do's. Mel had chosen to have rose buttonholes for the bridal party, the ladies of the wedding party, Angela, Jonathan's mum, nan and Mum, all had double rose buttonholes.

They looked more like corsages but they had them up on their left lapel, rather than round their hands.

Mel hadn't seen Mum and nan's outfits, but she knew they were both excited. They also had shoes, handbags and hats to match their outfits. Mel had decided to stay at the hotel the night before, in fact they all did. Nobody wanted to miss out, so they ended up booking all of the rooms, for the Friday afternoon. Mel and Tina wanted to have their nails done, then nan and Mum did, so Jonathan watched Nicholas so they could have some girly time.

Mel didn't really have a hen night, she remembered Tina's and didn't want to go down that road, so they were going to just have a couple of drinks that night in the hotel in her room, but Nicholas was going to be there, so she didn't want to take liberties and she needed to be up earlyish in the morning. But for this evening, they were going to have a nice time.

Mel's nails looked lovely. Her and Tina had the same shade as the bridesmaid dresses. Mum and nan had a French manicure, so they looked nearly natural. Once it turned 11, everyone left Mel. Nicholas was fast asleep, she said goodnight to everyone. "What time is the lady coming to do your hair, Mel tomorrow?" Nan asked.

"About 11am I think. The wedding isn't until 2pm, so that should be plenty of time, I suppose," she replied. She gave both her mum and nan a kiss on the cheek. They said goodnight and went to their own rooms. Mel went to bed, feeling like the luckiest woman alive.

She had a great son whom she loved unconditionally, a man who loved her and her son, but also her family, she couldn't ask for anything more.

The next morning, Nicholas didn't stir until after 9am. There was a knock at the door, it was her mum and nan, bringing in a bottle of cold champagne, with some glasses. "Do you know what time it is right now? To be drinking at this time of the morning. Come in then, let's not it go to waste," said Mel laughing. Nicholas was still snoring softly.

She opened the door up fully, they both came in and then in behind them waddled Tina. She was really big now, but she couldn't see her feet anymore, good job they were on the ground floor.

"What are you doing drinking at this time of the morning," she exclaimed, looking lovingly at the glass that was just poured for her. "Oh just the one then. I could put orange juice in it I suppose," said Tina.

"Maybe the next one," joked Mel.

"Oi, I don't remember you drinking while you were pregnant with our Nicholas," laughed Tina. The time went rather quickly. The ladies were knocking on Mel's door to do her hair. She had only just got in the shower.

"She won't be long, ladies, would you like a glass of champagne while you wait," suggested Jean. Those pair were incorrigible. Mel was soon out of the shower.

"Mum could you quickly wash Nicholas. I bathed him last night, before you lot turned up with drinks," asked Mel.

"Yes, of course, come on little un, let's get you ready," said Jean to her grandson. He gave her a huge smile. She took him into the bathroom. Mel had her bathroom robe around her, but no underwear on just yet. Her dress hanging up behind the door in one of those clothes protector bags, so it wouldn't get ruined.

Mel needed the loo, she excused herself, thankfully there was a separate toilet. She thought she needed the loo, but no, she threw up instead. "Oh dear," said nan.

"Oh well, not to worry," said Jean, they both knew what that was. She came out, she grabbed her underwear and disappeared back into the toilet. Then they heard her again.

"Definitely," said nan. At this point, Tina still hadn't got up, she did struggle now getting up, but she was still asleep. She wasn't needed yet, but she would know soon enough. Mel came out and apologised. Mum and nan smiled at her a knowing smile. Mel then came to the same conclusion.

"Oh well, I suppose it was going to happen sooner or later," she laughed. The hair stylist came over and asked if she wanted anything or to get started. Mel said to get started, just in case she needed to run to the loo again. The lady did a lovely job of Mel's hair and the bridesmaids.

Tina finally made an appearance while Mel's head was still stuck down the toilet. "What's that?" Tina asked.

"Mel's head down the toilet again," said nan.

"Again, how many times has she been in there then?" Tina asked.

"That's the fourth time," said Mum.

"Four times, well we know what that means. Do you think she knew?" Tina asked.

"I think she does now, if she didn't know already," said nan. Mel came back out. The hair stylist checked Mel's hair, thankfully it was fine. She had a similar style to Tina. Tina had swirling curls down one side of her head, she looked like a Greek goddess. Nan and Mum were crying slightly. Mel's make-up looked lovely.

They both had to get their dresses on. The bridesmaids were already finished. Nicholas was dressed. Elaine had brought Todd up, he looked lovely in his suit, same as Nicholas did. Jean took Mel's dress down and took it into her in the bedroom. Thankfully Mel had booked a suite rather than just a bedroom. Jean helped her into her dress.

She had long straight dress in ivory, with a bit of bling on the bodice part of the dress. She looked like a million dollars, she just had some trailing gyp on the side of her head. Tina had the same, but not as much. They both looked beautiful. Nan and Jean went to their own rooms and came back about fifteen minutes later.

Nan wore a soft peach and white dress, with a white cardigan, while Mum wore a snazzy purple and lilac dress, with a hint of white and a lilac cardigan. Mel and Tina looked at them both and started to cry. "You remembered," said Nan.

"Of course we remembered, what a beautiful touch, Nan and, Mum," said Mel, whose tears were all the way down her cheeks now. Mel and Tina hugged their mum and nan.

"We thought it would be a way of celebrating Jill and as if she was here with us today to celebrate. Well now three events," said Mum. Everyone was a little shocked, they didn't understand what was going on, but they didn't have to.

"It's an inside joke, Elaine, we'll tell you later on," said Mel.

"Right, are we ready to get going now then?" Nan asked.

"Oh hold on, Mel, let me fix yours and Tina's make-up. Those tears have left stains, it won't take a moment. There done, you both look beautiful," said the make-up artist. They all walked out of the room. Mel took Nicholas's hand, and Jean was watching Tina. She didn't want her to fall over, as she had said, she couldn't see her feet anymore.

The congregation were already seated. Mel was only a couple of minutes late. Jonathan had Jim as his best man, he was his only brother. When Mel got to the start of the aisle, her mum was holding onto her; nan was holding onto Tina for the time being, just to make sure she was OK. She waddled a bit but was OK. The other bridesmaids and page boys were behind.

George took Nicholas down the front to his mum and step-dad to be, so he had somebody to hold onto. Todd was being carried by Elaine, as he still couldn't walk. Thankfully he wasn't that heavy, but Elaine knew she wouldn't be able to do that for too long.

Mel was now at the front with Jonathan. The bridesmaids to her left and Nicholas was standing by both of them, with George holding his hand, but also keeping an eye on his wife. They said their vows and exchanged rings, which nan and Mum were watching and crying lightly again. Then they signed the register.

Mel was given their copy, which she asked her mum to keep holding Mel's bouquet until later as she didn't have a bag to put it into. They went back up the aisle holding hands and Jonathan had picked up Nicholas. Tina was holding onto George. They went outside for the photographs, because it was a beautiful setting behind and which made a beautiful backdrop.

They posed for photos for as long as they could, thankfully even though Nicholas was only 4, Mel had bought him one of those special needs prams. Todd had one also, it made it easier for the mums to push them and they didn't look out of place. They then went inside for their wedding breakfast.

Mel had chosen a lovely menu, but made sure there was stuff Tina and Sam could eat. So she started off with either garlic stuffed mushrooms, prawn cocktail or bruschetta, for the main course, either chicken, lamb or beef dinner. Mel wanted to make sure there was a choice. She didn't do that last time she got married; it was a set menu of one, prawn cocktail, chicken dinner and gateaux.

This time, she wanted a choice. So for dessert, strawberry cheesecake with a strawberry coulis, chocolate cake, sticky toffee pudding or a variety of desserts, with a bit of everything. Mel couldn't wait to try the stickly toffee pudding, but now she didn't want to even look at it. Once they had eaten, they had the speeches and then there was some relaxing music on, which Nicholas liked.

One of the guests came over to him and said hello. He said hello back. "So what's your name then, little fella?" she asked.

"My name is Nicholas!" He said. Mel and Jonathan were stunned.

"Hello, Nicky," she replied.

"My name is Nicholas, not Nicky, thank you," he told her. Mel and Jonathan couldn't help but laugh.

"Sorry, Nicholas, it was nice to meet you," she told him.

"Yes, it was nice to meet me too, bye," he replied to her. Mel and Jonathan couldn't contain themselves after that.

"I am sorry Aunt May, he hasn't been speaking for too long," said Jonathan.

"Not to worry, dear, he has to start somewhere!" She smiled at them both.

"Thank goodness she didn't take offense. Most people normally do you know, Jonathan," Mel said.

"Yes I know, but Aunt May is a real sweetheart, she's not offended by anything," Jonathan told her. "Would you like to dance, my dear wife?" Jonathan asked.

"Do you mind if we don't just yet, Jonathan?" Mel asked him.

"Are you OK, Mel? you look a bit peaky," he admitted, he hadn't noticed it until now. "Can we go somewhere a bit quiet for a moment?" Mel asked. "Mum, will you look after Nicholas for a few minutes please?" Mel asked.

"Yes, of course, I will see he won't go hungry," she stated. Mel led Jonathan by the hand and took him to one of the rooms to the side of where they were.

"Mel, what's wrong? You're not regretting getting married to me, are you?" asked Jonathan, looking crestfallen.

"No, of course not. You had better sit down, Jonathan," she said, he did as he was told. "Jonathan, our number of three, is going to be a number of four," said Mel.

Jonathan looked confused, "Are you sure, Mel?" He asked her.

"Well I think so, I have been throwing up all morning and it wasn't the drink, I hardly had anything and I can't even look at Sticky Toffee Pudding," she said.

"But you love sticky toffee pudding, so it looks like we are going to have a baby then?" He asked and she nodded in reply.

"But, Jonathan, we can't tell anyone until we have had it confirmed by the doctor or at least a pregnancy test," said Mel.

"I don't believe it, Mel!" He said.

"Are you mad at me?" Mel asked.

"How can I be mad at you when I am going to be a daddy," he shouted the last bit, so everyone at the wedding could hear him. He took Mel by the hand

and went back into the reception. He asked the DJ if he could have the microphone.

"Ladies and Gentlemen, Mum, Dad, Mum and Nan, we are going to have a baby. Mel said we shouldn't say anything until its confirmed, but I think what the hell. We were a family of three and are now going to be a family of four. I am so happy!" He told the whole reception.

He grabbed his wife and kissed her in front of everyone. Nicholas was fast asleep, so he didn't hear his parent's announcement, but he would be told later on with a social story. "Jonathan, how will we manage? I don't mean money, but with one special needs child. We could have another one you know," asked Mel.

"How will we manage, Mel. The same as everyone else, like everyone else does," Jonathan told her, then kissed her again.

The End